I0653873

slaughterville

Rod Glenn

www.rodglenn.com

A Wild Wolf Publication

Published by Wild Wolf Publishing in 2017

Copyright © 2017 Rod Glenn

First print

ISBN: 978-1-907954-65-8
Also available as an E-Book

www.wildwolfpublishing.com

more titles by rod glenn

The King of America: Epic Edition

Sinema: The Northumberland Massacre

Sinema 2: Sympathy for the Devil

Sinema 3: The Troy Consortium

The Killing Moon

Holiday of the Dead (contributor)

Wild Wolf's Twisted Tails (contributor)

Action: Pulse Pounding Tales Volume 2 (contributor)

No Chance In Hell

To the demon inside ...

Thank you Vanessa & Tony

Unhappy the land that has no heroes ...
No, unhappy the land that needs heroes
~ Bertolt Brecht

Foreword

This novel is based on my 2007 novel, Sinema: The Northumberland Massacre. With interest in a film adaptation of the novel, I was tasked with tweaking it to fit a cinematic audience. Unfortunately the first thing to go was my beloved original title, Sinema. There was too much confusion over what sort of film it would be. It needed to be blunt and to the point, hence Slaughterville emerged from the smouldering ashes of Sinema. As the original was released ten years ago, I also wanted to modernise it in the process of adapting it. It was during this process that the story began to alter in small ways, barely discernible ways initially. I say story, but it's more the feeling of the story, rather than the events and characters themselves.

Somewhere in this 2017 rewrite Sinema transformed into something more unsettling and surreal … it turned into Slaughterville.

For those of you who have read Sinema, I hope you enjoy this re-imagined story. For those of you that haven't, I hope you enjoy the ride.

A word of warning. This is a deeply unsettling novel – have no doubt about that. But, if you have the nerve, I think you'll find something engaging, interesting, unnerving, thrilling and down right terrifying.

Rod

prologue

23rd December. *Whoo-ee! This is better than a hog-killing!*

The blizzard reached a writhing frenzy of gusting, icy wind and driving snow, pierced only by a small shape, low in the black sky, being buffeted by the raw Northumberland winter. Angry, swollen clouds filled the sky, obliterating moon and stars. The sea of mature pines below was laden with a heavy coating of snow, the top layer whipping and swirling amongst the swaying treetops. Not a light could be seen.

The windscreen wipers of the Northumbria Police helicopter lashed frantically from side to side to preserve the pilot's view. Beads of sweat clung to his furrowed forehead as he fought with the collective lever and cyclic yoke in order to maintain altitude and bearing. Despite the gruelling task, he managed to whistle a cheery festive tune.

Good King Wenceslas looked out
On the feast of Stephen,
When the snow lay round about,
Deep and crisp and even …

The two plain clothed policemen in the back had remained silent for the best part of the journey from Newcastle Airport, but now, as they neared their destination, the older of the two finally spoke up with an irritated glance toward the pilot. "I don't think that's particularly appropriate, given the circumstances." The tall, almost skeletal, man looked swamped in his thick overcoat, scarf and woolly hat. His features were gaunt, the grey skin drawn tight across bony cheekbones and sunken around the eyes and temples.

The whistling stopped, but the pilot offered no apology.

His younger colleague, looking pale, rather hesitantly said, "How could this happen, Super?"

13

"We don't know the hows or whys yet, son; we just have the facts," Chief Superintendent Hewitt said flatly. *Three-fifteen AM ... phone ringing. "We've got a major situation, Sir ..."* He needed strong black coffee, a cigarette and a lot of answers.

Leaning forward in his seat, switching his attention to the pilot, he asked, "Any news of Wright or Mitchell yet?"

The frail helicopter rattled with a renewed assault from the elements, delaying the pilot's reply. There was a brief stomach-churning jolt as they dropped lower, but the pilot was quick to compensate. Without taking his eyes from the explosive fury of the snowstorm materialising out of the darkness beyond the windscreen, the veteran pilot said in a calm, even tone, "No, Sir. No further updates."

"Don't you think calling in the army was a bit excessive?" Sergeant Wilkinson was saying. The twenty-eight year old Geordie was only two months into his promotion to the rank and, for the first time, was feeling out of his depth.

Hewitt turned to stare at the younger man. "A bit excessive?" he repeated incredulously. "We've got multiple murders, a crime scene the size of Gateshead and suspect or suspects still at large. I'm going to use every damn resource I can, Sergeant."

He let out a sigh that turned into a wheezing, bronchial cough. Wilkinson opened his mouth to speak, but the old man offered a dismissive wave with his free hand as the other covered his mouth with a handkerchief. Once the cough had subsided, rasping, he added, "You're the local, Wilks; Division told me that you were born and bred in Rothbury, and that's not a kick in the arse off where we're headed." Shoving the hanky back into his coat pocket, he stared with rheumy eyes at his subordinate. "I'm going to need you on this."

Wilkinson took a deep breath and ran a hand across his bristly crew-cut. "Funny thing is," he said, frowning, "I'd never heard of the place till you mentioned it to me."

"Well you've heard of it now." As an afterthought, Hewitt added solemnly, "The whole planet will have heard of it by now ..."

Forest gave way to undulating moors, thick with snow-encrusted heather and coarse grasses. A solitary, isolated farmhouse, black and lifeless swept by below them. No beacon or searchlight offered to light their way, but they pushed on regardless, into the darkness, with bleak resolve. Woodland once again rushed up beneath them, heaving like black, turbulent water. The helicopter swung low over the twisted, nightmarish shapes then, abruptly, the village materialised out of the storm.

The small clusters of stone houses and shops were in darkness, apart from the illumination of flashing lights from emergency vehicles on the ground and dozens of bobbing beams from handheld flashlights. Snow swirled violently amongst the buildings and whipped at the deep drifts that had built up over two days of heavy snowfall. The figures on the ground appeared distorted and elongated, moving quickly from building to building, despite the shin-deep snow.

"Looks like the power's still out," Wilkinson said, grimacing at the prospect of leaving the cosy confines of the helicopter.

Hewitt grunted, but otherwise his attention remained fixed on the chaotic scene below. Whilst his face remained as grim and unmoving as a statue, his mind was boiling with unanswered questions. One elbowed its way through to the fore; was this nightmare over or just beginning? In response, a shiver danced across his bony shoulders.

chapter 1

15th June – Six months earlier.

The man lying on his back in bed blinked as the drowsiness from a disturbed night's sleep gradually ebbed away.

The dream was still fresh in his mind, crystal clear down to every last detail. It had all seemed so real, so perfect. He was by no means new to this dream – he had experienced it time and time again over the last few years. Sometimes small details would alter, but the message was always the same. And yet, this time it had seemed so much more vibrant, so insistent. The urgency could no longer be ignored.

He sat up, exposing a broad bare chest with a diminutive portion of fair hair. The red hair on his head was thicker, but closely cropped and receding. His chin had a dusting of fine stubble, and lack of sleep had left its bruised mark under his auburn eyes. The fat Labrador splayed beside him on the duvet lifted his head, curious at the disruption, then flopped back down, letting out a deep contented sigh.

The man swung his powerful legs off the edge of the bed, and gazed absently at the curtained bedroom window, his mind a torrent of thoughts and emotions. A fine shaft of sunshine stole through a gap between the two panels to offer a hint of a warm early summer morning outside.

The master bedroom of his modest three bedroom semi was decorated similarly to the rest of the house – plain magnolia walls and white woodwork with a generous helping of simple, but functional Scandinavian furniture and furnishings. However, what filled the room was anything but plain. Posters, pictures and memorabilia were scattered in random patterns across every wall and surface. A framed original film cell from *Alien*, accompanied by a petrified looking Sigourney Weaver, playing Warrant Officer Ripley, adorned centre stage above the headboard … *last survivor of the Nostromo.* Either side of it were similar cells from *Enter the Dragon* and *Scarface*. Bruce Lee, sporting nunchucks … *Do not concentrate on the finger or you will miss all that heavenly glory* … and Al Pacino in the iconic stance, complete with M-16 assault rifle … *Say hello to my little friend.*

Either side of the window were rows of postcards collected over the years and carefully stuck to frame the window on both sides. Michael Caine in *Zulu*, Martin Sheen in *Apocalypse Now*, Richard Burton in *Where Eagles Dare*, Woody Harleson in *Natural Born Killers*, Steve McQueen atop motorbike in *The Great Escape*, Anthony Hopkins in *Silence of the Lambs*, John Travolta and Samuel Jackson in *Pulp Fiction* and many more.

The door had another tribute stuck to it – a signed poster of Anthony Hopkins, again in his role as Hannibal Lecter, as seen by Clarice Starling through his glass prison ... *His therapy was going nowhere.*

All in all, the room, along with the rest of the house, was a not so subtle tribute to the silver screen.

He stood up, his muscular body, ordinarily pale, seeming more so – almost translucent – in the poor light. Preoccupied, he dressed slowly in jeans and a *Pork-Chop Express* t-shirt. As he slipped on a pair of trainers, he said, "Ju, asshole and elbows, come on boy." His accent was nondescript, lacking any local twang.

Jumanji snorted his displeasure, but complied, jumping down rather gracelessly from the bed.

The dog followed his master down the hall, past a huge poster of Michael Caine, cigarette hanging out of his mouth, from *Get Carter* ... *You're a big man, but you're outta shape.*

Still on automatic pilot, he went about his routine of making a cup of tea and two slices of toast with honey. His body was going through the motions as his mind played the dream over and over in his head. Slowly, it was solidifying; taking shape, evolving.

"I love the smell of tea in the morning. It smells like … breakfast," he muttered to himself with a distant amused look.

Sitting at a small breakfast table, he drank his tea out of a *Lord of the Rings* mug in silent contemplation, his gaze drifting out of the window to the postage stamp fenced lawn beyond. His thoughts were only interrupted briefly to tear off a piece of toast and cast it into the eager, salivating jaws of Jumanji. The Labrador swallowed it with one short gulp and sat, tail wagging furiously, for more. With only a mild awareness, he continued to eat the toast while his mind worked through his dream ... his plan. Could this be what some religious nutters call destiny? Only the writers of history could answer that.

As he swallowed the last dregs of tea, he seemed to snap out of his trance. At once, he stood up from the table and looked down to his faithful companion. "Come on, Ju, we've got some work to do."

Happy to be included, the dog let out a short, high-pitched woof and continued to wag his tail.

The man sat at a computer desk in his small cluttered box bedroom-turned-study under the watchful eyes of Paul Newman and Robert Redford, making their famous Bolivian last stand ... *For a moment there I thought we were in trouble* ... on the wall behind him and from a shotgun-brandishing Dustin Hoffman ... *Jesus, I got em all* ... above his computer screen.

The screen showed an installation bar nearing completion and the title, *Whitman's Country Guide: UK Edition*, emblazoned above a silhouette of the British Isles.

As he waited, he thumbed through a pocketbook of Zen meditations. Several of the short phrases held little interest, but he paused at one: *We shape clay into a pot, but it is the emptiness inside that holds whatever we want.* He stared at the words for some time.

The software pronounced the end of the installation process with a short sound-byte of Gerard Butler as King Leonidas, shouting, "This is Sparta!" After clicking through a couple of colourful welcome screens, he arrived at a menu screen with a number of filtration fields, allowing searches by place name, location, landmark or custom.

Sitting forward, he clicked on the *Custom* icon. This brought up a drop-down list of options to fill the first part of the equation with a greater/less than/equal to option followed by an empty field.

After taking a moment to study the different options, he chose POPULATION followed by < and then typed 500 in the empty field. The word *searching* flashed up briefly and was then replaced by an extensive list of place names.

Ticking the box entitled *Narrow Lookup*, he then opted for KILOMETRES FROM URBAN AREAS > 30. After a moment, the list began to shrink. After a couple of minutes of chin-scratching and adjusting his position in the swivel chair, he further narrowed the lookup; SNOWFALL/YEAR > average. Only a few left. Last, but not least, CAPITAL CRIMES (based on 2010-2014 Home Office statistics) = zero. One place name remained: Haydon.

His eyes widened as he studied the six innocuous letters. One? He glanced down at the book of Zen meditations and then back to the screen. Excitedly, he double-clicked the mouse over the name. An Ordnance Survey map of the village and surrounding area popped up in a new window with a few lines of text beneath it.

Haydon, Northumberland. Pop.392.

Set in the heart of England's border county, amongst the picturesque Cheviot Hills and surrounded by unblemished woodland and moors. A quaint village lost in time. Local attractions include Cragside House, Lady's Well, Rothbury, Wallington Hall, Hadrian's Wall, Northumberland National Park.

The highlighted words offered further information on the individual attractions. Clicking on Northumberland National Park opened up a new window that sent him to the park's official website.

Welcome ... *Northumberland National Park, the land of the far horizon – a landscape of limitless beauty from Hadrian's Wall to the Cheviot Hills.*

He clicked back to the map of Haydon and stared at the screen for several long minutes. His face remained unchanging, his eyes seemingly piercing through the screen to the tangle of cables and the wall beyond. After a minute, he nodded slowly and whispered, "Three-ninety-two? That would beat Pedro by at least forty-two." Questioning himself, he added, "What about Shipman though?" He scratched his chin in deep thought.

"Hmm, possibly as many as four hundred and fifty-nine, but only two-one-five confirmed, so officially not a problem." Besides, Shipman's cowardly injections were hardly Hollywood material.

A little googling rewarded him with the telephone number of the nearest Tourist Information Centre. The phone rang for a couple of minutes before a bird-like voice answered, "Rothbury Tourist Information."

"Hi, I wonder if you could help," he said, ignoring her abrupt tone. "I would like to visit a village called Haydon; do you know it?"

"Yes, it's not far from Blindburn. Business or pleasure?" Still a clipped tone, but a little more forthcoming. He couldn't help but imagine a skinny old maid with a long beaked nose and narrow, squinting eyes.

"Both," he replied with just a hint of a smile angling the corner of his mouth. "Is there somewhere nice to stay in the village itself or would I need to look further afield?"

"I'm pretty sure one of the pubs there is also a B&B; let me just check." He heard the receiver clunk onto the desk (obviously not heard of mute or hold buttons out in the sticks yet) and then heard muffled rummaging through a filing cabinet. State of the art … whatever next, the wheel? Just as he laughed out loud, he heard the woman say, "Here it is. Are you okay?"

Clearing his throat to suppress the snigger, he said, "Yes, fine, sorry got a bit of a cough."

"Right," she said, clearly unconvinced and unhappy at not being let in on the joke. "The Miller's Arms. It's a quaint little place right in the village itself."

He made a mental note to check the dictionary for the latest definition of quaint, as a vision of dust, draughts and foist sprung to mind. But, what the hell, it would all be part of the experience. "That sounds fine. Do you have their number?"

Always a business doing pleasure with you. As soon as he hung up, he dialled the number for the pub. A gruff, authoritative Scotsman answered on the third ring. "Miller's," was his succinct greeting.

"Hi," he said cheerily, "is that the Miller's Arms in Haydon?"

"Aye, what can I do for yer?"

Shifting back in his seat and leaning into the handset, he said, "Well, I'm planning a stay in the village for a while and I need a room. Do you have one free?"

"Nae problem. When do yer need it and for how long?"

The man smiled; he liked this man's friendly but no nonsense manner. "From the Second of July till probably December/January."

There was a short pause, presumably while the landlord calculated the length of the stay. "Five or six months, yer say?" Surprise and just a hint of suppressed delight. "Yer know we dunna tend to give better rates for longer stays, laddie," he added tentatively.

"What's your nightly rate?"

"Thirty-five; including a hearty Scottish brekkie cooked by my good lady wife." A hint of pride in his voice.

"I'll pay thirty and I'll pay monthly in advance – in cash. That's my one and only offer."

He could almost hear the man rubbing his hands together as he agreed. "And what's the name for the booking?"

His heart skipped a beat. Stupidly, he hadn't been prepared for that. What was he thinking? Why hadn't he taken the time to jot down a few notes before ringing to get his story straight? He sat forward and chewed his lip as his mind scrambled for options. A favourite film character sprung to mind, followed quickly by the logo still displayed on his monitor. The process took a mere three seconds. "Hannibal Whitman."

"Hannibal? As in the man with the elephants?"

"I … err …" Bemused, he said, "Yeah, but normally people associate it with Hannibal Lecter."

"Sorry, don't know that one."

Shrugging, he said, "I'm researching a book, you see."

"A genuine writer, yer say? That'll get the gossip-hounds waggin'. Yer written anything I'll know?"

"This is my first actually." The old landlord hadn't seemed to notice his discomfort, so his heart rate gradually slowed and he quickly regained his composure. "It's a dark thriller."

He wrapped up the conversation with the usual pleasantries, along with giving false address details and the happy acceptance that the first month would be paid in cash on checking in. The next step was to start planning and also to sort out his affairs for the time he would be away. There was Ju to consider, the shop and the house.

Perry should be able to take Ju and keep an eye on the house, but it would require a lot of faith to let him run *Movie Maniac*. Six months was a long time for him to cope on his own – it would be quite a directorial debut. He had been friends with the scrawny Tarantino wannabe since their Uni days in Newcastle, so trust wasn't an issue. But, thinking about it, there would be a need to restock new Blu-ray and games titles and assorted merchandise, rota the part-timers, but other than that the shop pretty much ran itself. His accountant would continue to handle the important stuff.

Nothing would change really. Hell, the little shit already pretended to the occasional hot girl that popped in that he was the owner. He had stumbled upon that little gem when he had interrupted the flow of bullshit to one such tight-jeaned victim by entering unannounced one night just before closing. Of course, being the friend that he was, he didn't spoil the line, but he sure as hell gave him some stick for it over the weeks that followed.

So, Perry would get his end away a bit more while he was away. The desperate fucker needed the help.

Chuckling, he turned to his dog and said, "He should get himself some of that Arcturan Poontang – as long as it ain't a male." Jumanji panted back at him, his face a picture of happiness.

chapter 2

2nd July. *I'm from the city ... Doesn't matter what city; all cities are alike.*

It took all of his resources, a couple of shady characters (acquaintances of a drinking pal down the Queen's Head) and the combined efforts of eBay, Gumtree and Craigslist to acquire all the equipment that he would need for his little adventure.

The most difficult part was arranging an address and occupation (in Cumbria) and National Insurance number for his new identity. The young Chinese gent had told him quite openly that the documentation would hold up to cursory background checks, but would not withstand intense scrutiny. He was certainly not going to be any *Carlos the Jackal*, but it would have to do.

Now, as he headed north along the A64 heading away from Leeds, his thoughts were of Jumanji. Leaving his faithful Labrador behind with Perry had been the hardest part of his adventure so far. Ju had sat at the front door of Perry's flat while they had discussed a couple of final shop issues, his big eyes full of wonder and his tail wagging. He had even let out a low surprised whine when he ruffled his head one last time and walked away without him. He would miss the dumb mutt terribly while he was away, but it had to be done.

His story to Perry was that he was off to Cornwall to hide out in a cottage so that he could write the long overdue novel that he had been threatening to write for the last ten years. He had even paid for someone via Fiverr to send regular postcards from Cornwall as if from him. Old school, but Perry would appreciate it.

This adventure was going to give him something amazing to write about, that was for sure.

A heady concoction of excitement and trepidation cast aside any lingering drowsiness from the restless night's sleep he had endured the night before. He had felt like a seven year old on Christmas Eve – before adult anxieties and the unveiling of the true Santa Clause had dampened the magic.

The image of his mum sneaking into his bedroom at three AM was still vivid. She had the red woollen stocking with his name penned in biro and the picture of a colourfully decorated Christmas tree on it in her hands and she had silently deposited it at the foot of his bed. He still remembered the pyjamas she had gotten the two of them that year – his had small cartoon karate fighters all over and his brother's had been racing cars – C&A's best.

In previous years, she had always managed to outwit and outwait the both of them. They had always been foiled in their attempts at pretending to be asleep, but that year, when his mum checked on him, he had successfully fooled her, and suddenly years of belief were abruptly shattered. At first he had felt deeply hurt and even embarrassed for not listening to Darren at school, but the next day, seeing his mum beaver away in the kitchen with never a second's rest, something clicked inside. A seven year old boy learned to appreciate his mum that bit more.

His mum had always worked damn hard, holding down tough jobs to put food on the table. He had always asked for EVERYTHING on his Christmas lists before that year. In the years to come his lists became far more frugal. He never told her that he had caught her; instead he had just carried on with the ruse for several more years, until a mutual acceptance just kind of settled that such things were just for kids.

The early morning was grey and drizzly; just your typical English summer day. Traffic was heavy, with the ants dashing to work or dropping the kids off at school. A lorry roared past in the outside lane, buffeting Hannibal's small Peugeot and spraying it with dirty brown surface water.

He shook his head with an expression of disappointment and sadness, but then, spying the exit for A1 NORTH up ahead, his spirits immediately rose once more.

The drive north on the A1 was unchanging and uneventful, so to ease the boredom, Han further formulated the character he was to become for the duration of his adventure. He would live, breathe, sleep and think as the Cumbrian writer, Mister Hannibal

Whitman – the shop owner from Leeds would no longer exist; there would only be Han Whitman. So, he began creating background and family, likes and dislikes, motivations and careers. He'd fancied being an actor when he was younger and had always done well in drama. *Stanislavski would have been proud of my character preparation*, he mused. Slowly, in the dark recesses of his mind, Hannibal Whitman began to take shape. *It's alive ... It's alive!*

Once every last detail had been finalised, he played them over and over in his head, so that he would be able to recall them without hesitation. Chatting incessantly to the windscreen, he discussed every aspect of his new life to the splattered fly-corpses encrusted there. He adopted a mediocre Irish accent for the unnamed person questioning him and replied in a cheery 'all too happy to tell' tone. After twenty minutes, he was both satisfied with his character and bored with talking to himself, so he switched the radio on and turned the volume up high.

I can feel it coming in the air tonight, Oh Lord, Oh Lord,
I've been waiting for this moment, all my life, Oh Lord ...

Chariots of fire.
Detouring from the A1, he took the A690 and followed the signposts through the former mining town of Houghton le Spring, all the way to Sunderland city centre. From there, he followed his sat-nav to drop the Peugeot off at a long stay car park. After paying cash for a full six months in advance, he rushed through the cold rain, passing late morning shoppers, to the nearest taxi rank. The Mac-Cab Mondeo that picked him up stunk of cigarettes, despite having a peeling 'No Smoking' sign slapped onto the front of the glove box. But that was refreshing in comparison to the fat driver's body odour.

As luck would have it, his journey did not last long. 'Davey' dropped him off outside a shabby second-hand car lot, aptly (or not) named 'Chris's Chariots'. If the faded lettering on the cheap amateur sign was anything to go by, it would be perfect. The sky had turned a purplish-grey and the rain was beating off the uneven pavement and the bonnets of the colourful variety of cars.

With the rest of his luggage safely stowed with his car to pick up on the way out of Sunderland, all he carried was a plain backpack containing a few important items. Shouldering the bag, he strode confidently around the littered and oil-stained forecourt, ignoring the pounding rain, until his eyes fell upon an old Daihatsu Sportrak. On closer inspection, its age seemed to be the only thing going against it; nothing that a decent service and a couple of new tyres couldn't rectify, at any rate.

The salesman, sensing a fresh victim, moved in for the kill. Angling his bright yellow and blue golfing umbrella to shield both of them, he said, "I see you're a four-be-four connoisseur, mate. Nothing more rugged and reliable than these Sportraks." Under his *Arthur Daley* overcoat he was wearing an expensive suit, but he made it look cheap. With a 'I want your money' kind of a smile, he added, "Me name's Chris and these are me chariots and, aye that does sound like more cheese than Edam, but try not to hold it against us."

Without waiting for a response, and with the chit-chat dispensed with, he ploughed straight into sales mode. "You can see she's in damn good condition and only two previous owners. She's a ninety-five with the 1.6 ELXi engine – real quick for a four-be-four. Seventy-three on the clock, and taxed and MOT'd. At this price it's a steal – already had two lads looking since I put it out yesterday. If I was one of them shandy-drinkin' southerners, like, I'd be saying 'I'm cuttin'me own froat, Guv'. But as am not, I'll just say this – let's take her for a spin and see for yourself, eh?"

Han did just that, and was pleasantly surprised. The ten minute drive around Sunderland's one way system wasn't too juddery, nor was the engine too noisy. He also managed to knock the price down to five hundred pounds, by paying cash there and then. Halfway through the transaction he looked at his watch and feigned horror. Apologising, he said that he had an important meeting to go to and would have to finish the paperwork off another day. Eager not to lose the sale, Chris did what Han hoped he would do. He rushed through the formalities, failing to check for any proof of ID when filling out the notification of sale and new keeper on the Registration Certificate.

Han was feeling pretty pleased with himself as he drove his newly acquired Daihatsu back to the car park to collect the rest of his luggage. Even the rain had died off to a fine drizzle.

Once back on the A1, he skirted around Newcastle and Gateshead via the Western Bypass. The bold view of the Angel of the North, looking down from a well manicured grassy hill at Gateshead's fringe, reminded him of a film, *The Prophecy,* starring Christopher Walken. In the film, angels had been locked in an ageless conflict because God had favoured man with a soul. Han had loved the idea of that film; especially the fact that many of the angels – mainly Walken, playing Angel Gabriel – had been portrayed as vicious amoral killers, whom considered man no better than livestock.

He made a mental note to dig the DVD out when he returned from his little adventure. Walken was huge favourite of his; an actor with a rare talent to give the appearance of being a total psychopath, without the need to prove it through actual violence. He could chat casually, smile, laugh, hell even smell a rose in such a way as to make you run for cover, leave the country, buy a bunker, lock the doors and buy a very big gun (to use on yourself, in the event that he actually found you, because you wouldn't want to piss him off by trying to shoot him).

Laughing out loud at that last thought, he reached across to the passenger seat where several audio tapes had been scattered on the cracked leather, after being hastily purchased in Sunderland from several charity shops. A minor bugbear about the Sportrak – no CD player or DAB radio, just old school tape deck and FM radio. He located the soundtrack to *The Lost Boys* and popped it into the front loader. As *Echo & the Bunnymen* started crooning about strange people, a contented smile settled across his face.

People are strange when you're a stranger,
Faces look ugly when you're alone,
Women seem wicked when you're unwanted,

27

When a stranger calls.

After taking the A696 turn off, he pulled out of the Newcastle suburbs and into Northumberland. He passed by the Northumbrian Police Headquarters at Ponteland with mild interest. The bustling historic town on the River Pont was heaving with activity. Further on, he caught a glimpse of a signpost for Darras Hall; famed estate where many of the North East's rich and famous lived, including a few Toon footballers.

Once north of Ponteland, the landscape became steadily more luscious and green. He found himself travelling through quaint villages, with even quainter names – Belsay, Barnhill, Kirkwhelpington. To kill time, he started imagining tabloid headlines for each village – THE BELSAY BLOODBATH, THE BUTCHER OF BARNHILL, THE CRAZED SMALL BUSINESS OWNER KILLER OF KIRKWEL-KIRK-WHELP-OH FUCK IT-OF KIRK.

After skimming the southern borders of Harwood Forest, a thick coniferous mass of spruce and pine, sloping gently north east all the way to Rothbury, he was approaching the edge of the vast sixty thousand acre army training estate at Otterburn when he located his next turnoff. The B6341 led him to a road with just the simple index of '68' on Google Maps on his mobile (no sat-nav in this old-timer, of course). It was narrow, twisting and pot-holed and ran parallel with the tranquil River Coquet. This was the road that would lead him all the way to his destination … Haydon.

The final leg of his journey into early evening took him through the quiet hamlet of Alwinton, at the south eastern foothills of the Cheviots, surrounded by rolling moors and grazing fields. He had to stop once to pull onto the grass verge to allow a battered faded blue Land Rover to pass. He took a moment to glance down to his left and saw a trickling stream down a shallow bank, covered with luscious grass and sprinkled with buttercups. Dreamily, he looked back towards the driver of the Landy, a grinning, craggy faced man with a thick head of white hair and bushy sideburns. The man waved a thank you as he passed by.

Three miles further along the small, bumpy track, he blinked and passed through the small cluster of stone buildings that was Shillmoor, then after the track crossed the river one more time, a couple of hundred yards further was the turnoff he had been searching for. Even with Google Maps he still managed to miss it twice. Overgrown shrubs and bramble crowded in on the junction from both sides, making it virtually invisible until you were on top of it. It was as if Haydon didn't want any visitors. He smiled at that. Oh, boy, this was gonna be fun.

He pulled onto the road and the sky immediately darkened. It was as if someone had turned a dimmer switch right down. At the same time the FM station he had been listening to threw out static instead of the mindless drivel of some annoyingly energetic DJ. He stopped the car and looked from the radio to the sky, craning his neck to look up through the grubby windscreen.

It was dark because the tree canopy stretched over the road, leaving only brief glimpses of the sky above. One mystery solved. He twiddled the dial on the radio and found nothing but static. He then picked up his phone and noticed that he no longer had any mobile service either – no signal or data.

"Bad service area, that's all," Han said, shaking his head at his slightly unnerved reaction. Still chastising himself, he switched the radio to medium wave and was instantly rewarded with an old crooner.

Fairytales can come true, it can happen to you if you're young at heart
…

It was after eight PM when he finally turned onto the main street of Haydon. The evening was growing dim and a bank of clouds had rolled across the sky to conspire to quicken the process. The street was narrow and lacking street lights, but well-maintained and lined with mature oak and sycamore trees. The first group of stone buildings to come into view were only two hundred yards from the road that continued on to Blindburn.

On his left, was a used car dealership that made Chris's appear mid market by comparison. Beneath moss and grime, gothic letters spelled out *Belmont Cars*. The small forecourt had a motley collection of aging motors that made his Daihatsu look fresh off the forecourt. To his right, was the modest stone steeple of St. Bartholomew's church ... Church of England, by the look of it.

A short distance away, Main Street parted around a well-groomed green with a park bench and, holding centre stage, a mighty oak which, with sunshine, would easily overshadow most of what was clearly the nucleus of the village. A Co-op mini market, Post Office, Merlin's Mea s (the '*t*' was missing from the sign), Little Bakery, Duck & Bucket Tavern, Jolly Moe's Barber Shop and, finally, the Miller's Arms Inn were all huddled around the dark, deserted Green.

All the premises were stone built, but each as individual as a human thumbprint. The Co-op, a squat stretched building; the Post Office, austere like a bank (it was amazing to see a small village with its own post office in this day and age); the butchers, shabby with a tired awning; Little Bakery, a picture of quaint England; the Duck, small but adorned with six overflowing hanging flower baskets in full blossom; Moe's, flamboyant ruby red woodwork and an old-fashioned red and white revolving pole, and the Miller's, an old coaching inn affair, solid and dependable.

Main Street rejoined itself and continued on to a car park and a disused train station. Two roads forked off Main Street; Bell Lane and, as he pulled up to the Miller's, he noticed the second was called Miller's Road (inspired). Main Street was wider at the old coaching inn, so there were three parking bays outside, one of which was unoccupied.

After parking, he jumped out with renewed energy, despite the long and tedious drive. His earlier ill-ease long gone. An old man, in a grubby overcoat that aspired to be as wrinkled as its owner, shambled past him into the pub.

"Evening," Han called after him with a cheery wave. The door slammed shut without acknowledgement. "Mean old bastard."

He followed the old codger to the entrance, but paused with his hand pressed against the tarnished brass welcome plate stuck to the centre of the wide oak door. Taking a moment to glance up and down the street, he muttered, "Perfectamundo," and then pushed the door inwards.

MOB, maybe Moby to his friends, was sagging at the cherrywood bar, adorned with half a dozen real ale pumps, along with a few lagers and beers that Han hadn't seen for years. *The one you've gotta come back for.* With rickety old washing machine shakes, he was awkwardly paying for a bottle of *Guinness Extra Stout* with a fist full of small change. None of your trendy continental beers here, just the old faithful.

An old vinyl-playing jukebox that looked like a throwback from the 60s was playing a Jim Reeves classic. *Welcome to my world … won't you come on in …* Apt.

As Han was taking this in, he gradually noticed that Moby and the burst-couch-chested barman, with a scowl and a silvery crew-cut were staring at him. No smiles, no curiosity, just cold hard stares.

Han offered them a smile. They turned back and continued with their transaction.

Now forcing the smile, he strolled over to the bar. Covering most of the walls was a wide assortment of military memorabilia; black and white photographs from various conflicts, maps, coats of arms, regimental flags, the cross of St. Andrew Flag (the National Flag of Scotland), a musket, a couple of helmets (one he recognised as British circa World War II), a flak jacket, bayonets, a rather lethal looking combat knife, and dozens of medals and ribbons hanging in a presentation case. In amongst the military memorabilia there were also dozens of vintage postcards depicting a multitude of saucy Benny Hill-esq encounters.

"Quite a collection, aye laddie?" the barman said with a deep, but unexpectedly friendly voice.

Assuming the barman meant his military collection and not his dirty postcards, Han said, "Damn straight. I'm guessing it'll be a safe bet that you used to be in the army."

The barman smiled. "Aye, yer got that right. Forty-two years in the Scots Guards; retired a couple of years ago. Served through one or two disagreements."

Han waited for him to elaborate, but when he didn't Han ordered a drink.

While the landlord poured him a pint of lager, Han continued the conversation. "Forty-two years, eh? Jesus. What rank?"

"Sergeant Major," he said, with obvious pride as he set the drink down. "I'm Joe Falkirk, the landlord of this humble drinkin' establishment. And my merry pal there's Tam Wellright."

As Han opened his mouth to respond, Moby/Tam spoke without taking his eyes off his pint. "I'm eighty-four and still grow me own veggies. Dig for victory … dig for victory …"

"You don't say?" Turning back to the landlord, he caught Joe rolling his eyes and laughed. "Nice to meet the both of you. I'm Hannibal Whitman; we spoke on the phone."

"Aye, of course – we've been expecting yer." He smiled and it was like the parting of the red sea. "Martha – the better half – has got yer room all ready for yer."

First night.

The room that would be his home over the coming months turned out to be spacious and bright, with a double bed, en suite bath and toilet. The furniture and furnishings appeared to have not been renewed for decades – pastel pink bathroom suite, highly polished teak desk and wardrobe and a floral high-backed armchair.

The curtains, carpet, cushions and bedding were a kaleidoscope of patterns and colours, but every surface was meticulously clean and a faint aroma of jasmine from a bowl of potpourri on the windowsill scented the air. Han was amused, but overall, pleasantly surprised.

After semi-unpacking – well, unzipping one of the cases and having a half-hearted rummage – he headed back downstairs to take Joe up on a courtesy bar meal to celebrate his first night as their guest.

Martha turned out to be a plump, grinning woman with a frizz of grey hair and energy to spare. Although a little overbearing – fussing over him like a long lost son returning from war – and the permanent grin that at times appeared to be glued in place, her toad-in-the-hole turned out to be first class.

The pub had filled up in his absence and 'Big' Joe – as the regulars seemed to call him – had been joined by a short, skinny girl with spiky black hair and tattoos called Lisa. She was perhaps seven stone dripping wet, but she commanded respect from everyone in the bar, including a group of three boisterous lads of the young, dumb and full of cum variety. Han noticed her eyes linger in his direction more than once. Maybe it was just that he was a new face, but you never know. He pretended not to notice and smiled inwardly. *She cannae take yer charm, Captain …*

He ordered a whiskey and made himself comfortable at the bar beside a slim redheaded woman in her early thirties. He nodded a greeting to her and was unable to help himself from eying the curves of her generous (cosmetically enhanced) breasts. Her slender hands were both wrapped around the stem of a glass of chardonnay, and Han noticed immediately, to his initial disappointment, a platinum wedding band.

"Janet, have yer met our new resident writer, Mister Whitman?" Big Joe's voice interrupted his thoughts.

"Nice to meet you, Mister Whitman," she said, offering him a hand and a glimpse at a perfect set of porcelain veneers.

"Han, please." He took her hand and returned the smile.

"Hannibal, hmm? Sounds like cannibal. I hope you don't bite." Her voice was – an old *Heartbreak Ridge* quote sprung to mind – as smooth as a prom queen's thighs …

They laughed as Big Joe said, "Watch out for this one, laddie. She's like one o'them femme fatales from a *Sam Spade* novel. She also happens to be married to the only quack in the area."

"I take offence at that," Janet replied, smiling playfully.

"What, being married to Larry or being a femme fatale?"

"Don't you come running to my Larry when your haemorrhoid problems flare-up again."

Han observed the friendly banter with detached amusement as the door opened to admit a tall, tanned man in his thirties. He strode up to the bar with the confidence of a cock in a henhouse. Boot-cut jeans and fitted sweater, dark tussled hair and designer stubble, carefully maintained to look like it wasn't maintained at all. He was a postcard for the pseudo-stylish and wannabe-famous. In his youth, probably captain of the football team too. Han disliked him instantly.

"A'right, Steve?" Big Joe said. "Usual?"

"Aye, BJ. Hi, Janet, fancy meeting you here." He smiled and there was something rather predatory about it.

"Steve," she replied a little sternly. "We have a new resident. This is Hannibal Whitman; he's a writer."

There was a brief flicker of annoyance in his face, but then it was replaced with a pretty good attempt at a sincere 'damn glad to meet ya' face. "Hey, Han. Steve Belmont of Belmont Motors; good to meet you."

"Likewise." They shook hands and his powerful grip said one thing; *this is MY henhouse*. Han kept his grip casual, not wanting to damage the man's fragile ego. Bless him.

Steve angled himself between Han and the femme fatale, and started a conversation, so Han took the hint and went back to nursing his whsikey. He was quickly rewarded with the skinny bum belonging to Lisa bent over in his general direction as she stooped to pick up a bottle of *Babycham* from a lower shelf. The movement briefly revealed a Rolling Stones red lips logo tattooed on the small of her back and a healthy portion of black thong.

"Ah, shite," Big Joe muttered under his breath, drawing Han's attention to the door.

A blonde had walked in. There was a hint of a previously very pretty woman, but now her face was puffy with blotchy skin, and dark bruised circles around bloodshot eyes. Her cheap jeans and blouse were creased, but precisely in reverse from the mighty Charioteer, Chris, she actually managed to make them look better on.

Steve and Janet both turned to look at the new arrival. Steve turned away quickly in disgust, but Janet's eyes lingered a moment longer.

"I dunna want nae trouble, Carol," Big Joe said, with a sincere mix of warning and compassion.

Hovering in the doorway, a picture of nerves, she took the hesitation as an opportunity to light up a cigarette with a trembling hand. After a couple of deep draws, the nicotine seemed to calm her and boost her confidence. "Campari and soda, Joe," she said with a passable attempt at nonchalance, thrusting the disposable lighter and crumpled pack back into her bag.

Big Joe relaxed and did as she asked.

She moved hesitantly to the bar and stood by Han. He did not feel overly happy at suddenly being thrust into a Checkpoint Charlie role between the obviously warring factions.

Nobody seemed to comment on her smoking, which was quite a surprise to Han. They must be a little more flexible with the smoking laws out in the sticks.

Taking another shaky draw on her cigarette, she turned to Han and offered a somewhat embarrassed nicotine-stained smile. "Hi, hun. What's your name?" There was the faintest tick just above her left eyebrow and her bloodshot eyes had a thousand-yard stare quality about them.

With the resignation that comes from knowing that a chain of events were now impossible to prevent, he replied in his friendliest, yet most non-committal voice possible. "Han Whitman. Pleased to meet you."

"I'm Carol Belmont; ex-wife of that adulterous bastard there."

"Ah, Christ." Scarcely above a whisper from Big Joe.

"Why don't you get a life, Carol," Steve muttered in an even tone, without taking his eyes off his glass of red wine.

Still looking at Han and maintaining the forced smile, she replied, "I had a life and you stole it from me."

Janet turned to her, her expression genuine sympathy. "Carol, please ..."

Carol whipped her head around with such ferocity that Han thought her head would surely fly off. Glaring at Janet, she hissed, "Save your pity. You'll need it for yourself."

Janet's face flushed almost as red as her hair, and she turned away back to her drink without another word.

To Han, it was a car crash; hypnotic rubbernecking to his morbid curiosities.

"I don't need this shit, Carol. Get off your cross." With that, Steve drained the rest of his red wine and strode out, without another word.

"Carol, why do yer have to start this in my boozer, eh?" Big Joe said, shaking his jowly face with his hands planted on his substantial hips. There was anger in his tone, but his face showed deep empathy.

Timidly, she turned to Big Joe, tears welling in her eyes. "S-Sorry, Joe. I just ..." Her bottom lip quivered and her voice faltered. With one swift movement, she drained her drink then stubbed out the remains of her cigarette into a *Skol* ashtray. With far less grace and dignity than her former husband, she fled into the night with tears streaming down her face.

There was a minute of awkward silence as Big Joe glanced from Janet, to Han, to the door.

"Quite the soap opera," Han said with a half-hearted attempt at humour. Big Joe just shook his head sadly and returned to rinsing glasses. Janet continued to stare into her drink.

"Going through Hell, keep going," Tam mumbled into his empty glass from the end of the bar.

Lisa walked through from the lounge, with several empty pint glasses stacked in her hands. "Was that Carol making a tit of herself again?"

"Give over, Lisa," Big Joe muttered with a scowl. Then, with a sigh, he added, "Can you serve Tam? He's dry again."

All in all, Han's first night in Haydon had been enlightening to say the least. The blend of excitement and trepidation that he had felt at the start of his journey was now

36

joined by a hungry curiosity for what would follow. There was so much to do and the clock was ticking.

chapter 3

3rd July. *The girl and the playground.*

Han awoke from the most restful sleep he had experienced in years, as the first rays of morning sunshine pierced the thin floral curtains. Despite the early hour, he felt refreshed and ready for the day. He swung his legs out of the bed and jumped up, yawning but smiling, his eyes wide and blinking.

With electric razor in hand, Han stared at his unshaven image in the mirror of his pokey en suite bathroom. He had switched it on and was about to start shaving himself when his hand had stopped less than an inch from the skin. The razor vibrated gently in his hand.

"Man, you look just like I feel," he said to his reflection.

Chuckling, he switched the buzzing device off and popped it back into its pouch. No more shaving, at least while on location. If he was going to be a writer, he was going to have to look the part.

After a brief stand up wash, he dressed in jeans and a *M*A*S*H* t-shirt, then headed for the door.

The lounge was deserted, apart from the ever fussing Martha. She swooped down on him the instant he sat down at the one table that had been laid out with cutlery, placemat with a Northumberland National Park scene, and a napkin. Her ample breasts, bulging in a plain matronly dress, swayed close to his face as she swept away imaginary specks of dust from the table.

After a considerable Scottish fry up that would block all but the healthiest arteries, followed by two cups of tea, he headed out into the cool fresh morning sunshine.

It wasn't quite nine AM, but the village centre already seemed a bustle of activity. The Co-op and the Post Office both had customers, Henhouse Steve could be seen leaving the former in a sweaty t-shirt and jogging shorts. Three older gents, two in obligatory beige overcoats and caps and the third in a tartan dressing gown and slippers, were stood around the bench under the mighty oak. They stopped their animated conversation on seeing the stranger in their midst. All three turned in unison to stare at him. There was no attempt at subtlety, just open distrust.

Han offered them a broad smile and then turned right to head down Miller's Road. Unlike Main Street, the narrow off-shoot was cobbled and far more in keeping with Han's mental image of a quaint little village. After passing S Priestly Chemists and a cluster of narrow terraced houses, Miller's Road ended quite abruptly. It was replaced by a gravel footpath that led into a dense wooded area of birch, oak and alder. Thick luscious branches intertwined above the path to offer a latticework canopy.

Not wanting to backtrack just yet, he decided to venture into the woods. The bubbling, dove-like call of a black grouse, somewhere within the woods, greeted him as he walked casually along the shrouded path. Vibrant bluebells and clumps of wild grass lined its edge, and a rustling of leaves rippled through the branches above with the caress of a gentle breeze that carried on it an array of woodland scents.

A five minute walk brought him into a bright picnic area with a swing, roundabout, slide and a wooden climbing frame. This quiet woodland sanctuary was clean and well-kept; the grass well-groomed and not a scrap of litter or an expletive of graffiti. It was bordered on the far side by a shallow, rocky stream with stepping stones that allow the walker to continue along the path beyond. Narrow dirt tracks led off on both sides of the clearing, leading deeper into the forest.

Dressed in an obscenely short denim skirt and tight low cut top, the barmaid – Lisa – stood at the swings pushing a little girl gently backwards and forwards. She hadn't noticed his arrival. There was a distant, dreamy look in her eyes as she gazed out past the stream. She looked pale and fragile in the dazzling sunshine.

The girl, maybe four, was also quiet and following her mother's gaze as she swung back and forth, accompanied by the rhythmic creak of the chains. As he approached, he could see a resemblance between mother and daughter, except for the thick curly blonde locks on the child.

Lisa was like a statue, only the briefest movement from one hand to keep the swing moving. Her daughter was just as still. Both staring, silent, at the stream. No giggles, no chat, just staring.

Beginning to feel uncomfortable and having crossed most of the distance, he felt compelled to say something. He said, "Hi."

"Fuck!" was her startled reply as she swung round to face him, her diminutive chest heaving almost out of her low top. Seeing that it was Han, she flushed red and composed herself, hoisting her top up to a more respectable level. "Sorry, you scared the shit out of us there."

Han laughed and, holding up his hands, he offered a brief apology. "This your daughter?" He bent down and smiled at the little girl who had now fixed her intense stare on him. She had wide, curious eyes, the same colour of stormy sea grey as her mother's.

"I'm four," she said matter-of-factly.

Feigning astonishment, he said, "Wow, I woulda thought you were at least five!"

She offered him a thin smile, but it was brief and followed by a shrug that said, 'yeah, typical *adult* thing to say'. She kicked her small legs off the ground to resume the swing motion and her gaze returned to the stream.

"Yeah, Haley weren't exactly planned," Lisa said awkwardly, almost apologetically. "But she's me little angel."

"Well, she's got her mother's looks, that's for sure," Han replied, with a flicker of a glint in his eye.

"Pretty smooth, Mister ...Whitman wasn't it?"

"Call me Han."

"And what should you call me?" She gave her daughter's back another gentle push then turned back to Han with a teasing smile brightening her fair complexion.

Her playful expression was infectious; he returned the smile effortlessly. "Why don't you be my Princess Lisa?"

She laughed at that, throwing her head back to expose more of the slender angle of her neck. Han was pleasantly surprised by how glowing and alive it made her look, despite her gaunt features. The short exchange had allowed him to move closer to the young woman, but as he ventured to gently touch her arm, Haley jumped down from the swing and squeezed in between them with a protective scowl on her face.

He backed off immediately, apologising to both mother and daughter.

"Haley, be nice, angel," Lisa said with an affectionate firmness. "It's okay, Han. Haley's just a little over protective sometimes."

The rest of the day was spent leisurely finding his way around the village and surrounding fields and woodland. He made a point of visiting each of the shops. His first stop was Priestly's to buy condoms, just to see if he could get a reaction out of the mid forties, prim looking bespectacled man behind the counter (a little positive thinking for Princess Lisa might have constituted a second reason). He was disappointed to receive only a polite 'good day to you' for his trouble from Mister Priestly himself, who then calmly went back to reading a well-thumbed and faded copy of Reader's Digest. Han couldn't make out the year, but it had illustrated cats on the cover that made it look vintage.

Crossing over Main Street, he then entered the Co-op to buy a newspaper, but was rather surprised that they didn't stock any. A husband and wife (young enough to be his daughter) were running the show there. He, Duncan Fairbank, seemed like the rugged outdoors type, but not far off being sent to pasture, but the wife, Loretta, was all smiles, with a look of Olivia Newton John about her (pre *Grease* badgirl unfortunately, but still very easy on the eye). As he was leaving, a very pretty blonde in her late teens almost bumped straight into him, saying, "Sorry I'm late, Mister Fairbank – oop! Sorry, sir!" She was flushed from running and clutching a purple bag protectively to her chest. She offered a melting-heart apologetic smile and stepped to the side.

Returning the smile, he said, "No worries, hun." His eyes only stayed on her for a moment, but it was enough to take in her Barbie-like frame, tight shorts over long slender and tanned legs, and a warm, intelligent face. *Sandys and Barbies*, he thought with mild amusement.

"No problem, Mand," Duncan replied, ignoring the near collision.

His next stop was the Post Office to buy a notepad from a stork-like older gent with a nervous twitch. The stumpy wife, with an acute dodgy hip, appeared from nowhere as soon as she heard a stranger's voice.

She was quick to introduce herself as Agatha (but you can call me 'Aggie') Smith, and, as an afterthought, waved a curt hand towards her husband, Leonard (or 'Lenny', presumably only when he was in favour, which was probably not that often). The husband offered what was somewhere between a scowl and a forced smile, which Han imagined as a plea. *K-kill me ...*

Outside the Owen and Momma Lift Post Office, he paused, one foot on the curb. A dusty green Land Rover, with *Bryce & Son* stencilled on the hardtop in faded white lettering, pulled up to the intersection. It slowed, before swinging out onto Main Street, giving Han a brief glimpse of a big bear of a man with a wide spade-like face sporting a deep frown.

Crossing over Bell Lane, he looked through the window at Merlin's Meats, but found neither an excuse nor the inclination to enter. The proprietors seemed to be a couple, based on a few simple observations; they were both fat, with similar glazed expressions and open, toothy grins, and both wore matching cords and woolly jumpers under blood-stained aprons.

It was clearly a local shop, for local people, he mused. He released a mock shiver and vowed never to buy *anything* from them. There were a few oddballs in the village, but gold medals had to go to the Merlins, aka Edward and Tubbs.

His final stop was Little Baker's, and what was a huge contrast to the demon butchers of Main Street next door. The aroma of freshly baked bread aroused his nose and taste buds even as the bell tinkled to announce his entrance. As he bought a sandwich, he discovered that Simon and Kim Little seemed almost normal for Haydon. They were friendly, but not overbearing and kept a beautifully clean – if a little chintzy –

shop. They were both in their forties, a little haggard looking, but, at least on the surface, happy enough with their lot in life.

Strolling back along Main Street, he decided to eat his lunch in the grounds of St. Bart's. The graveyard and gardens were on the unkempt side, but were pleasant enough, bordered by mossy dry stone walls and faintly scented with lavender. As he sat, a pair of chaffinches sitting high up on a sturdy branch of an oak in the corner of the graveyard, their white shoulder patches glinting in the summer sunshine, chirped to one another. He sat for a time, shaded by the branches of a sycamore, eating the sandwich and contemplating the various characters he had met so far.

It was not long before the resident vicar, obviously smelling the scent of a fresh agnostic quarry, appeared and headed in his direction. This man was at least six foot three, beanpole skinny with a shocking mess of ginger hair, still thick and red, despite his advancing years.

As he approached, the vicar surprised Han by producing a *Hamlet* cigar and popping it into his mouth. Lighting it with an old Ronson lighter, he nodded as he puffed. "Afternoon to you."

"Afternoon, Father," Han said genially after swallowing a bite of his sandwich. "I hope you don't mind me stopping for a spot of lunch in your lovely gardens."

"Not at all, friend. I'm not a Father, though, I'm a Reverend – Church of England, you see. Reverend Dunhealy; Morgan. Now, I know that sounds like I should be Catholic, but what can I do?" He grinned, revealing a mouth full of slightly stained and crooked tombstone teeth. "You must be the newcomer I've been hearing whispers of about the place."

Leaning back against the wood slats of the bench, Han grunted a short laugh and shook his head. "Sorry, Reverend. The gossip is far more reliable than your mobile service."

The reverend frowned and stared at him.

"I mean, news certainly travels fast around here."

The frown switched to a cheerful nod and he said, "Aye, there's nothing goes on round here without the whole village getting to know about it." There was a subtle hint of Scot to his accent.

Han stood up, dropping the empty wrapper into a waste bin beside the bench. He held out a hand. "Han Whitman, Reverend. Pleased to meet you." The vicar took it without reservation, but, for a split second a look of uncertainty passed across the old man's face. Han's strong hand gripped the slender, musical hand of the vicar's and he offered him a wide, cheery smile.

You're bugging me.

Several days passed as he began to find his feet in the small village of Haydon. Gradually, he developed a feel for the rhythm of the village and its strange array of occupants. During those early days, occasionally it would rain – heavy summer rain, richly scented with the surrounding woodland, grass and thirsty flora – then a few clear powder-blue sunny days would follow, before returning to chilly showers. Such was the climate of northern England (well, pretty much all of England for that matter).

He continued the gentle flirting with the skinny young mother, Lisa, who seemed only too flattered with the playful banter from an older, supposedly wiser, pretend writer. Martha persisted in fussing about him at every opportunity in her grinning motherly way, which, once acclimatised to, actually became moderately pleasant and comforting. For the most part, Big Joe left him to his own devices, apart from an occasional chat about life in the village. Tam Wellright would appear every evening at the same time and shuffle across to his same spot at the end of the bar, and, without a word, Big Joe would bring him his usual bottle of stout.

Janet and Loretta Fairbank dropped in one evening for a girly night without the husbands (or bits on the side). They made one or two whispered comments aimed in his direction that frequently ended with a giggle from one or the other. The Haydon cock, Steve Belmont, would never be far away when Janet was around, but Carol managed to keep her distance; Han only spotted her once, standing across the street from the Miller's while Steve was inside chatting, for a change, to Duncan, rather than Janet. It had been a cool, cloudless evening and a breeze licked the unkempt strands of her dirty blonde hair while she stood rigid by the curb side. A haunted expression was fixed to her rigid features. Unmoving and silent, she clutched a Co-op carrier bag with an unseen bottle inside like it was the secret elixir to everlasting life.

Over the placid shuffle of time, at a pace to relax even the most high-octane, coke-sniffing stockbroker from The City, the residents of Haydon slowly began to get used to his presence. The ever watchful eyes of the nosey-parkers and curtain-twitchers ceased scrutinising him quite so closely. Heads stopped turning as he passed by and skulking whispers moved on to fresh subjects. He waited patiently for guards to slip before commencing with his chores.

The first job was intelligence gathering. That meant surveillance, and that in turn involved breaking out some of his online purchases. All of his more sensitive equipment was stored in a combination-locked titanium luggage case which now lay open on his bed as he sorted through some of its contents.

An assortment of electronic devices had been laid out either side of the open case. There was a large clear plastic bag full of telephone transmitters, which were small white plastic devices that plugged into telephone wall sockets, a chrome high performance wall microphone and two dozen black transmitters, which were about half the size of a pack of playing cards. His high-spec laptop had been set on the desk and was fitted with a state-of-the art radio receiver and recorder that enabled the recording of multiple devices instantaneously, as well as listening while recording.

Every piece of equipment for the experiment had been purchased under his false identity and delivered to a PO Box in York that had also been opened using his false name. With a flair for the dramatic, he had dressed in ill-fitting clothes, a wide-brimmed fedora with a black curly wig beneath, sunglasses and a rather fetching Clark Gable moustache. Amazingly enough, the assistant hadn't even spared him a second glance. He kept his head slightly angled downwards the whole time and ensured he that he never once glanced towards the security camera. The bounty was retrieved without hitch or incident and, once back to his car, he had laughed all the way back home.

The telephone transmitters ran off the power from the phone line, so they would never need replacing. As a result, once in place, the phone bugging would be effortless. Room bugging was a different matter, as room bugs needed an independent power source. Unless you had the resources and contacts of the CIA, adequate technology was pretty restrictive. After a great deal of internet-based research, he finally chose the small black transmitters for their extended battery life (one thousand hours in standby mode or sixty-two hours of continuous transmission). They were the best his funds could reasonably run to, but the batteries would still need recharging from time to time which would be risky.

The Miller's was easy enough to bug with a transmitter on the phone (a classic red dial job) and one of the battery transmitters in the bar and lounge and both toilets (suckered to the underneath of tables and hand basins). The Post Office, the Co-op, Merlin's and Little's were also pretty straightforward for a man with a degree of patience (mainly battery transmitters concealed under a shelf here or behind some loose panelling there). A crawling sensation at having to buy some homemade sausages from the Edward and Tubbs double act was the only difficulty. A haircut at Moe's allowed the placement of a transmitter under the barber's chair and a relaxing rest on the Green gave him time to attach one to the underside of the bench.

Even Belmont's turned out to be simple enough; he just had to wait for Steve to jump into his old red Ford Capri to nip off somewhere (probably an illicit meeting with Janet) and then he just strolled into his unlocked portacabin and popped a transmitter under his shabby desk. He passed Steve's salesman, James Falkirk and mechanic, Paul Mason, chatting by the open bonnet of an Austin Princess 2200. Orange bodywork and black roof, just like a car his dad used to drive. He stood and stared at it, a bolt of lightning straight out of the dark recesses of his past.

Shaking off the weird feeling, he offered the two men a friendly wave and walked on. Neither gave him a second glance.

The Duck & Bucket proved a little more testing. The landlady, Tess Runckle, turned out to be a robust woman with big bleached-blonde hair and even bigger breasts. She dripped more gold than Mr T and laughed like Eddie Murphy, but she had a cunning eye and, without any subtlety at all, gave Han a look of pure suspicion.

With considerable effort and patience, he did eventually manage to plant a transmitter on the phone (a salmon pink push button trimphone) and another in the lounge, bar and gents. It was the ladies toilets that proved to be something of a Stalingrad, as experienced by the Germans in the winter of 1942.

Sitting beneath dozens of framed photographs and paintings, chiefly around the themes of birds and flowers, Han shifted in his seat and rubbed his bristly chin. He was growing impatient and beginning to convince himself that it was starting to show. Under the watchful eyes of grey wagtails, sparrows, thrushes and kestrels, not to mention Miss Marple-meets-Bet Lynch, he downed his third whiskey then stood up in what he hoped was a casual way. He arched his back and let out a resolute sigh. Offering the nosy landlady a sociable smile, which received a pencil-thin one in return, he turned towards the toilets.

His heart was racing as he approached the two doors, marked subtly with 'Cocks' and 'Hens'. Glancing over his shoulder, he could see that the busybody was no longer in view, but his pulse continued to race nonetheless. A nauseating feeling struck him that seemed at once undeniable. If this were a film, his next action would be known as a story decision. This was a major plot choice that would thrust our faithful protagonist/antagonist further on towards his goal. Suddenly, it was as if everything rested on this one task, which he reminded himself immediately was nonsense. As he reached the doors, he dropped his head down and, taking a deep breath, barged headlong into the ladies. Decision made.

Having positioned himself earlier to keep an eye on both conveniences, he knew already that the hens' were empty. After a cursory examination, revealing two cubicles and a wash area, he wasted no time in slipping a transmitter behind one of the two wash basins, pressing hard so that the adhesive back on the small device stuck firmly to the ceramic surface. With a sigh of relief, he flashed the back of his hand across his hot forehead. Not wishing to linger, he headed straight for the door, only to be confronted by Ms Runckle herself.

"Lost, Mister Whitman?" Her face was set and her tone accusing.

For a couple of very long seconds, Han was dumbstruck. His eyes were wide and staring and his mouth hung open slightly as fireworks exploded inside his mind. Then, recovering quickly, he said, "Little bit disorientated, I'm afraid." There was a feigned slur to his words. "Missed dinner ... I think that last one went straight to my head."

"Well, you just make sure it doesn't happen again. I wouldn't want you scaring my girls now." Her arms remained folded across her abundant bosom and her tone sustained an icy curtness, but she stepped aside and allowed him to pass.

Brushing past her, he received an eye-watering whiff of musky roses that reminded Han of something his Gran used to wear. Something from Avon, if his memory served him correctly. He started to walk away from the toilets, and then instantly realised his error. He spun and strode straight into the gents without so much as a glance in the landlady's direction.

Tess Runckle continued to watch the closed door to the cocks' for a moment longer, a look of reservation etched in her face that caused the thick foundation to crease around her pursed lips.

Opportunity Knocks.

A run of mild, overcast days slipped by as he persisted with carefully bugging key areas of the village. The incident with Tess Runckle had shaken him, although he was loath to admit it, but it was a stark reminder of the risks he faced. He re-doubled his concentration and maintained patience and vigilance at all times. His only indulgence, to help pass the time, was to build on his earlier successes with Lisa, maintaining a healthy banter between the two of them. He would make a point to chat to her in the street or in the pub, always flirting, but never over-stepping the mark.

Two blurred and eventful weeks had passed since his arrival when an opportunity arose quite out of the blue.

Han was sat at the bar, sipping his fifth drink of the night, and trying to ignore the smell of mould coming from Tam propping up his usual spot. He was staring at the packets of *Scampi Flavour Fries* on a board behind the bar, but his mind was running through hundreds of details on the residents, searching out the important ones that could be used to his advantage at a later date. The night had been slow, only a handful of patrons drifting in and out.

Lisa appeared at his side, a couple of empty glasses in her hands. She winked as she scooped up an empty tumbler beside him. She was dressed in a thin white blouse that revealed the lines of her bra underneath and the usual shortest of short skirts.

"Princess, you're such a tease."

"You don't know the half, darlin'," she replied with a wicked giggle.

Han's smile broadened and, fishing further, said, "I bet it's all just talk with you."

Lisa had turned to head back behind the bar, but that stopped her in her tracks. She turned to him, her expression mock-challenging. "I get off at eleven-thirty. Wanna find out?" There was a brief flicker of the tip of her tongue on her glistening lips.

A tingling sensation like static electricity rippled through his loins. *Fuck yes!* were the first words that sprung to mind, but instead, he opted for a more laid back line. "How could I turn down a princess?"

He caught Tam watching him as Lisa went back to work. The old timer had a strange look on his face, a mix of pity and antipathy. It was unexpected and out of place on the old man's usual slack features.

The old man turned away without comment and started rolling a cigarette with trembling, nicotine-stained fingers. As his swollen, arthritic joints worked to construct the smoke, he started humming a tune.

It took Han a few bars before he recognised it. *Devil in Disguise* ... Elvis.

You look like an angel,
Walk like an angel,
Talk like an angel,
But I got wise,
You're the devil in disguise ...

He had sunk another couple of whiskeys by the time Lisa appeared with her jacket and bag. "Ready to walk us home then?"

"My lady," Han said, taking her arm in his.

Tam had long since shambled back to his pit and Big Joe offered a farewell wave as they walked out into the cool night air. Han smiled back and saw no judgement or disapproval on the old soldier's tired features. There was the hint of a smile though.

Instead of heading back to her flat, Lisa led him towards the park. The trail was in pitch darkness as they made their way to the clearing. Lisa shivered and clung on tighter to Han's arm, angling her face up to reveal a contented smile. There was no breeze to rustle the canopy above their heads, so the only sounds were the crunch of their footfalls and the occasional hoot from the trees.

As they entered the clearing, Lisa abruptly broke away from him and ran towards the roundabout. Smiling, Han followed at a stroll.

"You've got to be old enough to be me dad," she shouted merrily, giving the creaking roundabout a gentle shove. It was an old wooden affair with gun metal grey hand rails. The faded red paint on the boards was cracked and peeling from regular use and the elements. Her gaze was distant and dreamlike as she watched it slowly rotate.

"You're a cheeky sod," Han replied, catching up to her and grabbing her round the waist from behind.

Squealing, she drew her gaze away from the hypnotic wheel and turned around to face him. Moonlight twinkled in his intense, auburn eyes and she caught her pale ghost-like reflection there. There was a moment's pause as they gazed at one another in the darkness, then she moved closer and kissed him, forcing her tongue into his mouth. Pressing close against her firm body, he returned the kiss with matching fervour, savouring the taste of her slightly minted saliva.

Han forced her back against the roundabout, grinding it to a sudden halt as the intensity of their kiss grew. He felt her hands move from around his neck down his body, caressing his chest then moving around to his buttocks. Pulling away from her mouth, he moved to her earlobe, licking and sucking the soft pink flesh. Then, leaving a silvery trail in his wake, he bore purposefully down the side of her neck, where the veins were pulsating with the sudden increased blood flow. She squirmed beneath him as their breathing intensified with every lungful of air.

Moving down to her chest, he continued to kiss and lick her hot arched body at the bony ridge between her breasts. He lifted his face away from her cleavage for a moment and, with a leering grin, ripped open her blouse. Lust overriding patience, he didn't trouble himself with unclipping the plain white bra, instead forcing it upwards, exposing her small, pert breasts. He descended upon her eager nipples, causing her moans to grow louder, laced with a deep hunger.

"Ah, yes, suck them hard," she hissed through clenched teeth, her tone guttural.

His face flushed with anticipation as he roughly yanked up her tight skirt, exposing skimpy black knickers. Without pausing, he wrenched the briefs down to leave her fully exposed.

He felt her tugging eagerly at his jeans and, in a moment, they were dropping to his ankles. His boxer shorts followed quickly to reveal the extent of his excitement.

"Fuck me," she snarled as her hands clawed at him.

Tossing her thin pale legs over his shoulders, Han jerked forward, plunging deep inside her and causing them both to cry out. Thrusting hard and fast, Lisa screamed out his name, urging him on. She bit on his lower lip as his groin slammed against hers and their groping hands gripped each other with wanton desperation.

As they both hastily approached a climax, a voice from the shadows behind them shouted, "You whore! What do you think you're doin'?"

Han's heart lurched into his throat and he instantly withdrew. She screamed again, but this time in shock, rather than ecstasy. Roughly pulling his jeans up, Han turned to face the intruder. "Who the hell are you?" He was breathing hard and red faced, but anger was rapidly overshadowing his embarrassment.

A scraggy young man, unshaven with long, matted brown hair and a grubby ill-fitting long coat, had followed them along the path and chosen the perfect moment to reveal himself. His hands were clenched in fists of rage and unadulterated hatred radiated from his blazing eyes. "I'm that bitch's boyfriend is who I am, you cunt."

Han finished buttoning his jeans and, taking his eyes off the intruder for just a split second, glanced to Lisa, who had managed to partially button her blouse and smooth down her skirt. Her knickers were, however, still down to her knees. He laughed, despite himself, then said, "What's this guy talking about, Lisa?"

"I'm gunna fuck you up, faggot," the young scrote continued, seemingly less than impressed at being laughed at and also unaware of the stupidity of his chosen insult. He closed the gap, his entire body a coiled spring, trembling with surging adrenaline.

Standing up, her face red and her lipstick smeared, Lisa said as evenly as she could muster, "Jimmy, you're not me boyfriend. How many times do I have to tell you?" Turning to Han, she added, "We used to see each other from time to time, that's all."

The cool night air invaded his receding passions as Han glanced back at Jimmy, then back to Lisa. "You used to see *that* guy sometimes?"

This appeared to snap the over-taut spring within Jimmy. He launched himself at his girl's defiler, hot breath and spittle surging forth from his snarling lips as he screamed, "You're a dead man!"

Han was ready for him, side-stepping and planting a solid punch on the side of the kid's jaw in one fluid motion. He felt the crunch of the jaw under his unyielding blow and was somewhat pleased to see a spray of blood splatter across Lisa's white blouse.

Jimmy staggered back, his mouth a bloody mess, but to his credit (or stupidity), he spun and thrust himself at Han a second time, screaming both in pain and frustration.

Han grabbed him easily and head-butted him on the bridge of the nose, instantly shattering it. Without pausing, he followed through with a swift knee to the crotch, doubling up the hapless twat.

Lisa was screaming and grabbing his shoulder. "No! You're killing him!"

Han stopped just before he connected with the kid's swollen sack for a second time. "Sorry princess, he attacked me here." His tone was matter-of-fact.

"Leave him alone; *please!*" She forced her way in between them and helped the gurgling kid to the ground. Blood and snot were oozing like glistening entrails from his broken nose. As his weak knees hit the moist grass, he instantly keeled over, with one hand over his gushing face and the other on his crotch.

Lisa was sobbing and tentatively touching the kid's mangy hair. "Jimmy ..."

Han shook his head and straightened himself up. His face looked pale in the moonlight, and several droplets of blood were drying on his cheeks and forehead. Mustering up all the tolerance he could manage, he said, rather sheepishly, "I'm sorry, Lisa. He took me by surprise – I was scared, I just reacted. I'm really sorry."

She didn't take her eyes off Jimmy. "Just...go, please."

"I could—"

"Please!" she snapped harshly, now kneeling beside the prone man who was coughing and spitting out blood.

"Bastard ... fucker ..." he was repeating feebly, between spluttering and groaning.

He watched her for a moment, fussing over the young lad like Martha did with him. Apart from Lisa's soft sobs, intermingled with soothing words, and Jimmy's mutterings, the park had become still and quiet once more.

"Okay," he said finally and left without looking back. His head was downcast as he walked back along the shrouded path. As he grew further away though, a smile crept across his lips. "You see that fuckin' head come apart, man," he muttered to himself and laughed. Bunny would've been proud of that.

Fog on the Tyne.

The following evening, Lisa tried her best to keep away from Han. He found himself chatting to the local livestock farmer, the big bear bloke from the Land Rover, John Bryce. He was as tall as he was wide, with hands like paving slabs, cracked and calloused from years of hard labour. His forearms would have put Popeye's to shame, but he assured Han that he had never seen the inside of a gym.

After passing pleasantries like, 'where ya from', 'what ya do', and Han finding out about Bryce's wife, Sally and son, Anthony, and a brief and thoroughly uninteresting mention of his sheep and chicken stocks, they moved on to chatting about the village and Han's initial thoughts on the place. Then, inevitably, the conversation turned to writing.

Bryce took a hearty swig of his pint of real ale, followed by a draw on his half smoked cigarette (no one seemed to give a shit about the smoking ban in this place). A mop of thick, dark brown hair lent a genial look to his otherwise hard, furrowed features. "So what's this book of yours about, Han?" His voice was a rich baritone, which, overall, reminded Han of a Geordie version of Tom Jones.

Han sipped his whiskey, savouring it for a moment, before responding. "It's a thriller about a serial killer stalking a remote Northumberland village," he said, and smiled at the raised eyebrow the answer rewarded him with. "That's why I'm here – to do a spot of research."

"Wey it's beautiful countryside, so you couldn't ask for a nicer setting. Although, the murdering part doesn't sound much good for tourism," Bryce added with a wry smile. "There's not enough stuff set in the North East. It's a damn shame – we've got the best people and the best locations in the world."

"Oh, I don't know. You've had some iconic writers and a few TV series and films. You even had Harry Potter."

Bryce frowned, but then said, "We do alreet with music I guess – that bloke from the Animals, er …"

"Burdon."

"Aye, that's him; Eric Burdon. That Bryan Ferry bloke, him from The Shadows, oh and the mighty Lindisfarne an'all o'ourse."

"You forgot Ant and Dec."

"Who?"

Han laughed and said, "Good one."

Bryce shrugged and went to take another swig of his beer. His pint still hovering, Bryce's eyes took on a glazed look and he appeared lost in thought for a while.

Han watched him with interest.

After a moment, he snapped out of it and, instead of finishing off his pint, he raised his glass in an impromptu toast, and said, "Well, your good health, and I wish you good luck with the book. Just divvent kill us off if I get in it, eh!"

Han laughed and, with a wicked glint, said, "Nobody's safe." Then, raising his own glass, he pronounced in the best Robert Shaw impression he could muster, "Here's to swimmin' with bow-legged women."

It was approaching midnight when John Bryce stood up with a lengthy sigh and headed for the exit. "Take it easy, mate," he said to Han with a broad grin planted on his round face.

"You too, big fella," Han replied with a friendly wave.

"Get oot, yer bum!" Big Joe jokily shouted from across the bar, then stretched his mouth wide open in a big yawn.

Bryce feigned a hurt pout. "Bloody charmin', that is, like!" Then, with another wave, he trudged out onto Main Street.

The cold, clear night caused a shiver to run across his wide shoulders. He let out a chesty cough then fished into his jacket for his cigarettes. After lighting up one, he started across the road towards the Green. It was bathed in darkness, save for a lone light above the Co-op. Despite the moonless night, he was still able to pick out a hunched figure sitting on the bench on the Green. As he grew closer, recognition dawned on him. She was shivering and rocking gently as she tightly hugged herself.

"Carol?" he said softly, squinting to make out the features of her downcast face. Her mascara was streaked down her cheeks and clear snot was dribbling from her nose.

"You okay, pet?"

As if suddenly awoken from a trance, Carol Belmont shot to her feet and rushed off the Green, heading further along Main Street away from him.

Bryce stopped in the middle of the road, watching her head towards St. Bart's and Belmont Motors. He opened his mouth to call after her; to attempt to help her in some way, but as she dashed away, he struggled to find the right words, any words. He somehow guessed that it would not be Reverend Dunhealy that she was searching for, although the old pastor would have hopefully been able to offer her far greater guidance than he.

Shaking his head sadly, he trudged onward towards Bell Lane.

With the last of the punters gone, Big Joe handed the keys to Lisa and said a gruff goodnight before heading for his bed. That left Lisa and Han alone.

She finished her few remaining tasks of collecting ashtrays and briefly wiping over the tables and the bar and then dropped onto the stool beside Han. She looked exhausted and forlorn.

She seemed to struggle with the right words to say for a time. Han waited patiently while she gathered her thoughts and, seemingly, some courage.

"Sorry I've been off with you," she said finally, her voice like a gentle rustle of reeds on a riverbank.

Han offered her an understanding smile and touched her slender wrist gently. Despite whiskies numbering near double figures, his head felt crystal clear. Solemnly, he said, "You don't need to apologise, hun. I just lost it; I don't know what happened. Jealousy, I guess." With his last shame-filled words, he hung his head.

They seemed to be exactly the words she was hoping to hear. Pulling his hand up to her face, she kissed his palm softly. Her voice strained to say, "You divvent need to be jealous. Jimmy's ancient history; he just cannat get it through his thick, coked-up head."

Drawing his hand close to her chest, she moved closer to him and looked deep into his eyes. Sighing, she said, "Jimmy had us hooked on coke and crack for five years; before, durin' and after me angel was born. It was so hard to break away from him and that shit, but I did it; for Haley's sake and for me own." She was trembling slightly and biting her lip anxiously by the time she finished.

To allay her fears, Han leaned forward and kissed her on her quivering lips. Gripping her hand, he said, "I know how hard that must've been to tell me. I understand, hun. I know about obsessions and how hard it is to fight them. How long you been clean?"

Awash with relief at not being judged, she said, "Six months."

"Good on you. It can only get easier – you're doing great and you have a wonderful daughter to help keep you strong."

She looked at him; staring deep into his eyes, searching for just the tiniest hint of insincerity. His caring eyes met hers, unblinking. With that, Lisa burst into tears. Han instantly pulled her to him and held her tight as she sobbed noisily and uncontrollably for several minutes. At first, she tried to speak; to apologise, to thank him, but the words were unintelligible and drowned out by her sobs.

As she cried, Han gently stroked her hair and pondered on this news. It would seem that fate had chosen the first one. That it would be such a worthless piece of excrement actually brought a smile to his face.

Pride and Punishment.

Jimmy Coulson groaned as he shifted his aching body. The bed sheets that covered his sweating body were stained with a concoction of piss, blood and semen, as well as lager and smears of drippings from the occasional bedtime junk food feast.

With a wired jaw, set nose and two black eyes, the man whose favourite middle school form teacher, Miss Savage, used to call 'Beautiful Boy', now looked like a car crash (and a one that you'd struggle to walk away from at that). Before his world turned to shit, the occasional girl in a nightclub or pub used to liken Jimmy to James Dean. Now though, he was skinny – bordering malnourished – with pale, blemished skin and bloodshot eyes.

His world had begun its downward spiral at high school. His looks and laid back attitude had earned him a prestigious spot with the in-crowd. When he started learning to play guitar in the first year, his popularity with the girls jumped up a few more notches. After a trip with mates down south to a music festival, he quickly found himself in cover band.

That had been the place where he got his first blowjob off some lanky chick who never gave him her name. It was also where he first sampled mescaline. Dabbling in a bit of recreational drug use also seemed to heighten his popularity even further, not to mention improving his guitar playing as well. He never quite got into the writing side; they had Crazy Don for that, but he did get pretty good with that battered sunburst Fender Stratocaster of his … until he *had* to flog it for gear, but that was later.

The mescaline opened the floodgates for him. He had skipped the dope stage when it had first started doing the rounds at school the year before, but after the festival, dope and mescaline quickly took over from beer. Then, one night in the toilets of a pub on the Bigg Market in Newcastle, two weeks into sixth form, he sampled his first line of cocaine. He instantly fell in love with the stuff; it made him feel more alive than he had ever felt before. It gave him boundless energy and his popularity with the ladies seemed to improve still further too.

By the time December came round, he was snorting lines daily and stealing from family, friends, shops … anyone to buy more of his white heaven. Fighting and disruption in class followed. Soon after the school washed its hands of him, the police came knocking. After a slagging match with his dad turned into a fistfight, he was slung out of his home with just a bin bag of clothes (not even full, come to think of it).

It was while dossing with a friend that he discovered a new saviour; Crack. He was penniless, kipping on the floor of a shitty bed-sit and, even though he had heard it was supposed to be highly addictive, he had thought, *fuck it*. Nobody gave a shit about him, so why should he? Overnight *everything* changed. He experienced his first whole-body orgasm and *nothing* in the world mattered after that.

As a state of unwanted consciousness seeped in through his sweaty pores, so did the creepy-crawlies. He shivered as he pulled his bruised and emaciated body out of his bed, scratching at the itchy sensation quivering across his clammy skin. Glancing at an orange Bakelite clock by the single sagging bunk, he saw with no surprise that it was gone four in the afternoon.

The bed-sit was a two room affair with the pokey main room, serving as bedroom, lounge and kitchen, and a tiny cubicle with a shower, sink and toilet as the second room.

A dirty homemade bong held centre stage in the middle of the stained carpet-tiled floor, surrounded by empty beer cans and vodka bottles, sweet wrappers, crisp packets and the occasional used condom. An old moth-eaten blanket had been nailed up to the window to impede the afternoon sunshine from invading the dank, sweaty feet and mould-smelling room.

He staggered naked to the stained toilet that was missing its fold-down seat and lid and urinated while scratching his backside. The upturned crucifix tattoo across his spotty back twitched with the flexing of his somewhat wasted muscles.

Yes, life was pretty good for Jimmy.

After dressing in grass and blood-stained jeans, he managed to find a nearly clean – once black, now charcoal grey – t-shirt then pulled on his black long coat and muddy trainers.

He stood in the doorway, trembling slightly and scratching at his arms. With no gear left, he was desperate for another hit to banish the bugs and lift his mood out of the depths of hell. But he already owed Steve Belmont for the last bag and, pulling some grubby coins out of his coat pocket, he discovered that he had precisely one pound thirty to his name. He was watched like a hawk in the village shops these days and he didn't have the money to go into Rothbury, so it was time to resort to one of his other professions – poaching from Bryce & Son. There was usually a few chickens, eggs or bags of tatties that he could get his hands on, that one or two of the less fortunate of the village would be happy to pay under the odds for, no questions asked.

Three or four chickens might be enough for a quick hit, with maybe some change for a meat pie from Merlin's.

He would have to be careful though as that big prick, John Bryce, had nearly caught him last time, and he had publicly threatened to hospitalise anyone caught stealing from his farm. Well, after what that new bastard had done to him, what sort of a threat was that? That Whitman was going to get his – he would make him suffer to his last stinking breath.

Opening the door, he paused a moment and turned to the rickety set of drawers to the side of the door which had two drawer fronts missing. A grey metal lock knife was perched on top, amongst empty cigarette packets and other assorted rubbish. He snatched it up and thrust it into his coat pocket.

chapter 4

Oh Mandy, well you came and you gave without taking.

Han sat at the desk with his laptop open and a cup of tea steaming beside it. Afternoon sunshine shone through the open curtains which rippled gently from a breeze blowing in through the raised sash window.

For several hours, he had been meticulously trawling through the sound-byte footage from the various bugs. It was mainly comings and goings or inane drivel, but the occasional interesting piece of gossip or notable item did show up from time to time. The important thing was that he was slowly building up a picture of the habits and movements of the villagers. His notepad already had pages filled with detailed notes on most of Haydon's residents. A dab here, a brushstroke there; the masterpiece was slowly taking shape.

He was tapping a pen against his teeth as the play bar slowly crept from left to right on each sound file. Loretta Fairbank and Sally Bryce were playing in his earpiece, chatting on the Green with neighbourly concern about *poor* Carol Belmont. His mind wandering, as it sometimes did, he wondered how Jumanji was getting on with Perry. His faithful mutt would be pining something chronic for him no doubt. He made a note to make a quick phone call later to see how they were both getting on. Mobile phone reception was nonexistent in and around the whole area, so he'd have to ring from the public telephone box by the Post Office (safer than using the phone in his room). He'd have to remember to withhold the number, so that the area code wouldn't give anything away. Perry would never notice such things of course (unless he had been smoking weed while watching reruns of *The Lone Gunmen*), but little details ...

As his Labrador drifted away from centre stage, Han found himself thinking of his past girlfriend; something he hadn't done for quite some time. She had loved Ju. He and Vanessa, his one and only long term adult relationship, had parted company nearly two years ago after six years together. She had wanted the whole package – marriage, kids, PTA meetings ... he had said he wasn't ready for that, that he wanted to do some travelling, see the world, experience more of life, before ending it. Strangely enough, she hadn't taken too kindly to that final comment. After a few weeks of bickering, arguing, then some crying, she packed her bags and went back to her parents in Derby. They spoke a few times in the weeks that followed, him telling her that he missed her and what they had together, and her telling him that she needed more and that she wasn't getting any younger. But then the calls became less frequent, and then in one final phone call, she had awkwardly informed him that she had met someone else. Those words had felt so final, like being nailed to the ground and looking up to see a bomb whistling its way down toward you. He had wanted to beg her to come back and tell her that he would do anything she wanted, but all he managed to force out was a murmured 'congratulations'. He could have sworn that he had heard a stifled sob before she thanked him and hung up. A year later he found out by chance that they were already married with a newborn baby boy. Close call there ... yeah.

While browsing through one of the Co-op recordings, a curious sound caught his attention, immediately causing his ears to prick up and to snap him back to the present. It was soft and barely above a whisper, so he cranked up the volume to full and pressed the earpiece tighter into his ear, straining to listen. It only took a moment to recognise the soft sounds of someone crying quietly to themselves. He listened for several minutes more before he caught the odd audible word.

"How ... used a condom ..."

"Ah, the plot thickens," Han said to himself, thankful to be distracted from the unsettling memories of Vanessa. He now recognised the voice. It was that pretty part-time assistant. Flicking through the notepad, he located the name, Mandy Foster, and wrote 'pregnant' beside it.

A thought occurred to him. He had bugged the phone box by the Post Office just in case – sometimes, for dirty little secrets, people didn't feel comfortable using their home phone or mobile (not that he had noticed any Haydon residents actually using mobile phones, but given that there was no reception, that wasn't unusual).

He located the sound file for the public phone and started it from the time when the crying stopped. It wasn't long before his instincts paid off.

Mandy's voice; shaky, fraught. "Dougie, it's Mandy."

"How you doin', babe?" Throaty Scottish accent, possibly Glaswegian. "You decided whether you wanna little trip across the border, eh?"

"Yeah, I gotta see you."

"I wanna see you too, babe. What about your kin?"

Emotion ripped great rents through her trembling tone. "I'm going to leave this Saturday – I can ring them when I get away from this place. I just gotta be with you."

There was a slight hesitation from the mystery Scot. Then, "Okay. Has something happened, babe?"

The sound of a sleeve wiping across a snivelling nose, and then, "Everything's fine, Dougie, honestly. I just need to get away from this place." After a trembling sigh, she continued, "I've got a friend in Shillmoor, so I'll walk down to hers after my shift and she'll be able to take me as far as Berwick. I'll get the train from there."

After an edgy goodbye, the sound file ran quiet. He clicked the pause icon and sat back in his chair with a slight creak from the tired old wooden joints. So, it would seem the test would not be on the druggie tosspot, but rather a knocked up runaway.

Well, it wouldn't take much to find out when her shift finished, so it would just be a case of tailing her into the woods. It'll take a couple of days before the friend or lover raises concerns to the parents. A missing person's would not be filed till then. Would they search the area in between Shillmoor and Haydon? Certainly, but doubtful before Tuesday or Wednesday.

Well, that gave him plenty of time.

Saturday morning arrived and he made a final check of the items that he would take with him; the more sensitive items were extracted from his combination locked case. Dark clothes, hunting knife, back pack containing: flashlight, *Jack Daniel's Old No.7* embossed *Zippo*, lighter fluid, hacksaw, zip ties, bin bags, gaffer tape, an army surplus trenching tool, camouflage netting, a second set of clothes including boots, bottled water and two twenty-four hour ration packs.

A shiver of anticipation, mixed with a healthy vein of fear, skipped through his tensed muscles. This day would be the true start of his adventure; the dress rehearsal before the live finale. After today, there would be no going back. He thought about that for a while. If there was ever a time to stop, it was now. He could pack up and leave this weird little village that seemed lost in time and never look back. He could then just carry on his normal shop life like nothing had ever happened. No one would ever know. But no, he would know. He would know that he came so close and then chickened out at the last minute. The dream was a calling and he had to see it through to the end.

He had a key for the side entrance, so that he could come and go as he pleased without having to go through the bar, so slipping out wouldn't be a problem. He had already politely informed Martha that he would be working undisturbed in his room all day, and had even recorded random typing, muttering and shuffling noises to play quietly on his laptop while he was away. There was a slight risk, even with the door locked, but he had also gotten Martha to make up some sandwiches to last him throughout the afternoon and insisted that he would be down for dinner for eight-thirty. That would have to be enough.

There was one final item that he would be taking. The case remained open on the bed. He rummaged inside a concealed pouch until his fingers brushed over a cool, angular surface.

The matt black 9mm Walther P99 felt good in his hand and instantly ramped up his excitement another notch. It was a compact, solid design and the favoured handgun of the more recent 007s, until Daniel Craig decided to go old school and return to the PPK. Perfect.

He pulled out a couple of magazines and loaded them with practiced care. Once full, he inserted one into the grip with a satisfying click. In one swift movement, he cocked the pistol and aimed at the mirror by the door. Adopting the more classic Connery accent, he uttered, "The name's Bond. James Bond."

His face took on a stern, *I don't take no shit,* look. With set bearded jaw line and fierce eyes staring unblinking down the sight, his handsome face looked the consummate rugged hero. Chuckling to himself, he slipped it under his jumper and tucked it into his jeans in the small of his back.

Absently flicking a few wayward strands of baby blonde hair out of her hazel eyes, Mandy handed the carrier bag over the counter. She thanked the last customer of the day, the plump, camp owner of Jolly Moe's hair salon.

"You're a sweetie, Mand," Moe Baxter said with exaggerated relief. He wore a crimson silk shirt open almost to the navel with a broken heart gold necklace and a thick rug of chest hair on show. In his fifties, with grey, slicked back hair and sideburns styled into points, contrasting with heavily tanned features, he was a man who wanted to grow old his way. "Mister Flibble would have been ever so upset if he missed out on his Saturday treat of sardines."

"Give him a big kiss from me," Mandy replied, forcing a smile through the tempest of tormented thoughts cascading around her embattled mind.

"Will do!" Moe said, accompanied by an infectiously beaming smile full of glaringly white teeth. With a wave of one jewel-encrusted, manicured hand, he swept out of the shop, leaving Mandy alone once more.

Duncan Fairbank popped his head round the door that led to the store room and tiny cluttered office. "Get yourself away, Mand. I'll lock up here; you just go enjoy your weekend. Your pay packet's in the usual place." He offered her a smile, emphasising his angular jaw line.

Mandy returned the smile with near sincerity – she always went a little girly over Duncan's *Marlboro* man smile. She slipped her hand in the drawer next to the till to retrieve the small brown envelope. She liked both Duncan and Loretta – they had always been kind and fair with her, and Duncan was still quite a hunk, despite his age. Maybe like Charlton Heston, but carrying a little extra weight. Glancing inside the envelope, she noticed that he had slipped in a little extra for her. "Thanks a lot, Mister F. That's really nice of you."

His voice drifted from the store room. "No worries, pet. You deserve it."

Duncan appeared in the doorway and watched her leave in silence.

Mandy carefully unlocked the front door of her parent's house, making sure not to rattle the keys. The door was a bit stiff, as usual, so it took a bit of persuasion to ease it open.

She crept along the narrow hallway, past her sleeping father on the sofa in the living room in front of the television (a Sony Trinitron in a wood veneer chassis). Mork and Mindy were hanging out in a record store, laughing at a customer's flapping hair piece. "I've seen wavy hair before, but never hair waving …"

Her mother would not be home for another hour or so, so that gave her plenty of time. The stairs creaked and groaned under her slight frame, causing her to pause and glance back down to the open living room door. Her father continued to snore softly amidst the drone of the television.

Mandy's bedroom was decked out in purples of all shades and dozens of posters of Steve McQueen, Warren Beatty, Farrah Fawcett, Michael Caine, Debbie Harry and Jack Nicholson.

She wasted no time; dropping down onto her knees, she pulled a purple sports bag from under the bed that was already full to bursting point. As she stood up with its not inconsiderable weight, she glanced around the room, running through a mental checklist in her head. She had already carefully chosen which outfits and shoes that she most needed to take with her, along with her meagre collection of makeup and jewellery and some photos. Adding her wage packet to the funds already in her purple purse, she quickly calculated that she had a grand total of two hundred and thirty-two pounds in cash. This would constitute the sum total of her worldly possessions from which to start her new life in Edinburgh with. Sod all.

Fighting back tears, she rubbed her eyes and heaved a sigh. She had to go, to be with Dougie. The thought of leaving Haydon and living in a big city terrified her. But they could have their own home, together; they could be a family. Her, Dougie and the baby. Since the initial shock result of the home pregnancy test, she had been even more surprised to realise that she actually wanted this baby; in fact, wanted it more than she ever thought she would. It would be hard at first; Dougie wasn't earning much with his brother in their window cleaning partnership, and she would have to get whatever temporary job she could until the baby came. She was also very close to her mam and dad and the thought of leaving them made her ache deep inside. But there was no other way; they wouldn't understand and they certainly wouldn't approve of Dougie. So he had made a few mistakes as a kid and done a little time, but he was a loving, decent man now. He loved her, and that was all that mattered.

She shrugged into her purple synthetic fur jacket and picked up the sports bag. It took all of her determination to tear her gaze away from the photograph in the plain silver frame on her bedside cabinet, which showed a pretty blonde haired girl in her early teens with proud, beaming parents standing behind, both with a loving hand resting on each of her shoulders … the life that she was leaving behind. After hovering in the doorway for another couple of gut-wrenching minutes, she finally turned and walked away, tears blurring her vision.

Han watched from across the street in the shadows, appearing to flick through a North East England *'Passionate about walking'* guide, as Mandy left her home for the last time. The cute nineteen year old was dressed in tight jeans, and what appeared to be a strange hairy purple monster. She had red eyes and flushed cheeks. Obviously an emotional departure.

Bell Lane was quiet and surprisingly devoid of activity for a Saturday afternoon. From his position near the intersection with Main Street, he heard a car drive past behind him. He ignored it and continued to watch the girl over the top of the pages of the leaflet.

Shouldering the stuffed bag with considerable effort, she walked quickly straight past him, without so much as a glance, onto Main Street and then headed back towards the B road that would lead her south east to Shillmoor. He noted that she had wisely opted for walking boots, rather than the heels that he had half expected her to wear. After waiting a short while, Han casually folded the guide and headed to the back lane that ran parallel to Main Street.

All the good things you deserve now,
Climbing, forever trying,
Find your way out of the wild, wild wood,
Now there's no justice …

The late afternoon sun was obscured by a bank of thick, grey clouds that were heading inland from the west coast. The air was still and warm; a close feeling that immediately drew beads of sweat with the exertion of the quick pace.

Mandy kept to the uneven and weed-ridden roadside as she headed at a steady pace towards Shillmoor. Her confident strides with the burden on her back betrayed a keen walker. It was tougher going for Han, fighting his way through the pine forest about fifteen yards in and back from the young woman. It was made all the more difficult by having to carefully place his footing at every step, so as not to alert his prey.

As she strode purposefully, occasionally hoisting the heavy bag back onto her shoulder, she picked over the events of the last few days. The finite details re-played on a seemingly endless loop, tormenting and drawing out her pain once again. Tears rolled down her glowing cheeks.

She pictured her mam, sobbing uncontrollably at hearing the news that her only daughter had fled, pregnant, to be with her ex-con boyfriend. She imagined the face of her dad, enraged, screaming that he never wanted to see her again, that he no longer had a daughter. She saw the face of Mister Fairbank; disappointed and disapproving - *she had always been such a sensible,*

68

reliable girl. Then, la piece de resistance, Dougie; what if he sent her packing as soon as he discovered that she was pregnant? *What's a matter with you, babe? I dinna want another kid. Got two already to that bitch, Cheryl, that I cannae afford.*

Struggling to keep pace, Han snaked his way between trees and clumps of wild flowers and bracken, ever watchful of his footfalls. His eyes darted between the broken outline of Mandy and the ground in front of his feet. It was as his eyes flashed back to the girl that, stepping onto a mossy, felled branch, his boot slipped, sending him face first into the mulchy forest floor and snapping several smaller twigs and branches with knees and elbows in the process. Stifling an angry curse, he scrambled to a crouch and cast a furtive glance towards Mandy's last position.

A flutter of wings disturbed the leaves in the forest canopy, but otherwise there was deathly silence.

She had stopped dead in her tracks and was staring into the shadowy trees with a look of unease etched into her pretty features. She was staring right towards him.

He froze, not even daring to breathe.

"Hello?" Her voice had an anxious edge to it.

Still holding his breath, Han watched and waited, ignoring the protests from his straining thighs. A brown and orange meadow argus butterfly wavered past his still face, then settled on a low branch in a rare spot of greying light. His eyes followed it hypnotically for a moment then returned to the girl.

She took one hesitant step towards the trees, still frowning, but then quickly changed her mind and spun back towards her destination. Heading off at a noticeably quicker pace, she glanced back one final time, her ill ease still apparent.

The whole sky appeared bruised and prematurely darkened as the cloudbank settled across the early evening sky. The wind began to pick up as Mandy rushed onward towards Shillmoor. Without pausing for breath, she buttoned up her jacket and hoisted her bag higher onto her shoulder. As the first droplets of rain struck the pot-holed road, Mandy glanced towards the heavens with scolding annoyance, diminishing any lingering nervousness.

"Fuck," she said simply to no one in particular. Her breathing had deepened from the exertion and strands of her blonde hair were plastered to her forehead.

"Bitch, isn't it," Han said nonchalantly, stepping out of the trees to her side.

"Shit!" Mandy jumped, flinging her arms out in a spasm that caused her sports bag to fly off her shoulder and drop to the damp road. She spun round to face him, her cheeks suddenly drained with fright.

"Sorry, hun," Han said, raising his own gloved hands in apology. "Didn't mean to scare you. I was just having a little walk through the forest. Weather's turning, eh?"

Mandy took a couple of uncertain, shuffling steps away from him, visibly shaking and her eyes wild. "You ... you're following me."

Han feigned surprised innocence. "Me?" Then, abruptly, there was a subtle shift in his expression and, as suddenly as he had appeared, he dropped the act. Shrugging, he said, "Busted."

The unexpected admission caught Mandy off guard. Fear was momentarily replaced by confusion. "What?" Disbelief, as if she didn't hear him correctly. She bent and picked up her bag, not taking her eyes off him for a second, adding, "I've got a boyfriend."

Taking another step closer, Han nodded apologetically and said, "Yes, I know." His tone matter-of-fact, he continued, "I've been following you since you left Haydon. I'm going to murder you and bury your dismembered body in the woods."

Any remaining specks of colour vanished from Mandy's face. A deep down primal instinct told her that this man was not joking. His features and body language were a relaxed facade, but the intensity in his eyes revealed the complete horrific truth in an instant. She staggered backwards as if struck by a physical force. "This ... this is Haydon ..."

Han glanced around and shook his head. "I don't think so, not any more."

"No ..." she managed in a breathless whisper.

Rubbing his hands together, Han said, "Okie-dokie. Here we go." He glanced up to the drizzling purple-grey sky and added, "This rain looks like it's going to get worse before it gets better."

Han's blasé attitude both confused and appalled Mandy as she stumbled backwards into the middle of the road. Her mind was surging with conflicting instincts and emotions, momentarily stalling the one most important one; self preservation. It all seemed so surreal; like a scene from some tacky teen slasher film, not real life. Haydon couldn't protect her.

Matching her slow pace, Han offered her a gentle smile, one that could've been mistaken as that of a proud and loving father. His tone was soothing as he said, "I think now's your cue to run. Screaming." The sneer that followed his last word was far from gentle; it was predatory and laced with inhuman malice.

Without needing prompting a second time, Mandy thrust her bag in Han's face with all her mustered strength and dashed for the tree line on the opposite side of the road. Her heart-stopping scream would have put Jamie Lee Curtis to shame.

Han caught the heavy bag an inch from his face and smiled at the unexpected flash of tenacity. Casting it onto his back with his own pack, he started to jog after her at a more sedate pace. He wiped droplets of rainwater from his face and chuckled quietly to himself. He hadn't quite known how he would feel at this stage, but so far it was quite enjoyable. Like *catchy-kissy* in the playground …

Mandy tore headlong into the forest, her arms flailing to cast obstructions aside. Branches and low shrubs scratched and clawed at her extremities as she threw herself unbound into the forest. Her throat quickly grew hoarse and her lungs ached from both screaming and flat out sprinting over uneven ground. The beating of her feet on the spongy ground and the lashing of branches against her face and arms seemed to conjure a cold clarity of mind that seemed almost unbelievable. The screaming was prematurely tiring her and the only person in range to hear it was the madman behind her.

She rushed on with only her panting breaths mingling with the snapping of twigs and rustling of leaves and foliage. The pungent smells of moss and damp earth tingled in her nostrils as she struggled to regulate her breathing.

She had to reach safety. She had to reach Haydon.

Droplets of rain broke through the canopy here and there, one hitting her cheek as she glanced upwards to the pinprick views of the dark sky. The already damp ground was turning to gluey mud with the worsening rain, sticking to the soles of her boots and making every step ever more laborious.

Daring to peek over her bobbing shoulder, she could not see the man chasing her, but her instincts told her that he was out there somewhere. Questions cart-wheeled through her mind as she forced herself onwards. Was this all really happening? Was the new guy in town really going to kill her and chop her up? It sounded absurd – like some sort of sick practical joke – and yet she knew it to be true. He was going to kill her. But why?

The last question stopped her abruptly in her tracks. Gasping for air and clutching her throbbing chest, she spun around to face the way she had just come. There were a couple of angry scratches on her forehead and left cheek and her hair was hanging limp and dripping from the continuing fine rain. She drew in a gulping breath then screamed at the top of her lungs, "WHY?" After another gulping breath: "Why me, you *fucking* nutcase?" The first question had been laced with anger, the second with desperation.

Han stepped out from behind a tree several yards away to her side. He was breathing hard and red-faced, but was utterly composed. "Why not you?" The question was put simply and with an almost resigned tone.

She shrieked and threw herself away from him, stumbling immediately over several roots that had broken the surface of the wet forest floor. Shaking his head in mild amusement, Han walked casually towards her, his own face reddened across one cheek by an unseen branch.

The hard fall scraped both her hands on rough bark and twigs and jarred a knee against a stump, but she was moving again as soon as she struck the ground. Crawling on her hands and knees, Mandy frantically scrambled away from him, crying out in pain and frustration.

The Walther sprung to mind first – he really wanted to have a play with that and its allure was strong. But no, that was not needed. He pulled out the hunting knife as he gradually closed the gap, his footfalls squelching in the mud as the rain continued to drizzle down around them.

She struggled on, shaking and crying, her hands and knees oozing blood that instantly mixed with the dark, gritty mud. Snot and tears dribbled from her face and were lost on the cold wet ground. As he loomed over her, rain spattering his head and shoulders, Mandy spun onto her back, holding her trembling, gory hands up in defence. Seeing the knife, droplets of clear water dripping from the tip of the jagged blade, caused the panic in her face to twist into utter terror. Suddenly the stark reality of it all crashed upon her. "No! God-please-no!" Raindrops struck her face, causing her to blink feverishly and smearing blood and muck down her cheeks in tiny rivulets.

"Sorry, Mandy, God isn't going to help you." His tone was morose, matching the sudden and unexpected sadness he felt inside. He couldn't quite understand this new feeling, but he had to finish what he had started. There would be time later for reflecting. "You're going to die here, and then after I've tasted of your flesh I'm going to chop you up and bury you. Your remains will never be found." He had no intention of eating part of her body, hell he liked his steak well done for Christ's sake, so the thought of a little raw long-pig almost made him gag. It just sounded like a cool thing to say that would hopefully banish the feeling of sorrow that now marred his earlier feelings of excitement. It was like a bitter aftertaste of a much savoured sweet.

Mandy screamed again, her features contorted with both rage and horror, and then all at once, she launched herself at him, propelling herself up using both elbows and feet with surprising speed. Her voice was hoarse as she spat, "Not if I kill you!"

Han was surprised by the counterattack and stumbled backwards with the force, his boots sliding in the mud. Snarling, she scratched and slapped at his face, blood and muck spraying from her clawed hands. He stepped back another couple of feet, before he recovered enough to block her next torrent of desperate blows. Then, as she blundered forward once more, half-blinded by rain and tears and muck and blood, he stabbed her in the stomach, burying the knife all the way to the hilt. It slipped into her with almost no effort at all.

She let out a soft gurgle and her attack abated at once. For a moment she just teetered in front of him, trembling, her arms still raised in readiness for a renewed assault. They were as close as lovers, his wet, mud-daubed face inches from hers. There was no pain in her face, just surprise. Attacker and victim stood staring into each other's eyes, panting. After the momentary pause, as rain pitter-pattered down over them, she toppled backwards, the knife sliding back out of her soft flesh, as if through water. The tip of the knife snagged on her drenched purple-monster jacket and she hung there, drooping like a sodden rag doll. A trickle of blood appeared in the corner of her mouth as she uttered, faintly, "But ... why?"

With the last syllable still adrift, he cast off the two bags with a shrug of his shoulder and then, at once, sprung upon her, straddling her slim wet denim legs as she landed flat-out in the mud. The sneer returned to his quivering lips as he ripped open her jacket and blouse to reveal her bra-less, rounded breasts. The sight of her pert nipples and soft skin caused him to pause. Her skin, being spattered with droplets of rain, looked porcelain in the failing light, with a pure, untouched innocence. Then his gaze fell upon the clean entry wound into her stomach with dark blood oozing out down her side. It reminded him of the unashamed lie of it and that abruptly renewed his fervour.

Lashing out in a sudden and violent frenzy, the knife plunged into her smooth stomach several times as she lay there staring up at him, her mouth moving and forming soundless words. Her gaze shifted beyond the man thrashing on top of her and settled on the canopy above them, fixing on one small pinprick view of the dark sky.

Why me? she asked in a rather detached fashion, as the darkness closed in.

Her abdomen and legs were awash with luridly red blood from multiple stab wounds as he lifted the dripping knife above his head again. A distinctive crack reverberated around the small clearing as the tip of the blade drove into her chest with such force that it caused an involuntary grunt to escape his lips. Lifting it once more, gasping, his face flushed with exertion, he drove it through the swell of her left breast, slicing her petite, pink nipple in two.

My baby. A single tear welled in the corner of one hazel eye as the canopy above her blurred and then disappeared into darkness. The tear slipped down the side of her face and into the hollow of her ear. Her eyes no longer blinked as rainwater splashed into them.

He continued stabbing her for several minutes, the blade making soft squelching noises, with the intermittent crunch of metal on bone. The sustained attack was accompanied by the soft patter of the rain, like a gentle backing track to his furious percussion. The rest of the forest stood silent, watching.

Finally, he fell off her, gasping and sweating and spattered with Mandy's sticky blood. The knife, held limply in one hand, was dripping with gore and small chunks of skin and flesh. He dropped it in the mud, unable to bear its weight a second longer. His rain-soaked body lay there for a moment, in the dark gruel mix of mud and blood, panting, with wisps of steam rising from his head and back of his neck.

The teenage girl lay still, her tilted face milky white, in stark contrast to the isolated drops of blood that mingled with the splashing rain. Her entire torso had collapsed inwards with the sheer ferocity and number of wounds, showing a pulverised mass of tissue, oozing shattered organs and pooling blood. Several splintered ribs poked out of the coagulating mass, and the muddy forest floor around her whole body was saturated with crimson.

With considerable effort, Han rolled onto his side to face Mandy's corpse. His gasps gradually receded to heavy breathing as the rain continued to fall around him. Its soft patter was the only accompaniment to his laboured breathing. His stare fixed upon her face for some time, studying her frozen expression. There was a hint of wistful sadness on her colourless lips and in the subtle lines around her dead eyes. The spots of blood on her face had now been completely washed away, giving her almost translucent complexion a freshly washed look. Droplets of rainwater dribbled off the end of her nose and eyelashes as those dead hazel eyes stared back at him.

The slab of meat in front of him had been a life, and he had cut it short. Mandy Foster was now dead, no more, and he was solely responsible. The test was over and the results were in. Passed.

With these revelations, Han suddenly burst into tears. His hearty sobs wracked his entire body as if electricity were surging through it. Tears streamed down his grimy face. Curling up into a ball on the sodden earth, he thrust his head into his gore-covered hands and wept for several minutes. His eyes were squeezed shut as the tears forced themselves out.

In the darkness, his mind recreated Mandy's corpse in front of him. Every little detail formulated in his mind; the tilt of her face, the droplets of water running off her nose, the stubby creamy piece of rib, gleaming from its rainwater wash, poking at an absurd angle from her side, her skinny blue jean legs, darkly stained from the mud, blood and rain. This teenage girl was dead and covered in gore, but quite suddenly her face shifted and the eyes blinked. When they flickered open, her warm hazel eyes had been replaced with red blazing orbs, burning with an intense hatred. The snarl on her curled, now ruby red lips had a wolverine quality to it.

His eyes snapped open and, with a gasp caught in his constricted throat, he flung his hands aside to scrutinise the body. It was motionless and her head was still turned slightly towards him, with her hazel eyes gazing blankly back at him. Nothing had changed.

Half laughing and half stifling another sob, he struggled to his feet, unable to take his eyes off Mandy's lifeless form for a second. A shiver ran through his cold, soaked body. After a moment, he rubbed his muddy hands on his jeans then wiped the tears and rain from his face. He let out a deep, trembling sigh and glanced around the gloomy woods.

"When you're slapped you'll take it and like it." His low murmuring voice sounded small and fragile, like a fly caught on the wind.

He stood there in the woods, staring down at the mutilated corpse, with the rain pouring down around him and the darkness closing in. The hard part was done. Now he had to clean up the mess and obliterate any traces of activity, then ultimately, continue with his preparations.

Yesterday's a dream,
I face the mornin',
Crying on a breeze,
The pain is calling, oh Mandy …

Over the following couple of days, word spread like a brushfire that Mandy had run away. Rumours were rife, ranging from a totally unsubstantiated allegation of an abusive father, through star struck dreams of Hollywood to something actually resembling the truth.

He had to wear a light daubing of concealer to hide a couple of red marks on his cheeks, but they faded quickly and appeared to go unnoticed.

Those first days thrust a torrent of emotions onto Han. Initially, he had an overwhelming feeling of regret and sadness; to have taken the life of such a pretty young girl. Someone who had their whole life ahead of them. A real person. After waking up during the night sobbing, and finding himself close to tears throughout the day, the sadness gradually made way for guilt, and even a sense of embarrassment.

A creeping paranoia set in, a feeling that he had missed some minute detail that police forensics would pick up on and lead them directly to him. He then started to wonder whether someone had actually seen him follow her that day. He was sure no one had – he had been extremely careful and vigilant – but still … Images of being caught, arrested and paraded, bound and beaten led to feelings of shame and humiliation. Ultimately those sickening feeble emotions settled upon a deep sense of resentment and anger, laced with a vigorous sense of fear and frustration.

Images of Mandy's ravaged body frequently flashed through his mind, both during the day and in the still, small hours. He could be talking to Big Joe or Lisa or John Bryce and her pallid, contorted face would replace that of the person he was conversing with. Once or twice he almost cried out, only just managing to check himself. Each time she would glare accusingly at him with those fierce burning eyes. There was a rage in those orbs that left him with a cold, crawling sensation.

Standing in front of the bathroom mirror, his eyes bloodshot and his complexion leaching a pale hue, Han gazed upon his haunted reflection. After letting the cold tap run for a few seconds, he cupped some of the cool water and splashed it onto his feverish face. His hands remained over his eyes for a time, before slowly drawing away and falling down to the rim of the sink. Looking back to his reflection, he noticed a faint flickering in his eyes.

Blinking, he rubbed his eyes vigorously then looked back at the mirror. The flicker was still there and his eyes had changed colour ... Hazel. "No!" he gasped aloud, his voice hoarse and distant. He squeezed his eyes shut once more and snapped them back open. Auburn eyes, bloodshot and fearful gazed back at him.

With a gravelly and wavering voice, he muttered, "I am reality. There's the way it ought to be, and there's the way it is." He let out a shaky sigh then shuffled wearily back to his bed.

Here come the Marines.

Gossip and general concern turned to alarm as news swept through the village that she had never made it to her friend's house in Shillmoor. Mandy Foster's name was on the lips of every single man, woman and child. Within hours, a growing sense of hysteria rose throughout the village. Nothing like this had ever happened in Haydon. Sure, it happened on the outside ... Newcastle, Morpeth, Rothbury from time to time, but never in Haydon. Haydon was ... different.

Two plain clothed police officers turned up the next day and started asking a lot of questions. Han chose that morning to take a trip into Rothbury, hoping to avoid having to use his dubious cover identity.

By the afternoon, the two detectives had called in a dozen uniformed officers and had organised more than fifty volunteers from the village to search the route between Haydon and Shillmoor. The search continued long after darkness fell, but the failing light made searching the woods increasingly futile and somewhat treacherous. It was with great reluctance, despite heated and desperate pleas from Mandy's parents, that the search was halted until the following morning. Ron Foster and several men from the village continued searching through the night, regardless. John Bryce, Duncan Fairbank and Doctor Herring accompanied Mandy's distraught father into the early hours and, despite their desperate efforts, they too finally trudged back to the village, dog-tired, dirty and dejected.

Erika Foster's agonised cries could be heard around the village as her husband stepped through the door, alone and hopeless.

The trip into Rothbury turned into quite a pleasant day out, and a much needed respite from the rising tensions within the closed community of Haydon. With the spire of All Saint's Parish Church dominating the skyline, and backed against the Simonside Hills, Rothbury was a bustling market town and tourist favourite.

Upon arrival, Han immediately felt the weight fall from his shoulders. The town was alive with walkers, caravanners, cyclists and bikers. The coffee shops were brimming with many enjoying customers enjoying the sunshine sat outside, sipping coffee or eating ice-cream.

A young couple walked by, both talking animatedly on their mobile phones. Everything seemed so normal – in stark contrast to Haydon.

Han grabbed a coffee to go and then chose to take a stroll and enjoy the fresh air. Seemingly drawn there, he found himself at the graveyard across the street from the church without even realising it. His feet seemed to draw him across the threshold without his conscious consent, and he soon found himself standing in front of a headstone depicting a mountain stream with a kingfisher upon a rock. On the bank of the stream was a fishing rod, creel and fish. The inscription read:

"But where's the auld fisher, sae bent and sae lame,
Wha cam' ilka spring wi' his rod ab' hois creel?
Death's ca'd him awa' to his lang latest hame,
An he'll wander nae mair by the stream le lo'ed well."

Although he struggled to read it, he grasped at once the sentiment, and felt surprisingly touched by the simple, but eloquent poem. Unnoticed, several tears rolled down his cheeks to moisten his rusty beard. What inscription would be etched into Mandy's headstone? He found out later from John Bryce that Walter Mavin, the Coquet Angler, had been a much loved figure who had reputedly trained Lord William Armstrong in the arts of fishing.

After mooching around the High Street, taking in an outdoor clothing shop and the Coquetdale Art Centre, he stopped for a light lunch at a café on Bridge Street. Satisfied by a ploughman's lunch, with his spirits lifted somewhat, he browsed a few more shops and galleries.

A walk down to Beggar's Rigg offered the perfect spot to sit and watch the river gently flow by. Several Mallard ducks had settled on the river, occasionally quacking to one another. He felt his tumultuous feelings settle, and a sense of calm embraced him as he sat and observed the quiet scene. The smell of freshly cut grass and the melodic buzz of bees added to his sense of well-being.

A people carrier pulled into the car park and a stressed couple with four kids in tow piled out, descending upon the picnic area accompanied by clattering, stomping and shouting. That was Han's cue to leave. Walking back to the High Street, he made a quick call to Perry to check up on how things were going with Ju and the shop, then stopped off at a florist to buy a bouquet for Lisa, followed by Soulsby's toy shop to pick up a little treat for Haley.

A short drive then took him to Cragside House, the former home of the inventor, Lord Armstrong. A walk around the vibrant, meandering gardens and lakes rewarded him with a glimpse of a red squirrel scurrying through the branches of a mighty Douglas fir.

On his return from Rothbury, he spent some time with Lisa and Big Joe, learning of the failed search. He made sure to tell them that he would be joining the search first thing in the morning to do whatever he could to help. Lisa seemed particularly comforted by his spirited offer of support.

The following morning, Han rose early. After dressing quickly in jeans and t-shirt, he went through to the en suite to splash water over his face. The vision he had seen in the very same mirror was still fresh in his mind, so there was a slight hint of apprehension as he paused to look at his dripping face. Only his mirror image, refreshed and calm, stared back.

Considering events, he felt he should still feel at least a little nervous, but strangely – and in complete contrast to the last few days – all he felt now was elation. His day out yesterday had more than lifted his spirits; it had renewed his conviction, and cleared his distorted vision. His gifts to Lisa and Haley had also been much appreciated, despite the shroud hanging over the whole village. His high spirits might waver when he eventually had to face the investigating officers, but for now, he felt good.

He was brushing his teeth as a knock sounded at the door. Han's heart skipped a beat. He had an idea who it might be.

Spitting frothy toothpaste into the sink, he shouted, "One sec – just brushing my teeth." He finished up quickly. No sense irritating them by keeping them waiting.

He swung the door open, to reveal two big men. The taller of the two, who had to be six feet four and looked like an all in wrestler, had short cropped salt and pepper hair and beard. His slightly shorter friend was balding with a tanned Latin look and a broad smile.

Latino spoke first, flipping open an ID wallet, to reveal his CID credentials. "Mister Whitman, I'm Detective Sergeant Mitchell and this is Detective Constable Wright." There was a slight Geordie twang to his accent; a posh Geordie or maybe attempting to hide his accent?

"Yes, of course. Sorry I missed you yesterday." Stepping aside, he gestured for the two officers to enter. "Please, come in." He finished drying his hands on a hand towel as they stepped inside, then tossed it onto the bed.

"Cheers," both officers said in tandem as they glanced around the room.

"We'd just like to ask you a few questions regarding the disappearance of Mandy Foster," Wright said, his accent subdued cockney. His genuine smile revealed cigarette stained teeth as he stood, feet apart with both hands thrust deep into his black trousers. He was broad-shouldered with the makings of a paunch, but he had the look of a man more than capable of handling himself.

"No problem. I'll try to help in any way I can." Han stood in the centre of the room with them. Suddenly the room seemed full and he felt at once self conscious. Folding his arms across his chest, he cocked his head towards the window and added, "I was just on my way to join the volunteers meeting on the Green."

"Yes, the landlord told us," Mitchell replied, popping his ID back into the inside pocket of his leather jacket. "Everyone's help is much appreciated. We thought we'd have a word beforehand, if you don't mind."

"Not at all." Han leaned casually against the desk where his laptop lay open, but switched off.

"Good; we won't keep you long," Wright said in a 'let's get down to business' tone. "First of all, can you confirm your home address and reasons for being in Haydon?" He flipped open a notepad, pulling a thin pencil from its spine.

"Thought you guys would be using iPads or something these days."

"Pen and paper's just as good," Wright said matter-of-factly, licking the tip of the pencil.

Han shrugged. "I'm surrounded by tech day in day out – I sell the stuff."

Mitchell raised his eyebrows. "I thought you were a writer?"

"I am, but writing doesn't pay the bills; not yet anyway. The day job is mobile tech – latest smartphones and whatnot." Picking up his phone, he said, "This one's just off the assembly line – blisteringly fast processor—"

"We get the picture," Wright politely interrupted, scribbling a few words onto the pad.

"Sorry, force of habit." Han popped it back onto the desk and said, "I had to save up twelve months of holidays and take some unpaid leave to be able to take this research trip."

Han proceeded to answer their questions, giving the false address in Cumbria and more background into his false identity. Wright was jotting down the last of his notes when Mitchell's mobile beeped in his jacket.

Shaking his head in irritation, Mitchell retrieved his phone and glanced at the screen. "Missed call. Bloody reception is useless around here."

Han nodded and said, "Yep, same with mine. I'm lucky to get one bar for miles around here, and then only briefly. Got to go into Rothbury to get a decent reception." He offered an apologetic smile.

Thrusting the useless phone back into his jacket, Mitchell asked, "Mind if I use your landline?"

"No problem."

Mitchell dialled on the cream pushbutton phone and received an immediate answer. "It's Mitchell, in Haydon ... *Haydon*. Thanks." While he waited to be transferred, he glanced towards Han and said, "So much for technology, eh? Back in the bloody stone age here."

Han shrugged apologetically. "Yeah, lots of black spots like these out in the sticks."

Mitchell turned his attention back to the phone. "Aye, you got it. Cheers." Hanging up the receiver, he turned to his colleague. "We've ID'd the boyfriend. Lothian are sending a couple of uniform round to question him."

"Result," Wright said, flipping shut his notepad with a flick of his wrist.

"Jesus, do you think he's done something to her?" Han asked with marked concern.

Wright shoved the pad into his jacket and said, "The boyfriend's always the prime suspect in these cases." Their eyes locked for a moment longer than Han felt comfortable with, but he met his stare and maintained the look of concern.

"But we're not ruling anything out at this stage," his colleague smoothly interjected. "Now, we've kept you long enough. Thanks again for helping with the search." His tone was relaxed and he offered Han his hand.

Han grasped it with conviction "I'm not religious, but I pray that she turns up safe and sound."

After seeing the two officers out, he sat down on the edge of the bed and let out a long, trembling sigh. As perfectly as that went, he was damn glad it was over and was suddenly acutely aware of how damp his armpits had become.

There was also his less than perfect identity. Would they run a check? Definitely. Would it just be a perfunctory one? It bloody better be. Would Mandy Foster prove to be his downfall? Maybe the test had been a bad idea; catastrophic even? The questions and concerns came in a surge, but, in the end, only time would tell.

Wright and Mitchell walked back downstairs and into the street without a word. The early morning was dull and overcast, but awash with activity. Across the road, on and around the Green, dozens of villagers and police officers were gathering beside the incident unit that had been set up there. As they observed, a police dog section van arrived.

Wright pulled out a crumpled pack of cigarettes and stuck one in his mouth. Lighting it with a *Zippo* sporting a red dagger, he muttered, "So, what do you think of our friend there?"

"Seems pleasant enough."

After taking a long satisfying draw, Wright said, "Yeah, I thought he was lying too."

Mitchell glanced back at the pub then thrust his hands in his pockets. "Hmm, but what about exactly? I can't quite make him out. He's a cool bugger, that's for sure. Not sure whether he has anything to do with this Foster case, but there's something about him."

Wright drew on the cigarette again before replying. "Yeah, don't think he's a killer, but there's something shifty about him. Shame we don't have enough probable to get a search warrant."

"A hunch isn't enough and all we've got is a missing person so far. So you reckon the bet still stands then?"

"Oh yes. She's definitely dead and I reckon it's foul play, mate."

"You always think it's foul play," Mitchell scoffed. "You have a disturbing lack of faith in the human condition."

"Ten years of the Marines'll do that to a bloke, believe me."

"And then you decided to join the force for some 'real' human misery? You're a glutton for punishment, mate."

They stood for a minute longer in silence, both men contemplating their thoughts. Wright finally dropped the used butt and crushed it under foot, much to the annoyance of his partner.

"I wish you wouldn't do that."

Rolling his eyes, Wright said, "He's probably just defrauding his company or something. Nothing that interests me."

Mitchell nodded. "Aye, command can run the usual checks while we get on with this search. Hopefully those Lothian lads can get something out of the boyfriend in the meantime."

"Only real lead we've got so far. Nothing from her friends, family or neighbours. For all intents and purposes she was a real girl scout."

"Homemade apple pie," Wright muttered while considering whether to spark up another cigarette or not.

"You're a sick man, Tone."

"Takes one to know one, mate." Wright grinned at him and slapped him on the back.

The Searchers.

The clouds burned off quickly to give way to a hot, still day that had all the volunteers and officers stripping off layers of clothing and dabbing at damp foreheads and necks. The search was slow and painstaking, covering each section of woodland and meadow between the two villages with slow, deliberate precision. Two dog teams assisted in the search, the two Alsatians eager and seemingly immune to fatigue, as they attempted to pick up a scent from the lost girl. They successfully followed her trail to the spot where she had ran into the woods, and even managed to stumble across the area of her final demise. However, a combination of the weather over those early days and Han's meticulous cleanup efforts left them bewildered.

The Forensic Science Service despatched a Scene of Crime Officer (SOCO) to the area to perform a comprehensive grid search of the sections the dogs appeared most interested in, looking for footprints, fragments of clothing, hair samples or traces of blood or other substances. Using a combination of UV lighting and vacuum sweeping and combing, the search revealed little except some recently disturbed ground; no human traces were found.

The SOCO, a hearty woman with a bright red nose, explained to Mitchell and Wright that both the recent rainy weather and the elapse of time stood against them. Various forms of local wildlife had also passed through the area which would make it even more difficult for the dogs. She had, however, managed to collect a number of samples which would be sent off to the lab for analysis and added that the scene, if preserved, could benefit from a more thorough investigation by a full team.

Mitchell, on her advice, argued with Command to pull in additional forensic resources, but his request was denied. Lack of evidence and restricted resources were sited for something that could ultimately amount to a runaway. The samples, in fact, turned out to be rat faeces, a fox hair and a woollen clothing fibre that was too degraded to be linked to the Mandy Foster case.

The sun was setting once more as the volunteers trudged, weary and dejected back to their homes. A second day of searching had again proved fruitless.

Han, too, plodded back with the rest, his t-shirt, with SHUT IT emblazoned across the stern faces of John Thaw and

Dennis Waterman, drenched in sweat. His jeans had several muddy marks up the legs and on the knees where he had stumbled more than once.

John Bryce walked alongside him, his broad shoulders rounded and hunched over, his face a mask of gloom. Janet Herring walked just ahead of them in tight shorts that clung to the toned contours of her rounded bum. Her tall, wiry husband, the good doctor Larry, walked with her, occasionally offering a comforting smile to her. He had a fleece tied around his jogging bottoms and his damp short-sleeved polo shirt revealed strong, outdoorsman arms.

He knew without looking that the strutting cock, Steve Belmont, was a few steps behind him. He had caught Janet glancing back towards him several times. Surely poor Larry must have some idea?

So what the hell did Janet see in Steve? Larry was certainly not the old, crusty bookish man that he had imagined him to be – he had an open, intelligent face and appeared fit, confident, and certainly had the good job to go with it. All in all, Larry seemed to have the right packaging to catch the right shopper, so why was his customer buying her meat from a new butcher?

And what about Steve? Han glanced back towards the tanned menace. Everyone else around him was dishevelled and grimy. He, on the other hand, was, in a word, pristine. Blue shorts over muscular legs, fitted (completely unblemished) white t-shirt, gold St Christopher medallion around his neck, sunglasses, tennis shoes.

Their eyes met and Steve exposed his pearly whites in an unconvincing grin. As he turned away, his eyes met the blue eye-shadowed blinkers of Tess Runckle, dressed in a gold two-piece track suit. She was staring – no, glaring at him. There was an accusation in her eyes that was unequivocal.

She had Moe, the maybe not so gay hairdresser, on her arm, patting her hand in a comforting fashion. Whether it was for her benefit or for his, he couldn't tell, but there was definitely a lover's touch in the way they moved together so closely. Perhaps only a fraction closer than friends, but Han noticed it.

All in all, it looked like a fucking freak show parade. He smiled at that, but the glare from Tess Runckle lingered on his mind.

Bryce stopped at the Bell Lane junction and arched his aching back. "You take it easy, mate. Probably see you in the Miller's tomorrow."

Han nodded, but his downcast eyes and his set jaw caused Bryce to pause before heading off. "You okay, Han?"

He looked up to him, concern marking his tired features. "I'm getting some funny looks from people. I think people are thinking ..." His voice trailed off, his point made.

Bryce laid a big hand on his shoulder. "Let us guess? That curtain twitcher, Tess, for one, eh?" Han nodded, dejected. "You divvent want to let the likes of her get to you, man. It's just 'cause you're the new guy, that's all."

"Yeah, but it doesn't change the fact that people are going to start thinking that I'm some kind of freak or something." Han chose his words carefully, but the more he spoke about it, the more he genuinely felt a twinge of sadness that people would actually be thinking ill of him. He was still the nice, polite guy he always had been.

"You are a freak, mate," Bryce said then laughed as heartily as his tired body could muster. His tone sincere once more, he added, "Look, divvent worry – you know that you had nothing to do with any of this and so will most of the *normal* people round here."

Han said a washed-out farewell to John Bryce and then crossed over Main Street to the pub. As he entered, he noticed the two plain clothed officers standing by the open door of the incident unit. Wright was smoking and Mitchell was sipping a hot drink out of a Styrofoam cup. Both were watching him.

As he slowly closed the door behind him, he noticed Tess and her camp-as-an-Abba-tribute-night beau make a beeline for the two detectives. For the first time since his arrival in Haydon, Han felt a very real knot of fear twist his stomach.

The smoking gorilla and his bum chum were already a little suspicious, but throw paranoid Bet into the mixing pot and they may start delving under the surface of his flimsy fake identity.

What if he had to abort everything? All his planning and preparation would be for nothing. But then, that would be the least of his worries.

His heart was racing as he rushed upstairs to his room.

"Detective Mitchell, dear," Tess called to the two detectives as she approached, hoisting her breasts up with one arm as a gesture of determination.

Moe squeezed her arm hard and said, with marked consternation, "I really don't think this is a good idea, Tessie."

Tess shook his arm off. "Don't you 'Tessie' me, Moe Baxter. That Whitman lad is shifty and I know it." She made one last adjustment to her plentiful breasts – squeezed to bursting point into the zipped up tracksuit top – and crossed the final few feet to the waiting officers.

"What can I do for you, Ms Runckle?" Mitchell asked in a strained-polite tone as he tossed his empty coffee cup into a nearby bin. Glancing at Wright, he saw his colleague briefly roll his eyes as he stubbed out his cigarette.

"It's that Mister Whitman – there's something definitely fishy about him," Tess told him sternly. She jabbed an accusing finger towards the Miller's and added, "I see him sniffing around town all day, *snooping* on folks. I even caught him going into the ladies at the Duck a while back, the pervert."

Mitchell listened with forced interest, nodding in the right places, as she talked about Haydon's stranger for several minutes, without seemingly needing to take a breath. Moe would occasionally try to inject a comment, but was always silenced by a harsh 'Shush, dear'.

He exchanged a look with Wright, who was pretending to write notes, before saying, with as much enthusiasm as he could muster, "Ms Runckle, we really appreciate this information. We are already looking into Mister Whitman's background, as we are a number of other individuals, in the course of our enquiries, and will certainly take this new evidence on board in our continued investigation." He felt as if the words rolled out like he was reading from a cue card and lacked any real sentiment, but it seemed to be exactly what the landlady wanted to hear.

Tess's face beamed with pride and she instantly pulled Mitchell to her breasts and gave him a vigorous hug. Before he could object, she then turned to Wright and embraced him too.

"Thank you, dears," she said with enormous relief and then marched off with Moe scurrying along after her. "See! I told you so!" she could be heard saying to Moe as they disappeared from earshot.

Mitchell stared after her, mouth agape.

"Bunch of fruitloops, every man jack of 'em," Wright muttered, lighting up another cigarette.

After several more days of investigation and searches, with Han helping where appropriate, but keeping a low profile for the most part, the search was finally called off. The incident unit was packed up and carted off with the last of the officers. Only posters remained in the shops and pubs, appealing for information. Similar posters had been put up all over the area as far as Morpeth and Hexham and appeals had been broadcast on local radio and television channels.

Mitchell and Wright were the last to leave. They strolled unhurriedly along Main Street back to their parked unmarked saloon, both deep in thought. Wright smoking, Mitchell chewing on a pencil.

Mitchell unlocked the car as they approached, shoving the mauled pencil back into his jacket. Opening the door, he paused to look at his partner. "I know his story checked out and he's Mister Nobody, but there's still something about him."

Wright leaned against the passenger door and took his half-smoked cigarette out of his mouth. While examining it, he said, "He's shifty, I grant you." Flicking the smoking butt into the gutter, he turned his attention to Mitchell. "But we got nothing on him whatsoever."

In the absence of the pencil, Mitchell chewed on his bottom lip. "Yeah, that is rather irritating."

Wright pulled open his door and, before sliding in, said, "Make you a deal; if the boyfriend turns out to be a dead end, I think we should continue sniffing round our squeaky friend here."

Mitchell recognised the conviction in his friend's eyes. He had seen it several times before on some of their tougher cases. "Deal," he replied.

An orange Datsun Cherry drove by slowly. The driver had bushy grey sideburns, greased back hair and a moustache. A cigarette was hanging out of his mouth and his eyes were fixed on the two detectives.

Wright met his gaze and watched him until the old car disappeared from sight. He glanced around the village and then back to Mitchell. "Can we get out of here now? This place is like the fucking Twilight Zone."

chapter 5

Joe's Heroes.

The Miller's lounge was empty, apart from Han who sat at a corner table, finishing off a portion of pork chops, chips and peas. The room felt uncomfortably stuffy after a particularly hot day, aided by some sort of baking frenzy that Martha had been possessed with. He was deep in thought and glad to be on his own. Apart from his time spent in his room, it was difficult to be completely alone around Haydon. He felt eyes on him all of the time. Some of it was undoubtedly paranoia, but some was justified.

Of late, his mood swung from elated, when with Lisa or when cultivating his blooming friendship with John Bryce, to melancholy when he would catch the eyes of Tess or one of her cronies glaring at him with open suspicion. And, occasionally, Mandy would speak to him at night, in his dreams. Although sometimes he wasn't sure whether he was asleep or awake.

Big Joe trudged through from the bar with an empty glass in his hand and a tartan tea towel tucked into his belt. He was red-faced, with sweat standing out on his brow. He sounded a little wheezy when he said, "Slow the night, laddie. Grub do yer?"

After swallowing the last couple of chips, Han patted his stomach theatrically and said, "Damn fine, sah. As usual."

"Glad tae hear it. Hope yer saved room for a wee slice of Martha's apple crumble; she's made enough tae feed the Otterburn ranges! And a whole lot better than the slop we used to get in the service."

"Always room for apple crumble," Han said with a smile. Sitting back, he took a sip of bourbon and added, "You must've seen a fair bit of action in the army, I bet."

The big landlord's expression changed. He stood silent, eyes downcast for a time. Han was beginning to regret broaching the subject, but then Big Joe spoke, his normally booming voice quiet and sullen. "I was already a veteran when they shipped us off. The young'uns were full of bravado, but us older blokes knew what was coming ..." His voice trailed off and he turned to look at an old black and white photo on its own to one side of the lurid postcards. It was faded and tobacco stained.

It was a group of soldiers in the jungle. Most of them looked too young to buy a pint and they were all emaciated. Sunken distant eyes, fatigues reduced to tattered rags. Some sitting on ammunition crates, some sagging against their Lee Enfield rifles.

Han frowned. The photo was significant, but why? It was clearly circa World War II, possibly Burma. Father maybe?

"Is that—"

Big Joe turned away and headed for the kitchen, muttering, "I'll get yer pudding."

Han opened his mouth to comment further, but decided against it. Instead, his mind wandered back to that Saturday evening in the woods with Mandy. He saw her dead face turn towards his with those red, evil eyes.

He knocked back the rest of his drink in an attempt to shake the vision from his mind.

A Nightmare on Miller's Road.

A thick soup-like fog oozed through the shadowy streets of Haydon, obscuring the moonless sky. Han stood rooted to the spot on the damp grass beneath the Haydon Oak, staring at the Miller's. The pub was in darkness, as were the surrounding buildings. Glancing about, frowning, he noticed that there was not a single light on in the village, not even shop signs. Had there been a power cut?

As he waited, a solitary howl lifted above the gloom, causing his heart to quicken. There was a lonely desperation in that canine cry.

Distorted by the creeping fog, Han thought he saw shapes moving behind the blackened windows of the Co-op and the Post Office. His pulse quickening further still, he noticed similar figures in other windows. As his mind struggled with this vision, new shapes appeared in the yawning darkness of open doorways.

A big, bloated form appeared in the doorway of the Miller's. Han's instinct was to run, to get far away from this foreboding place, but his legs refused to oblige. They seemed set on facing whatever demons awaited him.

The figures stepped out of the shadowy doorways and started to move towards him from all directions, shuffling with a slow awkward determination. They were human and he recognised them, but the way they walked – that stiff shamble – disturbed him. Something wasn't right about these people.

As they grew closer, he recognised Big Joe, but as his face took shape, he realised that the retired soldier had no eyes, just empty black sockets. His face was drooping, as if melted, with a glistening, waxy sheen.

Tam Wellright was lumbering along beside him, but he, too, had no eyes, along with a gaping bloody tear where his Adam's apple should have been. A bloated tongue lolled over thin, quivering lips.

Terror rose up into Han's throat like hot bile, but no sound escaped his lips. His body trembled from more than just the damp, slithering cold that seeped into his pores.

At once, he regained some bodily control. He spun around to see more villagers approaching, mere feet away. John Bryce, his eyeless, severed head held by matted hair in one hand, Carol Belmont, naked with her stomach ripped open, cradling her slimy intestines like a baby. They were grey and most definitely dead. Then the stench struck his nostrils like a head butt to the nose. The reek of death and decay; the stink of all that is rotten was too much. Spasms kicked at his stomach, causing him to retch noisily.

Still spinning, he stopped abruptly with Lisa right in front of him. Like the others, her eyes were hollowed out voids. Her pallid, rotting skin clung to her face like folds of muslin, yet her lips were luscious and ruby red. She held a bundle of bloody, torn rags in her cracked and bleeding fingers.

With a blank, dead expression, she outstretched her arms. A sick, crawling revulsion sent a shiver through him, causing him to gag once more, as he took the package against his will. Holding it in one arm, he peeled away the top layers of sticky, rank material to reveal a maggot-infested rotting foetus, complete with bloodied ginger hair and a shrivelled, blackened penis.

TAP TAP.

"Yours," Lisa uttered with a hoarse whisper, without moving her engorged lips.

TAP TAP.

Finally, a scream rose up from the pit of his stomach as the rest of the villagers closed in around him. Lisa's dead face offered a hint of a smile as she allowed the others to engulf his squealing, flailing form.

TAP TAP.

Han awoke with a scream anchored to his lips, gasping for breath. His face and chest were glistening with sweat and the balled up sheets felt damp to the touch. His chest heaved with a desperate effort to draw gulps of air into his lungs and his whole body trembled uncontrollably.

The room was silent and in darkness. A quick, wild-eyed glance towards the folding travel clock on the bedside table revealed that it was two seventeen AM.

TAP TAP – a light knocking on the door disturbed the stillness.

With considerable effort, Han heaved himself out of bed and padded, barefoot across the rough carpet, to the door. "Who is it?"

"It's me, you divvie," Lisa whispered through the door, suppressing a giggle.

With a nauseating, repulsive feeling still stuck to his skin like a feverish sweat, the thought of being in anyone's company was a welcome relief. He swung the door open and pulled her immediately to him.

Surprised and excited by his immediate response, she embraced him fervently, kissing him hard on the lips and running her hands down his naked body.

Kicking the door closed with a flick of his foot, he lifted her diminutive body off the floor and flung her onto the bed, which offered a creaking protest.

Laughing, she yanked her Grateful Dead t-shirt over her head, revealing her small breasts then quickly unbuttoned her jeans as she kicked off her heels.

Anticipating what was to come, he grew hard as he approached, much to Lisa's delight. Gripping her jeans at the thighs, he wrenched them off in one fluid motion.

Her knickers followed, leaving her naked and breathless on his bed. Han descended upon her, licking her inner thighs and tracing a line towards her exposed mound.

She moaned, gripping the sheets as he delicately savoured her sweet taste and greedily breathed in her musky aroma.

She cried out softly and gripped his head between her thighs.

Slowly, he progressed up her body, kissing and tasting every part of her. Moving to her stomach and across her breasts, lingering at her hard nipples. Her chest then neck followed as he worked up to her eager lips. Then the tip of his erection brush against her.

Clawing at his back, Lisa begged him to enter her.

Their mouths touched and his tongue slipped inside her. She could taste herself on his lips and it only served to fuel her desire.

As he eased inside her, she moaned further still and drew him in deeper. He buried himself all the way into her, until they were pressed tightly together, clutching each other like they would remain forever entwined. Then, slowly and deliberately, he withdrew almost to the tip.

She quivered, her mouth trembling and her body arching, as he slowly penetrated her once more.

They moved together unhurriedly for several minutes, savouring every second of their joining, before their needs grew beyond control, forcing urgency into their thrusts.

They came together, kissing and moaning, their bodies glistening and intertwined.

Holding each other, they tenderly kissed and whispered like forbidden lovers. After maintaining the embrace for some time, Lisa gently and reluctantly slid from under him and started to dress in silence.

Han sat up to watch her, resting on one elbow. The bed suddenly felt empty without her. Slipping the jeans over her bare backside, she shoved her knickers into a pocket and said, "I wish I could stay, but I've got to get back to Haley."

Han smiled and was surprised by the genuine affection in it. "I understand. Thanks for your company – I really needed it."

Lisa paused with one shoe on and the other in her hand. She looked closely into his eyes and tears started to well in her own. "Are you the real deal?"

Han matched her stare with a growing intensity, before saying, "Yes. Yes, I am."

A Slovakian exporter, Larry, his wife and her lover.

After a brief rattling of keys, the front door swung open to reveal Larry Herring in shorts and a sweat-soaked *Northumbria University* t-shirt. He stretched both calves several times on the raised stoop, before stepping inside.

The modest two-up two-down was in silence. Janet was out shopping and Kerris was in school. Larry had taken the morning off from the surgery to deal with several chores. One such chore was a package wrapped in grubby brown paper and tied with string. It had arrived in the post that morning to his private post box in Rothbury.

Grabbing the package from the foot of the staircase, he strode through to the kitchen. Popping the package on the breakfast table, he crossed to the refrigerator and retrieved a carton of grapefruit juice.

As he poured himself a drink, his eyes wandered back to the package. It was silent and unmoving, but something appeared to trouble the doctor when he glanced at it.

The post mark was Bratislava, Slovakia.

After gulping down the juice, he trotted upstairs for a shower.

The cool shower refreshed and invigorated his tired limbs from the five mile run, but the cleaning ritual was perfunctory, his mind ensnared by more important issues.

He dressed in jeans and a *Led Zeppelin* t-shirt, depicting their 1970 UK tour. After slipping on some sandals, he padded back downstairs and headed straight for the package.

Pulling up a chair, he sat and turned the package over in his hands several times. The troubled frown returned to his features as he examined every inch of the innocuous looking parcel.

After what seemed like an age, with a slight tremor in his fingers, the doctor snipped the string and carefully tore open the paper packaging. He eased one hand inside and rummaged through shredded packing paper until his fingers touched upon a slim, cylindrical object.

Holding his breath, he withdrew it. The small vial was all but empty, apart from a few of drops of clear liquid in the bottom. There was no label and no instructions or accompanying letter.

Still not daring to breathe, Larry carefully held the vial up to the light between thumb and forefinger. It could have been a drop of tap water or Evian or dragon's tears, but Larry knew exactly what it was. He had been waiting for it for three weeks, and many months more in actually sourcing a trusted, anonymous supplier, using the computer in the local library in Rothbury.

Larry had never listened to the gossip hounds when it came to the whispers of his wife with Steve Belmont, but then there had been that fateful night when he had returned early from the pharmaceutical conference in Newcastle. That night he was supposed to be staying overnight to catch up with a colleague over a few drinks on the Quayside. Unfortunately (or fortunately), Jim Pembroke had left early on hearing news of his mother being rushed in to hospital with a suspected heart attack. She had died early the next morning.

He had called from the hotel before leaving, but there had been no answer. Probably down the Miller's or round nattering to Loretta, he had thought.

February had been a cold and wet month and that evening had been no exception.

The Ford Escort splashed through the muddy puddles that had collected on Main Street throughout the day and evening. The rain was still falling, but had lost most of its earlier fervour, allowing Larry Herring to reduce the windscreen wipers down to their lowest setting. The absolute darkness was only pierced by the rare light from a veiled window.

It was closing on ten PM when he turned onto Bell Lane and then into the car park behind their home.

He climbed out, feeling weary, but relieved to be home. After popping the boot to retrieve his haversack and Barbour jacket, he walked around the side of the house towards the front door.

As he reached the side window, he noticed the light on and two figures caressing in the lounge. His heart skipped a beat and the hairs on the back of his neck prickled.

Peering through the slim gap in the curtains, Larry witnessed, with utter horror and disgust, Janet and Steve naked in the middle of his living room. They were both standing, kissing and touching each other's sweaty bodies, with Steve's hard on brushing against his wife's naked thigh.

Then, as if it could get any worse, it did. He saw his wife kneel down in front of that prick and take it into her filthy mouth.

His head suddenly began to swim, as if he had stood up too quickly after having several too many brandies. Staggering away from the window, a wave of nausea swept over him. Instantly, he emptied his stomach of the beef stroganoff, brandy and coffee that he had consumed earlier, onto the gravel path.

His quiet sobbing and retching went undetected for several minutes as the gentle rain continued to fall on his back and around him.

After wiping his mouth he composed himself then walked slowly back to the car. He threw his bag and coat back into the boot and turned the engine on.

He sat there with the motor idling for several minutes as the windscreen slowly misted, his expression blank, haunted.

Then, after switching on the fan, he eased it into gear and turned the car carefully around in the small car park. He then drove without a word out of Haydon and back to Newcastle.

Tears streamed unchecked down his face periodically on the long drive back, blurring his vision and twice almost sending him into a ditch. But he made it back, checked in, threw his bag into the room and went straight to the bar. He stayed there till eight the next morning, having gone through a full bottle of Hennessy XO at fifteen pounds a glass.

He finally drove back to Haydon at midday with a thumping head and several times over the limit.

Janet greeted him with a hug and a kiss, trying to force her tongue into his mouth, but Larry broke it off before she could manage it.

Remaining inhumanly calm, he managed to ask about her evening with even a little amiable smile on his face. And this year's Oscar goes to ... Doctor Larry Herring for his loveable-dickhead-arsewipe role in the 'Janet and Steve Affair'.

She had lied, of course. Had a couple in the Miller's then back to the house for a quiet night in front of the telly. Did you, dear? Ah, that's nice ... bitch. And Kerris asleep upstairs, was she? No more nightmares? Good ... whore.

After that day, Larry had remained the doting husband and had given his 'wife' dozens of opportunities to come clean. Clean? That would be a laugh after having that Steve Belmont's cock in her disgusting mouth.

But she never did, so after a while he had found himself spending more and more time at the library, searching the internet for a certain poison, a poison that would be totally undetectable in an autopsy. His search had led him to Saxitoxin, also known as Shellfish Toxin, and then to an unscrupulous supplier in Eastern Europe.

Just one milligram would kill the average human stone dead within seconds when taken orally or through injection. As the bitch-whore was no 'average' human, he purchased two milligrams.

So, this was the stuff that would kill his wife and the mother of their only daughter. Looking at the small unassuming vial, he considered that last statement, as he had many, many times since learning of his wife's infidelity.

He still loved Janet, as much as it pained him to admit it, but the hate had grown far, far stronger. The disgust burned inside him like molten lava, eating away at his insides; consuming every happy memory of their years together, every reason to stay his hand. So, killing Janet, although difficult, had not been impossible to come to terms with. What he had struggled the most with, and struggled still, was that Kerris would lose the mother whom she loved dearly.

There was a battle raging within his head and the final victor had yet to be decided.

He slipped the vial into his pocket, then collected the packaging and headed out of the back door to the public rubbish bin in the car park. After shoving the packaging deep into the bin, under crisp packets, cans and old newspapers, he trudged slowly back to the house, with the vial still resting against his hip.

Guess who's coming to dinner.

Han and Lisa crunched up the gravel lane towards the Bryce family farmhouse. The evening sky lent a soft red hue to the broken white clouds, and the warmth of the day still lingered. The air was still and fragrant with a myriad of wildflower and woodland aromas, but as they approached the farm, these gave way to the far fresher smell of manure.

Lisa was fidgeting nervously, constantly adjusting her short denim skirt and blouse. Her cheeks were flushed, and only part of that was due to the walk.

Han glanced at her and smiled. Sighing, he said, "You look fantastic, hun. Stop fretting."

Lisa stopped abruptly and, defensively, said, "This is a big deal for me. I don't *do* dinner parties." Her annoyed tone vainly tried to disguise her anxiety.

He turned to face her. Swapping the bottle of red wine to his other hand, he placed the free hand on her flushed cheek. "John's a good bloke, and Sally's supposed to be nice too, from what I've heard. It'll be fine." He kissed her soft lips then added, "It'll be a laugh."

Lisa let out a deep breath and said, "Wey, if they suggest charades I'm getting the hell out."

Han laughed and gave her a brief hug. "I'll be right behind you."

John Bryce swung the front door open on the first knock. Grinning, he said, "Welcome! Welcome!" Then, cocking his head to one side, shouted, "Sal, Han and Lisa are here!"

"How about letting them in then!" his wife called back from the kitchen with an exasperated tone.

"Brought you a bottle, big fella," Han said, shaking his hand.

Bryce took the bottle and glanced at the label. "Canny, you shouldn't have. We've got enough to sink a battleship already, so I hope you've got your drinkin' heads on!" He led them past a cluttered study to a spacious lounge. As Han and Lisa sat next to each other on one of the two old and cracked Chesterfields, Bryce went to a glass fronted wall unit with a flip down shelf. Dropping the shelf, he opened the glass doors to retrieve a corkscrew. As he uncorked the bottle, his wife appeared.

Sally Bryce was a tiny, frail looking woman with loosely tied-back mousy hair. She had piercing blue eyes that were framed by the gradual onset of crow's feet. Wiping her hands on a tea towel, she offered them a warm smile and said, "Hi, Han, nice to meet you finally. Hi, Lisa, how are you, pet?"

Han rose, quickly followed somewhat timidly by Lisa.

Sally waved a hand at them. "We don't stand on ceremony here, pet. You two make yourself comfortable." Feigning impatience, she turned to Bryce and added, "John, you big lug, get our guests a drink before they die of thirst."

"Aye-aye, divvent get your knickers in a twist."

Rolling her eyes, she said to her guests, "I'll be right back. I hope you both like lamb." With that she whisked off back to the kitchen.

Pouring the wine into four glasses, Bryce said, "Anthony's staying round his mate's tonight, so it's an all adult night. We haven't had one of them in years!" He chuckled at that. After handing out the over-filled glasses, he raised his in an impromptu toast. "Here's to a crackin' night." On reflection, he added more sombrely, "We could all do with it after recent events."

Raising his own glass, Han looked from Bryce to Lisa. She smiled back at him and now looked a little more at ease.

Hesitantly at first, she took a sip of her wine, and then proceeded to take a big gulp. He glanced at the dark liquid in his own glass for a moment, then followed suit.

Beat the Parents.

As August fell by the wayside, a warm September settled upon Haydon. Police activity relating to Mandy Foster's disappearance faded and, one by one, the posters disappeared from the lamp posts and notice boards. The two prying detectives, Wright and Mitchell, seemed to have drifted off into the ether. Even the nightmares had become less frequent.

Erika Foster became more and more reclusive, rarely venturing out. Her husband began spending a lot more time in both pubs, alternating between the two when things got a little out of hand. He drank and, as the night wore on, he would become steadily angrier, until he would snap. Anyone who happened to be nearby was likely to be on the receiving end of his temper.

Ron's increasingly erratic behaviour came to a head one night in the Miller's. As the evening progressed, Ron became louder and more animated, attracting concerned glances from several patrons. If he saw any of them, he chose to ignore them. He knocked back a pint and shouted for another.

His face furrowed, Bryce said, "Take it easy, mate." He glanced briefly to Duncan who was stood beside him at the bar.

Duncan offered an apologetic shrug. After a lip-biting moment, searching for the right words, he said, "I think I'm about ready to call it a night. What about you, Ron?"

Ron spun to glare at him, wavering slightly. His eyes were bloodshot and the dark growth on his chin – several days past the stubble stage – lent a pale tinge to his features. "Nah, divvent go yet, man. Loretta can wait."

There was a flicker of a cringe, then Duncan said, "Erika needs you, mate."

Ron waved a dismissive arm and turned back to the bar, leaving Duncan and John staring at each other. Wordlessly, they exchanged their concerns.

A young man, lost in an over-sized duffle coat with a spotty forehead, squeezed past Duncan to get to the bar. In the process, he knocked Ron's shoulder. Big Joe was now, reluctantly, pouring fresh pints for them.

Ron spun round to confront the person who had stumbled into him.

Not suspecting trouble, the lad in his late teens hardly spared him a glance, but muttered, "Sorry."

Ron's face reddened. *"Sorry?"*

"Ron, leave it," Bryce said, tensing immediately. Big Joe glanced up from the hand pump, sensing trouble.

The young man turned to him. Seeing the drunken man's growing anger, he at once said, "Sorry, man. Didn't mean to knock you, like."

Even in his drunken state, Ron was easily capable of grabbing the lad by the scruff of his jacket. He yanked him towards him and snarled in his face, "Sorry isn't good enough, you cheeky little prick."

Both Duncan and John lunged for him, dragging them apart.

His eyes wide and his voice shaking with terror, the lad cried, "Get off us!"

"Ron!" Big Joe bellowed, discarding the half-filled pint. His voice silenced the entire pub in an instant. "Get off the laddie, NOW!" He rushed round to the other side of the bar to join Duncan and John who were struggling to free the frightened youth.

"Got nee respect!" Ron shouted, shaking him roughly. Spittle flew into the lad's contorted face.

Big Joe reached them, puffing and panting. He grabbed Ron's shoulder. Ron, reacting, rather than thinking, lashed out, catching Big Joe across the chin with his elbow. The blow brought tears to the landlord's eyes, but he maintained his grip, and in a calm, sincere tone, said, "Ron, pal, it's time for yer to get yourself away home to Erika. She *needs* yer." The last three words came out almost as a plea.

Bryce and Duncan both relaxed their grips of his arm and coat. The fury ebbed away, leaving Ron looking tired and dejected. He released the young lad, who immediately backed away to his two friends who had been observing nervously from a safe distance.

"Take him home," Big Joe said, patting Ron gently on the shoulder. His chin was reddening from the blow, but he appeared not to notice. He glanced in the direction of the three lads. "I'll get you three lads a drink on the house, eh?"

Duncan and John escorted Ron out of the Miller's and down Main Street. They had walked only a few yards from the door when Ron stopped and turned to look at them. His eyes were wet with tears. His voice was heavy with emotion as he said, "I-I'm sorry."

Duncan put a hand on his shoulder. "It's okay, mate. We understand, honestly we do." Bryce nodded earnestly.

Tears openly streamed down his cheeks as he looked at his two friends with a mixture of desperation and despair. "I just … where is she? What happened to my baby?" He thrust his hands to his face as his knees buckled under him. Making no attempt to stop himself, he dropped to the pavement heavily. Sobbing, he cried, "Mandy!"

Duncan instinctively bent to help him. Bryce shook his head and said quietly, "Nah, mate. Give him a sec." Instead, they both placed a hand on each of his trembling shoulders as he sobbed uncontrollably for several minutes.

After the dinner party with John and Sally, which turned out to be a very enjoyable and drunken evening, Han and Lisa seemed to be accepted by the rest of the village as a couple. This amused Han and delighted Lisa. For Lisa, it was the most accepted she had ever felt. For Han, the settling into a relationship for the first time in years was a refreshing tonic. He felt at ease and composed … content even.

The majority of the villagers had come to accept him as part of the furniture, and his relationship with Lisa certainly helped cement that. The most notable exception being Miss Marple-meets-Bet Lynch. Tess Runckle was like a pitbull with a bone, refusing to give up on her theories and making no attempt to be discreet about them. Everyone and anyone to whom she spoke got the speech about *Mister Murder*.

The sideways glances from Tess and some of her cronies, including that camp goon, Moe (Sloth to his friends ... *Hey you guys!*), were really starting to get under his skin, despite his overall contentment.

He had decided, and Lisa, John and Big Joe all agreed, that the best course of action was to ignore it. She was the El Supremo of gossip, nay, the Goddess of Gossip, and everyone knew it. Who, apart from Sloth, would really take her seriously?

But still, it was irritating.

So, maybe he *should* go talk to her? Straighten things out once and for all. What harm could it do to put the old girl's mind at ease? Yeah, maybe that was best; clear the air. Then they could drink to each other's health. Aye, he could just see that happening ... not.

No, he should just leave well enough alone. Let the sleeping bitch lie.

I'm a firestarter, twisted firestarter.

Despite the warm, still evening, Jimmy Coulson shivered and drew his crumpled long coat together. In the back of his mind, he knew that the shiver had nothing to do with feeling a sudden chill, but it was still a comfort factor. The dressings had gone from his face, but around his eyes looked as bruised as ever and his nose had set with a slight kink on the bridge. The doctor at Rothbury Community Hospital had offered to reset it, but he told him where to get off.

He walked with shambling purpose down the road to Belmont Motors, his hands shoved deep into his pockets. He could see that the office light was still on and that Steve's vaguely shabby-looking Ford Capri was still on the gravelled bit of waste ground that served as the car park to the side of the forecourt.

As he approached, he met James Falkirk, Steve's salesman-come-assistant manager-come-dogsbody, and Paul Mason, the particularly greasy grease-monkey coming the other way.

"Alreet, Jimmy?" Paul said casually, talking through the rollie sticking out of the corner of his mouth. "Goin' to see the boss?"

Jimmy sniffed his dribbling nose and merely nodded, lacking the inclination to enter into an inane conversation.

Paul jabbed a grimy thumb towards the office. "Y'nar where to find him."

Jimmy muttered and walked past them.

"You look like shit, Jimmy," James jokily called after him. "You get hit by a bus?"

"Get stuffed."

James rolled his eyes and followed the bandy-legged Paul back to the village. "Junkie."

Jimmy continued up to the office, a single-story wooden semi-permanent portacabin, with cracked and peeling white paintwork. The light was on, but the blinds were drawn on the only window. He paused at the bottom of the two metal-rung steps, shivering ever so slightly. What sort of proposition did Steve have that would pay big bucks? It would solve his money problems, that's for sure, so did it matter? Did he care? He *needed* a fix so goddamn badly.

At the fringe of the car park, a figure watched, squatting behind an unkempt hedgerow.

Wiping cold sweat from his brow, Jimmy pushed on up the steps and shoved the door open.

Steve was sat behind his desk with his trousers round his ankles and Janet Herring sat in his lap, her leather skirt hitched up to her waist and facing away from him. She was bouncing up and down on him, moaning softly. He had his eyes closed and his head tilted upwards.

"Shit, sorry, man!" Jimmy blurted out.

Steve's eyes shot open and he turned to the intruder, startled and red-faced. "What the …?"

"Dipshit," Janet snapped, immediately leaping off and smoothing her skirt down. Anger adequately concealed the burst of shame she suddenly felt.

Pulling his trousers and briefs up to cover his flagging excitement, Steve growled, "How many bastard times have I told you to knock first, Jimmy, you retard?" The fury in his voice was joined by a slight trembling in his hands as he finished zipping up his trousers.

Jimmy quickly averted his eyes, staring at the various dull mediocre achievements on the wall, including several football awards dating back to high school. "Sorry, Steve, man, I didn't realise, mate, like. Just ... needed to see you 'bout that job."

While fixing his belt, Steve said in a more even tone, "It's Mister Belmont to you, Bungle, and I'm not your mate. Christ, it's not enough that we've got Carol spying on us at every opportunity, now we've got Pig-Pen here too."

As Janet straightened her blouse, muttering under her breath, Steve stormed over to the fidgeting Jimmy. He grabbed him by the collar and spun him round to face him. Pulling him close, Steve sneered, "You *ever* do that again and I will cut your balls off and feed them to you. You got that, you stinking pile of pig shit?"

Arching his neck back to try to hold his face as far away from Steve's as possible, Jimmy said quickly, "Yeah, Ste—I mean Mister Belmont. I understand, man, I'm sorry." Steve tightened his grip around the young man's neck, drawing the collar tight around his jugular. Gasping, Jimmy whispered hoarsely, "*Please!*"

"Steve!" Janet shouted, folding her arms across her chest.

After a quick glance at Janet's stern expression, Steve shoved him back against the flimsy wall, shaking several of the framed awards. He turned back to Janet, his face still flushed, but his expression changing to rueful. "Sorry about this, babe. Me and *Jimmy* here have some business to attend to. Can we continue this later?"

Grabbing her jacket, Janet snapped, "*No*, it's not alright, Steve. I'm sick of this shit. Larry will be back in an hour, so that's fucked everything now, hasn't it?" She snatched her bag from the desk and stormed past them.

"Babe, I'll make it up to you."

"I'm sick of all this sneaking around." She paused at the door and dropped her head to stare at the cheap lino floor. Tears started to well up.

Steve grabbed her and pulled her to him. "Sorry, babe – it's not going to be for much longer, I promise." Lifting her head gently, he said sincerely, "I'll have the money soon enough and then we can get out of this hole once and for all and start over together."

She sagged against him and slipped her arms around his waist.

He bent down to kiss her tenderly. At first she pulled away, but then returned it, hesitantly at first, then eagerly.

After she had departed, Steve wiped his lips and sat back down behind the desk. Jimmy shuffled across the floor after him, his head hanging down sheepishly.

"Okay, Jimmy. Here's the deal." Steve leaned back in his fake leather chair and put his hands behind his head. "I wanted to go over this at a more convenient time, but as you're here and you've bollocksed up my evening, now's as good a time as any." Staring evenly at a young man who found it difficult to return his confident glare lifted his mood somewhat. He continued, his tone almost jovial. "You're going to torch the lot for me, and it *has* to look like an accident beyond *all* doubt – I can't stress this enough, dimwit. Any sniff and we're both fucked. In return I'll give you enough blow to last you months. Plus, I'll throw in five hundred quid to keep you in toasties and sugar puffs." His smile had a predatory look to it.

With a glint of restored confidence, Jimmy rubbed his trembling hands together and asked sceptically, "What about a thou'?"

Steve sat forward purposefully and glared at him. "Don't get smart, boy. Do I look like Keith fucking Chegwin to you? This ain't pissin' Swap Shop; there ain't no bartering here. You take it or leave it."

Nodding frantically, Jimmy quickly said, "Sure, okay, okay, you got it, Mister Belmont." With his head still nodding involuntarily, he added, "I gotta take care of that Whitman wanker, too, like. I told you about that shit, yeah?"

Steve nodded. "Aye, whatever, as long as it doesn't interfere with the lot, you got that?" Looking the scruffy junkie up and down with open disgust, he added, "Now, I'll tell you when you're going to do it, when the time is right, but for now I want you to refresh your arson skills and work out exactly how you're going to do it."

Outside, the figure behind the hedge watched Janet Herring leave and walk back towards the village.

The sclera of two unblinking eyes appeared to burn through the twilight like white-hot metal. Grinding his teeth, Larry gripped the brambles at his feet in one hand and squeezed tightly on the thorns. A thin trickle of blood oozed between his clenched fingers and dripped amongst the weeds. His snorted breathing sounded feral.

A second figure, several feet inside the tree line, opposite the car lot, also observed Janet Herring leaving the portacabin. A trembling hand brought a cigarette up to thin, pursed lips. Carol Belmont drew in a shaky breath and blew out a cloud of blue-grey smoke into the still night air. Her wide eyes glowed with the embers from the tip of her cigarette.

Later that night, sat at his laptop, Han, too, eavesdropped on the exchange. He sat back in his chair as the sound file fell silent and rubbed his bearded chin, mulling over the development. Could it be used to his advantage? Possibly.

Day trip to Newcastle.

Steadily, Han and Lisa spent more and more time together. He had even been allowed to stay overnight at her flat. Haley had seemed nonplussed at his presence the next morning, but had just quietly taken her crayons and colouring book to the small plastic kitchen table and started colouring in farm animals.

The kitchen was cramped, with cheap council units and old battered appliances. The lino was cracked and peeling around the edges and toys and clutter littered the floor and every surface, but the place was clean. Lisa took pride in that.

Dressed in jeans and a t-shirt, depicting a prone Steve Buscemi and a looming Harvey Keitel, aiming pistols at each other, Han padded past the table in bare feet (careful to avoid stray plastic animals, a headless Sindy and several stuffed toys of all shapes, sizes and colours). He offered Haley a warm smile, but her look was distinctly noncommittal.

Lisa was standing at the kitchen worktop buttering toast. She was wearing a nightie that Han could swear was the double of a one his mum used to wear, which was both amusing and slightly disconcerting. Somehow, she still managed to make it look good though.

Han walked up behind her and kissed her softly on the back of the neck.

"Hey," she said smiling and turning to look at him. "Okay?" The question was clearly relating to the Walton's family scene that he suddenly found himself in.

He smiled and kissed her on the lips. "Sure, princess." Swiping a piece of toast off the Formica, he added, "Say, as it's a day of rest, why don't we take a trip to Newcastle and have a mooch around the Quayside."

Leaning against the kitchen unit, Lisa mulled it over while biting into a piece of her toast. Her gaze seemed lost for a time, before muttering dreamily, "Haven't been down there for years … haven't really been out of the village in … forever. Haley's never been." She seemed to shake herself out of the trance and turned to her daughter, bending slightly to come down to Haley's level. "What do you think, angel? You wanna go to Newcastle for the day?" Han smiled at the way Lisa attempted to speak more clearly when addressing her daughter.

"Is it safe?" Haley asked without looking up from her colouring book.

Han raised his eyebrows, but Lisa just smiled and said, "Of course, angel."

Haley carefully placed the crayon back into its carton and closed the colouring book. Looking at her mother, she said, "Alright, Mammy."

Han stared at the child, somewhat bemused, but then swallowed the rest of his toast and clapped his hands together. "That's settled then!"

The sunny morning drive through the countryside was pleasant, with light-hearted banter, intermingling with the occasional game of 'punch buggy' or 'mini nip'. Haley sat belted into the back seat of the Daihatsu with a big grin on her face, her colouring book and pens splayed out around her. As they left Haydon she had seemed pensive, worried even, but now the anxiety was gone. Every five minutes, she would point to a new wonder that caught her eye; three small grey wild rabbits munching happily on the grassy verge, sheep and cattle grazing in the fields, an immaculate sky blue 1957 Fordson tractor, making infuriatingly slow progress along the road ahead of them, the bottle-green, fast running waters of the River Coquet, with its mayflies and stoneflies buzzing above rippling water and along the overhanging wooded banks. Each new sight was a magical delight to the eyes of the small child.

Han could not help but smile as he caught her giddy expression in the rear view mirror. Glancing across to Lisa, he noted that she, too, held a similar look. She sensed his eyes upon her and turned to smile at him.

After a short stop in Rothbury for a cold drink, they crossed through the bustling seventeenth century village of Longframlington. Posters and bunting were still up from the annual Longframlington Show which had taken place only the day before. Driving leisurely through the village, Haley was quick to point out the Lion Trough Fountain as they cruised by. "Lion!" she exclaimed proudly.

"That's right, angel," Lisa said, turning in her seat to smile at her.

Once through 'Longfram', they joined the A1 and headed towards Newcastle. They took the Gosforth exit and drove through Gosforth High Street and past the Town Moors. Finally, around lunchtime, they drove into Newcastle City Centre.

Once they had located a car park on Dean Street, filled with trendy bars and bistros (and, remembered Han, the primary location for the jazz-fuelled northern film noir flick, *Stormy Monday*), they walked out into the sunshine onto the steep bank and headed down towards the Quayside. After strolling through the pedestrian area of the Side, bustling mainly with tourists and students, they walked under the Tyne Bridge and onto the main stretch of Newcastle's Quayside.

Haley, giggling and staring wide-eyed at the huge green bridge looming above them, skipped along in front of Han and Lisa, as they walked hand in hand. Ahead of them, the wide boulevard stretched out, with the white sleek arc of the Millennium Bridge crossing the gap between the ultra-modern Pitcher & Piano on the Newcastle side and the austere Baltic Centre for Contemporary Art on the Gateshead side. In between, next to the Baltic, was the mammoth glass and steel slug-looking Sage Gateshead Music Centre.

Han was amused to see Lisa's awed expression, staring at each new wonder like they were the Pyramids of Giza.

As they headed along towards the Millennium Bridge, Lisa slipped an arm around Han's waist and squeezed him close. "Thanks for this, Han. I've never seen Haley's eyes light up so much."

Kissing her cheek, he said, "My pleasure."

"It feels good to get away from Haydon," she added with the hint of a frown. "Sometimes it feels like Haydon is the only place that exists. The rest of the world is just a dream."

Han looked at her, but remained quiet. Instead, he gave her an encouraging squeeze.

As they passed a young Caucasian couple in shorts and t-shirts having their photo taken by an elderly oriental gent in a reverse cliché, Haley, still skipping, asked excitedly, "Can we cross the blendy-blidge, Mammy?"

"Bendy bridge, angel," Lisa corrected tenderly.

A quizzical expression set into the young girl's face as she considered what she had just said. After a moment's deep contemplation, she giggled to herself then continued on her way, singing to herself, "Blendy Blidge! Blendy Blidge!"

Han and Lisa laughed together and followed at a stroll. He caught himself glancing from Haley to Lisa. The warm feeling he felt inside was unmistakable. Was this what Vanessa had wanted to have with him? The whole family deal? He had to admit, it did feel good.

chapter 8

Tess of the Jabbermouths.

Two more weeks passed by with Han continuing to monitor the bugs, whilst spreading the majority of his spare time between Lisa and John. His frequent visits with Lisa were exciting and sensuous, and a much needed release from his endeavours. After their day trip to Newcastle, Haley had truly warmed to him and opened up, to a point when she accidentally started to call him daddy. She had caught herself halfway, but the power of that one syllable was enough to stop them both in their tracks. Lisa had apologised to him later, feeling deeply embarrassed, but pressing for a reaction. He had hugged her and said how much he cared for her, so it had been an unexpected honour. That appeared to be exactly what she had wanted to hear.

It was a night in sorting paperwork for Bryce, or 'bean-counter-night' as he would call it with a distinct lack of humour, so the big man wouldn't be showing his face in the Miller's tonight. So, after one of Martha's 'special' chicken in a basket meals and a couple of drinks, Han retired early to spend a few hours trawling through the recordings. Lisa was disappointed to see him go, but he said that he needed to catch up with his writing.

He passed several hours listening to inane banter in the Post Office, Merlin's and the Co-op, before catching an interesting exchange in the chemists.

Stuart Priestly was serving Carol Belmont her prescription. "Here's your repeat prescription, Carol. Same dosage as before."

Meekly, Carol replied, "Thanks, Stuart. Maybe this will be the last lot, eh?"

"Depression is a long term illness, Carol. Just take things one step at a time." A pause, then, reassuringly, "You'll be fine."

Quiet, then a moment later the bell sounded for the door opening. "Bye, Missus ... er, Carol." The clumsy goodbye was from Priestly's assistance, the chubby Brian Dobson.

The door slammed.

"She's still a bit sensitive about that, Brian," Stuart said.

"Yeah, I'm always putting my foot in it."

"And that's not all." Both men laughed.

"Dirty bugger! You just wait till I get you in the back later."

Han smiled. Jesus, this place had *everything* going on. Who needs *EastEnders* or *Corrie*, eh? He had no intention of listening to middle-aged Mister Priestly doing his twenty-odd year old assistant from behind in the stockroom, so before switching to the Duck, he popped on his room's mini kettle and stretched his aching back.

Glancing at his watch, he noticed with surprise that it was ten-fifty PM. The last of the punters would be supping up downstairs and in the Duck. It wouldn't be a late one, with it being a school night.

Sipping tea, he clicked on the relevant file and started skimming through, his posture and features betraying his disinterest. Mere minutes in, he caught his name being mentioned by the venerable Ms Runckle.

"Whitman is up to no good; I know it with every bone in my body," she was saying.

"He's a strange one, sure." Moe's voice. Bloody typical.

"He's always watching people – I think he's a pervert. Probably molested that poor girl out in the woods." Her irritated tone betrayed the matter-of-fact accusation.

A rumbling rage rose from the pit of his stomach. Pervert? Rapist? The cheeky bitch. Who the hell does she think she is? She didn't know *anything* about him. He hadn't raped Mandy; he wasn't like that. He wasn't some kind of sexual predator. That was so far beneath him.

"Hmm, not sure about that, sweetie. That's a bit harsh." Well, thanks, Sloth. Mighty kind of ya.

"Oh, what do you know, Moe Baxter?" He imagined a dismissive flurry of one clawed hand. "Just look into his eyes –

115

behind them is a sick and twisted mind. He killed that poor girl and I intend to prove it."

Pervert, sick and twisted? That's quite the accolade. Bitch.

Well, the time had most definitely come to have a chat with Bet Marple.

It was past eleven-thirty by the time he had pulled on a black sweater and quietly snuck downstairs. Using the side door, he slipped out into the street.

The night sky was layered with high altitude cirrostratus clouds, obscuring the partial moon. Only a couple of scattered beacons of light glowed dimly behind curtains to penetrate the gloom. One such light was still on in the bar of the Duck.

Casually (to a distant observer; closer inspection would have revealed a smouldering anger itching just below the surface), he strolled towards the open backyard, glancing around to check no one was watching from a window or the shadows. The yard had several kegs and empty crates stacked to the left side and three large wheelie bins to the right. In between, there was sunken access to the cellar and the backdoor.

The shrill cry of a small dog pierced the quiet from across the other side of the village. Han stopped in his tracks, furtively scrutinising the darkness around him. His pulse quickened, but then as quickly as it had announced itself, the dog fell silent. With the returning silence, it seemed the whole village appeared to settle once more. He crossed the small yard quickly and tried the door. Unlocked, like the rest of the village tended to be. Gently, he eased the heavy door ajar and peered into a darkened corridor lined with crates of bottles and boxes of crisps and snacks. He noticed with surprise that one of the boxes was Tudor Crisps, tomato sauce flavour. *A canny bag of crisps …* Were they making a comeback?

Stepping inside, he left the door open a crack and crept along the corridor, which led to the kitchen, then toilets, and finally opened into the lounge on the left and right into the bar.

As he approached the end of the corridor, he heard the clattering of ashtrays and someone humming an unrecognisable tune. It was coming from the bar.

116

Easing his head around the open doorway, he caught sight of Tess Runckle, several ashtrays in hand and a flowery apron stretched across her ample chest. After listening and watching for several minutes, he concluded that she was alone.

As she clattered and clanked her way through filling up the dishwasher, he slipped into the room and headed towards her, concealed by the wall. On reaching the edge of the bar, he heard her disappear through the back and start stomping upstairs. He followed, muttering under his breath in irritation. Vigilant of every step, the only sound he made was the whisper of fabric. Much of his initial anger had dissipated, only to be replaced with a faint feeling of embarrassment and awkwardness. But, unwavering and unperturbed, he continued on regardless.

The narrow stairs were carpeted and well maintained, so no creaks betrayed his presence. As he reached the narrow opening at the top, intersecting with a wood-beamed corridor, he heard shuffling in a room off to his right.

Edging off the last step, as his foot fell onto the landing, a floorboard groaned.

Silently, he mouthed, *fuck*. Holding his breath, he stared, unmoving down the corridor.

A wall mounted clock, with a cartoon mackerel tabby cat head as its face and whiskers for hands, ticked for several seconds. His suddenly too damn loud, thumping heartbeat appeared to fall into rhythm with it.

"Shirley? Holmes?" Tess made kissing noises from the other room.

There came a soft, rapid padding noise from downstairs and two chubby tabbies, one blue and the second, slower one, silver patched, streaked upstairs, past Han and along the corridor through the open bedroom door. Neither gave him the slightest bit of attention.

"Hello, my babies," Tess fawned over the two cats. They responded with loud satisfied purring.

Shirley and Holmes? For Christ's sake … how very apt. Well how about I introduce you to Professor Moriarty, eh? How do you like them apples?

As she continued to make kissing and cooing noises, Han slowly edged his way along the corridor. He was right outside the door when it was unexpectedly flung fully open and Tess strode out of the room. There was a moment when he thought she would just walk straight through him, but that passed in a blink.

She was still dressed (*thank Gawd and the man Jesus!*), but minus the apron. The look of disbelief was quickly replaced with a mixture of fear and outrage. "What the hell are you doing here, you sicko?" Her voice was defiant, but she took a hesitant step backwards.

Han raised both his hands in a non-threatening gesture and said quickly, "I'm sorry, Ms Runckle. I just had to come and see you – to try to make peace."

"Peace?" Now she stepped forward, anger flooding over the fear. "Get the hell out of my pub!" There was nothing like a nice bit of arrogance to cloud someone's perception of the true dangers of a given situation.

Trying to reason with her, he continued, but stepped back all the same. "You don't understand; I just want to straighten things up between us. You're saying terrible things about me that just aren't true." His tone remained apologetic and non-threatening, his eyes imploring her to be reasonable.

Tess thrust her hands on her hips, and said, "So you thought breaking into my home and sneaking upstairs to peek at me getting undressed would put me straight?" The hint of self-satisfaction in her voice was virtually unbearable.

Han had to suppress a shiver at the very prospect. "God no! I just wanted to speak to you after you closed up – just you and me. The door wasn't locked."

She stepped forward again and thrust an accusing finger towards him. "Let's see what the police have to say about it, shall we?" The fear had now completely vanished and she stormed forward, shoving him back to the staircase.

Han backed up, his arms still outstretched, shaking his head. "Please! You don't understand – I just wanted to set things straight between us. I'm not a bad guy, Ms Runckle and I had nothing to do with Mandy's murder."

118

Tess stopped dead in her tracks. A flash of fear returned to her red face. *"Murder?"*

Han dropped his hands loosely by his sides and sighed. "Bugger."

"You …" Words failed her. Being suddenly and unequivocally proved right, and faced with Mandy's murderer had quite the opposite effect that Han would have first thought. Instead of fear and flight, she stood her ground and, in an enraged tone, she snarled, "I knew it!" Whether caught up in the moment, or realising that words would not be enough, she suddenly rushed forward, snarling. There was a contorted witch-like savagery about her that took Han aback. Hissing, she shoved him with remarkable strength, causing him to stagger back to the top of the stairs.

Han opened his mouth to speak, but Tess beat him to it, ejecting her words like acid, "I'll *kill* you." Hot spittle sprayed his face.

"Jesus," Han uttered and blocked a slap that would have taken the side of his face off.

Tess's frenzied attack carried her forward right to the edge of the stairs. Her legs came to an abrupt halt with her slippered toes dangling over the edge, but her generously proportioned upper body continued for an instant longer, unbalancing her.

"N—" was the only syllable to escape her lips as she toppled over the edge, her feet kicking back as she tumbled head and flailing arms first. For a moment, she appeared to be floating in mid air, but the illusion only held for a split second. This was followed by a swift series of thumps as arms and legs bashed off steps and walls, then finally a sickening crack as her forehead struck the bottom step, twisting her neck into an unnatural angle.

Her twitching body slid down several more steps, shoving her head off the final step and a couple of feet across the floor, before finally coming to rest. The silent twitching continued for several seconds with Han looking on, silent and dumbfounded.

One of the fat cats, the silver patched one, appeared and started weaving in and out of his legs, brushing up against him and purring loudly.

"Ah so," Han said, trying to mimic David Carradine in *Kill Bill* as he looked down at the cat. In one fluid motion, he lifted his foot and stamped down on the back of the cat with a sharp crack. It instantly yowled in pain, but before it could react further, he kicked it down the stairs. The writhing creature toppled end over end and landed in a heap at the bottom of the stairs beside its dead mistress. There it lay, squirming and making a low mewing noise.

Han walked slowly down the stairs, staring at Tess and her crippled cat. As he stepped over her tangled legs, he muttered, "I'm a killer. A murdering bastard, you know that. And there are consequences to breaking the heart of a murdering bastard."

He stood at the bottom of the stairs for some time, mulling over the events. It was not what he planned, but it wasn't a disaster. He retrieved some surgical gloves from his jeans pocket and unhurriedly pulled them on.

First, he took each of her hands and rubbed them thoroughly through the agonised cat's fur. Then, after spending ten minutes retracing his footsteps and wiping clean any areas where his fingerprints might have been left, he departed the way he had entered.

The dark night was as before, and the village remained veiled in silence.

The next morning, Han awoke early and headed downstairs for his breakfast. As he walked into the lounge, he saw Big Joe and Martha talking, his wife with tear-streaked mascara.

"Hi," he said genially, then, his tone quickly shifting to concern, added, "What's wrong?"

Big Joe looked at him and seemed to size him up for a second, before saying, "Some terrible news ... terrible news. Tess Runckle – she's dead."

Rubbing her eyes, Martha said, "I used to say such nasty things about her, Joe. About her being a tart and such. How can I ever forgive myself?"

Han feigned disbelief. "Dead? How? What happened? Heart attack?"

Martha started to snivel and noisily blew her nose on a handkerchief.

"They took her away just an hour ago. Seems like she tripped on one of her cats at the top of the stairs. She fell and broke her neck sometime last night." Big Joe shook his head, deeply troubled. "Poor Tess. She loved those wee cats and this is what happens to her. It's no' right."

Han shifted, uncomfortably. "God that's awful. If there's anything I can do …" He let his voice trail off.

Big Joe attempted a smile. "That's decent of yer, laddie."

"And don't worry about breakfast – I'll sort myself out."

Sometimes they come back.

Word spread around the village like a bushfire. It was Tess Runckle's turn to be the name on everyone's lips. Moe Baxter had found her when he popped in to see her with one of Kim Little's Danish pastries. His anguished screams had been heard by several people on the street and nearby. The man was completely inconsolable and eventually had to be sedated by Doctor Herring.

Wright and Mitchell turned up mid morning, but their presence and questioning was low key.

Han was typing on his laptop at the desk when the anticipated knock came to his door.

"Yep, one sec," he said, saving the Word document and popping his notepad into the top drawer of the desk.

The door opened to reveal Wright and Mitchell's smiling faces.

"Ah, we meet again," Han said, waving the two detectives in.

Wright, walking in first, said squarely, "Yeah, we must stop meeting like this, Mister Whitman. And, I must say, you don't seem surprised to see us. Seems like every time we meet there's a murder or a disappearance."

Han was walking back to the centre of the room, but he stopped dead and turned with a look of utter shock on his face. "Murder? Jesus, who's been murdered?"

Mitchell closed the door behind him and replied, "My colleague's just a bit of a wind up merchant. We're still looking into Mandy Foster's disappearance, so the jury's out on that one." He walked around the room, his eyes scrutinising everything.

Wright picked up the reins, leaning against the desk. "Ms Runckle's death by feline misadventure seems to be a real tragedy, eh?" He glanced down at the screen of the laptop, briefly examining the icons on the desktop.

Han walked over to the bed and sat down, facing both men. "It's horrible. I couldn't believe it when Joe told me about it this morning."

"Yeah, I bet," Wright muttered without conviction.

Mitchell stopped, looking down at Han. He thrust his hands in his pockets and said, "You and her didn't get on very well, did you?"

Standing up to meet his stare, Han said, "That's a bit of an exaggeration. She liked her gossip and, me being the new guy in town, I caught some of the flak."

"She told us that you murdered Mandy Foster."

Han shot a glance towards Wright. "That's a terrible thing to say. It's ridiculous and you know it."

Wright raised his arms in mock defence. His tone turned genial once more. "Easy there, mate. Just telling you what she told us."

"So," Mitchell injected casually, "you can understand us being just a little concerned when the old girl pops it."

"Dunno whether you're keeping up with current events, mate, but let's just recap," Wright said with just a hint of sarcasm, flipping open his notebook just for effect. "New guy comes to town – that's you by the way – girl goes missing, old bird starts spreading rumours that new guy killed her, and then old bird dies in tragic accident. That about cover it?"

Han slumped back down on the bed with a despondent look ingrained into his features as Mitchell started pacing the room once more. "Yeah, I suppose it does." Staring intently at Wright, he said, "But what that doesn't cover is that Mandy girl will probably turn up some place in a few months, maybe down in London or something, and that Ms Runckle had probably stopped gossiping about me ages ago."

"She hadn't," Mitchell corrected, turning to gauge Han's reaction.

Han looked surprised. "Well, I'm sorry, but that's news to me. People must've just stopped mentioning it to me."

Han seemed weary when he lifted himself off the bed once more. Shoving his hands into his pockets, he said, "Look, I talked to Joe and Lisa about this a month ago when she was whispering about me. I suggested that I go talk to her to clear the air, but they both advised against it. They said that she was the town gossip and everyone knew it, so after a while she would just lose interest and move on to a new topic. I dropped it and, when I heard no more, I assumed she had too." His voice virtually imploring, he added, "Just talk to them about it."

"We will," Wright said flatly, his eyes settling back on Han.

Drawing a deep breath, and with a distinctly lighter tone, Mitchell said, "Okay, I think that about covers it. Thanks for your help, Mister Whitman."

Wright clapped Han on the back and grinned. "Don't take it personal, Mister Whitman. We're just doing our job."

Mitchell opened the door, but before walking out onto the landing, turned and, as an afterthought, asked, "By the way, how's the book coming on?"

Han managed a weak smile. "Not bad – onto chapter six now."

With that, both men departed, leaving Han standing alone with his mind in turmoil. He listened, breathing deeply, as their footsteps echoed, first along the landing, and then down the stairs.

The Funeral.

It was a dreary mid-week lunchtime as Reverend Dunhealy led the procession of pallbearers, followed by dozens of grieving friends and relatives of Tess Runckle out of the church and into the graveyard. Moe, Big Joe, her brother who had travelled up from Kent, and young Danny Little were amongst the pallbearers.

Martha, frequently dabbing her eyes with her handkerchief, and James Falkirk followed, along with the Fairbanks, the Herrings, Carol Belmont, sobbing hysterically, John Bryce, Sally and their scrawny son, Anthony, and a steady stream of others.

Most of the village gathered by the open grave, their faces downcast, and their mood matching the weather. They stood, solemn and silent, as fine rain coated their dark coats and jackets with a glistening sheen.

Han stood at the gate, at a distance, and watched silently. His features appeared pensive and pale in the poor light. Droplets of water clung to his hair and beard.

After some clearly poignant words from Reverend Dunhealy that Han could not quite hear, the coffin was slowly lowered into the ground. This signalled a vocal outburst from Moe, who dropped to his knees at the graveside. He caught sight of the camp barber casting a single red rose into the grave, along with many of his tears. He stayed there, kneeling on the sodden green felt for several minutes, crying uncontrollably with the Fairbanks's daughter, Jill, holding a tender arm over his shoulders.

A single tear escaped from the corner of one of Han's own auburn eyes. He was surprised by it, but accepted it for what it was.

Lisa appeared behind him and slipped an arm around his waist inside his jacket. "You okay, honey?" Her hair was dripping from the rain, but the concern in her eyes was for Han.

He glanced at her and offered a half-hearted smile. "Yeah, just sad, that's all."

The fine rain continued into the evening. The mood in the Miller's was no better than by the graveside. People talked in hushed tones in their small groups, clustered in corners or at the bar. Carol Belmont managed three large gins, before she could stand the company of her fellow residents no longer.

She had sat at a small table on the periphery of the lounge, alone and without speaking to anyone, except Lisa to briefly order her drinks. She had barely registered the familiar faces around her, the muted chatter or the clinking of the occasional glass.

Her mood was etched into her face, so people knew to give her a wide berth. But, even the background noise soon became unbearable for her, so she left without a word, with her eyes downcast.

The unrelenting rain quickly plastered her short blonde hair to her head, but she seemed oblivious as she walked unhurriedly towards her flat. The village appeared deserted or, perhaps, in hiding. The rain helped clear her head, but only worsened her mood.

Water was dripping from her nose, chin and the tips of her hair as she opened the door and stepped inside her dark, cold flat.

She shrugged out of her wet coat and hung it on a hook on the wall by the door, her movement automatic, unthinking. She then walked through into the small kitchen, her hair still dripping onto the cheap coarse carpet along the way. It was similar in size to Lisa's – crammed with basic units and old second-hand appliances – but not in cleanliness.

She headed straight to a wall unit with one dodgy hinge and retrieved a cheap bottle of 'shop's own' brand gin, half full. She grabbed a mixer glass from the next shelf, which had a meagre mismatched assortment of cups and glasses, then filled it to the top with gin. Remaining at the worktop, she proceeded to gulp down the entire glass.

She gasped as she finished and slammed the glass down clumsily onto the Formica surface. A dribble of gin dripped from her chin to the linoleum. She screwed her face up, but it was exactly what she needed. As she started to pour a second, a sob escaped her trembling lips. The bottle clattered back down as she drew her hand to her mouth, it too shuddering violently.

She turned and glanced around the kitchen, seemingly frantically searching for something … anything. Tears began to well up in her eyes as her hand remained clamped to her mouth in some desperate effort to quell her desolation. Her blurred gaze fell upon the several 'shop's own' packets of paracetamol tablets on the grubby table. She had bought them one packet at a time and, one by one, they had built up to a small pile that now whispered for attention.

With her head swimming, her legs felt suddenly like stilts on rough ground. She slid down the unit and landed hard on her backside, but registered no pain. She pulled her knees to her chest as another whimper escaped her lips. One word was forced with almost physical pain from them as her eyes remained fixed on the table. "*Please* ..."

Hugging her knees, she could no longer hold back the tears. They came hot and flooding and her body shook and rocked on the cold linoleum floor.

chapter 9

Let's evolve, let the chips fall where they may.

The Duck stayed closed for three weeks while the investigation was tied up. The inquest announced a verdict of death by misadventure and the case was closed. Han breathed a deep sigh of relief on hearing the news, but that relief was tarnished by the occasional appearance of Wright and Mitchell sniffing around the village. They didn't actually come back to speak to him, but they did ask a few questions around the village about him, and Wright offered him a friendly wave on one occasion.

After the third week, a relief manager was sent into the Duck by the brewery. George 'Geordie' Langdon turned out to be a tattooed, hard-faced skinhead who was more at home running rough-arse boozers in Newcastle's East End. His last position had been a pub in Byker; nothing more than a fight club with a liquor licence. There was a distinct ill-ease from the majority of the regulars on seeing Tess's temporary replacement.

He made himself at home quickly and, despite his appearance, and the decidedly cool reception, he turned out to be friendly and devilishly witty. He was certainly a breath of fresh air to the gloomy atmosphere left with Tess Runckle's untimely departure.

John Bryce persuaded Han to make a rare appearance to the Duck to offer support. He wasn't keen on the idea of bumping into Moe, but eventually he caved after several of John's pleas. Bryce, leading the way, angled straight for the bar, where both Danny Little and Geordie were serving.

The bar was bustling with activity. It seemed that a lot of villagers had had the same idea. Amongst them were Janet and Larry Herring, sitting in one corner, with Steve Belmont hovering at the bar (did he have no shame?). Duncan Fairbank and his young bride, Loretta, were sitting with Simon and Kim Little, Danny's baker parents, at another table.

Seeing the new arrivals, Geordie greeted them with a broad smile that revealed one front tooth missing and another broken to a jagged stump. "Alreet, lads? Me name's Geordie Langdon and it's a pleasure to meet you." The remains of his receding hair were a mere dusting of black and grey stubble. His forearms were littered with dozens of tattoos, some recognisable, like the NUFC crest and a British Bulldog chewing a cigar, but others had faded and distorted over the years to a mere patchwork of blurry blue lines. The St. George Cross was also tattooed on one side of his neck. His age was something of a mystery; Han could only place him somewhere between late thirties to late forties. His face was creased and an old blue-purple scar snaked down from his left temple to his jaw line. Weathered and gnarly skin darkened the ambiguity, but he had the keen, alert eyes of a younger man.

John stuck out a hand with just a hint of wariness. "John Bryce of Bryce and Son's farm. And this is Han Whitman, our resident writer."

Geordie shook both their hands rigorously with a hand marked with a blue swallow tattoo and half a little finger missing. "Writer, eh? Canny – I've been meaning to write a book for ages aboot me exploits in the pub trade. I've seen a thing or tee working Byker, Wallsend and Howden, I can tell ya."

Bryce laughed and any guardedness seemed to vanish. "I bet. Got a mate used to work down Wallsend as a rigger. He got half an ear cut off in a fight in the Raby on Shields Road."

"Aye, they've got two hobbies in there – drinking and fighting, and not necessarily in that order."

"Well, we just wanted to welcome you to the village. You've come at a bit of a rough time, so if people are a bit standoffish, divvent judge 'em too harshly."

The smile vanished from Geordie's weathered face to be replaced by a sincere nod. "Aye, they told us about it before I came, so I understand. Nasty business, like."

"Good to meet you," Han added amiably. His face appeared welcoming enough, but his mind was churning through a myriad of concerns for this new arrival. After a short pause, he added, "You should have a crack at that book – I bet it would be a helluva read."

The infectious smile returned. "That it would, like. What'll it be then, lads?"

Han observed him closely as he retrieved a mixer glass and filled it with a double whiskey followed by a pint glass, which he started pulling Bryce's pint into. He moved with a loose agility that Han had seen several times before; it was the unmistakable dance of a man who knew how to handle himself. As the froth reached the rim, the door opened, admitting Moe Baxter and Jill Fairbank, his co-worker.

As the other patrons noticed their arrival, the mood switched, taking on an edginess that hadn't been there a moment ago. A hush swept through the room as Moe walked up to the bar, his chin up and his chest out. A few eyes flicked from Han to Moe and then back again. Neither man appeared to notice.

Geordie noticed the mood change immediately and quickly finished serving Bryce to turn his attention to the newcomer.

"Hello," Moe said, standing beside Han, but keeping his eyes fixed on Geordie. His voice was slightly shrill. "Vodka Martini and, Jill, sweetie, what would you like?" A fleeting look to the slim, tanned woman standing behind him.

Jill glanced at Han, before responding. There was a slight hesitation in her response as she flicked a suddenly irritating strand of sleek ash-blonde hair out of her eyes. "Just an Orangina for me, babe."

Han took a big swig of his drink, then, setting the glass down onto the bar, turned to Moe. With sincerity, he said, "I was really sorry to hear about, Tess, Moe. I know how close you two were."

All eyes in the bar switched from Han to Moe. Bryce clenched his teeth and shook his head just a fraction, willing Han to take back the words, but knowing that it was too late. As he fetched the drinks, Geordie had one ear fixed on the conversation, sensing all too well, the prospect of impending conflict.

His jaw fixed, and his blue eyes blazing into the optics ahead of him, Moe said, "Don't talk to me. Ever." His voice was harsh, lacking its usual campness and his gaze never moved from the bar. "You understand me, Mister Whitman?"

Han nodded despondently, but before turning away, said, "Please, you must believe me. I had nothing to do with Mandy's disappearance or Tess's accident. It's totally unfair to blame things on the new guy, just because he is the new guy."

Moe's heavily tanned face reddened and the muscles flexed along his jaw line. "Tessy knew you did something to Mandy and you killed her for it!" The words were spat in a rising whisper.

Jill touched his shoulder, and said with deep concern, "Moe, please, don't do this."

Shrugging her off, he finally spun to face Han. Jabbing an accusing finger into Han's chest, he snapped shrilly, "You *killed* them both!"

Han pushed his hand away, not without force. "This is crazy!"

Bryce grabbed his arm, saying calmly, "I think we should go, mate."

"Aye, that might be a good idea," Geordie said apologetically. Unnoticed, he had managed to come from round the bar and was now standing behind the confrontation.

Standing up, Duncan shouted over to his daughter, "Jill, I think Moe might want to go home."

Not taking his piercing eyes off Han, Moe flatly replied, "I'm fine, thank you, Duncan. I came here to have a quiet drink."

Han opened his mouth to object, but thought better of it. Glancing from Bryce to Geordie, he resigned. "Don't worry, I'm going. I just popped in to welcome the *new* new guy." Glancing to Geordie, he briskly added, "*Most* people here have been really friendly; don't let this misunderstanding taint your image of the place."

Han walked out quickly, not wanting to give Moe a chance to respond. Bryce shrugged and mouthed *sorry* to Geordie and

Jill, then followed. The eyes of everyone in the bar followed them both out.

Bryce caught up with Han outside in the cool evening air. Sighing, he said, "Wey, that could've gone … better."

Han rolled his eyes. With bitter sarcasm, said, "Aye, the guy was gushing – it was embarrassing."

Bryce's laugh was short and hollow and his face turned serious. "Try to give him a break – he's really an alreet bloke. He's just, like, really upset and maybe a little misguided."

Patting the big man's shoulder, Han managed a smile and said, "Yeah, I know. Thanks for your support – it's much appreciated."

Bryce returned the smile then, in a lighter tone, said, "Let's go back home – to the Miller's. Big Joe'll think we've defected."

A gaunt figure watched them leave from the shadows in the side lane, staying close to the wall so as not to reveal a profile. Scruffy trainers stood fidgeting in a puddle. The two men walked purposefully across the glistening wet road straight towards the Miller's. Jimmy waited until they were inside before following, his grip tightening around the lock knife concealed in his pocket.

Han and Bryce made a beeline for the bar, to be greeted by Lisa's warm, friendly face. She offered them a heartening smile and immediately set about fetching their regular drinks. A feeling of well-being settled over Han, and he felt, not for the first time, the sensation of being on the set of *Cheers*. He half expected Sam and Diane to be arguing behind the bar.

"Everything okay over the road?" Lisa asked, clearly apprehensive.

Han smiled at her, grateful for her genuine concern. "Let's just say I prefer the Miller's any day of the week."

"Aye, yer know it makes sense!" Big Joe shouted from just out of sight in the lounge. "Miller's is where the real drinkers come!"

"Nosey!" Lisa called back, rolling her eyes. "Doesn't miss a thing, him!"

They quickly settled down to their usual banter, normally angling toward one film or another – only older films would hold

Bryce's interest – and this night was no different. This time, the topic happened to be war films.

"I hear what you're saying about *A Bridge Too Far* – a massive ensemble cast, epic scenes and stunning direction; Richard Attenborough at his very best," Han was nodding and saying. "That Sean Connery line does it every time for me – 'I've got lunatics laughing at me from the woods. My original plan has been scuppered now that the jeeps haven't arrived. My communications are completely broken down. Do you really believe any of that can be helped by a cup of tea?'" Both men smiled at that. Even Big Joe had paused with glass in hand to listen to the short monologue. "But for me," Han continued, "on the Second World War front, *Where Eagles Dare* has always been a huge favourite of mine. Big fan of Richard Burton – that and *The Wild Geese* and *The Medusa Touch* are three of his best."

"Aye, *Where Eagles Dare* is bloody brilliant," Bryce agreed, taking a sip of his pint. "Haven't seen those other two though."

"You haven't seen *The Wild Geese*?" Not for the first time when discussing films Han was genuinely gobsmacked. Shaking his head, he said, "But, getting back to *Where Eagles Dare* – the scene where he bluffs then double-bluffs everyone, including Clint, is just priceless. There's that great exchange between Burton and Eastwood after all the confusion – 'Lieutenant, in the next fifteen minutes we have to create enough confusion to get out of here alive.' To which, Clint replies, 'Major, right now you got me about as confused as I ever hope to be.'"

Bryce laughed heartily and said, "Jesus, Han, how the hell do you remember all this shit?"

The conversation continued, meandering through various war film sub-genres, before, several whiskeys later, Han felt the pressure building, so excused himself to go to the toilet.

Bryce, drinking pints of real ale, scoffed, "Bloody southerners cannat hold their drink!"

"How the hell can *I* be a southerner?" Han asked, glancing back at him.

"Anyone south of the Tyne is a southerner in my book."

"Yeah, yeah," Han scoffed, smiling. "I'll have to read that book someday."

He almost bumped into Tam Wellright coming out of the toilets, whistling a tune. "Sorry, Tam, didn't see you there," he said, stepping aside for the old timer.

Tam smiled his toothless grin at him, before shuffling away, and resuming with his tune. *There may be trouble ahead ...*

Oh, har bloody har, Han thought, without a grain of humour in sight. "Moby *dick*," he muttered as he walked over to the chipped and rust-stained ceramic urinal. They were old, but always spotlessly clean.

His mind was filled with thoughts of Tess Runckle, Moe Baxter, Mandy Foster and Lisa as he lazily pissed down the splash-back, so he failed to hear the faint creak as the door to the single cubicle opened.

Jimmy Coulson was visibly shaking as he stepped out from the cubicle, knife in hand. His hair and coat were still wet from the rainfall earlier that evening. Strands of long matted hair were plastered to his forehead and cheeks and a cold sweat stood out on his brow. He edged closer as Han, oblivious, continued to urinate.

As Han shook the last few drops and zipped up, Jimmy pounced on him. Han heard the rustle of clothing an instant before the impact and so managed to half step partially to one side.

The movement wasn't enough to dodge Jimmy, but it was enough to dodge the blade of his lock knife. Jimmy clattered into him with the full force of one shoulder, ramming Han against the urinal.

With a solid crack, Han's head bounced off the dull white tiles, sending sparks across his vision. Despite the blow, he recovered quickly and, working on instinct, parried a second blow by raising his left arm. The tip of the knife sliced through material and skin on his forearm, causing a sharp intake of breath, but at the same time dislodged Jimmy's grip on the knife.

The bloodstained blade skittered across the tiled floor and out of sight through the gap under the cubicle door.

"DIE!" Jimmy screamed in a juddering adrenaline and withdrawal fuelled frenzy. Without pausing, he thrust a clenched fist across Han's jaw.

The blow jerked his head back against the tiles, dazing him once more and causing a burst of pain in his face. At once, he tasted copper in his mouth from his lacerated tongue.

Stunned, Han flailed wildly with both arms in a vain attempt to force his attacker back. Jimmy leapt to one side, cackling manically in a high-pitched squeal. "Dead man, bitch!" Moving in a second time, he lashed out with one soggy trainer and connected hard to the back of Han's knee. White pain burst out from behind his knee cap, causing both legs to fold.

He hit the tiles hard, causing the side of his head to strike the ceramic edge of the urinal. His vision greyed and the sounds of Jimmy's insane laughing dulled and suddenly seemed far away.

His victim now sprawled and groaning on the floor, with renewed confidence, Jimmy rapidly kicked out again and again, belting him full force in the thigh and then the side.

At that point, the door crashed open. Bryce rushed in like an enraged rugby prop forward, followed by a puffing and wheezing Big Joe.

Jimmy glanced over his shoulder, his eyes widening as Bryce rammed into him, slamming him with lung-emptying force against the urinal and clipping his forehead off the tarnished pipe work below the cistern. With very little effort, the big farmer then flung Jimmy, screeching and thrashing, to the ground and drove one knee into his chest.

Jimmy managed a gurgle and a whimper as he stared up at Bryce's calm face.

"Yer ... okay ... Han?" Big Joe asked between gulping breaths as he composed himself in the doorway.

"You still with us, mate?" Bryce chorused, glancing away from Jimmy's red and sweating, contorted face.

Han groaned then painfully rolled onto his side. "I've ... been better," he managed. His jaw was quickly turning a deep purple and blood was oozing out of the side of his mouth, but as his head gradually cleared, he actually started to feel good. A tremendous feeling of euphoria enveloped him, tempering the pain that seemed to be pulsating through his entire body.

With his breathing regulated to some extent and the redness fading from his cheeks, Big Joe helped him to his feet, being careful to avoid gripping him by his bloodied left arm. With Big Joe's steadying hand, he limped over to Jimmy and Bryce. The pain in his knee intensified with the slightest bend and his side flared with each movement, but the heady feeling of rapture made the pain surprisingly inferior.

"Jimmy, are you nuts?" he asked simply, with a look of pity on his pained face (more for effect, than necessity). Looking down at the weakly struggling figure beneath Bryce's considerable bulk, he added, "Lisa dumped you – I'm sorry, but there's nothing I can do about it."

"Gunna fuckin' *kill* you," Jimmy snarled through the pressure being inflicted on his chest. Blood was trickling down the side of his face from a small gash in his forehead where his head had struck the pipe.

Finally, having fully regained his composure, Big Joe glared at Jimmy. "Jimmy, yer barred. If I ever catch yer anywhere near ma boozer again, I'm gunna break both yer legs, yer got that, sunny-boy?"

Looking up, Bryce asked, "You wanna get the police on this thieving, druggie piece of shit, Han?"

Holding his jaw, Han thought about it for a moment. More police involvement was all he needed. *No, let's keep this strictly in the family.* After a moment's hesitation, he said, "No, that'll just be more upset for Lisa. She doesn't need this aggravation." He continued to look down on Jimmy, shaking his head unhappily.

"This is your lucky day, *Jimmy*," Bryce said evenly then slowly eased himself off him and got back to his feet.

Rest, recovery and revenge.

Han refused to see Doctor Herring, so Martha ordered complete bed rest for a couple of days and allowed Lisa to tend to his wounds. He spent those days being waited upon by both Lisa and Martha. Big Joe's wife even brought him her homemade broth in bed. His wounds were superficial; the cut wasn't deep and the blows to the ribs and knee caused some inflammation and tenderness, but eased off after a few days. He had a stubborn headache for a while but that, too, passed quickly.

He sat in bed, a tray, a bowl with mere dribbles of Martha's broth left, and a side plate with half a crusty roll, laid on his lap. His thoughts wandered back to mulling over the different ways to kill Jimmy Coulson.

Well, there were particular gory options of course, like cutting the top of his head off and feeding him his sautéed brain (if he could find it), like Lecter did to Ray Liotta. Or drilling holes into him and slicing his Achilles tendons like *Hostel*? Or how about feeding him into a wood-chipper like Peter Stormare did to Steve Buscemi? All pretty cool.

Or there were the more classic approaches, like a carving knife; the preferred weapon of most nutters, like Michael Myers and Norman Bates. Or the chainsaw, as used by, well Leatherface mainly, or Ash; but he's technically a hero (albeit a useless selfish one), so can't really count him. Or there's always a big fish hook, as used by the ghouls in *The Fog*. So many choices …

One thing was for certain, and that was that he was going to *really* enjoy killing Jimmy Coulson. *He must suffer to his last breath … well that I can pretty much damn well guarantee …* Maybe he'd get himself a Hattori Hanzo sword.

For those regarded as warriors, when engaged in combat the vanquishing of thine enemy can be the warrior's only concern. Suppress all human emotion and compassion. Kill whoever stands in thy way, even if that be Lord God, or Buddha himself. This truth lies at the heart of the art of combat.

The nights grew steadily longer and darker. The wind bore an icy chill and the leaves browned, withered and died, leaving much of the woods around the village, save for the evergreens, skeletal in comparison to their summer coats. Halloween (hardly even spoken about, never mind celebrated in any commercial fashion) gave way to Guy Fawkes (a small bonfire on the Green, with foil-wrapped baked potatoes and small glasses of sherry), which quickly gave way to the first exasperated conversations of Christmas and how there was so much to do and so little time left, and how quickly it had come around again.

With the plummeting temperatures, the first winter frosts hit, causing treacherous conditions. For the first time since purchasing it in Sunderland, Han was truly pleased to have the four wheel drive reliability of the Sportrak.

December brought with it the first snowfall; a light dusting of snow that froze to a gravely layer on paths and windscreens that was the devil's own job to scrape off. Predictions, both from the met office and, more importantly, the locals, were that this winter would be a particularly bad one.

Older folk in the village looked particularly glum at the prospect, having lived through some horrendous winters in the past, but Han felt truly blessed and redoubled his preparations.

chapter 8

20th December. *Headed right for the middle of a monster.*

The early evening had already turned as dark as night and bloated snowflakes were falling steadily, teased by a light breeze. As they hit the icy ground, they remained where they lay. The Miller's lounge was deserted, apart from Han and the occasional appearance of Big Joe or Martha. A Norwegian Spruce had been placed in one corner, with a multitude of coloured lights, tinsels, baubles and ceramic ornaments, and several gold foil garlands criss-crossed the ceiling. The main bar had similar decorations, but instead of the tree, it sported a huge *Merry Christmas* banner above the bar. Tam had his usual seat at one end, and Carol Belmont had turned up earlier for half an hour when Han had just started tucking into a casserole that Martha had prepared for him. She had downed three doubles in that time, without saying a word, other than those necessary to order the drinks, then left as quietly as she had arrived.

As he finished his dinner, Han's gaze was drawn to the radio behind the bar that had been spewing out a grainy and monotonous string of local interest stories – farming being the main focal point – intermingled with the occasional golden oldie. But now it switched to the weather and piqued his interest.

"A large band of low pressure coming down from western Scotland is going to continue south, hitting north and western areas of Northumberland by eight o'clock this evening. Heavy snowfall is going to cause treacherous driving conditions across the north east and Cumbria. Temperatures are going to drop to below zero, taking into account wind-chill factors, and it's likely to hang around through Christmas Eve, all the way through to Boxing Day; where it will gradually move south, losing much of its intensity.

"Bad news for last minute shoppers, but great news for the kiddies, as it's looking likely that we'll have a white Christmas this year, for most of Northumberland at the very least. Snowball fight later, eh, Jon?"

The presenter laughed, and said, "No chance, Paul. I'm hibernating till spring."

Han could not believe his luck. This was just too good to be true.

"Sounds like a bloody nightmare, eh?" Big Joe said as he passed behind him with several plates in hand. "It'll look like Lapland come morning."

Han turned and smiled at him with an almost child-like look of joy. "I love the snow; there's something … magical about it."

"Typical bloody townie. Wait till yer experience a Northumberland winter!"

"I prefer city slicker, BJ!" he scoffed, chuckling agreeably. "Whatever. You'll be begging for spring after a couple of days of the stuff." Big Joe trudged through to the kitchen, shaking his head, but smiling all the same.

The next morning Han rose early and, drawing back the curtains, gazed out over Main Street and the Green. It was at least an hour before dawn and snow was falling steadily on a gusting wind. Rooftops and treetops had already succumbed to the white veil and it was starting to lie on the footpaths and side streets as well, but traffic had so far kept it down to a grubby slush on Main Street.

As he gazed into the swirling darkness, a shiver ran across his shoulder blades. The central heating hadn't kicked in yet to take the chill out of the air. Dropping the curtain back in place, he turned to face his room and clapped his hands together. "Time's a wastin'." Although whispered, the words were filled with anticipation

After washing, he began systematically stripping and cleaning every square inch of his room. Bedding was bundled up and squeezed into black bin bags. Martha had kindly left his cleaned and ironed washing in a basket outside his door, so that was added to the rest of his possessions and was all packed into the back of the Sportrack. The bedding would be destroyed along with compromised clothing later. He would collect the bugs and clean any other possible tracks on his rounds.

His chores took three hours, by which point he had worked up a sweat and a healthy appetite. A solitary sleeping bag lay on the bare bed, open and waiting. He would have some sporadic touching up to do later, but the main job was done.

Through scrutinising the sound files from the bugs, he had counted no less than twenty-eight residents who would be heading away to visit friends or relatives for Christmas. Another thirty-five were never missed on a day to day basis, so those sixty-three would be first. After a hearty breakfast, he'd make a start. It would be approaching the evening by the time he got through those and then he would hit the outer rim – including his good friend, John Bryce's place – and then work his way inwards.

John lingered in his mind for a moment. The big farmer had been a good friend to him, as had a few others in the village. Lisa was a whole different issue; he would come to her later. But, Bryce, bless him; he had been a good laugh, and he had good taste in films too, those that he had seen anyway.

He frowned, seemingly waging an inner war. The hesitation only held for a moment. "Food," he said to himself to sever the unwanted deliberation.

IT – Illness and Technology.

The evening sky was blanketed with thick, angry storm clouds, and rain was driving near horizontal across the dual carriageway.

The A1139, leading north towards Peterborough was clogged with crawling rush-hour traffic, and had been since Sam Potter had set off at five PM from Old Fletton High Street. Exhaust fumes plumed up from the scores of vehicles stretched out over all lanes, and headlamps and brake lights lent a distorted glow to the darkness. It was now approaching six, and he still hadn't made it to the Peterborough turnoff for Fengate.

The *Beautiful South* CD was, unusually, doing little to lighten his disposition. Their Latin-flavoured version of the *Blue Oyster*

Cult's classic, *Don't Fear the Reaper*, was normally a huge mood lifter for him, but now it just seemed to fuel his impatience.

All our times have come,
Here but now they're gone ...

Steam rising up from the bonnets of dozens of idling cars, vans and lorries, mingled with the rain to further reduce visibility. Another one hundred and fifty yards further up the road, Sam could just make out flashing blue emergency lights.

"For C-Christ's sake," he muttered to himself. The slim man was swamped in a thick winter coat and, with the heater on full, his face was starting to redden, and beads of sweat were beginning to stand out on his forehead.

The side windows were completely misted up, and the fan in his Ford Fiesta was struggling to keep the windscreen clear. He switched the heater down to half, and then wiped his sleeve across his side window for the umpteenth time.

The delay was going to ruin his likelihood of getting to his routine session at the gym. Natalie also wanted him to do the last round of Christmas shopping with her, so the prospect of fighting through all those crowds was giving him heart palpitations. The Exchange Server at work had gone down, causing him a huge headache from staff and the partners, and had meant that his routine work had to be shelved to sort out the mess of restoring over-filled mailboxes. So, tomorrow, and probably part of Saturday too now, was going to be all about playing catch up, just to get back to square one. So, all in all, he had had a crappy Thursday, and the evening was heading precisely the same way. Great.

It was while he was mulling over these thoughts that his mobile phone started ringing its *Star Wars Imperial March* tune.

Using his Bluetooth hands-free, he answered it after the second bar. "Hi, Nats, I'm r-running a bit late."

"Honey, I've got some bad news. Where are you?" Her voice was deeply concerned.

"S-stuck in t-traffic. W-w-what's wrong?" The stuttering always worsened with rising anxiety.

"Don't worry, honey," she said in her soothing voice. "But your dad's been taken ill. I've just come off the phone to the doctor – he's stable, but he's asking to see you. They think it's a good idea that you go up to be with him."

Sam's head grew light and he felt his breathing grow shallow. "I-Is it th-th-the an-angina again?"

"Yes, but it's a bad one this time. I've called the home and managed to switch some shifts and use up some holiday. I'm packing a bag, so we can leave as soon as you get here. I'll bring the prezzies and some of the food, so we can make it a little special, eh?"

Tears were welling up in his eyes. His father had been asking them to visit for Christmas just two days ago and Sam had, as usual, skirted around the subject in his noncommittal way. "O-okay, N-n-nats." His trembling lips then failed him completely.

"Don't worry, honey. We'll go up there together."

Tears rolled down his cheeks and his breath found substance as the cooler air began to circulate. "B-be h-h-home soon."

Kicking in doors and snowball fights.

The Rolling Stones were singing about brown sugar tasting *so good* through Jimmy's headphones. He was clutching the old scratched cassette player to his chest as he lay on his bed. A well-thumbed copy of *Fiesta* magazine, along with an empty packet of cigarettes and two empty cans of lager, one of which had been used as an ashtray lay splayed about him.

Through the gaps that the blanket failed to obscure, the window outside showed gusting snow buffeting against the grubby windowpanes.

Jimmy was oblivious to the knocking at the door as he lay with his eyes shut, listening to the music. His skin was pale and clammy and a trembling hand rubbed unconsciously at an itch on his forearm.

The door burst open with a crack and splintering of wood.

Jimmy scrambled at the headphones while sitting up in a panic, tape deck, cans and porn magazine tumbling in different directions. "What the fuck?"

"Knock, knock," Steve Belmont said evenly as he walked into the room, stamping dust, splinters and snow off his loafers. Glancing at his inadequate footwear, he added sourly, "Should've brought fucking snowshoes."

"Jesus, Ste – I mean – Mister Belmont. Me door!" Jimmy threw the headphones aside and struggled to his feet.

"Well, fucking learn to answer it in future." He shook his head and arms briefly to dislodge droplets of water from his leather jacket and dishevelled hair.

"Sorry, man; I was listenin' to some tunes, like." Jimmy shifted uncomfortably from bare foot to holey-socked foot, scratching his forearms, one after another.

Steve glanced around the room with clear disgust. "This place is a fucking cesspit."

"It's the maid's year off," Jimmy muttered defensively.

"Funny little prick, aren't you?"

"You want a drink?" Jimmy shambled over to the filthy kitchenette. Dirty cups and dishes lay scattered on every greasy surface, and the sink was full of shitty-brown looking water with two rusting pans half submerged.

Steve looked at him as if he was announcing his celibacy in an Amsterdam whorehouse. "Do I look like I've got a death wish?"

Jimmy shrugged and proceeded to run some cold water over a mug with more tea stains than pattern showing. Using a grimy fingernail, he scraped some mould out of the bottom of the mug, before tossing a teabag into it.

"Christ, Jimmy. You really got to straighten your shit out. This isn't healthy."

"It's all I got," Jimmy said flatly, a slight tremor to his words.

"Well, you'll have a lot more when you do the job for me. This spate of shitty weather coming in is perfect; emergency services will have a hell of a job getting through. So, I want you to fire the place on Christmas Eve. You got that?"

As he waited for the kettle to boil, Jimmy turned to Steve and said, "About the payment. I've been thinking …" He absently scratched the back of his hand until it was red raw.

"Dangerous, Jimmy-boy," Steve said with a frown.

"I-I've decided to try to get myself off the blow. The shit is killing us, man. I've lost Lisa, my job; it's destroyed me entire life."

"And you sit in your room and think … how will I ever get away from all this?"

"Eh?"

"*Bonnie and Clyde* … Warren Beatty …" When Jimmy just continued to stare at him, Steve muttered, "Fucking movie icon, you retard."

Jimmy drew in a wheezing breath then let out a rattling cough. Clearing his throat and wiping spittle from his lips, he said, "Whatever, man, I just want money, not the blow, for the job, like."

Steve folded his arms. His irritation was heading south. "Oh, do you?"

"Yeah, I'm not greedy or nowt, I just want it in cash instead of blow."

Steve mulled it over for a moment then his rising anger seemed to dissipate. He shrugged. "Makes no difference to me; you can have two grand cash. Take it or leave it."

Jimmy started to argue, but he had neither the will, nor the energy. Pouring hot water into his cup, he muttered, "Reet."

"Sorted." Steve clapped his hands together and rubbed them briskly against the damp chill in the room. "I don't want to know any details and I won't be seeing or speaking to you again. You'll get your money delivered through what's left of your door the following week … if you don't cock it up." Steve turned and strode out. In the doorway, he glanced back, saying, "Good luck with going clean. You don't have a prayer, kid. Oh, and, if you do cock this up, that will be the least of your problems."

As the afternoon drew on, the snow continued to cascade down from the burdened sky, growing steadily thicker. The wind had died down once again, giving the snowflakes a sense of tender serenity as they dropped vertically to the white-covered ground.

One or two people, disguised under thick layers of coats, hats and scarves, shuffled past, hands buried deep into pockets and their boots leaving their mark in the deepening snow.

Larry Herring pulled his Escort onto Main Street, carefully manoeuvring it at just above a crawl. Despite sticking to second gear, the rear end still managed to drift slightly in the worsening conditions.

He had to bring the car to a virtual stop to edge it around the tight bend onto Bell Lane and then crawled round into the car park. He would have to attach the snow chains tomorrow, if he was going to be able to use the car at all over the coming days. The car slid once more, tyres churning up the fresh snow, as he brought it to a stop in his usual parking space.

Turning the engine off, he paused inside the car, his thoughts turning to Janet. After offering still further chances for her to come clean over her affair with Steve Belmont, she was still doggedly preserving the illusion of a blissfully happy marriage and lying through her back teeth about her every whereabouts. With the fan off, the windows immediately started to mist up, obscuring his view of the brilliant white landscape around him.

The sickening disgust that he had once felt had been replaced with weary impatience for the final act, which would clearly be her running off into the sunset with her lover. Well, he had finally made a decision. She was not going to get her happy ending. She was going to die. *And frankly, my dear, I don't give a damn.*

Steve Belmont would have to wait; it would be far too suspicious if both of them died in a short space of time. But one thing Larry was good at was waiting. He would bide his time and perhaps a year later, when the time was right, Steve Belmont would die too. And, if possible, he would make his dying breaths excruciating. Maybe some sort of accident that would involve him having his dick ripped off. The thought of that was just too good to hope for.

He smiled to his reflection in the rear view mirror. His face looked gaunt and furrowed; sleepless nights had taken their toll over the last few months. But, now that the decision had been made, it felt like a weight had been lifted off his shoulders. The hesitation and the indecision had been driving him insane. Now he could act. Maybe, once it was all over, just maybe, he could find some peace again; just Special K and him. They could be a proper family together, without that cheating, scheming bitch.

After retrieving his case from the boot, he trudged through the snow in his wellies, with his jacket zipped up to the chin. The falling snow coated his hair and shoulders in moments.

The house was well lit and warm and smelled of Janet's cinnamon Christmas candles. As he entered she called from the kitchen, "That you, Larr?"

Larry smiled wryly. "Who else?"

"There's chicken breast in a creamy pasta sauce warm in the oven for you," she was saying as he hung up his jacket and tugged off each boot.

"That's great, dear. I'm starving."

Kerris came bounding down the stairs, all woolly jumper and masses of long chestnut hair, being careful not to dislodge the holly garland that snaked around the banister. "Hiya, daddy!" The young girl, not quite into double-figures yet, but already the tallest in her class, slammed into her father with a playful giggle.

"Hey, it's my Special K!" Larry gave her a long luxurious hug, holding onto to her long after he would normally have broken away. As he held her, smelling the fresh shampoo in her hair, he had to suddenly choke back a sob. His vision blurred and he had to blink several times to force back the tears.

Kerris looked up to him with her big brown eyes, a quizzical look on her button features. "Y'ok, daddy?"

Managing a smile, he said enthusiastically, "Sure, SK. Just really cold out there and I need a big warm hug from my gorgeous daughter."

"Have you seen all that snow, daddy? It's AMAZING!" Breaking away from his embrace, she jumped up and down on

146

the spot, grinning wildly. "Can we have a snowball fight? Can we? PLEASE!?"

"I thought you'd never ask!" he said, matching her broad smile. "You get ready and I'll meet you outside in two ticks."

Kerris screamed with glee and ran to the shoe rack to retrieve her boots.

Larry was smiling as he walked through to the kitchen. As was the tradition in their house, only the lounge, the hall and Kerris' bedroom were the three places where a few elegant Christmas decorations could be hung. It struck him then that he couldn't remember who had made that choice or why. There, he saw Janet finishing off a glass of chardonnay. She looked radiant; short leather skirt, low cut top, accentuating her thrusting breasts, high heels angling her toned calves and flowing red hair in loose ringlets. She licked her ruby red lips and smiled as she saw him admiring her.

Larry felt a stirring, but then, angry at himself, he quickly walked over to the refrigerator, to hide his expression. "Another glass of wine?"

"I'm off down the Miller's shortly, but yes, one more would be nice, thanks. SK is staying round Kimberly's tonight, remember. Are you going to join me later?" The question was posed casually, but Larry detected just a hint of caution in it.

Retrieving the chilled half empty bottle, he turned to the breakfast bar and filled her empty glass. "Sorry sweetheart; got to catch up on loads of paperwork. You have fun though. You meeting Loretta down there?"

A slight flicker behind the eyes. "Yes, just have a few quiet drinks and some girly chat. You won't be missing much."

"Duncan not going?" *Aren't we both the professional actors*, he thought with little amusement. Dustin Hoffman and Susan George, maybe?

She turned away to hunt for something in her bag. "Hmm? Oh no, buried in a stock take or something, Loretta was telling me."

With her back turned, Larry slipped the vial of liquid out from his trouser pocket and popped it open. "That's a shame; I might've popped down for last orders if Duncan was going to be

147

there." He paused, the vial suspended over the wine glass. His hand trembled slightly.

Still rummaging through her bag, Janet said, "Never mind, the four of us can get together for a few drinks on Christmas Eve maybe."

Larry ground his teeth and, in one swift motion, emptied the contents into the glass. "Yes, dear."

He popped the empty vial back into his pocket as Janet turned around, bag in hand. "I better go, Loretta will be wondering if I'm still coming. Are you able to drop Kerris round to Kimberly's later?"

"Yeah, sure," he said dismissively then, keeping his words conversational, added, "Don't you want your wine first?"

She walked up to him and kissed him softly on the cheek. "Can you pop it back in the fridge for me? I'll have it when I get in."

"Sure," Larry replied, with just a hint of frustration. "Have a nice evening."

Janet flashed him a brief smile and strode out, saying, "You too, Larr."

He heard the front door open and Janet shout, "SK, honey, stay near the door until your daddy comes out. I'm off now baby; love you!" As the door slammed behind her, marking her exit, Larry slumped down on a barstool.

After a moment's indecision, he retrieved the bottle and emptied the remaining wine down the sink. Then, very carefully, he poured every drop from the glass into the bottle. "Only a temporary reprieve," he muttered evenly.

Then, with purpose, he forced a smile onto his face and headed back into the hall to join his daughter outside in the snow.

chapter 9

The Dark Man is coming …

Dozens of distant, smoke-like voices drifted up to his room, as Han lay corpse-like and naked on his sleeping bag. Intermittent laughter punctuated the muffled drone of conversation and the foreboding tones of Johnny Cash playing on the jukebox. Han had returned to his room for an hour's rest. His clothes lay steaming on the radiator, one or two stains prominent against the dark material.

His eyes twitched and flickered behind closed lids and his breathing was laboured. Images flashed through his mind of the nightmare day. Stabbing, slicing, eviscerating … severed limbs, heads … and blood … a sea of dark, sticky blood.

He had assumed that the majority of the residents would be easy pickings. He had been wrong … very wrong. Young and old, man and woman, they fought like the possessed. Even those he caught in slumber opened their eyes and clawed at him as the knife slid between ribs to pierce the heart or into the trachea to suffocate, and yet they were still the easy ones …

Suddenly his eyes snapped open. He swung his legs down off the bed and stood.

Shaking loose the visions of the day's earlier struggle, he thought to himself, *Sounds like quite the party down there.* Then, with a deep breath, he said aloud, "And they haven't even seen the start of it." He dressed in the warm, damp clothes and, retrieving the Walther P99 from the bedside cabinet, slipped that into the small of his back.

Zipping up the thick black leather jacket, he caught a glimpse of himself in the mirror. Against the black jacket and jeans, his face looked pale. The thick ginger beard accentuated his jaw, but gave his cheeks a sunken, gaunt appearance. He suddenly felt very tired of the beard and wanted rid of it as soon as possible. As if to emphasise the point, he scratched the rough hair along his jaw line. Well, after the weekend, all being well.

Looking away from the image, he pulled on his black Kevlar lined gloves then grabbed his backpack. A hint of resignation in his voice, he said, "All right ramblers, let's get ramblin'."

He slipped out through the side door into the cold, dark early evening. It vividly brought back the memory of sneaking out that night to see Tess Runckle; old Bet Marple, bless her cotton socks and her bloody sleuth cats. He had come so far since then and the last six months of preparation all amounted to this one extended weekend. It was going to be more difficult than first imagined, but the goal would soon be in sight.

The snow was falling harder than ever and had been rejoined by a tempestuous, bitter cold wind. The soft orange glow, emanating from behind scattered curtained windows around the village, offered the only faint illumination. The wailing wind was like a distant ominous portent.

He trudged purposefully through the flurries to the Sportrak. It already had another covering of snow, so took a couple of minutes to clear with a gloved hand, while the engine warmed up. Snow chains had been fixed that morning, so once cleared, he reversed out of the parking spot in front of the Miller's and pulled round the Green to head along Bell Lane. The windscreen wipers worked hard to clear his view. The wind was whipping up such a frenzy that the driving snow took on the appearance of swarms of albino bees rushing out of the blackness towards him.

Judging by the thick, unblemished snow, no car had driven along the lane for some time. As he passed the good doctor's house on his left, he switched the tape deck on. Mick Jagger erupted in threatening tones and it immediately helped ease Han's nerves.

I see a red door and I want to paint it black,
No colours any more I want them to turn black,
I see the girls walk by dressed in their summer clothes,
I have to turn my head until my darkness goes …

150

Even with four wheel drive and snow chains, progress was pretty slow. He wheel spun half way up the lane, the chained tyres struggling to find purchase and churning up clods of dirty snow. After a couple of seconds, they gripped and the Sportrak bumped forward once more.

Chickens, Bryce and two smoking barrels.

Enraged, John Bryce stormed into the study where his steel gun cabinet stood to one side of a well-stocked bookcase. A vast array of agricultural, farming and veterinary books rubbed shoulders with William Blake, Edgar Allen Poe, Shakespeare, Anne Rice, Stephen King and H. G. Wells, to name just a few. In the bay window stood a small six foot Scots Pine, decorated with garlands and ribbons, baubles and twinkling multicoloured fairy lights. The larger one, a nine footer, held centre stage in the lounge.

Sally had heard the chickens going wild in one of the barns. That could mean only one thing; one of the little toe rags from the village, possibly Jimmy Coulson, were taking advantage of the poor weather to try to steal some of the stock.

The steel box cabinet contained a double-barrel Webley & Scott 700 12-gauge shotgun and a Bassett Supreme .22 semi-automatic rifle, plus a shelf with cartons of ammunition, accessories and cleaning equipment.

Bryce unclipped the Webley shotgun and glanced down at the various types of shot.

Sally appeared in the doorway and stomped over to stand behind him with her fierce blue eyes boring into the back of his neck. Her arms were folded across her diminutive chest as she tapped a hob-nailed boot on the scuffed floorboards. "Don't you even think of using buck or slugs, John Bryce. I don't want you killing anyone!"

Without looking at her, Bryce replied, "We've lost maybe fifty broilers and God-knows how many eggs from the layers out of the perches from them little shits."

Sally stepped forward and kicked him hard in the backside.

Bryce spun, clutching the sore cheek. "Jesus, woman!"

Sally smiled sweetly at him and said, "Pet, just use the birdshot. Please, for me."

Bryce sighed. He never could resist anything Sally ever asked him, not that she asked all that often. "Alreet, alreet," he reluctantly agreed. Grabbing a handful of shells, he shoved them into a deep side pocket in his jacket as he turned to his wife.

Sally kissed him on the lips then grabbed a red woolly hat. "Here," she said, perching on her tiptoes to tug it onto his big head. He still had to bend down a fair bit to allow her. "It's pretty cold out there, pet."

Bryce couldn't resist the urge to give her another kiss, this one more passionate than the previous. "Divvent worry, Sal. I'm gunna kick this kid's arse and then be back for a hot toddy within the hour."

A small head filled with a thick mess of curly brown hair popped around the corner. "Can I come too, Da?" Anthony had turned a teenager earlier in the year, but his size and features made him look more like ten or eleven. Bryce often insisted – not with his son present – that this was from his mother's side.

"Not this time," Bryce said, and with a nod, added, "but thanks for the support, son."

Sally pointed a stern finger to the stairs. "Up them stairs young man; it's time for your bath. I'll be up shortly to check on you." Her tone was stern, but she offered him a sly wink when his face dropped. That brought his cheeky smile back. He dashed off upstairs, taking the steps two at a time in his bare feet.

After locking the cabinet, Bryce made straight for the front door with angry purpose and swung it open, letting a gust of snowflakes into the hallway.

"John!" Sally shouted behind him, a look of supreme exasperation set into her features.

"Sorry! I'm goin'! I'm goin'!" Bryce quickly stepped out into the swirling darkness and slammed the door behind him, causing the bells on the holly wreath nailed to the outside of the door to jangle festively. He rolled his eyes and headed through flurries towards the barns.

The wind moaned through the old, dusty rafters of the cold, draughty barn. Several hundred flustered and clucking chickens scurried about on the barn floor, thick with sawdust, feed and faeces. The air was heavy with dust and feathers. In the gloom, trying to ignore the acrid smells of shit and urine, Jimmy Coulson had managed to bag four of their brethren. He finished tying the Hessian sack as it moved and jerked in his hands, and then carefully picked his way through the squawks and fluttering feathers towards the back of the barn.

These birds should last him till Steve's money came through, then no more sneaking around in the middle of the night for him. Although, there was of course one more night to do on Christmas Eve, but then that would definitely be it. Finito.

Shoving aside the two planks he had pried open earlier, he then shimmied through the thin opening facing the woods. As he slipped out into the storm, he heard the barn doors swing open.

"Right, where are you?" Bryce bellowed, igniting a flashlight and sweeping the beam from left to right, cutting through the hazy darkness. The shotgun was broken open over his other arm and snow and ice particles hung to his hat and clothing. Chickens scurried away in all directions as he pulled the doors closed with a shuddering clatter and strode through the startled throng.

Jimmy yanked his remaining leg through the gap and dashed across the white-cloaked grass, kicking up clods of snow ahead of him. Driving snow stung his face as he rushed to the comparative cover of the trees.

Bryce swept through the barn, squelching through the mixture of shit and feed and, as he reached the centre, the light fell upon the opening in the far corner with a small patch of snow building up just inside. "Sonuvabitch!"

Spinning round, Bryce dashed back across to the doors and back out into the storm. Biting snow lashed his already red face once more. Moving purposefully round the side of the barn, his body hunched over against the elements, he squinted to study the tree line with the trembling light. He adjusted his grip on the shotgun and, with a flick of the wrist, slammed the barrel shut and into a firing position.

The beam caught Jimmy's broken silhouette just as he entered the blackness of the forest.

"Fucker!" Bryce raised the shotgun to his shoulder and aimed down the sight, holding the barrel and the flashlight together in his left hand. The figure was gone before he could get a shot off. "Damn it," he growled with frustration, breaking the shotgun once more before giving chase. The thick snow clung to his boots in thick clumps, making running impossible. Reluctantly, he settled for a lumbering jog, while yelling curses at the trees. The cold was quickly creeping through the warmth of his jacket, causing shivers to run through his body. His fingers were already partially numb, as too were his angry red ears and nose. Snot started to dribble down onto his top lip, warranting an irritated swipe of a sleeve across his face.

"Little bastard," he muttered to himself. The words appeared to be sucked from his lips by the raging storm.

The Sportrak pulled over into the tall grass, just out of sight from the farm. The snow was a white blanket bellowing from the heavens, obscuring everything beyond ten yards. The trees either side of the lane were just grey shapes behind the white veil.

Han sat and stared out towards the Bryce farm, his expression pinched. He remained motionless for a time, hands fixed to the steering wheel.

Finally, he jumped out and headed at a trot towards the farm, raising an arm to guard his blinking eyes from the worst of the storm.

The cluster of buildings quickly emerged from the white shroud; three timber barns, a series of squat stone outhouses, and the two story main house, complete with a single story brick extension. He had visited the Bryce farm on several occasions, but seen through the storm, it looked entirely different; sinister even. Was this a manifestation of doubts for what he was about to do to his friend and his friend's family? Bryce had indeed been a good friend, and had even come to his aid when Jimmy Coulson had caught him off guard.

Wiping his face roughly with his raised arm, he shook his head angrily and continued on at a brisk jog. The ball had been put in motion with Mandy. Her face still haunted his dreams from time to time, but it had eased with Tess, so logically it would get much easier after this night was over. There was no stopping it now. It had to run its course and as long as he kept his eye on the ball and continued with the plan without pausing for thought, then that is exactly what it would do. Reflection would come after.

Han angled towards the door on the end of the extension, which he knew to be the kitchen. Drawing closer, he could see that the blinds in the large window along the length of the annex had not been closed and the strip lights glowed from within. A bright red Christmas garland was hanging inside along the top of the window and draped down the sides. He could clearly make out the country-cottage style kitchen, with a reclaimed welsh dresser, *Aga* twin oven and Belfast-style deep sink.

Unsurprisingly, the stable door leading into the kitchen was unlocked. He gently opened it and peered inside. The rush of warm air sent a tingling sensation over his cold, wet cheeks and he revelled in its comfort.

The kitchen continued into the main house, where the smaller, original kitchen had clearly started. At the far end, there was a chunky eight seater, rough-hewed dining table and chairs, complete with a three pronged brass candle holder with red, vanilla-scented candles and green bows.

Strong smells of coffee and fresh herbs, mixed with the vanilla from the candles, drifted into his nostrils and he breathed in deeply through his nose to savour the aromas. He slipped in and closed the door gently behind him, dampening the storm's frenzy immediately. Quietly, he rubbed his boots on the welcome mat as melting snow dripped from his clothing.

"You in bed yet, pet?" Sally's voice shouted from the hallway.

"Yes!" Anthony's high-pitched voice from upstairs. "Dad back yet?"

"No, he'll pop up to see you when he gets in."

Damn, John wasn't home. That was irritating and would throw a small spanner in the works. Still, roll with the punches. Unsheathing the hunting knife, he advanced along the kitchen to the doorway beyond the dining suite. Water dripped from his wet clothes onto the quarry-tiled floor as he edged closer, a look of grim resolve set into his ruddy features. The ice-crystals garnishing his beard were melting quickly with the sudden warmth.

He was a couple of feet from the doorway when Sally walked in from the hall. At first she didn't even register his presence, her mind clearly preoccupied with a dozen mundane chores.

"Who the hell—" Her eyes widened and hesitantly, she said, "Han?"

Han smiled, but something about the smile was wrong, twisted in some way. Even as she started to relax, instinct rang alarm bells in her head. Then she saw the knife. Alarm instantly spun towards panic.

"Oh my God! What have you *done to John?*" Her voice went shrill as her mouth dried up halfway through the sentence. Her eyes blinked repeatedly and the colour drained from her cheeks. Despite her words, she seemed unable to comprehend the situation she was now confronted with. It seemed just too alien; unreal.

Han advanced without saying a word, that *grin* fixed to his face.

One thing rushed through her mind which seemed to polarise her tornado of thoughts. "ANTHONY RUN!" Han leapt upon her, the smile transforming into a sneer.

The weight of his body slammed her against the low door of the under stairs cupboard, winding her and cracking her head off the wooden trim of the banister.

"Mam?" Anthony cried from somewhere upstairs, clearly distressed.

Dogs started barking and one, a shaggy black and white collie, appeared through the lounge door further along the hallway.

"Sorry, Sally," Han said simply as her wide eyes stared at him and her mouth worked wordlessly. Pinning her against the door with one arm, he quickly drew the blade up to her throat and sliced it clean open.

As blood gushed freely from the gaping wound, soaking the front of her sweater, she suddenly shrieked in his face, her features stretching and contorting almost impossibly wide. Blood and spittle sprayed Han as her teeth snapped at him, merely an inch from the tip of his nose.

Shocked, Han struggled to restrain her as she thrashed and kicked as the blood continued to gush down her front and pool around their feet.

The struggle seemed to go on for an age, but was merely seconds. She fell limp and Han allowed her to slid down into a sitting position, soft murmurs escaping her paling lips.

"Bu—" she managed in a hoarse whisper before she died.

Two things then happened in quick succession. Anthony appeared at the top of the stairs, dressed in paisley pyjamas, and the collie surged forward from the doorway, snarling and barking.

Anthony took one appalled look at the blood-soaked corpse of his mother and screamed. "MAM!" The shock caused him to stumble at the edge of the stairs and slide down half a dozen steps on his socks. Miraculously, he managed to stay on his feet.

Han turned to the dog, just as it pounced at him. Swinging the knife in a shallow arc, he sliced the dog across the muzzle. It yelped in pain as its blood splattered across the wall and a photograph of the Bryce family. Their son looked a few years younger in the picture; all sat, smiling for the camera, John proud and grinning, Sally slender and radiant.

Despite its injury, the dog shook its muzzle, spraying more blood up the walls and across the floor, and then surged forward again, its paws scrabbling on the varnished floorboards for purchase. The second attack lacked the ferocity of the first, instead staying low and rushing forward to lash out at the intruder's groin. Han leaped forward, gripping the knife in both hands, and landed, legs straddling the dog's back. The blade buried deep into the centre of its back, causing it to yelp once more and thrash out in agony.

He pinned it between his knees and, withdrawing the knife, quickly rammed it back into the dog's flesh several times. It dropped to the floor, squirming and whining softly. Without pausing, he turned and hacked at the dog's neck. The force of the strike all but severed its head. It lay dead before the knife was through to the other side.

The collie's head, hanging on by a sliver of tissue and skin, flopped to the floor as a dark pool of blood spread out around it, quickly mingling with its owner's.

Casting a quick glance up and down the hall, Han prepared for the Bryce's second collie to come charging towards him, but it was nowhere to be seen. As his eyes returned to the dead dog, the fur seemed to shimmer in front of his eyes. It became short and sandy coloured. The nearly severed head became fatter and more rounded. Suddenly, he found himself staring at Ju with matted, blood-engorged coat and hacked head. Its dead eyes stared accusingly at him.

The knife lurched from his shaken hand and clattered to the drenched floor as the wind rushed from his lungs.

A clattering commotion above him snapped him back to reality and the dog was at once a collie again. Han's head arched towards the landing where Anthony was now scrambling back up the stairs he had just fallen down, sobbing and screaming uncontrollably. Bending down to retrieve the knife, he took one final hesitant look at the dog, which was still the Bryce's collie and not Jumanji, then turned his attention to the boy.

"Hey, Anth, hang on there, big fella," he said in a strained-friendly manner, stepping over the bodies of the dog and Sally and walking to the bottom of the stairs. He was careful not to slip in the thick pools of blood spreading along the hallway and channelling along the grooves in between the floorboards.

Without even looking at him, Anthony screamed louder and lunged up the last couple of steps.

Suddenly, Han's relaxed demeanour switched and he thundered up the stairs at a sprint.

Scrambling along the landing on all fours, Anthony screamed one more time. "DADDY!" The terrified voice had a primeval quality to it.

Drenched and shivering, Bryce cursed as he tripped over a fallen branch and fell to his knees into the mush of mud and rotting leaves. He knelt there for a moment, taking advantage of the brief respite to catch his breath. His panting exhales clung to the air in front of him. The farmer glanced up to the black, skeletal canopy and the steadily falling snow, less disturbed by the wind within the restrictions of the forest. It pattered incessantly on his brow and numbed red cheeks. Shaking snow from his flashlight and shotgun, he struggled back to his feet and continued deeper into the forest. He could just hear the thief up ahead; in his panic to escape, he was making it easy for him to follow.

The storm was not letting up for a moment; it remained merely breezy within the forest, but up in the canopy he could hear the incessant howl wrenching at the upper branches. With each step, he was being drawn further and further away from the warmth and comfort of the farm. Sally would be getting worried by now.

He struggled on for several minutes more, before the thief's escape finally fell from earshot. Frustrated, he continued stumbling on for a short distance further, before angrily giving up the chase. It was a hard call to make and sent a short, sharp jab to his pride.

Despondent, he slumped against a pine, vibrant against groves of slender birch and their smaller cousins, the magical rowans. His fringe sticking out of the woolly hat was plastered against his dripping face. As he stood there shivering, the snowflakes and droplets of water continued to rain down through the blackness. The forest around him had fallen deathly silent, save for the soft hypnotic patter.

After taking a few deep gulps of air, he bellowed, "You come round here again and I'll fucking kneecap you, you got that you fuckin' pissant!" He hesitated, half expecting a reply. When none was forthcoming, he turned around and headed back to the farm. The shotgun felt like an unyielding ton weight in his frozen hands.

Jimmy paused and glanced behind him as the farmer's enraged voice echoed through the forest. His lank hair was plastered flat and he, too, was soaked to the skin. A violent shiver shot through his body, almost wrenching the heavy sack from his icy grip. He set it down, but held on to the drawn opening. While he caught his wheezing breath, he snivelled noisily then coughed up some bright green phlegm.

After a couple more dry coughs, through chattering teeth, he muttered, "Yeah, lick my balls. There won't be a next time." He was more determined than ever – he would use Steve's arson money to sort his life out. These four chickens would have to see him through somehow until then. This was his last chance to make something good out of his worthless, rotting cesspit of a life.

The Ford Fiesta struggled along the churned up snowdrift that was the B6341. Since passing through Rothbury, progress had been slow and treacherous, causing the unceasing snow to quickly build up on the roof and bonnet. If a snowplough had been through, it must have been quite some time ago. The darkness of the narrow country road was utterly unforgiving. Fences, hedgerows and tree lines shimmered by as one shade darker smears; lost shadows dancing in the storm.

Sam Potter was hunched over the wheel, red-faced and bleary eyed. Natalie Potter, a short, chubby young woman, was slumped against the passenger window, her spiky black hair splayed against the misted glass. An intermittent nasal grunt was all she had been capable of for the last hour.

The stereo was turned down so low that he couldn't hear what was playing over the drone of the fan. The warm air, combined with the back and forth motion of the windscreen wipers, conspired to seduce Sam's already tired eyes to grow steadily droopier. The weariness bore down on him like the weight of the ocean above a deep sea diver. It crawled steadily into the darkest recesses of his mind, corrupting him body and soul. Ceaselessly, it whispered to him ... *relent Sam, it's okay, Sam, lose yourself in the gentle comfort of my embrace.*

A bump in the road caused Natalie's head to bounce off the window. She stirred and turned to look at him, her own eyes as bloodshot as his. "You okay, baby?" she asked groggily.

Startled back to full consciousness, on reflex, Sam jerked the steering wheel, sliding the car into the deep snow bank to their left. They both jolted forward into their seatbelts as the car came to a sudden halt.

Natalie stared at him, open mouthed and all fatigue temporarily banished. "Guess that's a no then, honey?" She kept her tone light, despite the sudden thumping of her heart.

Trembling slightly, Sam said, "S-sorry, Nats. Was d-drifting off there."

The engine idled and the windscreen wipers continued back and forth as Natalie plucked a packet of cigarettes and a disposable lighter from her bag. She lit one before saying, "You need to get some rest, honey. We can't go on any more in this."

"Blindburn is o-only another f-few miles past ... past ... w-what's it called again?" Sam frowned and rubbed his eyes, searching his groggy mind. "Haydon," he remembered and shifted his weight in his seat to ease his aching back then let out a long, satisfying yawn.

Natalie wound her window down a fraction to let the smoke from her cigarette escape in bluish plumes. "No, let's go to Haydon. We can get a room at that pub we stayed in last year and then head out in the morning."

Sam shook his head. "W-what about D-Dad? I-I-I need to get t-to him t-t-tonight."

With her cigarette hanging out of her mouth, Natalie turned in her seat and grabbed his hand in both of hers. Her tone was kind, but firm. "No, honey. Your dad wouldn't want you to risk your life. We can get some rest then head out first thing. It's for the best, honey."

"H-Haydon's w-weird."

Natalie drew on her cigarette and thought about that for a moment. "True," she said finally, "but we've got no choice here."

A particularly strong gust of wind buffeted the small car, causing chunks of the thick snow piled on the bonnet to blow across the windscreen, fleetingly obscuring their view of the dark, wintry road.

As the wipers cleared the view one more time, Sam glanced ahead of them along the road, stretching into what appeared to be nothingness. A quiver crept across his shoulder blades. Reluctantly, Sam nodded and briefly sagged back in his seat.

It didn't work out, so I took a souvenir ... her pretty head.

Angry, cold and drained, Bryce trudged across the thick snow-covered courtyard to the farmhouse. The poor light and the storm obscured old footprints easily, not that his weary disposition would have spotted them in any case. The cold and wet seemed to have seeped right into his bones, flaring up all his old aches and pains, picked up over the years from a tough farming life. It certainly hadn't been an easy life, having started helping his father from an earlier age than Anthony was now, but he would not have changed it for the world.

As he drew nearer, the lights from the house offered improved illumination, so he turned off the flashlight and popped it in his pocket. He left the barrel of the shotgun broken over his arm. Grumpily, he pondered on how he would need to strip it down and thoroughly clean and oil the barrel, hinge and action after the beating it had taken from the elements. In actual fact, he didn't mind cleaning his guns at all, finding the process quite therapeutic, especially accompanied by Bob Dylan straining across threadbare lyrics. But his mood was such, that even the thought of a normally uplifting chore darkened his mood still further. The first thing he was going to do was pour himself a very large whisky to help ward off the icy chill.

The front door was unlocked, as it generally was when someone was home. Stomping his snow and mud-caked boots on the welcome mat, he swung the door open and called, "Sal, I'm back. Didn't get the bugger though."

As he stepped into the hall his blood ran as cold as his extremities. Glancing to his left towards the kitchen, he saw the floor and walls awash with swathes of congealing blood. Lying sprawled, amidst the expanse of crimson, was one of the dogs; it may have been Cody, but he couldn't tell for sure because of its head hanging off and facing away from him, partially submerged in the sticky mass. Its coat, too, was drenched across the back and hind quarters. It seemed an impossible amount of blood from a single dog. His hall had been turned into an abattoir while he had been running around in the snow chasing ghosts.

As the horrific scene began to sink in to his numbed mind, a wild panic swept over him. Then, registering just above the pounding of his heart, he heard soft crying coming from ... the cellar.

"Sally! Anthony!" he cried with an anguished tone, one notch from hysteria. Reacting, rather than thinking, he dashed to his right and around a short corner to the wide open door of the cellar. Cracking shut the shotgun, he stood at the top of the stairs, staring into the darkness down below. The fear of what he might find down there caused a moment of hesitation. They could have been ... they could be ... The crying continued; it was Anthony.

"Son! I'm coming!" Bryce started forward, but his boot clipped a low wire strung across the crest of the opening. He stumbled forward into the darkness, his shocked cry paving the way.

There was a rapid series of thumps, in harmony with the cracking and creaking complaints of the staircase, followed quickly by a thunderous crash, and the distinctive blast of both barrels of the shotgun discharging.

The force of Bryce's boot on the wire pulled the cellar door shut with a slam and half a dozen six foot logs piled behind it crashed down in front of the closed door.

Da dead Ron Ron Ron.

The howling wind buffeted the sash windows, causing several draughts between the cracked and rotting frames to flutter the curtains like restless spirits. Ron Foster sat slouched on the sofa, a can of lukewarm lager atop his rounded stomach and his chin resting on his collarbone. The sound of a distant chainsaw emanated from his nostrils. The white t-shirt stretched over his portly frame was stained with several blotches of beer.

The television showed the muted picture of Ben Cartwright and Little Joe arguing in the Ponderosa. A standard lamp lent a dimmed orange glow to the cosy room.

Erika Foster shuffled into the room in a floral dressing gown. Her eyes were bloodshot and sunken into purple hollows. Patches of cracked, angry skin had erupted on the backs of her hands and around her neck. She stood just inside the doorway for a moment and absently scratched her concealed thigh. She looked down at her husband with what, at first, seemed like impatience, but then her features softened.

She moved quietly over to him and gently removed the can from its perch. Popping it down on the coffee table, she then placed a tender kiss on his forehead. She managed a weak smile and stood up to leave.

"Touching," Han said from the doorway. Encumbered with thick clothing and equipment, he appeared to fill the entire doorway. The smile on his lips was friendly enough, but his stance was coiled.

Startled, Erika knocked the coffee table, sending the half full can of lager careening onto the carpet, spilling its frothing contents across the floor. Her husband grunted and stirred.

Han tutted and shook his head. "That'll stain if you're not careful."

"You!" With recognition came venom. "You *did* have something to do with our Mandy's disappearance!"

Ron groggily raised his head and blinked. "Wha? Eri?"

Han sighed and nodded grudgingly. "Yeah, yeah I did."

The admission stunned Erika into horror-struck silence and caused Ron to sit up, rapidly shaking off any drowsiness.

"Sorry, but yes, I followed Mandy into the woods and murdered her. I chopped her body into a dozen pieces and buried her out there." There was no passion in his words, just a faint impression of relief. It actually felt good to finally put Mandy's long-suffering parents in the picture and out of their misery. Hopefully it would ease their passing.

The words were not matching his body language or his tone. Ron stood up clumsily, saying, "Fuck you talking about?"

As the truth of his words sunk in, Erika burst into tears. Vehemently, she shook her head, uttering in a low, rasping voice, "No, no, God no, it's not true." She covered her streaming eyes with shaking hands as her mouth continued to work soundlessly.

Ron stood staring at Han, his mouth wide and slumber forgotten. Struggling to force the words from his disbelieving mouth, he stammered, "You ... *killed* ... my daughter?"

Han shrugged. "Someone had to be the first. Consider Mandy the lucky one."

Ron raised white-knuckle, clenched fists and, with the tone of a wounded bear, snarled, "I'm gunna rip you apart!" With that, he launched himself, cursing at his child's killer.

Erika wrenched her hands from her half-blinded eyes and, despair suddenly forgotten, growled, "Kill him, Ron!"

Han blinked and quickly brought his knife up and thrust it deep into Ron's sizeable stomach as he barrelled into him. A loud *oof* rushed from his snarling lips, but with a hatred-fuelled determination, he managed to grip Han's shoulders with vice-like pressure.

Drawing close to Han's face, Ron screamed, "You murdered my Mandy!" He shoved Han back into the doorframe, jarring his back. Encircled by a dark patch rapidly spreading across his t-shirt, the knife slide out of his stomach and caused him to double over in an agonising spasm.

In spite of the temporary sting in his back, Han reacted immediately. He raised the dripping knife into the air, his face set with resolve.

With balled up fists, Erika yelled a warning at her husband. Ron had a moment to glance up from his bent over position in time to see the knife descending towards him.

The blade barely faltered as it entered through Ron's upturned eye, smashing through the fragile bones in the back of the socket and penetrating the brain. His body dropped to the floor with the suddenness of a massive brain haemorrhage. The weight of the body yanked the knife out of Han's tight grip.

As Han bent to retrieve the knife, he glanced at Erika. She was standing motionless, dead eyes staring at him – through him – her hands flexing between outstretched talons and fists, a low rumble emanating from the pit of her stomach.

Unnerved, he quickly shoved a wet boot against the dead man's neck and wrenched the knife out with a wet sucking sound. Blood and fluid spurted forth from the gaping wound as the blade tore free, darkening the pastel-green shade of the carpet and spraying the wall and sofa. A fleeting vision of the Bryce hallway, complete with family portrait, doused with dripping gore, sparked across his mind's eye.

"*Ronnie*," she whispered whilst not taking her eyes off Han.

He stepped over Ron's dead, bleeding body. A twitch snagged the side of Erika's mouth. To Han, it resembled the hint of a smile.

He closed the distance and held the knife in front of him. To his surprise Erika grabbed his wrist and plunged the knife into her own stomach. The shock caused him to release his grip and shrink away from Erika's cold touch.

Not taking her eyes off him, she proceeded to draw the sunken blade across her own stomach. Her only reaction was her twitching mouth as her intestines spilled onto the carpet.

She uttered a single word, "*Haydon*" and then fell to the ground, dead.

Han couldn't help but bring a gloved hand up to his mouth to stifle a cry. Shaking his head, he said, "Who ... *what* are you fucking people?" Still shaking his head, he retrieved his knife and quickly backed out of the room.

He stumbled back out in the storm, saying, "Just get on with it ... Get this fucking freakshow over with."

Reverend end.

The church of St. Bart's was shrouded in darkness as Reverend Dunhealy walked down the central aisle towards the altar. He rolled an unlit cigar between his thumb and forefinger in thoughtful contemplation. The low moan of the wind whistled through the eaves, sounding like a lonely wolf calling from a distant hilltop.

Four six foot stained glass windows, depicting St. Bartholomew, St. Oswald, St. Matthew and St. Mark, gazed down upon him. St. Bartholomew, looking forlorn with long flowing beard, Oswald, with proud, angular features, Mark's rounded, cheerful face and Matthew, wise and craggy.

A noise behind him caused him to stop abruptly and turn around. He stood, motionless, his breath caught on the cold air in front of him, and his temporarily forgotten cigar dangling down by his side. Meditation dissolved to unveil realisation. "So … you have come for me now."

Shadow and movement to his side. The Reverend turned slowly. Standing below St. Oswald, complete with halo encircled crown and sword pointing to the ground ahead of him, he noticed a figure bathed in shadow.

"Mister Whitman," he said without surprise.

"Yes, Father." Han stepped out of the shadows, his face grinning and ghostly white against his glistening black clothing. In a strained effort to add levity, he said, "I have the devil in me, Father."

The Reverend examined his cigar and shook his head sadly. "No, Mister Whitman, you're not the devil." He glanced up at Han and added, "But you have unleashed him."

Dunhealy's calm demeanour further unnerved Han. His voice straining, he sung, "*You look like an angel … walk like an angel … talk like an angel*" and moved purposefully towards the Reverend.

The Reverend stood his ground and continued to roll the cigar.

The singing helped regain his confidence and he steadily got louder. "*But I got wise … you're the devil in disguise … oh yes you are!*" He reached the Reverend and they stood in front of each other. Han stopped singing and took a deep breath.

"This is *Haydon*, Mister Whitman," Dunhealy simply said.

"I *am* the devil," Han replied, grinning.

The Reverend smiled back at him with what looked like pity in his eyes.

Anger rose inside Han. He didn't understand what was going on. Nothing was going to plan. "Fuck you!" he said and buried the hunting knife into the Reverend's chest.

Dunhealy let out a soft rasp and dropped his cigar. Sagging, he managed, "I will ... pray for you."

Han pulled him close and said, "I don't want your fucking prayers, old man."

The Reverend coughed and managed that pitiful smile once more. "You *will*."

Han yanked the knife out and proceeded to stab the Reverend in the face until he was utterly unrecognisable. Somewhere in the frenzy both men toppled to the stone ground.

The Reverend's pulped face was angled towards the stained glass window depicting St. Bartholomew with three flaying knives on his cerulean robes. Breathing hard, Han glanced up at it and muttered, "Well, at least I didn't skin you alive." Attempting a hollow laugh, he added, "Or cut your heart out with a spoon."

He continued to stare at the lifeless body, his mind replaying the day's events ... Sally ... Erika ... Dunhealy ... the others. What was happening here? This wasn't right.

He gradually regulated his breathing and, with considerable effort, pushed himself to his feet. Straightening himself up, shakily, he said, "I'm gonna execute every mother-fucking last one of ya."

Icy snow crystals stung at Jimmy's red, dripping face as he shuffled through the ankle-deep snow towards the door to his bed-sit. He was soaked and shivering, with thick green snot running from his nose to congeal in the week old stubble on his upper lip. He was too drained to bother wiping it away anymore. The cold had sapped every bit of strength from his aching, malnourished muscles.

The village appeared to be completely bereft of life, with just a solitary orange glow from a bedroom window from across the street to act as a beacon on such a stormy night. He hadn't seen Main Street, so he assumed there would be a few people still revelling in the Duck and the Miller's at least, but here, there was nothing but the howling wind to keep him company. He thought for a moment of the warm and laughing people in the pubs, toasting each other and wishing each other a happy Christmas. The thought made him feel intolerably lonely, and chilled him to the core.

The sack was unmoving as he dragged it unenthusiastically along behind him, having stopped briefly to wring the necks of the four birds. It was a chore that he never had quite gotten the stomach for, despite having done it many times before.

As he reached the front door, he fumbled with his numb hands to retrieve the key from his cold and wet jeans. Cursing as his alien hands refused to cooperate, he then noticed that the door was already ajar.

Too weary to care, he shoved the door aside and struggled into the dark musty hallway. There was no sound coming from his landlord's flat on the ground floor, so after shaking some of the excess snow free from his coat, he trudged as quietly as he could be bothered upstairs.

The door to his bed-sit was still broken so he nudged it aside and staggered in.

Without even troubling to push the door closed behind him, he slung the sack towards the kitchenette, shrugged out of his coat and boots and collapsed onto the bed. His eyes closed and sleep embraced him almost immediately.

Life was good to me 'til now.

A quiet snoring drifted up from the king-size bed positioned against the fire breast wall of the spacious, decadently furnished bedroom. Three layers of complimentary voiles draped across the window, silk scatter cushions were splayed, top and bottom over the burgundy bed covers, and plush, crushed velvet wallpaper hung on every wall, broken only by paintings and photographs of cats (mainly Persian), and wall-hanging brass candle holders. The darkened room was hushed except for the rhythmic sounds emanating from the sleeping figure. Above him, on the fire breast wall, a sizeable oil painting adorned centre stage, depicting Moe Baxter on an opulent gold and jewel encrusted throne, stroking a fat Persian cat on his lap.

In sleep, Moe had managed to find an inner calm that eluded him in waking hours of late. It had been aided with several vodka martinis and a couple of sleeping pills, but the result was the same.

There was a faint creak from behind the door. After a moment of silence, the brass doorknob turned slowly and the door eased open a fraction. Jill Fairbank eased her head round the door to check on her boss and friend. He appeared to be sleeping peacefully for the first time in weeks. She paused in the doorway for a while, watching him. He had been through so much. It had not been well known, and most of those who had known had scoffed, but Moe and Tess had been involved in a meaningful relationship for several years.

He acted the camp clown at times, but he was a warm, sensitive man who had grown a deep love and respect for Tess over the years of their friendship. The village gossip had always suggested that it was just a thinly veiled attempt to hide his homosexuality, but, contrary to popular belief, Moe had never had those tendencies. He had, however, remained a virgin until much later in life, and over the years had developed deep anxieties towards intercourse and the opposite sex.

It had been Tess who had finally stripped away those years of apprehension. She had done it out of friendship at first, insisting that, as friends, she would help him with what had become a deep-rooted issue in his life. But out of that joining, they had connected on a much deeper level and a full relationship developed.

Moe had told his only other close friend, Jill, all about their relationship as it had developed, so Jill understood more than anyone the pain Moe had been going through since his partner's death.

Content that Moe was sleeping soundly, Jill quietly closed the door with a soft click and returned to the sofa bed in the lounge where the big Cream Point Persian, Mister Flibble, was already asleep in the centre of the thick rumpled blanket.

The generous living room, decorated royal blue and cream, with vibrant green velvet curtains and potted yucca and spider plants, was lit by an Egyptian-style ceramic table lamp. Since the heating had turned itself off an hour ago, a chill was creeping in to the old house.

She tied her hair back into a ponytail then quickly undressed out of her wool leggings and sweatshirt. Shivering, she grabbed a bed shirt from the arm of the sofa, but before putting it on she stopped still, standing in her underwear, bathed in shadow.

It was Mister Flibble who had caused her pause for thought. The cat didn't appear to be breathing, but in the poor light, it also appeared that there was a dark stain spreading out around him on the cream blanket.

"Flibbles?" she asked hesitantly, the shirt held close to her breasts. Slowly, she stepped forward and reached down to touch the still cat.

As the tips of her fingers touched the fine, luxurious fur, something beneath the blanket twitched.

Jill jumped and a startled cry escaped her lips as a large form took shape squirming under the blanket. "What the hell?" What was mild concern turned to alarm. She drew her hand back to clutching the shirt against her chest.

The movement pushed the cat onto its side and Jill caught a glimpse of a deep gash in its stomach. Then, slow and deliberate, a fully clothed Han sat up, the blanket falling away to his waist. The grin on his face was tipped way beyond joy and hovering somewhere around insanity. "Mister Flibble is flobbled, I'm afraid."

"You *bastard*," Jill said and dropped the shirt.

Han whipped the cover off, revealing the bloodied hunting knife in his other hand. "And then some."

"So, you are the *pervert* Tess said you were," Jill said and something changed in her eyes. A hint of mischievousness. Her hand drew up to her chest and touched the side of her breast. She unclipped her bra and let it fall to her feet, exposing her breasts and erect nipples. "You want to fuck me?"

Han gawped at her and couldn't help but feel a tremble in his groin.

She smiled and the tip of her tongue touched her lips.

Han blinked and said, "You people are all batshit crazy."

171

"This is *Haydon*, babe." With that, she slid her knickers down her tanned thighs.

Han jumped to his feet and stabbed her between her perfect breasts. Her face contorted as she toppled over with Han on top of her. "You like it rough," she rasped.

Han recoiled and stepped back, saying, "Jesus!"

Jill lay on the sofa bed, eyes staring up at him, blood dribbling under her breasts. Then her legs slowly began to part.

Han moved in quickly, brought the soiled knife up to her head and, with one swift thrust, rammed it into her ear. Her body twitched.

For good measure, he forced the blade deeper still into the side of her head, scraping through bone and cartilage. Blood ran freely, dripping off her earlobe and the hilt of the knife. A mushy, squelching sound accompanied its steady advance, until the blade was fully submerged. Wisps of her soft, splayed hair rested on the back of his gloved hand. He gazed at the delicate ash-blonde strands for some time as her faint tremors finally dissipated, then, with great effort, he withdrew the knife, wiped it on a fold of blanket and rose to his feet.

He walked quickly into the hallway and to Moe's room.

He made no attempt to be stealthy as he flung the bedroom door open and strode in. Moe Baxter was still fast asleep, facing him on his side, undisturbed by Han's clunking footfalls, or the brief confrontation in the lounge.

Impatient, irritated, nervy and just a little aroused, Han crossed quickly over to the side of the bed and knelt down in front of the sleeping man. The blade slowly rose to within millimetres of Moe's flabby chin, the steel glinting briefly from the soft light in the hall. There was silence, save for his hushed snoring.

"Drop your cock and grab your socks!" Han yelled, drill sergeant style, in the hairdresser's face.

Moe made a grunting noise and his eyes blinked open. "*You.*"

"Hey, Moe, how ya doing, big fella?" Han said, accompanied with a near hysterical laugh. "Christmas has come early, dickhead."

For a fleeting moment, Han thought he saw flames burning in Moe's eyes, such was the intensity of the hatred emanating from his glare.

Han did not give him any more time to react. He thrust the knife into his snarling mouth.

Perhaps we can frighten the ghosts of so many years ago ... with a little illumination.

A groan lifted up through the dusty gloom. The cellar was in complete darkness, except for the tiniest sliver of dim light squeezing through the gap between door and floor at the top of the stairs.

A second groan followed, then the slow, scraping movement of boots on the concrete floor.

John Bryce sat up on the cold floor, his mind dazed and reeling. He tentatively touched his forehead and was unsurprised to feel a congealing gash, the main cause of his pounding head, no doubt. His body was aching and stiff all over from the numerous knocks he had taken on his rapid decent down the stairs.

The cellar smelled dusty and dank and forced an involuntary cough to escape his lungs. Pain erupted in his chest from its force; possibly a cracked rib. Clutching his sore ribs with one hand and leaning back on the other, he tried to make sense of recent events.

It took a few moments for his scrambled brain to reshuffle everything back into order. *Cody dead ... blood-splattered walls ... Anthony.*

"Anthony!" His voice was shrill and loaded with fear.

The cold and dust seemed to consume his cry. Silence was his answer.

After carefully standing, favouring a possible sprain, he edged towards the bottom of the stairs where the light switch was. His hand eased along the rough stone wall until it hit the plastic casing of the switch.

The vociferous click was a harsh, dead sound in the confined space. The single naked bulb in the centre of the room remained dark. He flicked it on and off a couple more times, but to no avail. "Shit," he muttered in frustration. Fighting back the urge to cry out a second time, he remembered the flashlight in his pocket.

Praying that the fall hadn't damaged the bulb, he fumbled to retrieve it and tried the switch. An orange beam struck the far wall, revealing shelves crammed with boxes of toilet rolls, cleaning products and an assortment of household items.

Sucking in a breath and holding it, he swept the beam across the room. It quickly fell upon an unmoving bare leg.

"Sally!" He rushed over to her, but stopped dead as the beam revealed the rest of his wife's body. She lay twisted in a crumpled heap, drenched in blood and with wide staring, lifeless eyes. The colour rushed from his face and he felt a sudden urge to vomit. "*Sally* ..." The repeated word was feeble, like the rustle of reeds.

The rising panic was impossible to stem. "Son!" Sweeping the beam further across the room, it fell upon, what looked at first, like a small bundle of rags in the corner.

Bryce staggered forward, nausea flooding his head; threatening to spin him into oblivion. His knocks and pains were completely forgotten, all consumed by a desperate dread. As he approached, he saw tufts of hair poking from the top of the bundle, and an arm and a leg sticking out to one side.

Drawing closer, he realised that the head and limbs were not attached to the torso. Anthony had been dismembered and the parts deposited unceremoniously in a pile in the corner of the room. A small chrome Dictaphone had been placed neatly next to the head, but the batteries had died, silencing the deception while the farmer lay unconscious.

Bryce stood motionless, staring down with unblinking eyes at the body of his son.

Chapter 10

There's a number on the wall for all of us, angel, and if tonight's the night they pick mine, so be it. After you, sweetheart.

The backdoor to Lisa's flat opened with an audible click after a simple turn of the key that Lisa had freely given him. Han stepped into a narrow hall with a steep set of stairs in front of him. Gusting flakes of snow blew in behind, prompting him to quickly shut the door. In the darkness, he could make out the closed door at the top of the stairs that led to the kitchen. A thin strip of light pierced the darkness at the foot of the door. The kitchen light was on.

He ascended the stairs swiftly but quietly. At the top, he paused to listen at the door as dripping, icy water pooled around his feet. After a moment, he eased it open and crept inside. The kitchen was deserted, but the door to the hallway was open and the muffled sounds of a television could be heard from the lounge. Carefully picking his way through Haley's usual discarded plastic animals, headless dolls and crayons, he crossed to the hall.

The lounge door was ajar. Peering inside, the room was lit only by a lamp in the corner and the flickering images from the television. Han recognised the film immediately.

"No, no! Don't you touch that, little lamb. Don't touch my knife, that makes me mad. That makes me very, very mad ..."

He managed a smile, his first genuine moment of levity since the killings began. It helped renew his resolve.

Reluctantly, he drew his eyes away from the screen. The back of the sofa obscured whoever was lounging on it, but he could see two slender dangling feet kicking lazily off the edge. In the gloom, he could just make out dark toenail polish.

Han already knew who the babysitter was. He had met her several times. She was a cute high school girl; fourteen or fifteen, if he remembered rightly, but already with quite a figure on her.

Kelly Mason, Paul Mason's daughter, was Lisa's regular choice of babysitter. She was a little introverted, with Marc Bolan fixation, purple streaks in her hair and nose and tongue piercings. A younger Lisa in the making.

Scarcely breathing, he eased the door open further then slipped into the room. He crept the short distance to the back of the sofa and peered over the top.

Kelly was lying on her front with her head resting on one arm, engrossed in the film. Good taste in films. Shame really. Her long, messy hair was splayed out around her, covering most of her *T. Rex* t-shirt.

As he stood, watching Kelly watch the film, a thought occurred to him. Slowly, he drew his hunting knife as he crouched down on his haunches behind the sofa. After taking a moment to judge where her midsection would be, he then brought the knife back and immediately thrust it forward.

A startled cry, part shock and part pain, followed. He quickly withdrew the freshly bloodied blade and vaulted over the back of the sofa to land in front of the squirming girl. Another scream caught on her lips as she gasped for breath. She stared wide-eyed at the intruder standing before her.

"Surprise," Han said. With a wave of his knife hand towards the television, which splattered a few droplets of blood across the carpet, he added, "Who'd you expect? Robert Mitchum?"

Tears welled in her eyes and through gritted teeth, she said, "Just kill me."

Her composure was disconcerting, but not unexpected given what Han had already seen. With an irritated click of the tongue, he obliged.

The struggle was brief. He stood up from Kelly's still, bleeding body and considered his handiwork. Beads of sweat stood out on his forehead. The young girl's chest had been stabbed repeatedly and her head slumped to one side, a frozen grimace etched into her features. The blue fabric of the sofa was awash with the pooling dark stains of her blood. The position she had naturally fallen into was a vivid reminder of Mandy's after his first, virgin kill.

A flash of burning orbs caused him to blink momentarily and he had to steady himself on the arm of the sofa.

Not wishing to linger over the teenager's body or the memories it ignited, he walked out of the lounge without looking back. He headed instinctively for the smaller of the two bedrooms. This door too, was slightly ajar. He paused with one bloodstained, gloved hand on the doorframe.

A look of uncertainty flickered across his sweaty face. He stared at the door for quite a while, a frown burrowing dark lines into his features. Killing these people was a chore, and more than a little unsettling, but that was not what stayed his hand. An image of Vanessa formed in the back of his mind; her dreadfully sad look unmistakable and undistorted by time. The spectral image seemed to waver, and suddenly, in her place, Lisa was staring at him, her look of horror enough to draw the hairs up on his arms. Her black, gaping maw formed soundless words, pleading. As the vision faded, he glimpsed her eyes turning flame red, and her mouth contorting with rage.

He drew a long, shaky breath, then planted his palm firmly on the door and pushed it open.

He slowly crept towards the bed. It was as he noticed it to be empty that a screech jolted him and caused him to spin around. Haley had been hiding behind the door and now launched herself at him.

Han caught the flailing child in mid jump, dropping his knife in the process. She slapped him in the face with enough strength to cast stars dancing across his vision. Then her small hands grabbed his throat and started to throttle him.

Han staggered backwards, gasping, "Christ! Fuck!"

Haley was laughing a high-pitched squeal as she ferociously tried to choke the life out of him.

Han managed to tear her off him and threw her across the room. She slammed into a wardrobe and the cheap flat pack furniture folded in on itself, the door and sides landing in a heap on top of the child.

Haley growled and shoved the panels aside.

Han dashed over and as her head emerged, eyes glaring, he grabbed it and gave one savage twist. There was an audible crack and the child struggled no more.

Han recoiled from the body and his hands shot up to his mouth. He bit down on his knuckle to stifle a sob and tears rolled down his cheeks.

He turned away from the dead child, unable to bear looking at her. He was shaking uncontrollably.

Still sobbing, he stumbled into the hall and back into the kitchen. Still trembling, he poured himself a glass of water and gulped it down. He coughed then retched, dropping the glass in the process. It smashed at his feet, but he was oblivious as he held his head in his hands and wept.

"Come on Tam, if yer wanna lock in, get yourself along to the Duck," Big Joe said to Tam's slumped form on the edge of the bar. There was still good humour in his tone, but it was starting to wear thin. He folded his arms over the top of his big stomach. After a moment, the old timer grunted, stepped shakily down from his stool and made a poor attempt at straightening his overcoat.

Lisa trudged through from the lounge, yawning. Flashing Christmas tree earrings dangled from her lobes, but her demeanour lacked the cheer the novelty earrings suggested.

"Git yourself away, lass," he told her.

Leaning against the bar, she stifled another yawn and said, "Do you mind if I wait for Han? I was hoping he'd be back by now."

"Nae botha," Big Joe replied with a shrug. "Where's he been the neet? He missed Martha's minced pies."

"Said he had a couple of people to see in Rothbury — research for the book."

"Lucky he's got that jeep of his, with this foul weather." Big Joe watched Tam as he slumped back against the stool, mumbling to himself. Shaking his head, he said to Lisa, "I'm sure Martha'll make a fresh batch tomorrow."

Lisa rubbed the back of her aching neck and nodded, too tired to respond.

Tam finally struggled back to his feet and muttered something that might have been a goodnight while he wrapped a moth-eaten scarf around his scrawny neck. He shuffled precariously to the door and left without another word. Snow had been gathering up against the door and flakes blew in as the old man forced his way out into the storm.

"Be careful, Tam!" Big Joe shouted after him.

The door slammed shut behind him. Tam pulled his coat tight around his frail form as he shuffled through the deep snow. The icy wind whipped his thinning grey hair into a frenzy and blasted his ruddy, broken-veined cheeks. At the intersection with Miller's Road, a dark figure was waiting for him.

Tam stopped, the wind rocking him unsteadily on his feet. He stared at the figure through rheumy eyes and smiled. It was a thin, humourless smile. "What do you want?"

Han wiped fresh tears and melting snow from his face and moved closer to him to ensure that the old man would hear him clearly over the gusting wind. "What do you think I want, you mean old bastard?"

Tam laughed; it was more like a cackle, bearing what stained teeth remained in his mouth. "My turn, eh?"

Drawing the knife from under his jacket, Han sneered, "Let's just say; there may be trouble ahead."

Damn your love, damn your lies.

The lights flickered as Big Joe locked the front door. Glancing up to the ceiling, he muttered, "Ah shite, that's all we need."

"I've never seen it as bad as this," Lisa said from her slouched position on one of the bar stools. She was staring wistfully at one of the curtained windows, resting her chin in the palm of her hand.

Big Joe paused, listening to the low howl of the storm raging outside. "Aye, worst un I've seen in maybe twenty years."

"Looks like Bedford Falls out there, eh?"

Big Joe had to think for a minute then smiled. "Oh, aye." Attempting a James Stewart impression, he added, "You want the moon, Mary?"

179

Lisa laughed at the attempt. "Stick to the day job, Joe."

"Bloody cheek," Big Joe said then laughed with her.

A frown touched the edges of Lisa's tired features. "God, I hope Han's okay."

The landlord turned to her and offered her a reassuring smile. "Dunna ye worry. Han'll be fine. If he didn't get away from Rothbury in time, he'll just have to stay the night. There's plenty folk'll put him up."

Lisa lifted her head off her hand and returned the smile. "Thanks, Joe," she said sincerely.

Scratching his stomach, Big Joe yawned and said, "Right I better get off to bed before Martha starts wondering where I've got to."

"Don't worry, she won't." Han was standing in the doorway which led to the kitchen and staircase. His dark clothes were wet, crumpled and torn in a couple of places. Darker stains were spattered across his chest, legs and arms, and several smeared spots of blood were visible on his forehead and cheeks, despite the moisture from snow, sweat and tears. He was just finishing off a hastily hacked piece of homemade bread that he had swiped on the way through from the kitchen to satiate his grumbling stomach. It helped calm his fraught nerves, a little.

Big Joe and Lisa both performed a double take before recognising the panting, animal-like man lurking in the doorway, gulping down the remnants of some bread.

Big Joe frowned. "Han? Is that you? Ye look like you've been dragged through a hedge backwards."

Lisa stared at him and he saw something behind her eyes, something like grief. She then seemed to suppress it and said, "Babe, what have you done?"

Han stepped further into the bar and wiped breadcrumbs off his wet beard. Reluctantly, he said, "Everyone's dead. I killed them." As he spoke he felt his anxiety rise once more, and with it, dread.

"This is *Haydon*, laddie," Big Joe said, shaking his head. "Ye have no idea what you've done."

180

Han ignored Big Joe and continued to stare at Lisa. Her features were changing subtly, something simmering below the surface. "I killed Tess and Mandy too," he said apologetically.

"Martha?" Big Joe asked and took a step towards him.

Han now looked at the landlord and nodded sadly. "Yeah, her too."

Big Joe's jaw flexed. "Ye shouldn't have done that."

A tear dripped from one of Lisa's eyes.

Han stepped closer and sighed. "I'm sorry."

"No, but you will be." In one fluid motion, Big Joe swiped up an ashtray from the bar and swung it at Han's head.

Han stepped back and brought his own weapon up in a short upward swipe, tearing open Big Joe's forearm and cutting his faded thistle tattoo in half.

The landlord grimaced, but did not break off the attack. With his uninjured arm, he shoved Han backwards. His jowly face contorted into a maniacal grin. "Naebody fucks with Haydon."

Han stumbled into a table, but was surging forward again in seconds as Big Joe switched the ashtray to his good hand.

Lisa folded her arms and without conviction, muttered, "No … please." The words were hollow, lifeless.

Big Joe started to bring the ashtray down to connect with the top of Han's head, but the younger man was a fraction quicker. Han stuck the knife into the landlord's fat stomach, causing a short, sharp gasp to escape Big Joe's blue, snarling lips.

The ashtray clattered to the floor as Lisa looked on and shook her head.

"*Bastard* …" Big Joe uttered and threw his hands around Han's throat.

Han tore the knife loose, splattering blood across the bar and floor. As Big Joe sagged, Han jabbed the knife in his throat.

Big Joe's eyes rolled into the back of his head as he keeled over against the bar. The cherrywood bar creaked with the impact from his shoulder and head, clinking glasses stacked on the shelves behind. With the front of his shirt awash, and the colour literally draining from his features, Big Joe slid face forward into a crumpled, dead heap.

Lisa slowly began clapping.

Han turned to her, frowning. Every goddamn person in Haydon was weird, but for some reason he thought Lisa would be different ... normal.

He walked over to her and said, "Everyone's acting bloody strange in this place, princess."

She stopped clapping and folded her arms once more. "That's what happens when you try to fuck with Haydon, *babe*."

"What is it with this *Haydon* bullshit?" Han asked, anger getting the better of his fraught nerves.

"Just tell me one thing," Lisa said in a low, even tone, "you haven't harmed my angel."

Han stopped, mere feet away. "Angel?" he said, incredulously. "Fucking angel? Demon more like!"

There was a moment of complete silence. Lisa did not move, nor even breathe.

"Look," Han said, "I didn't mean for ... us to happen. I'm sorry, okay?"

Lisa remained deathly still.

"It's nothing personal, Lisa, but I've got to keep emotion out of this." He was genuinely apologetic, but also beginning to feel a rising fear. Continuing, he added, "If it's any consolation, I tried to make it quick for Haley, I really did."

What came at him was scarcely human. Claws and teeth and hissing. Wide-eyed, Han slashed out with the knife again and again, backing up the whole time as the woman whom he had shared a bed with tried to rip his face off.

Lisa finally collapsed, bleeding profusely from multiple stab and slash wounds. Still, she tried to crawl across the floor towards him, her eyes staring into Han's soul.

Han stepped back, panting and bleeding. He levelled the knife, but then Lisa finally stopped moving and her head slumped against the floor. Her eyes continued to stare at him, lifeless, but filled with hate.

But now old friends are acting strange,
They shake their heads, they say I've changed ...

182

With hunched shoulders and knife dangling loosely by his side, Han backed up to the bar, not daring to take his eyes off Lisa for a second. Only once he was behind the bar did he look away long enough to fill up a half pint glass with whiskey.

His hand was trembling as he brought the glass to his lips. It stopped an inch away from his mouth as he caught his reflection in the mirror behind the row of optics. His face was pale and sweating with smears of fresh blood drying on his cheeks and in his beard. He had several angry red scratches from Lisa's terrifying assault and dark, bruised rings encircled bloodshot auburn eyes.

He stared deep into the eyes that reflected back at him, studying them, venturing well beyond them. Tears welled up then dribbled down his cheeks. Suddenly his head began to spin and his legs felt like leaden weights. He slammed the glass down hard, splashing some of the whiskey on the bar. His hands covered his face as he sobbed uncontrollably.

Kicking and a' gouging in the mud and the blood and the beer.
Despite having been closed for a couple of hours, the Duck & Bucket still had several patrons sat in the bar at various stages of inebriation. In addition to Geordie behind the bar, Simon and Kim were sitting with their son, Danny at one of the small tables in the corner and Duncan and Loretta were sitting at the bar.

Cilla Black was singing on the jukebox.

Something tells me something's gonna happen tonight …

Downing the dregs of his pint of lager, Geordie said, "Anyone dry?"

Knocking back the rest of his pint, Duncan cheerfully said, "Another pint of your finest bitter, barkeep, and a white wine for the lady!"

"Aye, two more here too, Geordie," Simon said, referring to himself and Danny, who was looking pale and staring down at the three quarters of a pint still in front of him.

Kim glanced at Danny then turned to Geordie. "Don't get Danny another – I'll take him home in a bit. I'll have a quick gin and tonic though before I go."

"Oh, baby, something tells me ..." Duncan sang merrily along with Cilla, to Loretta's mild amusement.

"I'm fine," Danny slurred and carefully clutched his pint in both hands to help steady the pitching and drifting room.

Geordie grunted and shook his head. "Think your ma's right there, Dan. Bedtime for you like, you fuckin' lightweight."

As Geordie began filling pint, the lights flickered once and then died. With them, the music was also abruptly silenced, and the twinkling fairy lights on the rather small, skeletal Christmas tree in the bay window winked out. Looking up from the half filled glass, he glanced around the room that was now swathed in darkness. "Bollocks."

"This crap happens almost every year round here when the weather turns particularly bad," the shadowy form of Duncan said, with mild irritation.

"You could've just told us to sup up, Geordie!" Simon shouted from the darkness. "This is a bit extreme!"

"Anyone know if Tess kept any candles or a torch anywhere?" Geordie asked, setting the pint aside and scrutinising the gloomy shelves below the bar. "Cannat see shite, man."

"I think ... I'm gunna ... be sick," Danny uttered through a salivating mouth, staggering to his feet in a hurry and knocking his stool clattering to the floor.

"Hang on, nee one move till I get some light on the situation."

Kim fumbled for her son's arm in the gloom. "Don't worry, Geordie, I'll take him to the toilet. Don't want him redecorating in here."

"Didn't Tess used to keep some candles in the cupboard under the till?" Loretta asked no one in particular. "I'm sure that's where she got them from when this happened in January."

As Geordie fumbled around in the darkness, Kim helped Danny towards the toilets.

"I still can't believe she's gone," Lorretta muttered, looking down at her nearly empty glass of wine.

Duncan groped for her hand in the darkness and gave it a squeeze. "Aye, this kind of thing doesn't happen in Haydon, love."

"Gunna be sick," Danny muttered as he and his mother clumsily made their way through the gloom. "Gunna be—" His voice was cut short by a distinctive whoosh, followed immediately by a slicing of flesh and the briefest, soft gurgle.

Danny, suddenly a dead-weight, toppled, taking the much smaller Kim with him. She landed heavily on his stomach, confused and dazed. "Danny?" Feeling up his chest, her hands touched warm stickiness. Her voice shrill, she repeated, "Danny!"

"Kim? Danny?" Simon called, standing up and squinting towards his wife's voice. "What's wrong?"

Duncan and Loretta both got to their feet too at the sound of Kim's penetrating voice.

"Found some candles!" Geordie said. "All of you just stay calm!"

"*Kim*," a voice whispered in her ear, hot breath a mere inch away. The darkness and picking Danny off so easily lent Han some of his lost confidence. It was short-lived.

He had expected Kim to recoil in horror, but instead, she turned to face him and whispered back, "Good of you to join us, Mr Whitman."

Han sucked in a breath and stabbed her in the face, taking a step backwards in the process.

She screamed and it felt like his brain was vibrating inside his skull. She came at him and he stabbed her again and again until she collapsed.

Simon cast aside a chair and the table and rushed in the direction of his wife and son, bellowing in a voice alien to the man's small frame, "How *dare* you!"

Duncan forcibly detached himself from Loretta's and headed towards the Littles. "Si, I'm with you!"

With a sinking feeling and a flurry of regrets for accepting the temporary job, Geordie hastily pulled out a candle and box of matches from the cupboard below the till. Quickly, but calmly, he lit up a candle.

185

As the darkness lifted a notch, Simon stopped short of stumbling over the bodies of his wife and son. They were lying together, seemingly embracing each other in death. Despite the poor, almost liquid light, Simon recognised the blood and stillness immediately. "No ... no, no, no," he said over and over as he turned to face the figure bearing down on him.

Han grabbed him on the chin with one sticky glove and pulled Simon towards him. The baker came willingly, sneering and lashing out with his fists. Han blocked one, but the second grazed his temple, stalling his attack.

Duncan smashed a glass against the bar and rushed forward, swinging the jagged glass at Han's neck. Han stepped back at the last moment and the glass plunged into Simon's face, opening up his cheek and bursting an eye.

"Sorry, Si," Duncan muttered, turning to Han.

Simon raised a hand to his ravaged face and shook his head. "That hurt, you plank."

Han swiped the glass out of Duncan's hand and head-butted him. As he stumbled back, nose bloodied, Han slashed open his throat and then kicked him in the chest. Duncan fell back, slipping in the pooled blood and his head caught the edge of a table with a sickening crack.

"Duncan!" Loretta cried then took a sip of her wine.

Geordie had set the candle down and was staring at the ensuing chaos. "Who the fuck is that?" Instinctively, he grabbed an empty bottle of *Newcastle Brown Ale* from a crate at his feet and proceeded to smash the base of it off the bar top. "You fuckin' want some, do you?" His eyes flicked from the intruder to Loretta calming drinking wine then back to Han.

Simon was stepping forward, spitting blood and covering his oozing eye. Han moved in to meet him and rammed the knife through his hand and into his already ruined eye. With effort, it slid all the way to the hilt. Simon twitched and his one good eye stared unblinking at Han.

Han cast Simon's body aside and turned to Geordie and Loretta. His rising anxiety was suddenly joined by the crushing weight of exhaustion. He sagged, knife dangling by his side.

Geordie planted one hand on the bar and vaulted over. "Come on then, motherfucker!" Without taking his eyes off the intruder, he added, "What the fuck is going on? Who is this twat?"

Loretta glanced up from her empty glass and, with an irritated flick of her hair, said, "Han Whitman."

Geordie scrunched up his face and said, "The fucking writer?"

With considerable effort, Han sheathed the knife and drew out the Walther. He wasn't going to take any chances with the Byker Brawler.

"Fuck." Geordie tore his eyes away from the pistol long enough to glance at Loretta. "You just gonna sit there, like?"

She shrugged, but otherwise did nothing.

Turning back to Han, he growled, "What is your fuckin' malfunction?"

Han sighed and managed a tired smile. "Get the fuck off my obstacle, Private Pile."

"Eh?"

The crack of the pistol discharging in the confined space left a ringing in their ears. Geordie flinched, half ducking at the sound, but Loretta just continued to sit there, playing with her wine glass. Geordie recovered immediately and glanced at the smashed optic behind the bar.

The shot had gone wide, but there was something hugely satisfying about finally discharging the Walther. It was almost as if the handgun completed him somehow and it certainly seemed to immediately improve his mood and his energy.

Acknowledging that he was out of options, Geordie took the only chance he had; he surged forward screaming, "COME ON!"

It took a fraction of a second to adjust his aim. Geordie had cleared the distance in no time, but, as he swiped the broken bottle towards Han's head, the gun spoke first.

The bullet tore through his throat and exited out the other side, lodging in the bar a couple of feet from Loretta, who glanced at it and then back to her glass. Geordie's momentum carried him forward into Han and both men fell to the floor with a scrambling clatter.

On top, and with blood pumping out of his throat, Geordie snarled through red teeth, spitting blood in Han's face. Struggling with the skinhead's solid weight, Han squirmed to pull the pistol out from under his thigh.

"… Kill *yeee* …" Geordie spluttered, blood and saliva dribbling down his chin in gooey threads. The bottle lost, he struggled to bring his hands up to Han's throat.

As Geordie's slimy hands tightened around his neck, Han managed to dislodge the pistol from under his leg. The barman's grip was vice-like, despite his wound and immediately caused Han to gag. With rising panic, he yanked the gun up to Geordie's temple and pulled the trigger. The recoil nearly jerked the pistol clean out of his hand as Geordie's head was wrenched to one side with the impact.

Blood pumped out of the entry hole in Geordie's temple and brains and splinters of skull spilled out of the exit wound and splashed on the floor. Self-control forgotten, Han thrashed out, shoving the barman's still twitching body off him and struggled to his feet. He blinked and coughed from his near throttling, holding his red throat with his free hand and the still smoking pistol in the other.

Loretta shook her head and pushed her empty glass away.

Breathing heavily, the fatigue returned with a vengeance, burrowing into every joint and muscle with an unchecked tenacity. It had been a long night and there was still plenty yet to do. But at least the worst was over. His thoughts returned to Lisa momentarily; her face; cute, sexy, smiling, but then it transformed into the creature that leaped at him, clawing and screeching. Although banished almost as quickly as it had appeared, its presence left its mark, tainting him. Gritting his teeth, Han walked over towards the Duck's last living occupant with pistol in hand.

Loretta turned around from the bar and stared at him. There was no emotion in her eyes and she said, "Welcome to Haydon."

Han shot her in the forehead.

chapter 11

Two's company, three's a bloodbath.

The dimmed spotlights and shag pile rug in front of a burning fireplace mingled with the gentle tones of Elvis Presley to offer a warm glow to Steve Belmont's living room.

> *I just can't help believin',*
> *When she smiles up soft and gentle,*
> *With a trace of misty morning,*
> *And the promise of tomorrow in her eyes ...*

Steve padded across the floor in bare feet and a bathrobe, carrying two bubbling champagne flutes. Janet, also dressed in a bathrobe, was curled up on the leather sofa.

Handing her one of the glasses, Steve said, "Here you go, love."

"Storm's still raging out there," Janet replied dreamily. "I'll tell Larry that I stayed with Loretta, rather than walk back through that." She sipped the champagne and savoured the fizzing bubbles on her tongue.

Sitting down beside her, he gently caressed her flowing red hair and took a sip of his champagne. "Won't Loretta get pissed off with all the covering she's doing for you?"

Pushing a hand between the folds of Steve's robe, Janet stroked his hairy chest while contemplating the question. After another sip, she said, "Loretta knows that I'm going to leave Larry and that I'm just waiting for the right moment. She's not happy about the lying, but she's doing it for me, as my friend."

"She's a good friend."

"Yes, she is." Turning to him, she looked deep into his granite eyes and said, with mounting emotion, "We're doing the right thing, aren't we? I mean, what's best for everyone, including Larry?" Her eyes were beseeching.

Steve moved his hand from her hair and touched the side of her hot cheek. "Of course, love. You two haven't been happy for years, so it's going to be best all round. It'll be hard for Larry and Kerris at first, but once the shock is out of the way, everyone will be much happier in the long run." He kissed her on the lips, then added, "I love you and I want to spend the rest of my life with you."

Closing her eyes, with a dreamy smile on her lips, she leant forward to return the kiss. She maintained the embrace for a moment then eased herself up, saying, "Just going to freshen up a little."

Steve nodded and flashed a warm smile as she walked into the hallway to the bathroom, dabbing the corner of one eye with the sleeve of her robe.

Finishing off his glass, Steve stood up and headed back across the room. The kitchen was partitioned from the living room by a solid breakfast bar with a couple of bar stools.

He set the glass aside on the worktop and crossed to the refrigerator to retrieve the bottle. As he opened it, a noise caught his attention from the living room. The King had been halfway through *Bridge Over Troubled Water* when the music abruptly stopped after the line, *I'll take your part, oh, when darkness comes.* Glancing over his shoulder, he saw Han standing in the middle of the room and looking at him. Muddy water was pooling at his feet.

Steve stood staring for a moment and then the spell broke. "Whitman." With a growl, he added, "You made a big fucking mistake coming here."

Wisps of steam were starting to rise from his wet clothes as he stood there and forced a smile. "I'm going to murder you and your whore, Janet," Han said. Surely, here was a tosser that he could get some real pleasure in killing. There had been a lot of shocks – and more than a few genuine scares – along the way, but surely he could enjoy this one.

Standing, naked, save for the bathrobe, Steve considered his options, whilst taking a gulp of champagne from the bottle. He wiped his mouth with the back of his hand and said, "Well, you'll just have to settle for me, dickhead. Janet's not here."

190

Han took a moment to glance around the room then shrugged. "Ah well, not to worry." Trying to conjure up some enthusiasm, he raised the pistol and aimed it at Steve's chest.

Steve eyed the gun whilst taking another drink of champagne. "So, what's it all about, Alfie?"

Janet was about to step out of the bathroom when she registered the two voices. She froze, hand on door handle, frowning.

Waving the gun dismissively, Han said, "It's nothing personal, Steve. Although, unlike a lot of the others, I will quite enjoy this one." As an afterthought, he added, "You're a arsehole, Steve. That should be reason enough."

Only a slight twitch betrayed Steve's irritation. "Fuck you, Whitman." Then with a snort, he added, "Think you're friggin' tough coming in here waving a gun about? You're nowt but a coward. Put that gun down and let's settle this like men. I'll fucking show you who's the boss round here, you little runt." He stepped up to the threshold between the two rooms.

Han actually managed a proper laugh, cocking his head to one side with amusement. "Nah, I have neither the time, nor the inclination for a roll around in the hay with you ... not after the fucking night I've had. So, let me just say, fuck you, eh?" With that, he fired.

The bullet tore into Steve's shoulder, spinning him round. Cursing, he dropped to the floor and ducked behind the breakfast bar. Clutching the rapidly widening patch of red spreading through the robe, Steve shouted, "You dirty little bastard! I'm gunna kill you!"

Janet clamped a hand over her mouth, which at first looked like it was to stifle a scream, but it was actually a snigger. She quietly back away from the door.

Rolling his eyes, Han let out a sigh and walked towards the kitchen. "Steve, I can't be bothered with this shit, man. It's been a long night ... a long, weird, fucked up night ... and I've still got a few more to sort before I can get some sleep."

"Well, sorry for making your life difficult, you whiny little prick," Steve said.

Pausing, Han touched the tip of the Walther to his chin and savoured the burnt, acidy whiff emanating from the barrel. "I know you were gonna pay Jimmy to burn down that shithole of a car lot so you and Janet could skip off into the sunset together."

Steve raised an eyebrow and cocked his head up. "You have been a sneaky little twat, haven't you?"

Han took a step closer then said, "You'll be glad to know that I'm still going to burn the place down for you, but I'm also going to stick yours and Janet's bodies in there so everyone can find out about your sordid little affair."

Grimacing as he touched the seeping wound in his shoulder, Steve said, "What do I care? I'll be dead. Tell me, why do you want to kill people in Haydon anyway? Why Haydon?"

Closing the gap, Han said, "No point in explaining it to you, Steve. You're about to die, so it's not really that important to you. Plus, I'm not really the monologuing type; I'll leave that to the Bond villains."

Glancing round the kitchen worktops for inspiration, Steve muttered, "Nee botha, mate, but I've got news for you, Haydon doesn't die so easily." His eyes fell upon the champagne bottle mere inches away. He grabbed it, wincing at the flaring pain in his shoulder. He shifted into a crouch on his haunches and waited. Pins and needles ran down the length of his arm and exploded in a hot tingling sensation in the tips of his fingers.

"Come out, come out, wherever you are," Han said in a low whisper, beginning to enjoy himself. "Or I'll huff and I'll puff and I'll blow your fucking brains out."

As he reached to within a foot of the breakfast bar, Steve jumped to his feet and lashed out with the bottle. The base whooshed past Han's nose, clipping the bridge and drawing a trickle of blood.

Han backed off, saying, "Easy tiger, you very nearly took my head off there."

Steve didn't bother with further dialogue. He roared and threw himself over the worktop.

Han stepped back hastily and opened fire twice in quick succession. The two rounds punched Steve in the chest, stalling his advance and leaving him in a crumpled slouch over the worktop. One hand swung limply over the edge and, after the second swing, the bottle slipped out of his grip and smashed on the laminate floor. Blood oozed from the gunshot wounds, pooling on the worktop and dribbling down the lounge side of the breakfast bar.

"Well, you died pretty easily, shithead," Han said and turned away to make a sweep of the flat. Swinging the door open to the bathroom, he peered in and scanned the spacious room, checking behind the door and casting a brief glance at the freestanding bath.

He hovered in the doorway, scrutinising the gloomy room and listening intently for some time. Content, he finally withdrew.

Janet lay still in the bath for several minutes, eyes closed and breathing softly.

After a time, she opened her eyes and smiled. She climbed out and tip-toed into the hallway. The front door at the bottom of the stairs was ajar, with snow gusting in through the gap.

She then walked into the lounge and looked at Steve's body draped over the breakfast bar. A wide patch of blood had spread out from base.

"Oh, Steve," she muttered softly, shaking her head. "What did the bad man do to you?"

Thumping footsteps sounded from the staircase.

Janet turned to the doorway, hands on hips. "Eager for seconds," she said and licked her lips.

Carol Belmont appeared in the doorway, her drenched hair plastered messily to her head and her thin denim jacket soaked through. Her cheeks and nose were bright red from the cold, but they could not mask her accusing glare. "Shouldn't you be with your husband, you whore?"

Janet feigned a hurt expression.

Carol stormed into the room towards her. "The door was open, so don't even st—" She stopped suddenly as she saw Steve's blood-drenched body. "What the ... Steve? *Steve!*" She rushed forward and clutched his limp arms, skidding briefly in the man's pooled blood. She grabbed a hand that was sticky where blood had dribbled down his arm from the shoulder wound. Despite having cried herself dry earlier, tears still managed to squeeze out of her inflamed tear ducts as her unhinged mind soaked in the scene. She tenderly lifted his head and looked into his staring, dead eyes.

Oblivious to all the blood, she threw her arms across his back and buried her face into the soft material of his robe. Muffled sobs wracked her body, sending violent shivers down her arched back.

Sighing, Janet said, "Han Whitman has taken it upon himself to murder the good people of Haydon."

Carol turned her damp, crimson face towards the timid voice. "And he just let *you* live did he?" The venom in her voice was unmistakable.

"I was in the bathroom. He didn't see me," Janet replied matter-of-factly.

Still holding on to Steve, Carol hissed, "So you hid while Steve was murdered?"

Janet stepped towards her. "It's sensible to pick your battles, Carol. You know that."

"Why don't you just fuck off and cower in some stinking hole while your doting husband is murdered too?"

Janet's mouth opened with dawning realisation. "Ah yes, Larry … Kerris … oh, not *Kerris*." She turned and ran towards the bedroom, casting off the bathrobe along the way, unaware and uncaring of her nakedness or the cold.

As Janet quickly dressed, Carol entered behind her. "So, Larry is worth saving, but Steve wasn't?" She stared with disgust at Janet's toned and tanned, naked backside as she threw on a blouse.

Without looking up from the leather skirt she was now pulling up over her thighs, Janet said, "Fuck you, Carol. I don't have to explain myself to you."

"Might've been an idea to explain it to your husband or daughter though!" Carol fired back, clenching her fists into tight balls.

194

Janet paused while zipping up the skirt. She shot Carol a searing glare. "That's none of your business, you withered old cow."

As Janet finished dressing, Carol stomped over to the trimphone on the bedside cabinet. "Bitch," she muttered under her breath as she picked up the handset and pressed 999.

After tugging on high heeled boots, Janet wrapped up in a coat and a silk scarf.

"Shit!" Carol spat. "No dial tone."

Janet headed for the door. "Shocker," she muttered, her tone laced with mock surprise.

"Well, I'm coming with you!"

Janet cast an irritated glance over her shoulder. "Do I give a shit?"

The crows do a nice line in withering irony.

Janet and Carol fought their way out into the blizzard, Janet setting the pace at a confident stride, seemingly impervious to the treacherous conditions. The storm showed no signs of abating and snow had piled up into great drifts against the darkened buildings and scattered cars. The black sky was a torrent of gusting snow. The village had a desolate, menacing feel, like the stone and bricks themselves were silently plotting.

The deep drifts made for slow progress as the two women made their way towards the Herring household. There was no other living soul in sight, nor a single beacon of light to temper the darkness.

As they arrived, with Janet leading, they found the front door open and several inches of snow gathering in the hallway.

"He wouldn't ... not Kerris," Janet said, wiping dripping stands of hair out of her eyes. Her scarf and coat were encrusted with snow.

As Janet stepped across the threshold, Carol, shivering, both from the freezing temperatures and from tattered nerves, grabbed her shoulder. Whispering, she said, "He might still be in there?"

Janet turned and glared at her. With an even tone, she uttered, "Then we kill him."

The intensity in Janet's eyes caused Carol to take a step back. Hesitantly, she said, "Okay."

Janet walked in first, caution slowing her steps. Thoughts of Steve were forgotten and Larry's face only lingered a moment. Her thoughts were filled with Kerris and Kerris alone.

With a mixture of fear and impatience, Carol said, "Well, go if you're going."

She had not realised that she had stopped completely. Without turning, Janet snapped, "Shut the fuck up." Then, slowly, she stepped forward.

The hallway and living room were both in darkness, but the kitchen ahead of them, its door open a crack, was well lit. Glancing briefly in the living room, she continued forward to the kitchen. Carol followed, her grim, dripping features apprehensive. Her chattering teeth were impossibly loud in the uneasy silence.

Janet placed a hand on the door and, holding her breath, she pushed it inwards.

The air already filling her lungs was joined by another sharp intake of breath, accompanied by a torturous croak. Larry was sitting at the table, facing the door, with a disposable syringe poking out of each eye and a neat slice across his Adam's apple. Blood had trickled from the corners of his eyes and poured down his chest from the neck wound. His favourite *Led Zeppelin* t-shirt was drenched all the way down to the crotch of his jeans.

Sitting in the second chair, was Janet's nine year old daughter, Kerris. She was dressed in her favourite woolly jumper that her Nan had knitted for her last Christmas. Her head had dropped forward, her long, wavy chestnut hair obscuring her face. The blood that had seeped down her chest, with shocking similarity to her father's, was as appalling as it was unmistakable.

Hyperventilating, Janet stumbled forward, uttering, "Kerris? Baby?" She savagely cast one of the chairs aside, which crashed into the cupboards. Bile rose up in her throat, forcing her to gag noisily.

Carol walked in behind her and gasped at the horrific sight of the doctor's and young girl's murdered bodies, sitting as if waiting for dinner to be served. "Jesus Christ! What the hell is going on here?" She backed up, slamming hard against the doorframe. The impact caused her to cry out involuntarily, screeching, "No, please!" Realising it was just the doorframe and not the murderer, she drew in a shaky breath.

Wrenching her eyes away from studying every minute detail of Janet's dead family, Carol glanced around the room. But one urge took over, as it often did in times of crisis. Spying the refrigerator, she headed straight for it as Janet stood, sagging in front of her dead daughter, her trembling hands gripping the edge of the table in an effort to stay upright on her rubbery legs.

"*My baby* ..." Janet's voice sounded pathetic and isolated. She didn't even realise that the voice was her own. She was transfixed with the top of her daughter's head, willing her to move; just a twitch ... anything.

"I need a drink," Carol muttered, gulping down the taste of bile in her own throat. Opening the refrigerator, she plucked out a nearly empty bottle of chardonnay. The cold bottle trembled in her hand she studied it for a moment, her thoughts suddenly consumed by the small amount of wine sloshing in the bottom. Yanking the cork out, she raised it to her lips.

Suddenly, Janet appeared at her side and viciously swiped the bottle out of Carol's weak grip. "You drink enough." Her words were distant and her eyes were fixed on a point beyond the confines of the kitchen. Without pausing, she up-ended the contents into her dry mouth, gulping down every last drop.

"You bitch. I need a drink!" Carol spat and pushed her love rival back with a hard shove. It was born more from frustration and fear, than real anger.

Janet opened her mouth to reply, but her features turned first to confusion, and then contorted with pain. The bottle dropped out of her hands and smashed on the tiled floor. She flashed a seething glare towards her dead husband.

Still irate, but frowning, Carol said, "What's the matter?"

Wheezing and clawing at her skin, Janet suddenly began to convulse. Her legs buckled and she fell to the floor, twitching and foaming at the mouth. Her pallid, clammy skin rapidly turned blue.

Terrified, Carol backed away to the periphery of the room. "Janet? What's wrong?"

After several more seconds of thrashing, she abruptly stopped and her head lolled, lifeless to one side with her tongue protruding, purple and bloated.

Carol stood, staring at the unmoving woman in an ungraceful heap with her skirt hitched up to her waist and her intimate parts on show beneath the leather trim. She stared at the woman's vagina for a time. "Well, the carpet matches the curtains," she muttered to herself. Then, shaking her head, she said, "No ... this can't be happening ..." Her voice trailed off and she dropped to her knees in front of Janet. Spittle and foam had gathered in the corners of her mouth and on her chin, and her eyes had rolled back into her head, leaving gleaming white orbs staring madly towards the bodies of her husband and daughter.

Clasping her head in her hands, Carol bent forward, as if to pray to the East. With her head on the floor, close to Janet's, a low moan emanated from her rigid lips. Gradually, the pitching wail grew to a blackboard-scraping, raging squeal.

They're only red from all the tears that I should've shed ...

Tired, cold and aching, Han trudged slowly along the darkened corridor to his room. He opened the door with a trembling hand and all but fell into the room.

After locking the door behind him, he struggled out of his wet clothes and dropped like a dead weight onto his bed, oblivious of the ingrained blood on his hands and face. Shivering, he pulled the flap of the sleeping bag over his naked body and half-heartedly tugged at the zip. Without even the strength to shift his body to allow the zip to close, he abandoned it and hugged the two sides together instead.

The shivers took him for several long minutes as his aching body adjusted to the warmth and comfort of the bed. It had been a very long night, but, apart from the absolute weirdness of everything – and some of the residents being downright terrifying – it had, for the most part, been successful. He just had a few stragglers to finish off in the morning, plus a sweep through to ensure no fingerprints or incriminating evidence was left behind. Then, his little adventure and experiment would be finished. He could then go back to his life with Jumanji and *Movie Maniac*. A growing desperation to return to the life he once knew – to some sort of normality – took hold of him. Emotionally, he felt threadbare and nearing the bottom of his well.

He wondered absently, as sleep gently embraced him, calming his shattered nerves, how much poontang Perry had been getting while he had been away, and whether Ju would remember him after all these months. Ju, of course, would be delighted to see him, but Perry, on the other hand, well, that would be the end of his reign of power. Poor Perry; at least he'll have got his end away a few times while he'd been in charge. *My gift, to you ...*

As the darkness closed around him, the images of his scrawny friend and his fat, panting Labrador faded and were replaced by a parade of Haydon residents, led by a half rotting, badly stitched together, Mandy Foster, resembling Tim Burton's *Corpse Bride*. Tess Runckle followed, her head lolling at an obscene angle. Every other face passed by, including Sally Bryce, looking like Sissy Spacek at the end of the prom in *Carrie* and carrying Anthony's head, Moe with the hilt of a hunting knife protruding from his mouth like a swollen tongue, Steve Belmont with gaping, cartoon-style holes in his chest that offered glimpses of the next person in line. They all had different injuries, but they all bore one identical characteristic – the empty, black sockets for eyes.

Finally, the cold, dead face of Lisa appeared before him, her eyeless sockets empty chasms. Her grey lips pulled back to bare a set of yellow impossibly over-sized fangs. The black hollows of her eyes suddenly lit up in flames. An intense fire burned within them, captivating him as the sneer grew into a gaping roar.

chapter 12

22nd December. *The morning after the night before.*

Having awakened from a restless, tormented sleep, lying on the stone floor next to the bodies of his wife and child, Bryce stiffly forced himself to his feet. He had no recollection of drifting off to sleep, but his body had clearly needed it. Stretching his back, with his senses returning to him, he stared at his dead son and felt a burning fury rise up inside him.

His stomach grumbled for attention, but that only fuelled his anger. Rummaging through his jacket, he retrieved a crumpled packet of cigarettes and lit one, drawing deeply on it.

Using the now weak beam of the flashlight, he located the shotgun. After a cursory inspection, he ejected the spent cartridges and reloaded. He paused to glance towards the far wall where his small wine rack lay with several shattered bottles lying in pieces in a pool of red wine. In the gloom it looked just like more blood to Bryce, and he couldn't help but glance back at his dead son.

Tearing his attention away, he continued to scrutinise the rest of the cellar. He spied a hatchet on his cluttered workbench and, hanging on a hook beside the bench, his tool belt. He clipped the belt round his waist and slipped the hatchet into one of the spare loops.

He was not surprised to find the door jammed. In the back of his mind, he had the vague recollection of a crashing clatter as he fell through the doorway, which he had been fairly sure wasn't just his bulk thundering down the stairs.

Several attempts at connecting his shoulder to the door resulted in a slight cracking of wood and a bruised shoulder. Frustrated, he raised both barrels of the Webley and stepped down a couple of steps.

He took aim at the handle and catch and squeezed the triggers. The gun boomed and spat forth an orange tongue of flame, shredding a one foot square section of the door around the handle and adjacent frame.

Shards of light spilled in, distorted by the churning smoke. Coughing and dispersing the smoke with one hand, Bryce peered through the ragged hole. He could make out a couple of the logs barricading the door from the other side.

Cursing, he reloaded and took aim at the top hinge. The blast tore away the top corner of the door. Reloading quickly, he aimed at the bottom hinge and opened fire again.

The door spun ninety degrees with the weight of the logs behind it then dropped to one side. Ignoring the thick, pungent smoke, Bryce ducked through the opening and pushed aside several of the logs.

As he emerged into the hallway, he was bathed with dull morning light. Despite it being diminished somewhat by the continuing snowstorm outside, he still found himself squinting after his forced captivity in the darkness of the cellar.

He was covered in muck and dust, mingled with blotches of dried blood; some of it his own, some not. He had a graze and purple bruising across his forehead and the tears and snot had smeared muck into black streaks down his cheeks, lips and chin. He stood at the opening for a moment and spared a forlorn glance back towards the cellar, then headed straight for his gun cabinet.

Face down on his grimy sheets, Jimmy awoke with a sudden start. On reflex, one arm lurched upwards, knocking his lager can-come-ashtray off the edge of the bedside cabinet and sending it spinning across the already filthy floor. Ash and dog ends spilled out amongst the dirty clothes and rubbish.

He lifted his head with considerable effort and blearily gazed at the mess. "Fuckssake," he muttered then coughed several times. Sitting up, he wiped his snotty nose across the back of his hand and yawned. A tremor rippled down his spine as he coughed some more then spat a thick wad of mucus into a mouldy mug that he found down by the side of the bed.

He glanced in the bottom of the mug and cringed.

After setting the mug aside on the cabinet, he flung his legs off the side of the bed and struggled to his feet. A brief stretching caused the audible cracking and grinding of various joints. After another bout of coughing, he retrieved a damp packet of cigarettes from his coat and lit up.

Sluggishly, he made himself a cup of tea which had to be drunk black as the milk had gone sour. The hot drink, followed by another cigarette, caused him to rush to the toilet and empty his bowels noisily into the toilet.

He returned to the kitchen feeling almost human, but still a little shivery, and proceeded to pluck and gut the chickens from the night before, with his third and final cigarette now dangling from his dry lips.

He unceremoniously deposited the four carcasses into his grimy refrigerator and ran some cold water over his slimy fingers. Wiping them on his jeans, he then pulled on wet boots over holey socks and trudged over to the open door. He retrieved his coat on the way, also still wet from the night before.

He cast an irritated glance at the damaged door and muttered, "Prick," before heading out into the hallway.

Opening the door to the street, he discovered that snow was still falling heavily and the ground had a covering of more than a foot deep. The wind had died down somewhat, allowing the snow a more sedate descent. The sky was leaden, but the brilliant white offered a lustre to the scene that was quite breathtaking. Taking in the Disney Christmas, picture-postcard scene, he noticed with a hint of surprise, that there were no fresh footprints or car tracks to be seen on either the road or paths. Surely that weasel across the road, Lenny, would have been out walking that mongrel of his by now? His fat bossy wife made him go out with it come rain or shine.

He needed to find buyers for the chickens pretty sharpish, otherwise he'd have a pretty miserable Christmas. Who was he trying to kid? Every Christmas was a miserable Christmas. Father Christmas wasn't going to be dropping any presents down his chimney this year. Come to think of it, the fat bastard never had.

Pulling his collar up, Jimmy buried his hands into the damp pockets of his coat. After a loud sneeze, he headed down the street, squinting against the icy flakes.

Slivers of grey light poked through a thin gap in the floral curtains, offering a suggestion of the morning outside. The bedroom was small and cluttered with two single beds, wardrobe and a matching dressing table.

Sam Potter stirred in one of the beds, as Natalie rested soundlessly in the other. He let out a sigh as his blinking eyes adjusted to the poor light. Thoughts of his father flooded back, causing him to immediately sit up.

Checking his watch, he said, "Nats, w-wake up, hun. I-it's after e-eight-thirty." As Natalie muttered something inaudible, Sam jumped out of bed and began his routine of stretching exercises.

Rubbing sleep from her eyes, Natalie glanced over her shoulder to Sam, who had now dropped to the carpet and was rapidly performing push ups, to the creaking displeasure of the floorboards beneath. Her voice croaky, she said, "Jesus, Sam, can't you even miss *one* morning?"

Puffing, Sam replied, "No!"

As Sam moved on to sit ups, Natalie finally dragged herself out of the cosy bed, farting loudly in the process. "Oops," she said mildly.

Sam paused, mid-sit up and glanced at her. She smiled sweetly back at him. Rolling his eyes, he continued with his exercise.

Sitting on the edge of the bed in bra and knickers, Natalie rummaged through her cavernous shoulder bag, through lipsticks, deodorant, tampons, tissues and mobile phone to find a packet of cigarettes and lighter. After lighting, she took a long satisfying drag.

Catching a sniff of the smoke, Sam stopped abruptly again and stared at her. "I w-wish you wouldn't d-do that."

Natalie wrinkled her nose at him. "Ah, get over yourself! You're the health freak, not me."

Getting to his feet, Sam said, "B-but y-you pr-pr-pr-"

"I know," Natalie interrupted. "I'm trying, baby, I am. But it was a stressful night and it'll be a long day too, so just let me enjoy this one little scrap of happiness."

Sam sighed and grabbed a towel and a toiletry bag. "Just g-going to the bathroom. Be b-back in a minute."

Nodding, Natalie took a draw on her cigarette then said, "Shame their only en suite was taken."

Hot water had steamed up the small bathroom as Sam scrubbed his body with an exfoliating mitten. After washing thoroughly, he methodically rinsed off the shampoo and shower gel from his slim, toned body.

The door opened with a creak, causing Sam to pause with his hand hovering over the control dial for the shower. "Nats?" he asked, hesitantly.

A figure approached the frosted shower curtain, embossed with dolphins leaping across its surface. He felt the hairs on the back of his neck raise as the unannounced person approached. "Nats, i-is that y-you?" he asked again more sternly.

The curtain was suddenly yanked back to reveal Natalie dressed in a red and black silk kimono, grinning mischievously.

"Ha ha," Sam muttered derisively.

Glancing down at his groin, she smiled and wet her lips. "I think baby wants to play."

Smiling, despite himself, Sam said, "I'd love t-to, Nats, but we gotta s-see my dad first."

Natalie sighed and nodded. "I know, darling." Lifting her Kimono, she stepped over to the toilet and plonked her plump bottom onto it.

Sam had always been a little uncomfortable with Natalie using the toilet in front of him, so he towelled off quickly and headed back to the room to dress.

Sex for dinner, death for breakfast.

Once they had both dressed and packed, Sam and Natalie headed downstairs to the lounge with their bags. The country-style pub lounge was in darkness with the curtains still drawn and the Christmas decorations turned off.

Whispering, Sam said, "He w-was called J-Joe, right?"

Nodding, Natalie, loudly announced, "Joe, it's the Potters. Did you want us in the lounge for breakfast?"

Stopping in the middle of the lounge, they both listened for a reply from the kitchen. Silence. No sizzling bacon, no rummaging; no smells of cooking at all for that matter.

Frowning, Sam looked at his watch. "W-we said n-nine for breakf-fast. It's ten past n-now."

Natalie shook her head. "Not everyone's as anal as you about being on time *all* of the time."

"It's not a-a-anal at all. It's good m-manners."

Shrugging, Natalie muttered, "Whatever." Walking over to the doorway to the kitchen, she peered in, saying, "Hello, anyone there?" The kitchen was deserted and untouched. All utensils and pans were still neatly stored on racks and the surfaces cleaned to a gleaming shine. All except a single wooden chopping board with a few remaining crumbs. Turning, Natalie said, "I don't believe it; looks like they've slept in."

Sam's cheeks flushed. Agitated, he wrung his hands, saying, "Th-th-this is ri-r-idiculous. W-w-w-we p-p-p-"

"Don't worry, darling," Natalie intervened, cringing at how rapidly his stuttering could worsen. It pained her for him to be so unmercifully attacked in that way. Soothingly, she added, "It's no biggie."

"Y-y-yeah, bu-bu-but-"

"Sam," Natalie said sternly, walking back over to him. "It's not a crisis. We can pick up a sandwich from a shop on the way."

His lips pursed, Sam glanced around the room for a moment, before saying, "O-o-okay."

Grasping the handles of the holdall that Sam had dropped at his feet, Natalie headed through to the bar with her own backpack in her other hand. Sheepishly, Sam followed.

The bar was similarly dark and deserted, but as they rounded the corner of the bar, they caught sight of the bodies of Big Joe and Lisa. They both lay as they had fallen, both with wide, dry patches of blood spread out beneath them. Even at a distance, Natalie could tell by their colour that they had been dead for several hours.

She gasped and clamped a hand to her mouth, simultaneously dropping both bags at her feet. The noise of them hitting the wooden floor was like a gunshot in a graveyard.

"W-wha—" Sam started, but abruptly cut himself off when his eyes caught the reason for his wife's shock. "Oh my God!" he said and, in some distant part of his brain, was surprised at how clearly it came out.

Trembling, Natalie dashed over to the end of the bar where she had spied a red dial telephone. Grabbing the handset, she thrust it against her ear and dialled nine. She stopped with her finger about to dial it a second time. No dial tone. "*Shit,*" she hissed.

Sam fumbled in his jacket for his mobile. He was less than surprised to find no signal. "Sh-shit," he echoed. Glancing apprehensively around the room, his mind raced through their options.

Natalie turned to look at him, her expression taut with suppressed panic. "Let's just get the hell out of here. We can call the police on the way."

"G-good plan."

They both rushed to the front door, carefully stepping round Lisa's outstretched body. They tried not to look, but Sam couldn't help but notice how young and small she looked. So frail and so … dead. After fumbling with the lock and bolts, Sam yanked the door open. Flurries of snow blew in, and the build up of snow at the door tumbled inside in thick clods.

"Christ," Sam muttered. Shielding his eyes, he forced himself across the threshold. The breeze rippled over his short, mousy hair and blew flakes into his eyes. He quickly made his way to the thickly blanketed Fiesta.

Natalie stepped out into the street after him, but as she turned, squinting at the car, two arms reached out from behind her and yanked her violently back into the pub. The holdall dropped, half submerged into the snow, but the backpack was flung back through with her.

Sam reached the car and turned back to spur his wife on. Seeing that she wasn't behind him and that the holdall was dumped in the snow, Sam's already unravelling nerves stretched to breaking point. "Nats!" His voice was shrill and frantic.

Without waiting for a reply, and the car momentarily forgotten, Sam rushed back along the trench he had just made, back to the open doorway. Snow was scattered several feet inside the entrance, but there was no sign of Natalie.

Desperate, Sam stepped inside, shouting, "Nats!" He just caught a glimpse of Natalie struggling with a hand over her mouth and being dragged backwards by a figure dressed in black. They disappeared around the corner, heading into the lounge.

Rushing forward, he cried, "Let her go!"

As he reached the corner, Natalie was thrust into his arms. She was making gurgling noises and had a deep gash in her throat. "NO!" He grabbed her with both arms and she sagged against him, fighting for breath. Blood was gushing freely down between her cleavage.

Despite the wound, she managed to utter, "Run … my love." As he shook his head, refusing to leave her, her eyes rolled back into her head and the gurgling, wheezing sounds ebbed away.

"God, no, please!" he wailed, cradling her in his arms, rocking gently back and forth.

"Picked the wrong weekend for an impromptu visit, friend," Han said, stepping out from an alcove bathed in shadows. With bright eyes and a healthy pink glow to his cheeks, he looked refreshed and eager to meet the day. He had even managed to have a quick invigorating shower (followed by a thorough clean up of the room afterwards). His red hair that had grown over his ears during his months in Haydon was swept back from his face and his beard smoothed and groomed.

Sam glared at the man through tear-filled eyes. The only word he could manage was, "W-why?"

Han touched the tip of the bloodied knife to his bristly chin in quiet contemplation for a moment. Then, on reflection, said, "Been hearing that a lot lately."

Sam gently set Natalie's body down then spied a discarded ashtray down beside the bar with spots of dried blood across its glass surface. As soon as he begrudgingly rested Natalie's head against the floor, he lunged for the discarded ashtray.

Han, caught off guard by the sudden movement, reacted too slowly, surging forward a fraction too late. Sam grabbed the ashtray and, in a crouch, spun round and swiped.

Han's momentum carried him into the blow, striking his stomach with full force. He doubled up, winded and gasping. Sam took the opportunity to go for the kill, raising the ashtray over his head.

Grimacing, Han lashed out with the knife, causing Sam to jump backwards before managing to bring the ashtray down on his head. Han hastily staggered upright, coughing, with the knife held out defensively in front of him.

Sam glanced from the knife to his dead wife, and made a decision that he would probably regret for the rest of his life; however short or long that might be. Fear temporarily conquered anger and so flight overrode fight. Clutching the ashtray, he turned and sprinted for the front door.

Laughing a half hysterical-half coughing laugh, Han shouted, "Coward! Just when we were getting to know each other!"

Sam dashed out into the snow. It seemed to be easing off somewhat, making the Green and the buildings across the street now easy to distinguish. Ignoring the car, he staggered out into the middle of the road, his feet leaving a deep churned up rut in the snow from the entrance of the pub.

Terrified and utterly clueless as to his next course of action, he did the only thing he could think of. "HELP! H-help me, there's a mur-murderer on the loose!" It felt like a hopelessly stupid thing to do, but as Han appeared in the doorway, still clutching his stomach, two men appeared in the street; one emerging from Bell Lane beyond the Green and the other trudging along past the disused Glitzy Bingo Hall at the top end of Main Street.

Han stepped out, ready to give chase, but then he too saw John Bryce and Jimmy Coulson approaching from different directions. That in itself wasn't a problem. The problem was that Bryce appeared to be armed with a rifle.

Considering his options, Han decided upon a tactical retreat. He disappeared back inside the Miller's.

"Help me! P-please! He's k-k-killed my w-w-w—" His fumbling mouth failed him completely and he screamed out in frustration.

Both Bryce and Jimmy started to run towards him. Bryce, armed with the Bassett rifle, immediately cocked it and brought it up across his chest as he crossed the Green to the screaming stranger. Jimmy thrust a hand into his coat pocket as he rushed towards the hysterical stranger, clutching the lock knife concealed within for some measure of comfort.

"What's going on? Who the hell are you?" Bryce shouted at him as he approached. "Some murdering bastard has killed my wife and son."

"Fuck's goin' on?" Jimmy echoed, bewildered and out of breath. He coughed a couple of times and spat into the deep snow before continuing on to join them.

Shaking, Sam thrust a finger towards the Miller's. "A b-b-bearded man in th-th-theere; h-he's just k-k-killed my Natalie." His stuttering gremlin was taking control, as his voice coach used to tell him.

Bryce turned and took aim at the open doorway. There was no one to be seen.

Jimmy glanced nervously from Bryce to the newcomer, gripping the hilt of the knife in his sweaty palm. An itch crawled up his sleeve, but he fought the urge to scratch.

The breeze had died down to a gentle whisper and only a dusting of tiny flakes continued a leisurely descent. The fine powder coated the three men's hair and shoulders as they stood clustered together in the deserted street.

Still aiming down the iron sight at the Miller's, Bryce demanded, "Who the hell are you?"

"W-we arrived l-l-late last night. C-c-c-" He had to stop to take a deep breath, before continuing. Tears were streaming down his flushed cheeks.

Bryce and Jimmy exchanged a glance.

"Caught in the st-st-storm heading to s-s-see my dad in B-b-b-"

"Blindburn?" Jimmy finished with obvious impatience. Turning to Bryce, he said, "You have any idea what's goin' on, like?"

Keeping the rifle pointing at the pub, Bryce turned to the two men. "You and me got unfinished business, you little prick. While I was out chasing you off me farm, someone broke in and killed Sally and Anthony. *Butchered them.*" He spat the last two words through clenched teeth.

Jimmy stepped back from the raw emotion in the big farmer's tone and features. "I-I didn't know, man."

Turning back to the door, Bryce muttered, "How do we know that the murderer isn't you, cityboy?"

Sam gaped at him and raised a fist still clutching the ashtray, shaking with fury. "My WIFE! He slit her throat!" The tears were dripping off his quivering chin.

Jimmy raised his hands defensively. "Woah, alreet, I think he's alreet, Bryce."

"Well, it ain't a local killing everyone, as you well know, *Jimmy.* This is fucking Haydon! Where the fuck is everyone else?"

Jimmy looked around the deserted street. Suddenly the solitude struck him. Despite the weather, there should have been a few people about, especially with all the shouting. And the kids ... they loved the snow. "He cannat have killed *everyone* ... not *here* ... could he?"

Bryce switched his attention from the sight to stare at Jimmy then, slowly, he glanced around them, his eyes frequently diverting back to the pub. No open doors, no faces at windows. No fresh tracks in the snow – other than theirs – come to think of it. But still ... "Impossible." Looking back to Sam, he snarled, "Who *is* he?"

"B-beard, ginger h-h-hair, stocky—"

"Whitman?" Both Bryce and Jimmy chorused.

"That cannat be right ... not Han." Bryce dropped the rifle to his side in disgust. "I know he's not one of us, but still ... he's a fucking writer!"

210

"Makes perfect sense to me," Jimmy said, nodding, scratching his stubble with a grubby, red hand.

"You shut the fuck up, boy. You've been gunnin' for him since he started seeing Lisa. The bloke's a friend of mine."

Jimmy's eyes widened and, with force, smacked the side of his own head. "Lisa! Oh, Christ! Was there anyone else in there?"

Sam nodded, his eyes drawn back to the dark entrance. "A really big old man and a slim, young dark-headed woman."

Jimmy grabbed him by the scruff of his jacket. "That's Lisa! Was she … alreet?"

Sam backed off from the scruffy young man, shoving his hand away. "Th-th-they were both d-d-d—"

"No!" Jimmy surged forward again, grasping for the newcomer's collar. "Divvent say that!"

"Christ." Setting his jaw, Bryce growled, "Talking's over." With that, he stormed towards the Miller's, aiming the rifle from the hip.

Jimmy turned away from Sam. "Bryce! Where the hell you goin'?"

Bryce continued towards the pub, muttering, "I'm gunna kill the bastard, whoever the hell he is."

Jimmy considered Bryce's words then rushed after him. Shakily, Sam followed. With Bryce leading, the three men marched towards the pub. Bryce kicked the door in and entered, sweeping the rifle left to right. It was empty, apart from the bodies.

Glaring at the bodies of Big Joe and Lisa, Bryce said, "This bastard is dead."

Stepping in behind him, Jimmy's eyes were immediately drawn to Lisa. Ignoring Bryce's warning, Jimmy rushed over to her and dropped to his knees beside her body. "Lisa … what's he done to you?" He hesitantly touched her pallid cheek. The chill to her skin caused him to recoil immediately and his eyes grew watery. Scarcely above a whisper, he uttered, "I'm sorry."

Sam hovered in the doorway, unable to take his eyes off Natalie's body. She lay exactly where he had left her only a short time ago. Undisturbed. Still. *It's no biggie*, her voice sighed soothingly to him. The words managed to draw him one step back from hysteria.

Bryce studied the stranger. He was an outsider, but no murderer. He didn't look like he could fight his way out of a paper bag, but one more body might help. "What's your name?" he asked.

"S-Sam."

"Well, Sam, I'm John and that's Jimmy. Now, you stay by the door while we take a look around." With that, he moved through to the lounge, stepping carefully around Natalie, the barrel of the rifle leading the way.

"*Jimmy*," Bryce hissed firmly as the younger man remained squatting beside his dead former girlfriend. The young man's face was set into a grimace, but he had managed to choke back the tears before they could break through.

Reluctantly, Jimmy got to his feet and tore his gaze away from Lisa's dead, open eyes. Once his eyes were averted, he was able to catch up with Bryce at the threshold to the lounge.

Sam waited, shivering, both from the cold and a mixture of adrenaline and fear. While he waited, his eyes drifting back to Natalie every so often, the minutes ticked away. After the two locals had disappeared into the lounge, he heard no further noises from within the pub. The breeze tickled the back of his neck and an occasional wispy flake would drift into the open doorway.

Glancing up to the heavens, he noted that the sky was still filled with a swollen, angry cloud covering, so the respite seemed to be only a temporary one. And, eyes darting up and down the street, still no other soul had appeared to question the antics of the three frantic men. It seemed that they were indeed the only survivors to this madman's rampage.

His attention promptly returned to the interior of the pub, and inevitably, to his fallen wife. Her face was pointing away from him, but if it wasn't for the blood, he would've sworn that she was just sleeping. Since awaking not so long ago, everything had happened so fast. His mind was only now starting to catch up. Natalie was dead. *Murdered.* And his dad ... what of his dad?

As he waited, his rattled nerves dissolved still further and, along with it, the last shreds of his patience. What was taking them so long? As he stood, hugging himself against the cold and more, the thought crossed his mind that this killer, Whitman, could have gotten to John and Jimmy too. If he had indeed murdered dozens of people already, what could two more possibly do to stop him? Even if they did have a gun and one was the size of that giant, Andre, from *The Princess Bride*. Well, slight exaggeration there, but still … And, if that was the case, what would he do then?

What would he do then? What *could* he do? He was one man, unarmed and fucking useless. What the *hell* could he do? He was good with servers, with firewalls and routers; that was what he was good at. You need to configure administration rights on SQL Server 2017? Well, Sam's the man. But fight a mass murdering psychopath? Forget it. He had never even been in a fight since high school, and only then, just a couple of stupid little punch-ups over his stuttering from one of the resident Neanderthals. He seemed to remember losing those too. Split lip, bruised cheek and sore ribs sprung to mind.

Maybe he should just run. Take the car and run to Blindburn to alert the police. He could be with his dad too – he needed him more than ever. Yes, that's what he should do. He had been waiting far too long already. *The killer must've gotten to them too. They're dead already and Whitman is on his way here to kill me too. What the hell am I doing still standing here? A fucking lamb to the slaughter! Get in the fucking car RIGHT now!*

As he made the decision to run, footsteps could be heard in the lounge and a shadow danced across the opening. Sam's eyes widened and his breath caught in his throat. His body tensed in readiness to bolt.

Bryce appeared in the doorway, gun held loosely in both hands. Shaking his head, he said sullenly, "Not there. We did find Big Joe's wife, Martha, though. In bed with her throat slit." Anger rising once more, he added, "Fucking … evil."

Appearing behind him, Jimmy added, "Aye, *and* Whitman's room empty – no Whitman and none of his shit either, like. I

213

reckon we can safely assume that it's definitely that bastard behind all this."

Walking back across towards Sam, Bryce muttered, "Certainly *looks* that way."

The three men walked out into the street. The air was cold and still as they stood, looking around the seemingly deserted village. A smattering of flakes lazily drifted earthwards. As they walked towards Sam's half submerged Fiesta, Bryce summed up their situation. "So, phones are out. Both me Landy and pickup had all tyres slashed and so have the other cars I've come across since walking into the village."

"He's cutting us off," Jimmy snorted. "So he can pick us off at leisure."

"M-mine looks o-okay, but it's g-g-going to be tough t-t-trying to get to Blindburn in these c-c—"

"Yeah," Jimmy added, "that piece of shit isn't gunna get far."

Sweeping the gathered snow away from the window and door of the driver's door with the sleeve of his jacket, Sam muttered, "Well, it's all we've g-g-got."

As Sam slipped behind the wheel, Bryce, with a reluctant Jimmy, proceeded to dig away the deep snow from the rest of the windows and the tyres. Jimmy's bare hands quickly numbed and his body shivered uncontrollably. Hugging his hands under his armpits, he stamped his feet in a vain attempt to warm his chilled bones. "Picked the perfect weekend, like."

Glancing up from the rear passenger side wheel, Bryce said, "I think that was the idea." His own bare hands were shaking, so he took a moment to blow hot breath over the icy wet fingers. "Could do with a hand here, *Jimmy*." His words were laced with fizzling irritation.

The engine groaned, but didn't manage to turn over with the first try. Cursing under his breath, Sam waited a moment then turned the key a second time. This time, almost begrudgingly, it turned over with a splutter and the expulsion of a cloud of dirty smoke from the exhaust.

"In b-business," Sam said, leaning out the open door.

Bryce and Jimmy finished clearing away some more of the snow, before piling into the car. Lifting the passenger seat, Bryce smiled and pointed to the back seat. "Get in."

After Jimmy, Bryce jumped in, causing a creaking groan from the suspension. He had to hunch his large frame over to avoid hitting his head off the roof. Cradling the rifle on his lap, he said, "You're gunna have to take it really slow and keep it in second to give yourself a bit of extra traction."

Nodding, Sam put it into gear and slowly applied the accelerator. After a juddering, wheel-spin start, they slowly pulled out of the parking bay into the road. The wheels crunched through the deep fresh snow, unsteadily and frequently losing their grip with a wheel spin that would thrust gouts of mucky snow up past the side windows.

With the fan on full blast to de-mist the windows, they could barely hear the impact of a bullet striking the bonnet. It was Bryce who noticed the plume of snow thrown up by the impact.

"Hell was that?" Bryce squinted through the hazy windscreen and instinctively switched off the fan. Instead of waiting for the fan, he quickly started wiping the misted windscreen with his hand.

"We—" Sam started.

"Quiet."

A second shot struck the bonnet just above the radiator. Without the noise of the fan, the crack of the gunshot was just audible over the idling engine.

Bryce's eyes grew wide. "Oh, that son of a bitch." There was mild amusement in his tone when he added, "He's shooting at us."

"Shit!" Jimmy said, lunging into the slim gap between the two front seats. "Let me out!"

A third shot struck the front grill, releasing a jet of hissing steam from the radiator.

"Sit back, you little prick," Bryce snapped as Jimmy forcibly wedged himself further between the two seats, shoulder and one leg jammed over the top of the hand brake.

215

Calmly, Bryce said, "Sam, how about you get us outta here?"

Sam snapped out of his daze and, on reflex, stepped hard on the accelerator. With better traction on the right tyres, the small car lurched forward and swung around at the same time.

In rapid succession, two more bullets struck the car, one punching a penny-sized hole in the corner of the windscreen, and the second, striking the driver side door, causing Sam to shrink away.

Another bullet struck the driver side front tyre, immediately deflating it to the wheel rim.

"Well, that's that," Bryce said. "We're not going anywhere in this. Try to get us over the other side of the Green so we've got a bit of cover." Winding down the window, he slid the barrel out.

As Bryce stared down the sight, trying to locate the position of the shooter, Sam, pale and sweating, struggled to turn the car around. On three good tyres, the car spun and swerved, seemingly under someone else's control.

As another bullet shattered the side window next to Jimmy, causing an involuntary scream, the car lurched into the wrought iron fence bordering the Green, next to the Haydon Oak. All three men lurched forward in their seats, Jimmy striking his forehead with a glancing blow on the back of Bryce's seat.

"Out," Bryce said as he shoved his door open and crawled free into the thick snow.

Sam needed no encouragement. He was out and scrambling across towards the Post Office, without bothering to turn the engine off. Jimmy frantically struggled with the release catch on the seat, his shaking hands struggling to cooperate. "Bryce!" he cried in a terrified voice.

Bryce was up and running when he heard Jimmy's cry. He spun and lunged back at the car as another shot rang out, punching a hole in a patch of virgin snow a couple of feet away.

Ignoring the gunshot, Bryce lent inside the car and yanked hard on the headrest. The seat tipped forward with a resounding crack and Jimmy immediately spilled out, landing on his back in the snow.

216

"You fucking abortion," Bryce growled, as he dragged the flailing man by his grubby coat collar with one hand and gripped the rifle in his other.

Another gunshot reverberated in the air. Bryce's teeth snapped together as he felt it tear a hole in his jeans below the knee, nicking the skin in the process. With Jimmy on his feet – of sorts – they both scurried for cover down Bell Lane, where Sam was already waiting, flat against the wall and breathing heavily.

"Oh, you better watch out, you better not cry," Han whispered quietly to himself. "Better not pout, I'm tellin' you why, Hannibal is coming to town." He allowed himself a broad smile. With the bulk of the hard work – and madness – behind him, he was actually starting to feel a lot better. Having an extra pawn in the mix was a slight irritation, but he wasn't a local, so that was something! The most irritating thing was that trying to hit anything over a distance with the Walther was nigh on impossible. He was a little annoyed that he hadn't considered the need for something more accurate over distances; something like John's rifle. Maybe he would help himself to that later.

After checking that the three figures weren't moving anywhere for the time being, he gently shut the sash window and drew the curtains closed. Turning away from the window, he glanced at the bed where Moe Baxter was laying in eternal slumber with his mouth a gaping, gruesome mess. Blood had soaked into the pillow and sheet in front of his face and had dried to a crusty stain.

His head lay on one side, with that twisted snarl fixed into his ashen features.

Han folded his arms, with the pistol still in hand, and with a reasonable attempt at a disappointed tone, said, "Ah, don't look at me like that, Moe. It's not my fault; the voices made me do it." He forced a laugh, but in truth, the longer he stared at Moe the quicker his levity ebbed away.

He caught his reflection in the dressing table mirror, his white face contorted into a sneer. The vision stayed his laughter, and he turned to stare intently at his features. His face was at once unrecognisable to him, and the shock of this dropped his jaw open.

A face slowly materialised to one side of his shoulder. As it took shape, the void where its mouth was supposed to be worked soundlessly. Gradually, a button nose took shape, then small ears with stud earrings, then dark spiky hair.

Lisa stared at him with empty holes for eyes. Han could clearly see the bedroom wall, complete with mounted feline pictures, through the blanks where her eyes should have been.

Lisa's dead mouth worked to form soundless syllables. YOU ... WILL ... DIE.

Han blinked wildly to dispel the ghastly vision then rubbed both eyes vigorously with his free hand. When he looked again, his former lover was gone.

A chill crept through his body and he suddenly became aware of his breath hanging in the air in front of him. Unnerved, he hastily left the room.

What's a little reunion without a little drama?

The three men remained flat against the side wall of the Post Office for a couple of minutes. Sam and Jimmy regaining their breath and settling their nerves, but Bryce just staring up at the dark sky.

"Cheeky fucker," Bryce said and glanced back around the corner. Main Street was as they had left it, and no other soul had yet to appear. The only sound to be heard was Sam's battered Fiesta as it continued to idle, combined with a soft hissing coming from the ruptured radiator.

"He's changing positions," Bryce said. "Time to move."

On his haunches, with his back against the wall and his head in his hands, Jimmy muttered, "Where to?" Then, slowly lifting his head out of his hands, he continued, "I hate to be the voice of reason here – goes totally against me character, like – but there *is* nowhere to go!" His cheeks were damp from unseen tears.

"Quit griping," Bryce retorted with marked impatience.

"I like griping."

Bryce shot a glare towards him, but Jimmy refused to meet his stare, instead focusing his eyes on the opposite wall.

Sam smacked the palm of his hand against the icy, wet stone wall with a resounding slap. "Sh-shut up!"

Bryce and Jimmy turned their attention to him, surprised by his sudden outburst. The man wasn't a local, so wasn't coping too well. The same could be said for Jimmy, of course, but that was because of the shit he stuck into himself.

"Sorry, Sam," Bryce said.

"Well, we got to think of something," Jimmy said. "We cannat just sit here holding our dicks."

Bryce rolled his eyes. "Well put." He bent down to examine the graze on his calf. The material around the rip in his jeans was dark and sticky and blood had seeped into his sock and boot. With an irritated snort, he drew back up to his formidable height and said, "We need to get off the street so we can work out a plan."

As the three men considered this, Sam caught sight of movement out of the corner of his eye. He snapped his head to one side to stare down the lane. Renewed adrenaline coursed through his body as he scrutinised this potential new threat. It was a bedraggled woman, staggering towards them along the lane. Her features were slack and emotionless and her arms dangled loosely down by her sides.

Without taking his eyes off her, Sam nudged Jimmy and whispered, "L-l-look, wh-who's she?"

Both Bryce and Jimmy turned to see who was approaching. They both recognised her immediately. "Carol, over here!" Bryce called to her.

She appeared not to notice, continuing unsteadily along the middle of the snow-covered lane. Her ankle boots were thick with snow and her jeans were soaked through. Despite the cold, she wore neither hat, gloves nor scarf, and her denim jacket was open to reveal a thin blouse. Her teeth were visibly chattering and her bright red hands, poking out of the sleeves of her jacket, were shaking.

Bryce rushed over to her, shouting to Jimmy, "Keep an eye behind us!" He slowed as he reached her and, after setting down the rifle against the wall, gradually raised his arms, beckoning. "Carol, it's John. Are you okay, pet?" He gently placed his hands on her drooping shoulders and caught a strong whiff of brandy on her breath.

Carol seemed neither to recognise him nor even register his presence. She tried to continue her journey, so Bryce gently restrained her, forcibly halting her swaying progress. Her feet continued to shuffle in the snow for a moment, seemingly unaware that her body had halted. "Carol, it's me," he said again and tenderly squeezed her shoulders. This time her eyes slowly lifted from the snowy ground up to meet Bryce's. Her teary, bloodshot eyes were glazed at first, but after a moment, they fixed on him and recognition followed.

"John?" her hoarse voice murmured.

Nodding, Bryce said, "Aye, pet, it's me. You look freezing."

"Steve's dead," she said dreamily. "So's Janet ... and Larry ... and their beautiful little girl. I-I had to have a drink."

Buttoning up her jacket, Bryce said, "Loads of people have been killed, Carol. It looks like it's Han Whitman." Turning to the others, he said, "We've got to get her indoors – she's freezing."

"My place is no good," Jimmy said, glancing from Main Street to the discarded rifle.

"The farm's too far, so we'll have to try for an unlocked door."

Stamping his feet to ward off the creeping cold, Sam looked around, searching for options.

His mind reeling, Bryce struggled to think coherently. After a moment, he said, "Carol, you mentioned Janet and Larry. Is their house locked? Have you come from there?"

Sagging into his arms, she started crying softly on his shoulder. "Please don't make me go back there." Her anguished, whispered voice was pleading.

"We've got to get off the street, Carol. It's our best option."

"Anyway," Jimmy injected, "I thought you'd be happy."

Bryce glanced at him – it was fleeting, but enough to halt a stampeding buffalo. In response, Jimmy raised his hands in mock apology then begrudgingly struggled to his feet.

"*Come on*," Bryce said. Turning to Carol, he said in a more soothing tone, "Come on, pet, let's get you into the warm." He stooped to retrieve his rifle, before gently leading her back towards the Herring household.

Jimmy noticed the farmer's slight limp, but remained silent and pensive.

chapter 13

We're the cavalry. It would be bad form to arrive early; in the nick of time would do nicely.

Skidding and wheel-spinning along the one and only artery between Shillmoor and Blindburn, the muddy Northumbria Police Land Rover made slow and erratic progress towards the Haydon turnoff. A snowplough had made a fleeting dash between villages in the early hours, leaving six foot snowdrifts either side of the road, but since then several more feet of fresh snow had built up on the rutted surface.

The rolling Cheviot Hills and moors to the right of the road were blanketed with a brilliant white, broken only by intermittent stick-like trees – coal-black against the hoary backdrop – hedgerows and the occasional dry stone wall. The River Coquet, to the left, normally a trickle, was fast flowing and swollen with snowmelt, its normally shallow rocky riverbed lost beneath churning, icy water.

Within the warm confines, a uniformed police constable fought a battle of wills with the wheel. Accompanying him were Mitchell, in the front, and Wright in the back, his head lolling against the window, snoring.

"Worst weather I've seen up these parts since I was a kid," the young driver, scarcely into his twenties, said in earnest.

Wright stopped in mid-snore. Without opening his eyes, he muttered, "And when was that? Last week?"

Rolling his eyes, Mitchell said, "Ignore him, lad. He's always grumpy in the morning." As the windscreen wipers worked tirelessly to clear the spray, he squinted to see the Haydon turnoff. "There it is," he said finally. "Christ. You did bring a couple of shovels, Bainbridge?"

"Aye."

"We're gonna need 'em."

The Land Rover slowed to a skidding halt by the junction. The snowplough had thrown a huge drift into the side road, blocking it completely up to waist height. The road beyond was untouched with deep virgin snow.

Rubbing an ache in his neck, Wright eased his big frame out of the four wheel drive and stood by the roadside, eyeing the obstruction. Mitchell and Bainbridge joined him as the engine idled. The snow had died with the breeze, leaving the breath of the three officers' hanging in the air in front of them. Mitchell suppressed a shiver and let out a sigh.

"You think they don't want any visitors?" Wright said with mild irritation as he plucked his cigarettes out of his coat. "Should we radio in for the snowplough? Get him to sort out his mess?"

Mitchell shook his head. "The ploughs are working overtime to try to clear the main routes; they won't have time to clear these secondary ones for ages yet. Do you want to hang round here waiting?"

Wright thought about it for a second as he lit up with his red dagger lighter. "Not particularly."

"Well, we might as well just clear it ourselves."

Wright turned to the young constable. "You heard the man. Jump to it."

The dejected look Bainbridge gave him was enough to raise Wright's flagging spirits. Zipping up his coat, he said, "Only joking, mate. Come on then, it won't move itself."

Between the three of them, they managed to clear a path in under an hour. As they finished, snow was starting to fall once again.

Glancing up at the solid roof of cloud above them, red-faced and puffing, Mitchell said, "Bloody typical. We better not hang about too long or we're likely to be stuck here for Christmas. Can't say that Shelly would be too happy about that!"

"Can't have you missing the kid's first Christmas, mate," Wright said sincerely, blinking flakes out of his bushy eyebrows as he cast his shovel into the back of the Land Rover. His face, too, was red from exertion and beads of sweat stood out on his forehead.

"I'm supposed to be going to my girlfriend's parents for Christmas dinner," Bainbridge said conversationally, adding his and Mitchell's shovels to the pile of equipment in the back of the four wheel drive.

"Nobody cares," Wright said evenly, then smiled at the resulting puppy dog eyes. "I'm joking! Jesus, you're bloody sensitive for a copper."

The slim officer shrugged defensively, but the gesture barely registered within his bulky florescent high visibility jacket.

The front door to Janet and Larry Herring's home had been left half open and trampled snow had built up just inside the hallway. Pushing the door fully open with the muzzle of his rifle, Bryce peered into the darkened corridor. He could see all the way through to the kitchen, where he could just make out slender legs lying crumpled beyond.

He stepped inside, followed by Sam who was helping Carol, then Jimmy bringing up the rear. After checking the living room, they moved in to the kitchen where the bodies of Larry, Janet and Kerris met them.

Bryce stopped in the doorway. Despite everything that he had already seen and having a very good idea at what he would find here, the sight of the entire Herring family lying dead still caused him to pause. He recovered quickly, wiping the back of his hand across his dry lips, he turned to Sam and said, "Take Carol into the living room and sit with her there while me and Jimmy sort things here."

Nodding, Sam gently coaxed Carol back down the hallway.

Folding his arms across his chest, Jimmy said angrily, "How come he gets the fucking babysitting job while I get shit detail?"

Bryce had started to fish his cigarettes out of his coat, but he paused to glare at Jimmy. "How about you grow the fuck up and start acting like a local, eh?" As Jimmy stared defiantly back at him, grasping for a witty comeback, Bryce continued. "She's been through the mill long before all this shit – she's on medication. She's got an excuse, what's yours?"

"It's the gear, man," Jimmy said, as if stating the obvious.

"You've got a smart mouth, Jimmy," Bryce snarled and stepped closer to him. "You've been a stain on Haydon for years."

Despite Bryce's intimidating frame, Jimmy held his ground, looking up to the much bigger man. "Sticks and stones, *John*. I divvent answer to you or neebody."

"You're a worthless layabout who got his lass onto drugs, got her up the duff, and then dumped her like steamin' shit." Bryce bent closer to him, willing him to take a swing for him.

Despite his best efforts, Jimmy could not help but lean away from Bryce's huge face, but with the farmer's last words, his own anger overruled his fear. "She dumped me! I loved Lisa!" With that, the tremors returned with a vengeance and he had to grip both arms in fear that he would shake himself apart.

Sam popped his head around the door of the living room. Glaring down the hallway at the two men hovering at the threshold to the kitchen, he snapped, "F-f-f-for fuck's sake! W-w-what's the matter with y-y-you people?"

Bryce straightened up and entered the kitchen without another word. After a moment, still trembling, Jimmy followed. Before starting, Bryce produced his remaining two cigarettes and handed one to Jimmy.

They worked together in silence to lift the three bodies and set them outside in the car park at the back of the house. The snow had started once more and a powdery layer quickly built up covering the Herrings where they lay. After locking up, they briefly wiped over the bloodstains and swept up the broken glass, then beckoned Sam to join them.

Bryce filled the kettle and switched it on as Jimmy and Sam took seats at the patio table, the former trying hard to cast out the images of Kerris' and Larry's blood that had just been cleaned up. Spooning instant coffee into mugs, Bryce said, "I think we should secure this house and wait it out." Glancing over his shoulder, he asked, "What do you two think?" His expression was unreadable.

They both nodded wearily, but remained silent.

"We need to get weapons for you three an' all. We cannat just rely on Bertie."

"Bertie?" Sam and Jimmy asked in unison.

"The Bassett," he said with a nod towards the rifle leaning against the cooker.

"Ah." Sam and Jimmy exchanged a glance, Jimmy rolling his eyes and Sam shrugging.

"Anyway," Bryce continued, irritated at the interruption, "we need to sort summit out for you. Wish I'd brought the Webley as well. Either of you two done any shootin'?"

Sam shook his head, but Jimmy said, "Aye, once or twice. Me dad used to have an old double-barrel."

Bryce thought about it for a moment, then said, "Much as I'd hate to trust you with a gun, I'd prefer at least two of us armed than not."

"Touchin'," Jimmy muttered, absently scratching the back of one hand.

"Means a trek to the farm though," Bryce mused. "Not sure we should risk it – we'll be out in the open. The only thing we've got in our favour is that he's not a very good shot. Either that or he was just toying with us."

"So we just stay here like sitting ducks?" Jimmy said, exasperated, but could think of nothing better to suggest. He continued scratching, moving up his arm. Bryce caught the action out of the corner of his eye, but refrained from commenting.

"I-if we w-w-wait for him, we can try to t-t-turn the t-tables on him; su-surprise h-him for a change," Sam suggested, carefully trying to regulate his speech. The effort appeared to tire him quickly.

Bryce appeared to mull it over as he finished making the coffees. Passing them out, he said finally, "Think that might be a good idea. There's only one of him; there's three of us—"

"Four." Carol had appeared in the doorway, wringing her hands nervously. Her tear-streaked face and bloodshot eyes exaggerated her haggard features, prematurely ageing her, but there was a determination in the back of her eyes that was unmistakable.

The three men stared at her as Bryce handed her a steaming mug of coffee. As she gripped the mug in both hands, he offered her an encouraging smile and repeated, "Four."

"Like t-the mu-musketeers," Sam said and managed a weak smile.

Jimmy frowned. "It's three musketeers, ya div."

"Four including D'Artagnan, you prat," Bryce said with a smirk.

"Wey, pardon me," Jimmy said. "Get a load of the English professor here."

Bryce shook his head, but he grunted a half laugh.

Sam offered Carol his seat and propped himself against the kitchen units, sipping his coffee.

She seemed reluctant at first to leave the imaginary sanctuary of the doorway, but then, hesitantly, Carol stepped forward and eased herself into the chair. She sat in silence, warming her hands on the hot mug and contemplating the dark brown liquid.

"You want to talk about it?" Bryce offered tentatively.

She remained quiet, seemingly transfixed by the steam drifting above her drink. But just as Bryce was about to change the subject, she let out a sigh and spoke. Her voice was hushed and gravelly, but once she started she seemed adamant to finish.

Carol proceeded to tell them everything that had happened, first at Steve's house, then finishing with Janet drinking the wine. The three men listened in silence, nodding occasionally. At the mention of Han's name, Bryce nodded slowly, but otherwise remained stone-faced.

When she had finished and sat back in morose contemplation, Bryce took the reigns, and explained his view of events leading to their meeting. He took a swig of coffee before skirting past the macabre discoveries of his wife and child, but otherwise recounted events quietly and matter-of-factly.

Sam had to turn away at the fleeting mention of Bryce's murdered family, brushing tears from his eyes in the process. Everything had been a constant blur since he and Natalie had strolled down into the bar that morning, unaware and totally unprepared for the chain of events that were about to unfold around them. He had not even had time to grieve for her ... his Natalie, his love. She had been taken from him in the blink of an eye; by a stranger, for seemingly no reason whatsoever.

He assumed that Bryce had not dealt with his demons yet either, and somehow, he doubted the poor man ever would. He had not only lost his wife, but he had lost his only child too.

Carol seemed to be one stage ahead of Sam and Bryce. She had been through an emotional meat grinder and somehow, through her strength and courage, had managed to come out the other side with her sanity stretched painfully thin, but intact nonetheless.

Jimmy was a different enigma altogether. He had lost the girl, Lisa, but she had been a former partner, clearly with a lot of water under the bridge. Sam struggled to justify his thoughts, but he felt that Jimmy was not even in the same city when it came to loss. Those thoughts were instantly followed by guilt. What did he know of Jimmy; of his life and his relationship with Lisa? Nothing. He was just prejudging, based on his appearance and the brief mention of drugs. With that, he cut off that train of thought altogether.

Looking up from his coffee, Bryce picked up on one of Carol's earlier comments. "The wine that killed Janet ..." he said, casting a glance to the refrigerator. "What if he's poisoned other stuff?"

"Wey, we've already had some of the milk and we're all still breathin'," Jimmy said, but fell silent to ponder further.

"And Brandy," Carol muttered without lifting her eyes from the patio table.

Bryce leaned back against the kitchen cabinets and glanced around the room, frowning. After an awkward silence, he finally said, "Guess we cannat really worry about it."

Sam nodded solemnly, saying, "Doesn't d-do us any g-g-good."

Beneath a pile of corpses, lying massed,
By bloody pool—rattling, gasping his last.

The police Land Rover drove slowly along Main Street, its occupants glancing left and right. The snow was falling heavily again, and with it, the wind was picking up once more. Freshly deposited powdery snow was being whipped up into swirling snow devils. Despite the worsening weather, they expected to see some activity, but all they saw was empty streets and dark houses.

As they pulled into an empty parking bay at the Miller's, all three men glanced over to the freshly covered Fiesta that had been abandoned after crashing into the fencing around the Green. Both doors were still wide open, but the engine no longer idled.

"Someone had too much to drink late last night?" Wright asked, sceptically. "That's not our friend's is it?"

Getting out, Mitchell said, "No, he's got that Daihatsu remember."

"Don't see it." Wright slid out after him, glancing up and down the street. "Fiesta ... too modern for these weirdos. They all seem to favour bangers."

"I think they'd prefer the term *classic*," Mitchell said.

Ignoring him, Wright said, "Bit quiet, innit? Even for a farty little place like this."

Bainbridge joined them, saying with a smile, "Alien abductions, eh?"

"Pucker up your arse then, boy. Don't want any anal probes prodding about up there, do you?" Wright said, followed by a wink. The fine snow was catching in his hair and eyebrows and clinging to the fur trim of his hood.

Shaking his head, Mitchell said, "Bainbridge, you stay with the car."

"Aye, and keep your wits about you." The young PC expected a laugh or a wink to follow, but Wright's expression remained serious. He frowned and glanced around the seemingly deserted high street.

The two detectives strode over to the door and, Mitchell, in the lead pushed it open. Both men entered the darkened bar. Shaking the flakes from his coat, Wright squinted in the gloom as he shoved the door too behind him. The room was still and cold, his breath pluming ahead of him.

"Mister Falkirk? Mister Whitman?" Mitchell called out. "It's Northumbria Police; Mitchell and Wright." Remaining a few feet inside the room, he studied the bar and archway through to the lounge. Nothing appeared out of place, but lengthy shadows hid a multitude of sins.

"Now, I know this place has always been a bit ... weird," Wright said in all seriousness, "but I'm getting a funny feeling here."

Mitchell grunted and walked towards the lounge. After a moment's contemplation, Wright followed. As they approached the lounge, Mitchell called out again, "Anyone there? It's the Police."

His foot slipped on the wood floor, nearly throwing him onto his back, but Wright shot a hand out to steady him. They both looked down to see smears of a dark sticky substance. Mitchell bent down and touched a finger to it.

"Oh, great," Wright muttered as they both recognised it instantly.

"Call for back up," Mitchell hissed, adrenaline quickly pumping through his body. He cautiously crossed the threshold into the lounge.

Wright retrieved his mobile, glanced at the signal and cursed. "No fucking signal, as usual." Glancing behind him to the door, he whispered, "I'm going back to the car to radio from there. You stay where you are till I get back, then we can sweep this place properly."

"No argument here," Mitchell replied, looking at something out of view from Wright. "We've got a major problem here."

Having taken two steps towards the door, Wright snapped his head round. "What is it?"

"Three bodies here; carved up by the looks. One of them's the landlord."

Wright suddenly wished he was back in the Marines. "Could do with an SA80 right now, mate."

Whispering harshly, Mitchell said, "I didn't think we'd need armed response for some fucking fraudster."

"Back to the car," Wright ordered, stalking slowly back to the door, his eyes darting over every shadow. Mitchell followed, walking backwards back into the bar. As he retreated, he pulled out his stumpy telescopic baton and extended it with a flick of the wrist.

Wright opened the front door and peered up and down the street. After a brief inspection, he dashed across to the Land Rover. Pulling the passenger door open, he said, "Get on the radio, we've got—" He cut short the sentence.

PC Bainbridge was slumped back in the driving seat, his throat cut and blood pumping down his chest from the fresh gaping wound.

"FUCK!" he cried out in shock. Extending his own baton, he rapidly checked the back seats then under the four wheel drive as Mitchell joined him. "Bainbridge is dead," Wright told him as he stood up again.

"Christ, get on the bloody radio then," Mitchell snapped, scanning the street for any movement.

Wright leaned back into the car and cursed immediately. "Radio's fucked too!"

Glancing in, Mitchell could clearly see that it looked like someone had taken a hammer to it. "I don't believe this. This is a nightmare!"

Wright shot him a glance. "Easy, mate. This is fucked up, but we're professionals. There's nothing we can't handle. Okay?"

Mitchell nodded, angry at himself for the momentary loss of control. "What's the betting that the phones are out too?"

"You'd get lousy odds from any bookie."

Staring at the Co-op and the Post Office, Mitchell said, "Where the hell is everyone? They can't all be dead. That's ridiculous."

"If there are survivors, they're probably hiding somewhere and waiting for the cavalry."

"That would be us then?"

"Yep."

"They're going to be sorely disappointed!" He tried a half-hearted laugh, but it came out as an angry grunt.

They both stood in silence for a moment, considering their options and scanning doors and windows for any movement. Finally, Wright said, "We're ineffective against this threat. Much as I hate to say it, but we should take the Landy back to Shillmoor – we came through there and that was all hunky dory. We should be able to call for backup there."

Mitchell nodded, solemnly. "You're right."

Wright quickly walked round to the driver's side and opened the door. Carefully, he eased Bainbridge out and laid him down in the snow. He stared at his wide, mildly surprised eyes for a moment then gently brushed his hand over them, closing them for good.

He reached back into the car and groaned. "Where … oh shit, no."

Mitchell crouched down to look through the open passenger door at him. "What now?"

"No keys. Someone's royally fucking with us." Growing concern marred his expression.

"Jesus!" Mitchell's mind was reeling and finding it difficult to catch up. "Don't suppose you can—"

"Nope," Wright answered, anticipating the question. "Guess that's a no from you too then?"

Mitchell kicked the door hard enough to slam it into its frame. "Shit!"

There was silence for a moment, broken only by the low moaning of the wind. Snow was building up quickly over their hair and clothing. After what seemed like an age, Wright leaned back out of the car and slowly closed the door. Looking around, he said, "Well, that kinda limits our options somewhat."

"No shit, Sherlock." Options were being dismissed in his mind quicker than he could even consider them. Mitchell grappled with the one remaining option and it left a very sour taste in his mouth.

Wright walked back around the passenger side, his face set to dour deliberation, his baton held tightly in his grip. With an angry grunt, he flipped his hood back over his head.

"We've got no choice but to search for survivors and an alternative means of communication or transport," Mitchell said simply. With his mind made up for him, Mitchell felt a sliver of control returning. Zipping his leather jacket up, he cursed his stupidity for not bringing something warmer.

"Aye."

Scratching his chin, Mitchell said, "So what do we know? We've got multiple murders, so far all seemingly knife attacks, but if there are many more deaths out there, it is likely that a firearm could be involved. We don't know as yet whether this is definitely Whitman's work, or whether it is the work of one or more assailants, but we do know that he is at least skilled with a blade. How am I doing so far?"

"Spot on." Wright glanced across at the abandoned Ford and a thought occurred to him. "I'm guessing that the driver of that Fiesta saw something, possibly the bodies in the pub, and tried to make a run for it. One of the tyres is out, I can see that from here, but I'm going to take a closer look. Cover me."

Mitchell looked at him incredulously. "Are you taking the piss? *Cover me*? What with? If a sniper pops up at a window, you want me to throw my baton at him to keep his head down?"

Wright stared back at him, thoughtful, as flakes of snow continued to settle in his hair and goatee. Shaking some of the snow free, he said, "You know what I mean." With that, he ran for the car at a hunched sprint, his clumping feet throwing up clods of snow behind him.

Apprehensively, Mitchell kept watch as Wright made his short dash to the car. He scanned doorways and windows for any lurking danger; a flicker of a curtain, the dancing of a shadow. Wright reached the car and began a cursory examination of it. It didn't take long to see why it had been abandoned in a hurry. Waving his colleague over, Wright crouched down between the car and the Post Office.

Mitchell did not need any other hints. He sprinted across to his partner after only a brief hesitation. Ducking down with him, he asked, "So what's the story?"

"Bullet holes for one – nine millimetre by the looks. By the placements I'd say a pistol, rather than a subbie, so we've got that in our favour. Can't see any traces of blood, so the driver didn't get capped here, at least."

"So we may have at least one survivor then."

Wright nodded as his eyes were drawn back to the dark, yawning opening in the Miller's. His gaze shifted upwards, then across to Moe's. After sucking his teeth, he said, "Reckon the shooter was second floor – the pub or the barbers."

Mitchell placed a hand on the snow-covered bonnet. "No residual heat, but in this weather that doesn't tell us much."

Wright nodded in the direction they had just come. "I noticed disturbances in the snow too – middle of the street and over there." Mitchell followed his eyes towards the entrance to Bell Lane. "Difficult to tell with all the fresh snow over the top, but certainly looks like one or more people on foot. Whether that was before or after the attempted getaway is anyone's guess."

Mitchell chewed his bottom lip and glanced up at the snow-filled sky. "Weather's getting worse by the minute too." After a moment's contemplation, he added with an air of resolve, "Well, let's see if we can find ourselves a survivor."

"And maybe a killer too," Wright said with a glint in his eye.

Something strange is happening in the town of Stepford.

Sam stood at the sink, in silence, washing the dishes from their recent meal of sandwiches and crisps. Glancing up at the window in front of him, he was not surprised to see the snow continuing to fall heavily. Despite only being lunchtime, the weather gave the illusion of it being dusk. Doing a mundane task like the dishes lent some sort of flimsy reality to the whole situation. The feeling of being slightly out of time only added to the strangeness. Bryce had left them to check the doors and windows, while Carol returned a block of cheese, butter and a bottle of salad cream to the refrigerator.

Perched on the edge of the table, Jimmy watched Sam and Carol, biting his grubby fingernails. It all suddenly felt like an episode of *Happy Days* for him. A madman out there had murdered hundreds of people, and all these people could think about doing was the dishes. "You know, you don't need to do the dishes, like."

"I don't m-mind."

"They're dead," Jimmy said harshly, suddenly angry.

Sam glanced over his shoulder, frowning. "W-w-we're intruding i-i-in their h-home. H-h-have s-s-some respect."

Jimmy looked down to his hands, ashamed at his outburst. The anger hadn't been meant for Sam; he didn't quite know where it had come from or who it was supposed to be aimed at. No, he did know; Whitman. That bastard was going to pay ... somehow. He had got the drop on him once, so he could do it again. Next time there would be no Bryce or Big Joe to pull him off. He would cut him up, like Whitman had done to Lisa.

Carol had stopped by the refrigerator to listen to the short confrontation without looking directly at one or the other, but as Sam turned back to the sink full of soapy water, Carol's attention turned to Jimmy. He was trembling and occasionally he would scratch at his arm or back of his hand. Jimmy had always been a social outcast in the village, much like she had become over the last couple of years with her very messy and very public break up with Steve.

She still couldn't quite accept their situation as real; it was more like a vivid and surreal nightmare. Almost everyone she had ever known, apart from a few scattered distant family members, Bryce and Jimmy, were all dead. Steve, Big Joe, Lisa, Moe, Tess, Duncan ... she just couldn't quite get her head round it.

Maybe if she clicked her heels together, and chanted, *there's no place like home,* maybe Glinda would allow her to wake up in her bed. God, she needed a drink. She recognised the dull throbbing behind the eyes, reaching round to the temples as the onset of a hangover. Wonderful. She also hadn't taken her medication today yet either. Tentatively raising a hand to her mouth and breathing into it, she realised with some embarrassment that she had a bad case of dragon breath to cap it all off. She needed toothpaste or vodka. One or the other. Preferably both.

Interrupting all their thoughts, Bryce stepped back into the room, saying, "Everything's secure. He's gunna have to break a window or kick a door in to get in here, so at least we'll have warning." Placing the rifle on the table, he added, "So now all we need is a pack of cards."

Drying his hands on a tea towel, Sam asked, "H-how l-long do you th-th-think we'll be st-stuck here before the p-p-police get here?" His thoughts turned to his father, gravely ill in bed only a few miles away in Blindburn.

Bryce thought about it for a moment. He hadn't really considered how long they might have to wait; he had been concentrating on an inevitable encounter with Han. "Could be a day, could be three. Your guess is as good as mine. But what I do know is that you cannat lose contact with a whole community without alarms being raised eventually."

"He'll find us before then, won't he?" Carol said and unconsciously hugged herself in a vain attempt to draw some comfort from somewhere. She *really* needed a drink ... a bloody strong one, but she had already consumed the only alcohol she had been able to find before she had met up with the others ... Larry's brandy. At the time, deep down, she had hoped that the brandy would kill her, like the bottle of wine had killed Janet. She had never felt so alone and had wanted it all to end. Now, with all that had happened, she felt some frail kinship with her fellow three survivors, a kinship that, for now, banished all thoughts of suicide to the dark recesses of her mind. She was pretty sure that they would be revisited again sometime soon though.

"Probably," Bryce replied, after giving the question some thought. "Whatever his game plan is, he's gunna have to make sure there's no one left that could recognise him. He's gunna search high and low until he finds us. And when he does ..." His voice trailed off.

"And when he does," Jimmy continued, "we'll gut the twat." He pulled out his lock knife and whipped open the blade with a sharp flick of the wrist. The brief act of bravado banished his tremors momentarily.

"Put it away," Bryce told him evenly. "If or when the time comes, we'll fight him alreet. We've all got scores to settle."

chapter 14

Mi casa, su casa.

As the already poor light rapidly deteriorated with the onset of dusk, the storm steadily grew in intensity, completely obliterating any previous signs of activity. The wind had picked up to a howling gale once more, throwing an eerie beckoning moan through the deserted streets and lanes. The gusting snow had become as thick as static on a television screen, obscuring all but faint hints of what lay beyond. The Northumbria Police Land Rover stood completely covered, with drifting snow reaching the top of wheel arches. Only a slight mound on the road beside it indicated where the body of PC Bainbridge had been laid.

Several isolated lights across the village suddenly winked out as one, bathing the village in total darkness.

The lamp in the corner of the Herrings' living room extinguished with them. As one, the four occupants stood up and glanced nervously around the shadowy room.

"Fuck happened?" Jimmy whispered harshly. He immediately sought the security of his lock knife and clutched it between his trembling hands.

"Hang on," Bryce replied and edged over to the window. Easing open a narrow gap, he peered into the night. He could only see the faint outlines of darkened buildings, obscured by the surging snow and claustrophobic darkness. "Looks like the power's out across the whole village."

"Great!" Jimmy spat, kicking out at the sofa. While opening and closing the blade of his knife, he started pacing anxiously like a caged beast. "Just bastard great, like!"

"For Christ's sake, Jimmy," Carol muttered. "I'll see if I can find a torch or some candles."

Bryce retrieved his flashlight and switched it on, being careful to obscure the faint beam with his hand and aim it down at the carpet. "Here, take my torch – it's not great, but it'll help. Sam, go with her."

Snatching the flashlight, she said sternly, "I don't need a chaperone."

Bryce looked with sincerity into her frightened eyes and said, "Safety in numbers, pet. We should always stick together, or at least stay in twos."

"Aye, in the horror films, when people get separated, that's when they get picked off one by one," Jimmy commented dryly.

Bryce glared at him. "Jimmy, you're a great help, you know that? You just divvent know when to shut up." Jimmy's shadowy form stopped and looked in his direction. His free hand moved up to his mouth and started chewing on his fingernails.

Sam stepped over to Carol and touched her shoulder gently. "C-come on, Carol."

With the dim flashlight leading the way, Carol and Sam made their way carefully to the kitchen. Tip-toeing and conversing in short whispers, they systematically searched through the cupboards and drawers, until Carol came across a box of white candles and a box of matches.

"Got some," she whispered with relief.

"G—" Sam stopped abruptly. A distorted outline of a figure passed fleetingly by the window. His heart started racing and his mouth suddenly ran dry. Backing up towards the doorway and pointing, he stammered, "W-w-w-w—"

Frowning, Carol turned to the window and instinctively retreated in Sam's direction. "You see someone?"

"Y-y-y-yes!"

For a moment they both held their breath in the quiet darkness. Carol extinguished the flashlight and shoved it into her pocket. Their hearts were beating hard and fast, the pressure causing their ears to throb hotly, and seemingly loud enough to betray their presence. All became still and the seconds stretched out in front of them until ...

The door handle moved with an audible click.

Sam gasped and, trembling, took another step back towards the open doorway. Carol, her legs suddenly feeling like jelly beneath her weight, stopped and thrust out a hand to the worktop beside her. Her fingers fumbled in the gloom for a weapon ... anything. The candles in her other hand clicked together softly with the shuddering of her body.

The handle stopped moving.

Within the confines of his own head, Sam's laboured breathing sounded like a freight train. He wanted desperately to shout out to Bryce, but his dry mouth refused to cooperate. Instead, his eyes hunted through the gloom, searching, like Carol, for a weapon of some kind.

As his eyes spied a knife rack in the corner, the door burst open with a piercing crack, causing both Carol and Sam to cry out and the former to scatter the candles and matches up into the air. The dark, looming figure who had shouldered the door open stepped inside.

Carol's free hand grabbed an object and instantly hurled it towards the intruder as Sam made a desperate dash towards the knives.

The mug hit Wright with a glancing blow across the forehead, causing him to let out an involuntary yowl. "Police! Stop right there!" One hand held his baton defensively out in front of him as the other, with his flashlight, shot up to his injured face.

Mitchell pushed past his dazed colleague, similarly brandishing his own baton and flashlight, the beam dancing across the walls and the two frightened occupants.

As Sam grabbed one of the knives, Bryce and Jimmy rushed in from the hall. Carol had instinctively grabbed a second mug and held it above her head, ready to throw.

With Bryce aiming the Bassett and Mitchell aiming a glaring flashlight beam at one another, and everyone brandishing weapons of one description or another, everyone paused for a few disquieting seconds, unsure what to do.

Mitchell broke the spell. "Detectives Mitchell and Wright. Northumbria Police CID."

"Oh my God!" Carol cried out with a mixture of joy and relief. She cast the mug, skidding, back onto the worktop and, putting the hand to her mouth, said, "God, sorry!"

240

Rubbing his forehead, Wright said, "Don't worry, love. Under the circumstances I'm not gonna do you for assaulting a police officer."

Lowering the rifle, Bryce said, "It's Han Whitman. The murdering bastard's gone on a rampage."

"Well, that substantiates what we were suspecting," Wright said. "You're the first survivors we've come across. And we've come across a lot of people." He chose his words carefully.

"H-have you c-cordoned off the v-v-village?"

"Yeah, you cannat let this twat get away," Jimmy added. "He'll leg it if he sees the likes of you, like."

Before replying, Mitchell gently pushed the door closed, applying a little force to squeeze it back into the frame. Then he turned to them with a concerned look on his face. "Things aren't quite that simple."

Placing the knife onto the worktop with a shaking hand, Sam said, "W-w-what does th-th-that mean?"

"Divvent tell us it's just you two?" Bryce asked. He looked from one officer to the other. Their faces were grim and revealed more than any words could.

"'Fraid so, chief," Wright said, leaning against the refrigerator and pulling out his cigarettes and lighter. Lighting one, he said, "Phones aren't working and he took out the radio in our Landy." He didn't think it appropriate to elaborate on poor Bainbridge.

"Took *out*?" Jimmy snapped, his voice crackling over the last word. "Who is this wanker? Charles Bronson? James fucking Bond?"

"Calm down, young'un," Mitchell said. "We're overdue by a couple of hours already, so questions are being asked and suspicion is being raised. I'm confident that additional units will already be on the way."

"Confident?" Jimmy repeated, suddenly feeling quite sick.

"What are you a parrot?" Wright asked, taking a draw on his cigarette.

"Aye, soon to be a dead one. Deceased, passed on, ceased to be, stiff, bereft of life, off to meet my maker. An ex-parrot."

"Bleedin' comedian too."

Ignoring the confrontation, Mitchell continued. "First, we need to know everything you know. We know bits and pieces, so hopefully you guys can fill in a few blanks."

"Can I take one of 'em?" Jimmy asked with a nod to Wright's smoking cigarette. With mild irritation, Wright offered the packet around and was even more irritated when both Bryce and Carol accepted too.

Between Bryce, Carol and Jimmy, the three of them explained the recent events to the two officers, broken only by the occasional *uh-huh* or a brief request for clarification.

Once they had finished, Mitchell poured himself a glass of water at the sink and took a long, satisfying drink. Then, turning to the waiting audience, he said, "That information will help us a lot." His eyes settled on Bryce's rifle. "Now, I see you're armed and, at this stage, I don't give a rat's ass if you've got a permit for that. What we're going to need is for you four to hole up here while we continue our search for Whitman and any other survivors."

It was Carol who beat the others to it, crying out in desperation, "No! You can't just leave us!"

"You're safer here," Mitchell said.

"He's armed n' all remember," Bryce injected. "I assume you two aren't?"

"Don't worry about us, mate. We've got sharp sticks. He's not gettin' nowhere." Wright flicked the stub of his cigarette into the sink and smiled; it said, *'just let him fucking try'*. He then took the glass from Mitchell and finished off its contents.

"You better take the rifle then," Bryce said without conviction.

Both Jimmy and Carol opened their mouths to protest, but Mitchell silenced them with a wave of his hand. "No, I wouldn't be comfortable leaving you without a weapon. We'll be fine – we're working methodically house to house. We're trained professionals."

Mitchell turned to leave, saying. "Barricade this door when we leave and, if anyone comes knocking without announcing themselves, you have my permission to shoot first and ask

242

questions later." He stared at each one of them in turn to emphasise the point. "I mean it."

Following Mitchell, Wright paused in the doorway to say, "Smoke me a kipper, I'll be back for breakfast." Then he, too, disappeared into the night.

The four of them continued to stare at the door for several seconds, before Sam eventually walked over to the door and jammed it back into place. "P-pass a chair."

Mother's milk.

Larry's Ford Escort had been transformed into a vaguely car-shaped snow sculpture. Crouched behind it, sheltering from the biting wind and concealed from view, Han had followed the two detectives and then lain in wait. As it became obvious that they were spending longer than necessary in there, his mind began to wander; perhaps to take his mind off the bitter cold and the stinging in his ears.

He started humming at first then, ever so quietly, he starting singing, "I feel so bad, I got a worried mind, I'm so lonesome all the time, since I left my baby behind on Blue Bayou."

I'm going back someday, come what may to Blue Bayou,
Where you sleep all day and the catfish play on Blue Bayou ...

The dining room was warm and the smells of the Sunday roast were causing the young boy to salivate and his stomach to grumble in anticipation. Roy Orbison's voice was both haunting and tragic as it drifted up from his mother's Bush record player and radiogramme, set inside a veneered cabinet.

The young boy was sat at the teak dining table with his chin resting on his arms, a dreamy look lost in his eyes. His thick shock of dark ginger hair hung almost to the collar of his t-shirt. He sat up as he heard his mother walking through from the kitchen. The front of his t-shirt had the faces of Adama, Apollo and Starbuck, set against a star-filled backdrop with the Battlestar, Galactica, leading the rag-tag, fugitive fleet on a lonely quest ...

A woman in her thirties walked through. She had luscious red, curly hair flowing past her shoulders and wore an orange and green floral apron

243

over bell-bottom jeans and a polo-neck shirt, tight across large breasts. She was wiping her hands on a London souvenir tea towel. "Nearly ready, sweetheart," she said with a warm smile. "Your dad should be back from the club soon."

His father spent quite a bit of time in the working men's club, and quite a bit of time away working, but he didn't mind, especially on a Sunday. He and his mother would listen to her old record collection – dozens of singles, LPs and Reader's Digest Box Sets; The Swinging Sixties, The Fabulous Fifties, Golden Greats of the Fifties and Sixties, The Great Transatlantic Hits, Elvis Greatest Hits, Golden Hit Parade ... The two of them would sit and chat while a whole host of favourites would tantalise tenderly in the background. Needles & Pins, Teenager In Love, Poetry In Motion, Run around Sue, Oh Carol, Venus in Blue Jeans, Duke of Earl, Mr Tambourine Man, Groovy Kind of Love, True Love Ways ... the list was endless.

The warmth of the memory had temporarily abated the cold reality as he watched the two detectives leave the doctor's house. His head and shoulders were now coated with fresh snow. Kneeling, unmoving in the foot deep snow, had soaked his jeans through, and, with the warm memory fading fast, the icy wet quickly crept back into his bones. But the wait had been worth it.

They had spent longer than usual in Larry's house, but someone else slamming the door after the gorilla left confirmed it. It would seem that one or more of his missing flock were holed up in the doc's house. That saved him a job. *Thanks, fellas.*

Whispering to himself, he said, "So, you've told them to sit tight and that help is on the way, while you two are going to be the heroes and hunt down the villain?" He thought about that for a moment. "The villain? That would be me, right? Well, I suppose that's fair, given the circumstances. I can play the Joker to your Batman and Robin."

Watching Wright and Mitchell walk back to Bell Lane, he mused, "Nicholson, Romero or Ledger ... or even Leto for that matter? Tough call that. Nicholson's was sinister without the complete psychosis of Ledger or Leto, but Romero was the original and mad as a box of frogs."

244

"How about Jack Romero?" he considered, standing. "Classically mad and sinister." After brushing the snow from his legs and shaking it free from his upper body, he followed the two detectives. *Jack Romero, eh? A great name to use for the sequel. Could be misinterpreted as a reference to George A. Romero, the zombie maestro, but there certainly wasn't anything wrong with that.* He really was feeling quite upbeat. In a low, but cheery tone, he sung, "Dan-a-dan-a-dan-a-dan-a-batman!"

The two shapes trudged doggedly along Bell Lane, shin deep in snow and hunched over against the raging elements. They kept their flashlights switched off, not wanting to register their presence to prying eyes. Shivering, Mitchell shielded his eyes against the driving snow with his flashlight hand and pointed ahead of them with the other, cradling his baton, saying, "We need to check everything on the Miller's side." He had to virtually shout for his colleague to hear him over the roar of the wind.

Wiping snow and icy water from his face, Wright nodded, wobbling his hood comically, then slowed to a shuffling crawl as they approached the junction with Main Street. "The shooter's going to know that his time's running out. He won't have sat waiting for us to show our faces – he'll be out looking for us." Tilting his head back the way they had come, he added, "And them." A strong gust whipped the hood from his face and fluttered his hair in short grey/black flames, drawn on the wind.

Wiping more snow from his face, Mitchell said, "Yeah, could be anywhere by now. What are the odds of him cutting his losses and doing a runner, do you think?" He plucked a handkerchief from his coat pocket and wiped his red, dribbling nose.

"Zero," Wright replied immediately, jamming his hood back onto his head and briefly shoving his numbed hands into his marginally warmer armpits to try to bring some feeling back to them. "This bloke is on a rampage – he wants everyone dead, and that now includes us. This maniac obviously doesn't give a damn that we're coppers or that more will be on the way. He's started something here and he intends to finish it."

Shoving the wet hanky back into his pocket, Mitchell muttered, "Wish we could've taken the rifle."

"Woulda been bloody handy right now, aye."

"But they need it more, right?"

Wright glanced at him, blinking snow from his eyes. "Bloody joking, aren't you? But it was the only thing we could do, us being the good guys, and all that."

"Oh aye, what was all that sharp sticks bollocks?" Mitchell asked with a half grunted laugh.

Chuckling, Wright said, "Dunno, shit just tends to pour out sometimes when I open my trap. Sounded pretty cool at the time though, eh?"

"Plank." Squinting through the snow and the darkness, Mitchell regarded the silhouetted buildings across Main Street with suspicion. "Suggest we move further back along Main Street and cut across the road at the edge of the village. Then we can search everything that side from top to bottom."

"Fine by me." Feigning an optimistic tone, Wright added, "Maybe some of our esteemed colleagues might join us for a pint in the Miller's by then, eh?"

"Aye, let's hope they send more than a couple of bloody uniform too."

"Well, if some donkey at headquarters thinks we've just crashed or gotten ourselves stuck up here, they might well do. But, on the other hand, they'd be hard pressed to ignore the lack of radio or telephone contact, even with those eventualities."

As content as he could be that no one was in view, Mitchell edged out onto Main Street and headed towards the church, with Wright following close behind. Shapes and shadows seemed to dance just out of view, lost within the snowstorm, teasing and defying the blurred vision of the two officers. Several times one or the other would stop, raising their baton in readiness, only to realise that it was nothing but a swirling snow ghost. Even the wind appeared to collaborate, whispering not quite recognisable words astray amongst the buffeting frenzy.

After barricading the door with a couple of chairs, Sam and Bryce joined the other two in the living room. A single candle flickered on the coffee table in the centre of the room, offering a warm orange glow that seemed to take a sliver of the chill from the air. Sitting on the arm of a chair, Bryce said, "Maybe I should've given them the rifle."

Slouched in the other armchair, Jimmy sat forward, saying, "Are you mental?" He scratched the back of his already angry red hand, wincing at the pain, but continuing nevertheless.

Carol was sitting on the sofa, with her legs tucked under her. She bit at a knuckle, before saying, "I've got to agree with Jimmy on that, John."

Bryce shrugged. "They're out there searching for him and we're in here. There's four of us and we've got the place secured, so who needs the gun more, eh?"

Neither Sam, nor Carol could return his stare. Even Jimmy glanced down at his hands when Bryce turned his attention to him. He looked at the angry scratch marks on the backs of both hands, but after a moment's hesitation, he looked up once more and matched his stare. He muttered, "They're coppers; they're trained for this sort of thing, like. It's what they're paid for."

Too tired to get angry, Bryce said simply, "They're not paid to get killed, son. They have armed units for this kinda thing. They're out there armed with truncheons, man. Han's got a gun – it's a big difference. Kinda like fishing with hand grenades."

"Well, they should've stayed with us then," Carol said, resting her head on her hand. Her face appeared gaunt and exhausted in the orange glow. Fatigue was creeping in with the hushed, cosy atmosphere.

"They're doin' their job. They might not like the situation, but they're still doing it. You gotta respect that."

"H-he's gonna g-g-get them t-too, isn't h-he?" Sam managed and regretted it immediately. Sitting next to Carol, he pulled his knees up to his chest and hugged his legs. He chewed on his bottom lip and glanced around at the others. They all remained lost in their own thoughts for a while.

247

Yawning, Bryce turned to him finally and shook his head. "Nah, divvent think like that, mate. Just 'cause they haven't got guns, that doesn't mean they're stupid – they're gunna be bloody careful."

Jimmy opened his mouth to speak, but closed it again. For once, he felt a wisecrack might be inappropriate. Instead, he took a chunk off the tip of a jagged nail with his discoloured incisors and thought about soft, pure white powder, lined up on a spotless mirror, with a twenty rolled up beside it. Or better yet, hot, bubbling liquid in a tablespoon. The thoughts made his mouth salivate and sent a tremor through his aching, clammy body.

The silence became unbearable. Quite unexpectedly, Jimmy surprised himself by saying, "Steve was gunna pay us to burn down the car lot."

The others turned to look at him, confused and surprised. "What are you on about?" Carol asked, but as the statement sunk in, it grasped her attention with both hands. She sat forward, waiting, frowning.

Jimmy shrugged. Too late now. "He was gunna pay us two thousand to torch the lot for him. He was gunna use the insurance money to bugger off with Janet somewhere."

"Now, Jimmy—" Bryce started, his eyes trained on Carol's open-mouthed expression.

Carol cut him off. Her voice was a little shaky, but she maintained her composure well. "It's okay, John. It's just what I expected. We've all got our secrets."

Jimmy looked at her with imploring eyes. "I'm sorry, Carol."

"Don't be. I was going to kill myself anyway." It was delivered like a throw away comment, but her face revealed no humour.

"D-d-don't say that, Carol," Sam said, sitting upright, appalled. He leant over and rested a hand on her hunched shoulders.

She sat back and offered Sam a brief, but thankful smile and patted his hand gently. She took a moment to massage the bridge of her nose, her eyes downcast. Then, scarcely above a whisper, she said, "Doesn't matter. Didn't have the nerve to go through with it."

Bryce and Jimmy glanced at one another.

"You've got friends here, Carol," Bryce said, reaching across to take her small hand in his. "We're your friends."

She looked up at him, her eyes growing watery then quickly looked away again, withdrawing her hand too.

"I-it takes more c-courage to keep going you know," Sam added, his own eyes growing teary at the sight of Carol's grief.

She couldn't look at him, but she fumbled blindly with one trembling hand to gently touch his hand once more.

Another awkward silence settled over them. Then, Jimmy, feeling like a burden had been lifted off his shoulders, said, "That's a reet corny line that, mate."

Sam turned to him, a look of deep wounding in his bloodshot eyes. Jimmy offered him a wink, accompanied by a cheeky grin.

Gradually, Sam's expression relaxed and he muttered, "Twat." That mustered a couple of laughs, and even a weak smile from Carol.

Big trouble in little old lady's house.

Snow continued to cascade down from the black sky as Wright and Mitchell fought their way along the back lane. The snow had gathered to almost knee height, making even the simple task of walking particularly strenuous. Both men were panting and sweating as they pushed open the peeling, green back gate and entered.

The walled yard was sheltered somewhat from the unrelenting wind, but the unlit house lent not a shard of light to its cold, wet enclosed stone walls. An outhouse ran along the right side of the yard and dozens of barren, snow-filled plant pots of all shapes and sizes ran along the wall to the left. The deep snow was untouched.

Soaked and shivering, the two men shuffled past a dustbin over to the back door. Pausing to wipe his drenched face, Wright pressed an ear against the wood and strained to listen over the low moaning of the wind.

Using a crowbar that they had stumbled across in a previous yard, Wright jammed it into the gap between door and frame just above the lock and yanked hard.

He was rewarded with splintering wood and the door popped open. Mitchell was through the opening before the door banged against the interior wall, flashlight in one hand and baton in the other. Wright immediately followed, brandishing the crowbar.

They found themselves in a country cottage-style kitchen with floral patterns clashing with herbs on walls and curtains. The room was cold and smelled vaguely damp.

A clatter of crockery preceded a muttered curse from Wright as he cracked a knee off the edge of a low standing trolley with a china tea service set out on it.

Mitchell swung the flashlight beam round at his colleague. Irritated, he said, "You okay?"

"Peachy fucking keen, jelly bean," Wright replied at a whisper, rubbing his throbbing knee.

"Glad to hear it. Shall we announce ourselves with a fanfare in the next house?"

"Ha bloody ha."

The two detectives moved through the kitchen to a narrow, musty smelling hallway. The walls were cluttered with gilded framed oil paintings of various Northumberland, North East and North West locations; Cragside, surrounded by mature woodland, the battlements of Alnwick Castle seen from the Lion Bridge, puffins nesting on the Farne Islands, the Roman Bath House at Ravenglass and Hadrian's Wall at Bardon Mill, were but a few.

The beam of light paused at an open doorway leading to the living room. As they cautiously approached, the rhythmic ticking of an unseen clock rose above their breathing and the intermittent creak of a floorboard.

Mitchell reached the doorway first and swept the beam across the room. A faded patterned sofa and armchair, both complete with doily armrest and headrest covers, were crammed into one end of the room around a 1964 Zenith television set.

The right-hand side of the room was home to a dining table and sideboard.

Dividing the two areas was a Grandmother Clock, the source of the ticking. As the light paused on it, the clock chose that moment to chime the half hour.

The beam danced across the blown vinyl wallpaper as Mitchell jerked with the sudden burst of noise. His baton raised on reflex, ready to strike an unseen attacker.

Wright leaned close to Mitchell's ear. "Little twitchy there, mate?"

His pulse throbbing in his ears, Mitchell took a deep breath before responding. "Thought I saw something in the corner of the room there, actually." A deep frown marred his troubled face as he swept the beam into the corner that concerned him. A coffee table with a short, scraggy-looking artificial Christmas tree lay lurking within the shadows. The flashlight glinted off several coloured baubles.

"Aye, them cobweb pixies can be a pain in the backside, eh?"

"You're telling me," Mitchell said, rolling his eyes. He turned away from the door and headed further down the hall towards the front door and the staircase. Wright afforded the living room one final, fleeting glance then followed.

A dark figure slid out from behind the open door in the living room and stepped out into the hall behind the two detectives. Han stood in the hallway, his piercing auburn eyes glaring at the two men. A sly grin played across his face.

"I'm getting a bit fucking tired of this sneaking around crap," Wright muttered. "Maybe we should just go back to the others and wait there for the cavalry."

"Inclined to agree with you, mate," Mitchell said with a sigh as he approached the bottom of the staircase. "Make this the last one, eh?"

"Best news I've—" Wright paused in mid sentence, his keen senses screaming a sudden warning to him. As he started to turn he felt a sharp pain in his back.

Mitchell turned in time to see his colleague drop to the carpet like a felled tree, his face contorted with pain. Han was standing over him with a bloodied hunting knife in hand and a broad smile on his lips. He was soaked through, but coiled to strike.

"Drop the knife!" Mitchell roared, raising his baton. "Tony, you okay, mate?"

"Been better," Wright gasped through gritted teeth, one hand clutching at the knife wound in his back. After a sharp intake of breath, he added, "Stove his fucking head in." His body writhed and squirmed as he attempted to drag himself away from his attacker.

"Think that might be what's known as excessive force, Detective Wright," Han said, keeping his eyes fixed on Mitchell.

"Gig's up, Whitman," Mitchell said evenly, tightening his grip on the cold hard handle of his baton. "Drop the knife; you're under arrest. This is your *final* warning." He took a step closer, to within kicking distance of Wright.

Wright managed to roll onto his side, against the internal wall. Blood was splattered on the cream carpet and all down the back of his jeans. He took a trembling hand away from the wound to gaze at the dark blood that had drenched it. "*Fucker*," he whispered.

Han appeared to think about it for a moment then said, "That's a generous offer, Mitchell. But I'm disinclined to acquiesce to your request." After a moment, he added, "Means no."

His face wracked with pain, Wright muttered, "You're just a walking cliché, aren't you, you fucking prick."

"Sticks and stones, love."

At that, Mitchell stole the opportunity to attack. With the baton raised, he rushed forward, swinging it in a tight downward arc for Han's head. Han anticipated the move and side-stepped, raising his blade to slash at the detective's throat.

Mitchell wrenched his head backwards at the last moment, allowing the blade to just nick the skin on his Adam's apple. Ignoring the trickle of blood dribbling down his neck, Mitchell surged forward again, shoving Han's knife hand aside and impacting with his chest.

Both men staggered backwards then fell in a crumpled heap close to the living room door. Han let out a grunt with Mitchell's weight bearing down on top of him, but still struggled to angle the knife round to attempt to stick him in the side.

Mitchell expected it, so immediately slammed the baton across Han's hand, causing him to cry out in pain and release the knife. Quickly adjusting his position, so that he was sat across Han's chest, he raised the baton again and slammed it down across his forehead.

Han's grunts were cut short.

Mitchell glanced across at his friend. Wright's eyes were closed and the grimace was softening. "Tony! Hold on, mate!" Jumping off Han, he grabbed the discarded knife and rushed across to his partner's aid.

Gently easing him over, he lifted his blood-drenched coat and shirt to examine the puncture wound in his lower back, just to the left of the spine. "Christ," he muttered to himself.

"No," Wright uttered with a rasping voice like dry kindling, "but nice of you to say."

"Stay with me, mate. I've got to find something to stop this bleeding."

"Whitman?"

"He's out cold; don't worry about him," Mitchell replied, easing his friend back to the floor. "You're my priority right now."

"*Kill* him," Wright said with utter conviction. His squinting eyes fixed on his partner with an intensity that overshadowed the pain.

Mitchell had pulled out his handkerchief, but paused to meet his friend's stare. "Can't do that and you know it, mate. No matter what the evil bastard's done. It's got to be by the book, unfor—"

A gunshot rang out in the confined hallway, causing a ringing in Mitchell's ears. A neat bullet hole appeared in Wright's temple, and a splatter of blood and brains emptied onto the carpet from the ragged exit wound.

"NO!" Mitchell screamed, dropping the useless handkerchief and cradling his dead friend. He turned towards the source of the gunshot, his eyes blazing with rage.

Han was standing, holding the side of his head with one hand and the smoking Walther P99 in the other. An angry mark was rapidly blossoming where he had been struck with the baton. "Think you should've listened to your dead partner there, Mitchell." In mock disbelief, he asked, "Haven't you *ever* watched a horror film? *Dumb!*"

"Sonuvabitch," Mitchell muttered weakly, his shoulders sagging and his eyes growing moist.

"And then some." As an afterthought, while continuing to rub his throbbing head, he added, "That fucking hurt by the way."

Switching his stare from the pistol to Han, Mitchell spat, "Good! Here's hoping for a fucking brain haemorrhage!" He glanced down at his dead friend and then back to Han. "Just fucking get it over with, you evil bastard."

"I will, if you don't mind. I'm already way behind schedule here, and I've still got the others to sort out at the old doc's place."

A flash of fear played across Mitchell's face.

"You two were kind enough to show me where they were hiding, so thanks for that."

"Joke's on you, dickhead. We told them to switch to another location after we left as a precaution." He took one last look at his dead partner's closed eyes. There was a sense of serenity to his features that he had never quite seen in him while he had been alive.

Han smiled. "Nice try, Officer. Pardon me for not trusting you, but I think I'll just nip down there and check first, eh?"

After gently setting down Wright's head, Mitchell stood up and set his shoulders back in defiance. Sardonically, he said, "Waste all the time you want, Whitman. I'm sure there's hours before reinforcements arrive."

Mitchell was rewarded with the briefest flicker of irritation. "Best not hang about chatting then," Han said evenly and pulled the trigger.

The bullet zipped past within an inch of Mitchell's ear and shattered the small frosted glass pane in the door. The time between realising that he was still alive and his body reacting was a mere fraction of a second. The report echoed round the house as he broke for the front door.

Cursing the residual foggy effects of the blow to his head, Han aimed and fired again. This time the bullet caught the fleeing detective just below his left shoulder blade, causing him to stumble forward into the door.

Crying out in pain, Mitchell fumbled with the catch and swung the door open. Gusting wind and snow struck his face as another bullet whipped past him into the night. He fell out into the frenzied storm and managed to slam the door shut as yet another bullet struck wood from the inside.

Not wishing to hang around, he stumbled as fast as he could back towards Bell Lane. The wind and icy snow stung at his face and hands, thrashing at his open, flapping jacket. He staggered, agonised and half blinded into the night.

chapter 15

I'll huff and I'll puff and I'll blow your house in.

Pushing a corner of the curtain aside, a face briefly appeared at the darkened living room window, peering out into the storm. Inside, Jimmy cocked his head towards the others, straining to see their outlines in the dark room. The flickering candle only managed to lighten the gloom one shade of grey. "Did you hear owt there, like?"

"No," Sam muttered, his head resting on the arm of the sofa with his eyes closed.

Bryce sat forward in the chair, cradling the rifle in his hands. "Push back the curtains. Someone might see." He blinked and rubbed his tired eyes.

Reluctantly, Jimmy complied and turned back in the chair. "You can say Whitman, Bryce."

Annoyed, Bryce turned back to him and replied, "You divvent have to tell me that, boy."

"Just seems like you're still in denial to me." His tone was less confrontational, just mere disbelief.

Their eyes locked, despite the gloom, and Bryce said, "Divvent go there."

Carol raised her head from the other arm of the sofa, lying next to Sam. "John, take it easy. Jimmy, leave it." Shifting her position, she added, "We've all just got to try to be patient. Help should be here soon." She so desperately wanted to believe that, and even more desperately needed a drink. Anything. *Special Brew* would do. Her eyes were drawn back to the mantelpiece where a single Christmas stocking hung in the centre from a small hook. Even in the gloom she could read the sown label that read KERRIS.

There was silence as everyone contemplated the validity of Carol's last statement. After a moment, breaking the awkward silence, Jimmy said, "I spy with my little eye—"

Bryce and Sam groaned as Carol hurled a cushion at him.

Silence descended once more, but then it was Sam's turn to break it. "Sh-show me the way t-to go home." His strained voice sounded frail and desperately lonely.

There was silence for a moment, but then Jimmy chorused, "I'm tired and I wanna go to bed." A smile warmed his pale, fatigued face. Even the tremors appeared to abate momentarily.

"Cuz I had a little drink about an hour ago," Carol joined in wistfully, imagining a large vodka and orange cradling in her hand, the ice clinking melodically as she lifted it to her parched lips.

Reluctantly, Bryce flatly added, "And it went straight to me head."

Slapping the arm of the chair in time, Sam continued with gentle enthusiasm, "Wherever I may roam."

All four, with even Bryce cracking a smile, continued, "On land or sea or foam, you will always hear me singing this song, show me the way to go home."

Sam actually managed a laugh. Despite everything they had been through, and were still going through, their desperate heartaches were fleetingly forgotten. Joined, and strengthened, in song.

"Didn't know it was foam, like," Jimmy said, smiling. "Learn summit new every day, me old twat of a da used to say."

Persisting solo, Sam continued, "Boom, boom, boom, sh—" A hammering on the front door abruptly cut him off.

Through the darkness, four sets of eyes darted between one another.

"The coppers?" Jimmy asked tentatively.

"Well, whoever it is they're knocking instead of breaking in, so that's got to be a good sign," Bryce said.

The knocking grew louder and more urgent. "Open the door!" It was Mitchell's voice, strained, but unmistakable.

"Christ!" Carol cried.

Bryce jumped to his feet, followed quickly by the others. "Jimmy, come with me. You two wait here; just in case." He grabbed the rifle and headed for the door.

Catching him at the doorway, Jimmy whispered harshly, "Just in case *what?*"

"Just … in case, alreet?"

Sam and Carol gathered in the centre of the living room, furtively glancing from window to door as Bryce and Jimmy disappeared into the hallway. Their eyes met briefly and they both saw a reflection of their own fear.

As Bryce reached for the front door, Mitchell's voice shouted again. "For Christ's sake hurry, man!"

Bryce quickly unlocked the door and disengaged the chain. Mitchell fell into the hall even as the door was still opening. Bryce caught him, dropping the rifle in the process with a loud clatter.

Jimmy dropped to his knees, scrambling for the gun.

"Wright dead," Mitchell gasped. "I'm hit … back." He was soaked, exhausted and shaking violently. Wind and gusting flakes swept into the hallway with him.

Bryce drew his hand away from the detective's back and discovered that his palm was smeared with blood. "Jesus, divvent talk, mate. We'll get you inside." Struggling to be as gentle as possible, Bryce hoisted one of Mitchell's arms around his shoulder, causing an agonising cry from the detective. Then he helped him through to the living room with the detective's drenched boots dragging along the carpet, all strength utterly spent. After re-locking the door, Jimmy followed, holding the rifle in trembling hands. He was breathing hard and the shock had brought the tremors back with vehemence.

As Mitchell was set down on the sofa, he managed, "Whitman … on his way."

Sam and Carol exchanged horrified glances.

"Fuck," Jimmy spat, pacing the room from window to door. "Jesus, man, if they cannat fuckin' sort him, what chance have we got, like?" The tremors were intensifying by the moment, turning him into a chattering wreck.

"Calm down," Bryce said, his tone even. "Anyone know any first aid?"

"M-m-my cer-certificate's a c-couple of years out of d-d-date, but yeah, I'll do m-m-my best," Sam stammered. The thought of occupying his mind was extremely appealing and he rushed forward to assist.

"I'll help," Carol added, moving with him.

Bryce backed away as Sam and Carol stooped over the stricken man. Turning to Jimmy, he ordered, "Give us the rifle, son. Now."

Jimmy looked at it, reluctant to lose the sense of security that it offered, however tenuous it might be. "I—"

"Just stop right there, boy, and hand it over." Bryce stepped closer.

Jimmy considered, for a second, attempting to hold on to the weapon, but as Bryce reached him, he offered it willingly. He dug into his coat pocket for his lock knife. "Suggest you two tool up, when you're finished with him," he said, flicking open the blade.

"*Tool* up?" Bryce repeated, shaking his head. "Who do you think you are? Edward G. Robinson?" He checked the magazine was fully loaded then looked back at the wired young man and added, "This isn't the movies, son. This is real life. This is Haydon."

Jimmy stared at him and, maybe it was the fact that the drugs were all but out of his system, but Bryce's last words garnered new meaning. There was a truth in those words that he had not been able to comprehend for so many years. Slowly nodding, he said, "Aye … this is Haydon."

Mitchell cried out as his jacket and shirt were hastily ripped off and cast onto the floor. Sam clumsily applied pressure to the bullet wound in his back as Carol gently held the detective in place, whispering, "Shh, it's okay, you're going to be okay, pet." She glanced up and caught Sam's eye. A look passed between them, but neither of them said a word. Sam turned back to the bleeding wound.

The sound of breaking glass upstairs stopped them all in their tracks. For a second nobody could breathe.

"He's-inside-the-fuckin'-house!" Jimmy cried, the words rushing out as one. He thrust the knife in the direction of the door, the blade twitching at the end of his outstretched arm.

"We're gunna take him; here and now, Jimmy," Bryce said and his lips curled into a thin smile. "You with us, son?" He stepped closer, looming over him, and gripped his quivering shoulder in his strong grip. Their eyes met. "For *Haydon*."

Jimmy's eyes were wild and his body continued to tremble from a massive dose of fear and adrenaline, aggravating his usual tremors. But, through taut, dry lips, he managed, "Aye."

Sam and Carol had eased Mitchell into a recovery position on the sofa with his shirt tied into a makeshift bandage over one shoulder and under the other. Both were now brandishing kitchen knives and looking expectantly to Bryce and Jimmy.

"You two stay here; we're going upstairs to finish this." Bryce cocked the rifle and shoved aside the door to the hallway. Jimmy half-heartedly followed, his shaky knife seemingly leading him on.

"Shouldn't we all be sticking together here?" Carol called after them, fighting to maintain some composure.

Forcing his face to one side, to speak more clearly, Mitchell muttered, "Drawing you out ... Stick together." The colour had rapidly drained from his face and his lips had a blue tinge to them.

Carol stared down at Mitchell's contorted face, his eyes tight shut against the pain. Her jaw dropped open and she turned back to the open door. "JOHN!"

Bryce paused with his foot on the first step of the staircase. He glanced at Jimmy behind him, then back up the stairs. He opened his mouth to shout back towards the living room, but closed it again without making a sound. Slowly, cautiously, he began ascending the narrow and steep staircase.

Jimmy watched him for a moment, his heart pounding like an earthquake and his legs welded to the spot, but then, after a further moment's indecision, he shadowed the farmer's footsteps.

A rising panic gripped Carol as her eyes darted around the room, the knife following her eyes in short, jerky movements.

Sam bent down to touch the side of Mitchell's face one more time, before moving over towards Carol who had drifted into the middle of the room again. "D-don't w-w-worry. J-J-

John'll get him." His eyes and his trembling demeanour suggested a very different alternative.

Bryce reached the top of the stairs and popped his head onto the landing, looking both left towards one bedroom and the bathroom, and right towards the second, smaller bedroom … Kerris's room. The landing was in darkness and the three doors were all closed. He had checked the upstairs a couple of times, so he was already familiar with the layout. Nothing seemed amiss.

He stepped out onto the landing, with Jimmy close on his heels. "Watch our backs," he whispered, turning towards the young daughter's bedroom. Jimmy followed, keeping an eye on the other two rooms past the stairs.

Courage is not the towering oak that sees storms come and go; it is the fragile blossom that opens in the snow.

Turning wildly on the spot in the middle of the living room, Carol thrust a hand up to her moist forehead, rubbing frantically at her throbbing head. "This is insane! He's just one man!"

Sam gently touched her shoulder. "Yes, e-exactly." He offered her a pathetic attempt at a smile then quickly returned his eyes to alternating between window and door. There was terror in his own eyes, but one thing had sprung to mind to focalise his thoughts; Natalie. Her killer was upon them, but he would not succeed; for Natalie's sake.

As Sam's eyes turned away from the window for the umpteenth time, it suddenly imploded with a thunderous roar of smashing glass. The brick that had caused the devastation sailed through the fragile barrier and struck Sam in the side, near the kidneys. He doubled over in agony, crying out. The kitchen knife dropped out of his hand.

Carol appeared to turn in slow motion, her face twisted with horror. Seeing Sam bent over in pain tipped her over the edge. Screaming and wielding her knife, she ran at the destroyed window. The curtains were flapping wildly in the gusting wind and flurries of snow blew in onto the glass-peppered carpet.

Casting the curtains aside, she glared out into the tempestuous night and screamed, "WHITMAN!" It was a rage-fuelled, animal cry.

Still bent over and clutching his side, Sam gasped, "Carol! Get back!"

Carol stepped back, turning back to Sam. At the same time, the blade of the hunting knife shot through the gap in the curtains and cut through the air at neck height.

The blade sliced the side of Carol's neck, releasing a spray of blood across the living room, then withdrew as quickly as it had appeared, offering the briefest glimpse of a gloved hand. Screaming, she staggered back from the window, clutching her wounded neck.

Sam bent down to retrieve his discarded knife, grasping it weakly and then staggered over towards Carol. He held the knife out in the direction of the window and grabbed her arm with his free hand. "G-get out into the hall!"

"Stick together," Mitchell whispered from his prone position on the sofa. His voice was distant, dreamlike.

"Carol! Sam!" Bryce shouted as he rushed into the room, rifle in hand. Jimmy was right behind him, but stopped in the doorway.

Pointing to the window with his kitchen knife, Sam said, "He's t-toying with us."

Bryce reached them and gingerly looked at Carol's wounded neck. "Doesn't look too deep, pet. Divvent worry." She looked back at him, but her eyes failed to focus on his. Instead, she looked down at her hand, smeared with her own blood.

"This wanker is really pissing us off, like," Jimmy said from the doorway.

"He's gunna pay," Bryce muttered, staring at the curtains as they continued to bristle in the wind. Several droplets of blood had spattered across the curtains and carpet. Carol's blood. Images of Sally and Anthony flickered across his mind's eye. Their blood spilled on the cellar floor. Their mutilated corpses discarded in the cold dark. Butchered at the hands of

Hannibal Whitman … a man who dared to call him a friend to his face.

Bryce started walking towards the window. There was inevitability in his stride that was impossible to ignore.

"Bryce?" Jimmy asked from the doorway, concern temporarily overriding fear.

"Han!" Bryce bellowed as he approached the window. "I'm coming for you, Han!"

"John! No!" Sam shouted and lunged for him, ignoring his own knotted pain.

Without pausing, Bryce dove through the window. His silhouette seemed to hang in midair, framed by the billowing curtains for an instant, and then he was enveloped by the swirling night.

"No!" Carol cried, taking an unsteady step forward. Her free hand seemed to be drawn to the ragged hole, beseeching.

Two gunshots rang out above the roar of the wind. Everyone held their breath, but the only reply was the unrelenting, lonely cry of the storm. The wet curtains perpetually flapped and snow continued to blow in through the shattered opening. The temperature in the room had dropped like a stone, making the occupants shiver and revealing their panting breaths.

Jimmy stood in the doorway, making no attempt to abate his trembling limbs. Bryce was gone, probably dead. The copper was dying or maybe even dead already, Carol was hurt and Sam looked like a lost puppy. "What the fuck are we gunna do now?"

"Boo."

The voice was whispered close to Jimmy's ear. He recoiled so violently from it that he cracked his head and shoulder off the doorframe, yelping in pain. He fell, staggering into the living room, cursing and twisting to see the source of the voice. Since the start of the nightmare, Han Whitman had grown into something of a mythical beast in that time. Jimmy was suddenly desperate to catch a glimpse of this person; this monster. He didn't actually expect to see the Whitman as he had previously known him. He expected some drooling, hairy creature with blood-dripping jaws. *When the wolfbane blooms and autumn moon is bright …*

Han stepped into the doorway behind him, smiling like Sylvester with Tweety Pie in his grip. He was dressed in his torn, black clothing which was drenched through and splattered with stains, but it was Whitman and he was still very much human. "Why don't you build a fire and sing a few songs?" he said with a chuckle.

Carol and Sam both spun to stare in horror at the voice of the very man of their nightmares. His face was pale and dripping wet, but his auburn eyes glowed with the intensity of burning embers.

"Cumbiah's always a popular choice."

Shaking off the throbbing pain in the side of his head, Jimmy fixed his stare on Han, and at the pistol he held in his hand, pointed predominantly in his direction. "*Wanker*," he muttered under his breath.

Mitchell stirred for the first time in a while on the sofa. He laboriously lifted his head and twisted his neck in Han's direction. "You," he rasped, "are under arrest."

"You," Han mimicked, "are dead." The barrel of the Walther switched from Jimmy to the prone detective in one sudden movement and discharged with a twitch of the wrist. The gunshot struck Mitchell in the centre of his back, punching a coin-sized hole and spraying a fine mist of blood into the air. The detective's head slumped back down onto the sofa and he stirred no more.

"NO!" Carol screamed, renewed tears streaming down her face. Her knife dropped loosely down to her side.

"Bastard!" Sam chorused. Stepping in front of Carol, he waved his own knife towards Han. The gesture was vaguely threatening in a desperate sense.

Jimmy quickly scrambled to his feet and he, too, raised his knife towards their attacker. He drew in a deep gulp of air in a futile attempt to contain his shattered nerves. His whispered voice was lost in the gusting wind. "Haydon ... *Haydon* ..."

As Han watched with mild amusement, Carol stepped to the side of Sam and finally raised her own knife. Seeing Sam and Jimmy's defiance reinvigorated her own. Through clenched teeth, she too muttered, "Haydon ... Haydon ..."

The three stood together, two men and one woman, each with a knife held out in front of them. A drug addict, a drunk and an IT manager. The three blades twitched and trembled, but maintained their aim directly at Han. Their eyes betrayed their terror, but the clenched jaws struggled with determination.

"Three Musketeers, eh?" Han said and snorted.

"There was four actually, dickhead," Jimmy corrected, his face set into a scowl that was a fraught attempt to hide his fear.

Han nodded, but his smile disappeared beneath his thick glistening beard. "Not anymore." Leaning casually against the doorframe, he added, "To be honest, I'm knackered after all this running around. You certainly didn't make this experiment easy for me, I can tell you. You can be happy with that, at least."

"E-experiment?" Sam asked, frowning.

"Yep, to see if I could beat the record."

"The record?" Carol injected. "Number of murders?" She was shaking her head, struggling to understand – to even remotely begin to comprehend – what this madman was saying.

Keeping the pistol aimed at the group in general, Han sighed, then said, "Something like that, but I can't be bothered to go into a Bond baddie-style monologue, as I said to Steve Belmont before I shot him, so let's just crack on, eh?"

"Fine," Carol said as evenly as she could muster. "Screw you." Her knife had lowered towards the floor, but now she yanked it back up with renewed determination.

Straightening up, Han said, "I may have deserved that." A thought suddenly occurred to him, frowning, he added, "Oh, just one more thing, where's Janet?"

Jimmy and Carol fired confused looks at one another. "You losin' track of who you murdered already?" Jimmy asked with a snort of disgust.

Han opened his mouth to protest, but then closed it as fast. *Larry, you old dog. Good for you!* After a moment, dismissively, he said, "Never mind then." His aim settled on Sam and then he added, "Okey-kokey pig in a pokey."

With a quick glance, Jimmy followed the barrel of the gun to Sam. One simple thought occurred to him in the blink of an eye. *He deserves life more than me.* As Han squeezed the trigger,

Jimmy lunged to one side, snarling, "No!" The bullet struck him, instead of its intended target. He dropped to the ground, clutching his bleeding abdomen with a mixture of shock and pain contorting his face.

Both Carol and Sam were shouting his name and surging toward him, but he was only vaguely aware of it. Instead, he looked down at the bullet wound that was pumping his lifeblood out onto the carpet. He was surprised that after the initial blow that felt like a kick from a hobnailed boot, the pain wasn't too bad. A throbbing not unlike stomach cramps.

"Jimmy, you never cease to surprise," Han said, shaking his head. The smile had returned to his lips. "You found a bit of backbone – well done!"

Carol and Sam crouched down beside him as Jimmy turned his attention to Han and spat, "Wanker." His spittle was discoloured with spots of blood. "Always wondered what it'd be like to get shot with something other than a needle, like." He even managed a weak smile.

Cradling his head, Carol said, "Don't talk, pet."

An image of Natalie in her favourite lotus-embroidered kimono, smiling affectionately, flashed before Sam's eyes. It remained anchored there like a sudden blinding glare. He sprang to his feet and launched himself at Han, screaming, "DIE!"

Surprised by his ferocity, Han swayed back on his heels. His recovery was instantaneous. "Nah," he said simply and shot him twice in the chest as he reached half way.

Sam staggered forward a couple of steps, his features fixed with a twisted look of hatred. Two neat holes had appeared in his jumper and a dark stain was rapidly spreading around both of them. Then, after tottering for a moment, with his eyes still set on Han, he toppled forward onto his face. His knife bounced away harmlessly into the corner of the room as his limbs settled and his body went still.

"God ... *no* ..." Carol uttered feebly, cradling Jimmy's head close to her breast. Tears were streaming down her face as she looked from Sam's body to Jimmy's ashen face.

"Nearly there, folks. This will all be over presently." Han ejected the magazine from the handgrip of the pistol, popped it into his pocket, and slapped a fresh one into place. As he cocked it, movement down the hall caught his eye.

Bryce had slipped through the open front door and was now aiming the Barrett at Han. His hair was plastered and snowmelt was pouring down his face, but his features were calculated; all except the eyes. There was something resembling rapture in them. Behind him, and licking at his coat, the storm raged on. Dancing snowflakes whirled into the open doorway around his feet.

Han kept the gun and his body facing Carol, but his head slowly turned to greet the new arrival. His smile was forced, but his tone remained jovial. "Hey, John, nice of you to join us. So glad you didn't miss the party."

"I couldn't quite believe it at first – not my mate, Han. Han wouldn't butcher me wife and boy." His tone was matter-of-fact. "But here you are." Despite the cold and wind, the rifle remained unmoving in his frozen hands.

Glancing from the barrel of the rifle to Bryce's eyes, Han said, "Well, if it's any consolation, I'm sorry, big fella. None of this was personal."

Bryce actually laughed. "Oh, I'm afraid this is very personal indeed."

Dropping his pistol to his side, Han shrugged, saying, "I'm not a monster – I'm just a normal bloke who undertook an extraordinary test." Lightening his tone further, he added, "Look, all this'll be over soon and I'll go back to my normal life and then the doctors, investigators and psychologists can ponder over it for decades to come. Books will be written, films will be made, but no one will ever understand why."

Bryce raised his head away from the gun sight and shook his head sadly. "Is that what this is all about? Notoriety? Make you more famous than John Wayne?"

Han frowned. "John Wayne? That was what you went with?" With a grunt, he added, "Nah, it's not about petty vanity, old friend."

"You have no friends here," Bryce said, aiming back down the sight.

"Sorry," Han said, in apparent earnest. "No one will ever know who did this or why. That is the point."

"That's no point at all," Carol snapped at him, still clutching Jimmy.

Han glanced at her briefly. "Exactly!" He seemed pleased that at least one of them understood.

"You're no longer welcome in Haydon, Mister Whitman," Bryce said. "And *Haydon* reacts violently to any threat."

Han blinked – a flash of fear – and then threw himself to one side, at the same time, firing a snapshot towards Bryce.

Smiling, Bryce opened fire.

Han's bullet lodged in the ceiling as Bryce's sailed through the space where Han's head had been only a second earlier. Acrid smoke plumed in the hallway, curling snake-like from both weapons.

Even as Han's shoulder slammed into the wall, jarring him, he was squeezing the trigger a second and third time, each report booming.

Bryce stepped back into the awaiting embrace of the storm. In an instant, he was gone.

Han righted himself and fired one more round out into the darkness as Bryce's outline disappeared amidst the raging blanket of snow. In frustration, he yelled, "Bryce! I thought you were made of stronger stuff!" With his anger directed at the open doorway, Carol appeared out of the corner of his eye and flew upon him.

Her knife slashed at his shoulder, ripping both material and flesh. He grunted loudly as hot blood jetted down his arm. Using the Walther whilst pivoting, he parried with a sharp blow to her wrist. The bloodied knife was cast down the hallway towards the kitchen.

Carol cried out in pain and frustration, but rushed at him once more regardless. Her hands were balled into white-knuckled fists.

Han punched her solidly in the face with the butt of the pistol. There was a resounding crunch as her nose shattered and blood splattered across her face. The blow caused an explosion of intense pain, blinding her and sucking the strength from her legs. She staggered back into the living room a couple of paces, with gouts of thick blood oozing down her face then dropped to the ground in a crumpled heap. Moaning softly, she grasped at her smashed face.

"What is this?" Han asked, holding his burning shoulder. "A tag team?"

Aiming the pistol at Carol's whimpering form, on her knees, he said with an exasperated sigh, "I'd love to hang around to chat, but time is short, Carol." He stepped closer, the muzzle a mere couple of inches from her forehead and pulled the trigger. There was an audible click, but no loud report. Rolling his eyes, he muttered, "For the love of God." Looking down at Carol, he appeared uncertain for a moment. Then, gathering himself once more, he said, "I'll come back for you two."

Jimmy was slowly and painfully crawling across the floor towards Carol. He paused, gasping, "You're a dead man, Whitman. Nobody fucks with *Haydon*."

Han stared at him then said, "Fuck you and fuck Haydon!" Regaining his composure, he added, "You're dancing with the devil here, son, and the song is coming to an end. When it stops there's going to be me, and that's it." Offering him a smile of condolence, he added, "Haydon is *dead*. You're just its last dying gasps; its death rattle. Just get over it." He turned to the front door, but before he left, he added, in an Arnold Schwarzenegger burr, "I'll be back." Then, gritting his teeth against the pain in his shoulder, he sprinted towards the open door where the storm and darkness awaited.

Jimmy struggled across the floor, dragging himself along by his straining fingers. The blood oozing from his abdomen left a slug-like trail across the carpet in his wake. Exhausted, his head slumped down with his outstretched fingers just able to touch Carol's leg. In a low whisper, he managed, "Carol … Carol …"

Still clutching her bleeding nose, she turned to Jimmy. Her watery eyes opened and managed to focus on the young man splayed out on the floor. Seeing that he was still with her seemed to centre her reeling mind. Muffled by her hands, she uttered, "Jimmy."

Lacking the strength to lift his head off the floor and with his eyes tightly shut, Jimmy muttered, "Listen to us, Carol ... get out ... of here ..."

Carol took the hand from her ruined nose and manoeuvred on all fours to face Jimmy. Her bloodied hand tentatively touched the side of his pale, furrowed face. "I'm not leaving you, pet."

Jimmy forced his eyes open and stared fiercely into hers. With renewed conviction, he said, "No! Get out of here! He's gunna come back and finish me off. That's just fine with me, like – I'm fucked anyway." Pausing to gulp in air, he then continued in a more gentle tone. "You can still escape – hide ... till the rest o' the coppers arrive. Please, Carol – do it for me."

Tears streamed down her face as she listened to his plea. Holding his cheek with her hand, she snivelled and said, "No, I can't leave you here."

Jimmy's eyes closed once again, but his lips managed to say, "No ... someone's got to survive ... to tell people ..."

Carol's eyes narrowed. "Han Whitman will not leave Haydon alive."

The driving snow stung at his face as Han waded through the drifts building up at the side of the doctor's house. His head throbbed, his shoulder stung and sticky blood was oozing down his arm. Every joint ached and he was acutely aware of how so very dog-tired he felt. It seemed like the night would never end, as if it were some form of perpetual purgatory for his sins against the good people of Haydon. Good people of Haydon? That was a joke. They were fucking lunatics, every goddamn one of them. He just desperately wanted it to be over. He wanted out of this nightmare town ... this nightmare. He needed the reassurance of his old life and the comfort of Ju's loving touch. He felt cold ... cold to his soul.

Blood was dripping from his sleeve, splashing the brilliant white snow with crimson. The dark and the blizzard were closing in around him, making him feel enclosed, despite being outdoors. It sapped his fading strength with alarming speed.

The storm still showed no signs of letting up, the black sky utterly hidden by a blanket of seething storm clouds. The wind whipped up the lying snow like playful nymphs as it continued to deepen still further.

As he rounded the corner, he lent back against the cold wet stone, gasping for air. He reloaded the Walther then stole a moment to grip his wounded shoulder, clenching his jaw against the flaring pain.

After a few seconds of catching his breath, he glanced round the corner back to the front door. The darkness and the thick falling snow combined to distort his vision. Squinting, he struggled to see the opening, and struggled further to see if there was anyone there.

His mind started playing tricks on him. Shapes and shadows danced amidst the swirling snow, each one threatening to materialise into John Bryce. There were others there too. Was that Mandy? Steve? A small shape – childlike – almost close enough to touch, sailed by.

His heart was racing in his chest. There was something very wrong with this place. Maybe he should just take his chances and cut and run. Haydon was going to swallow him whole as if he had never existed.

"No," he said aloud, his voice sounding frail and lost. He *had* to see this through … to the end. One thing was for certain, John Bryce would not run. John would hunt him down with his dying breath.

"Aye, you're right there."

Han recoiled away from the voice, banging his head against the wall in the process.

A huge, hulking shape emerged out of the storm. Bryce appeared much bigger, even for his normally sizable frame.

Han raised his pistol, but Bryce swatted it away with a swing of his rifle. Han cried out in renewed pain and grasped his hand where the barrel had struck him. "Who the fuck are you people?"

A grin cut into Bryce's stony countenance. "We are Haydon. And nobody fucks with Haydon."

"What does that even mean, you fucking lunatic?" Han screamed in his face. Laughing hysterically, he added, "Is this Stepford? The fucking Twilight Zone?"

"No," Bryce said, still smiling, "we just protect our own here. *Haydon* protects us." Stepping forward, he sneered, "You will regret fucking with Haydon for the rest of your very short existence."

As Han went for his knife he thought he saw something change in Bryce's face. It might have just been the lashing flurries swirling around them, but his eyes widened and blind panic took hold.

Lying still on the floor, Jimmy's shallow breathing was the only noise to be heard above the moaning wind blowing in through the curtains. Carol was nowhere to be seen. His head was light from the loss of blood and his mouth dry. Occasionally, he half-opened his eyes to peer with blurred vision at the arc of the room that he could still view, including the door to the hallway.

A loud bang startled him, wrenching his eyes open once more. His foggy mind thought it to be Bryce's rifle at first, but he quickly realised that it was the front door slamming. The call of the storm diminished only a fraction with it and there was a moment of near silence, save for the flapping of the curtains. Then, footsteps approached and Jimmy's eyes grew wide. After what seemed like a lifetime, a blurred figure appeared in the doorway.

"B-Bryce?" Jimmy asked in a croaky voice.

"'Fraid not, kid," Han uttered and slumped against the doorframe. His was staring blankly at the window and his whole body was trembling.

Jimmy studied him for a time then, managing a crooked smile, said, "I bet you regret coming to Haydon now, eh?"

Han choked back a sob and raised a shaking hand to his mouth. "Jesus wept." He was unaware that he had spoken. The words seemed to waver in the darkness.

"Scared ya, did he?"

Han shot a glance over his shoulder and then focussed on Jimmy for the first time. "Carol leave you?"

Jimmy coughed and said, "Oh, she'll be waiting out there for you." He closed his eyes and the words were all but a sigh that seemed to evaporate as they drifted loose from his blue-tinged lips. The tension in his body had abated, leaving him almost restful as he lay splayed out on the carpet, surrounded by his own blood.

Han walked over to the prone figure and tears openly streamed down his face. His movements mechanical, he angled the pistol at Jimmy's head.

Jimmy just lay there, eyes closed.

A flash of movement pricked Han's dull senses. Carol jumped up from behind the sofa and launched herself towards him. Han reacted far too slowly. She slammed into him with teeth-jarring force. There was a tearing of flesh as her knife struck his arm at the bicep, slicing deep into flesh and taut muscle. As they both staggered backwards, the gun dropped from his suddenly feeble fingers and clattered to the floor.

The new searing pain jolted him into action. Screaming, he spun and cracked her across the side of the face with the back of his other hand. The action renewed the pain in his shoulder and sent fresh warm blood oozing from the wound. For Carol, the blow sent flashes dancing across her vision and knocked her back into the coffee table. Her legs buckled as she sprawled backwards over the top of it, casting the candle and tea plate across the floor. The stump of candle puffed out as it struck the carpet, melting a small hole, and banishing the soft orange glow.

"Bitch!" he screamed at her, clutching his wounded arm as it hung limp and useless by his side. Blood was now pouring freely down both sleeves and dribbling onto the carpet.

Bending down, he painfully retrieved the gun in the better of his two hands, cursing and gasping under his breath. As he rose, a sound just below the drone of the wind caught his attention. Standing, bleeding, he strained to hear.

Then, as the sound grew louder, he recognised it … sirens.

Scrambling to find her feet, Carol screamed, "No! I'll *kill* you first!" Her fury grotesquely warped her features.

Gasping, Han swung the pistol on her, crying, "Fuck you!" He fired several rounds at her.

Screeching, Carol scrambled spider-like behind the sofa. Several rounds whizzed past her, lodging in the wall or zipping out into the storm through the window. One grazed the side of her face, slicing a burning groove across her jaw line, and then a second struck her hip. Her face was numbed from its earlier pummelling, so only barely registered the heat from the graze, but her hip exploded as the bullet shattered her pelvis. She slumped, in helpless, squirming agony behind the sofa, clutching her leg and waist and totally immobile.

Han kicked the sofa, nudging it aside enough to see her.

Carol's agonised cries abruptly stopped and she stared up at him.

Han looked down at the bloodied face of the woman. She was suddenly still, relaxed almost. He aimed the Walther at her head.

The sirens were much louder.

His finger touched the trigger, but then another sob escaped his taut lips. The gun wavered.

"Just do it," Carol said with irritated resignation.

"I ..." He aimed at her one more time and then, shaking his head, he lowered it.

Without another word, he turned and ran to the door.

In the doorway, he stopped abruptly and turned back, causing blood to spray across the door and frame. His eyes swept the room; Sam, Jimmy, Carol. "*Haydon,*" he uttered and then was gone.

Lying behind the sofa, Carol gripped her wounded hip and bit hard into her bottom lip to control the pain. Her face was caked in the dried blood from her smashed nose, with both nostrils blocked from thick blood and snot. Fresh blood was dribbling from the gash across her jaw and pooling around her waist from her pelvis. She was shaking uncontrollably, but she slowly turned her gaze to the door and a smile touched her lips.

chapter 18

Slaughterhouse blues.

The Northumbria Police helicopter set down, throwing up gusts of snow, in the middle of Main Street, between Moe's and the Green. All directions were awash with flashing lights and activity amidst the swirling maelstrom of the continuing storm. Sergeant Wilkinson jumped down first, then turned back to help Chief Superintendent Hewitt down from the passenger cabin, whist shielding his eyes from the clouds of snow being tossed up by the rotor blades.

Hewitt took his hand begrudgingly and dropped into the thick churned up snow, freshly gouged up by dozens of police, emergency and army personnel. The street was filled with Land Rovers and other four wheel drive vehicles, with a myriad of different markings; Police, Ambulance and Northumberland National Park Search and Rescue Team, as well as several with the woodland camouflage of army units out of Otterburn Army Training Estate. Two further canvas-topped four-tonne Bedford trucks were parked further down the street, next to Belmont Motors. In amongst all the flashing lights, people in thick winter clothing rushed to and fro.

The first thing Wilkinson noticed was that a sizeable number of those rushing around were armed, including the soldiers and what looked like the entire Armed Response contingent of Northumbria Police. A cordon had been set up around the village with armed sentries and temporary gates set up to block the main entrance into the village. Unseen sniper teams would no doubt be setting up in vantage points in and around the village as well.

Overall, his initial thoughts were that of a war zone, not a crime scene. Wiping snow from his eyes, he noticed rows of black body bags laid out by the roadside further up the street beyond the Miller's Arms. As he watched, more were placed there by shuffling soldiers and paramedics with each passing minute.

A uniformed police officer approached them at a stoop, holding his hat down with one hand as the wind from the rotor blades blew the snow from the top of it. As he approached, the helicopter lifted jerkily off the ground and rose up into the darkness, buffeted by the high winds.

"Chief!" he called to them above the din with more than a hint of relief in his frayed voice. He was panting hard from the cold and exertion, the cold air betraying him with every hot breath.

"Hasslebrook?" Hewitt asked, taking the man's hand.

"Yessir. The search has uncovered over two hundred bodies so far, including Detective's Wright and Mitchell and PC Bainbridge."

Hewitt let out an angry grunt then asked, "Survivors?"

"One so far, but she's in a critical condition, so we have not been able to glean any information from her at all yet. We managed to persuade the air ambulance to fly her out about ten minutes before you arrived. They don't normally fly at night or in these conditions, but under the circumstances ..." His voice trailed off, unsure how to finish.

Hewitt nodded, content for him to leave it there.

"Still no suspects?" Wilkinson asked almost dreamily, his head unable or unwilling to move beyond the body count, and reeling to digest the sheer scale of the nightmare unfolding around him. With the helicopter gone, the swirling snow died down somewhat and the roar of the wind with it.

"We have one; a certain Hannibal Whitman who Wright and Mitchell were up here to interview."

"Could one man possibly be responsible for all this?" Wilkinson uttered, his eyes starting to stream from the icy snow. He wiped his face with a gloved hand and glanced from Hasslebrook to his superior.

"Nothing's impossible, son," Hewitt said evenly, ruffling his collar against the bitter wind. He stood and surveyed the chaotic scene in silence for some time as fresh falling snow quickly coated his hat and shoulders. The faces of everyone who passed close by, including Hasslebrook's, had a haunted sheen to them. Some mass primeval fear had been evoked from within this place. Even the air, despite the icy wind, felt … tainted somehow. They were doggedly going about their duty, ingrained training heaving them through this frozen hell, but this was one night that none of them would ever forget. The men and women around him would take these scenes to their graves, and would most probably have many a restless and sweat-soaked night from this day forward.

A young constable stepped out of a house across the road, clutching a Santa Clause hat close to his chest. He appeared dazed and confused as his gaze switched from the impossibly vivid red hat to the dark pandemonium around him. As Hewitt watched, squinting, he realised that the officer was weeping openly.

The events in Haydon would join the ranks of the Moors murders, the Ripper murders, Hungerford, Shipman, the Wests, but it would top them all by a long, long way. If it was Hannibal Whitman, then he had single-handedly managed to wipe an entire village off the map.

"This bastard has to be the devil himself," Wilkinson muttered, his face deeply troubled.

Hewitt tore his eyes away from the young constable to the sergeant, then after a moment's contemplation, said solemnly, "Maybe. He wears many disguises." He continued to look upon the frenzied scene around them, then, as an afterthought, he added, "Well, what I say is, when you're dealing with the devil, praise the Lord, and pass the ammunition." His words were flat and humourless, and his sunken eyes settled on the black tree line of the woods beyond the borders of the village.

A killer was out there somewhere; a killer who was indiscriminate of age, race, gender or creed. This monster had to be stopped. As that thought consumed him, his chest began to tighten with the onset of another coughing fit.

The poundin' of the drums, the pride and disgrace,
You can bury your dead, but don't leave a trace,
Hate your next-door-neighbour, but don't forget to say grace,
And you tell me over and over and over and over again my friend,
Ah, you don't believe we're on the eve of destruction.

epilogue

9th January.

The entry bell tinkled as the door opened to admit a new arrival. The movie and game store was crammed with wall and free-standing shelving, overflowing with games and films and all manner of merchandise. Posters of films, past and present, adorned every square inch of wall and ceiling space; from classics to modern gore-fests and everything else in-between. A big flashing red and blue neon sign on the far wall above the counter boldly declared, MOVIE MANIAC. To the left of the sign, a poster menacingly declared, *Man is the warmest place to hide*, and to the right; *A motion picture destined to offend nearly two thirds of the civilised world. And severely annoy the other third.*

A skinny man with badly pock-marked skin and greasy brown shaggy hair stood behind the counter, reading *Empire* magazine, dressed in a faded *Snatch (Stealin' stones and breakin' bones)* t-shirt.

As the newcomer approached the counter, Perry kept his eyes glued to the interview of cult horror director, John Carpenter.

"How you doing, dickhead?" Han said, offering his startled underling a weary smile.

"Jesus, man!" Perry said, clapping a hand onto the glass top counter. "Scared the shit outta me there! Was just reading an interview with JC – the unholy one."

"Cool; I'll have to have a read after you." Han was clean-shaven with a recently cropped crew-cut and dressed in jeans and a t-shirt. One arm was tucked under his leather jacket in a sling. Most of the bruising on the side of his head had faded as had the grazes.

"Hey, what happened?"

"Fell off my damn bike, would you believe?" Han said with a dismissive wave of his free arm. "A branch skewered my arm.

279

Nice gash in my other shoulder too. Got great scars to show you."

"Bummer. Mind, you never could ride for toffee."

"Your heartfelt concern is touching, mate."

Perry grinned at him. "Good to have ya back, buddy."

Shrugging off his jacket, he slung it over the counter and said, "Cuppa wouldn't go amiss."

"No probs, bro." Perry disappeared into the back office and proceeded to fill a kettle. "So, you got the book finished then?"

Han pulled up a stool and sat at the counter, glancing around at the old place; the shelves, posters and wall-mounted flat screen televisions depicting a muted trailer for the latest blockbuster. His eyes settled on a poster with the faces of Gene Wilder and Marty Feldman which declared, *The scariest comedy of all time!* Somewhat distant, he replied, "Aye, just about. Doubt it'll ever get published though."

Popping his head round the doorframe, Perry said, "Doesn't matter, bud. It's a major achievement just to get it written."

"True," Han said, but could not draw his eyes away from the screaming head of Gene Wilder with a shock of mad scientist hair.

There was a clattering of cups which finally broke the spell as Perry said, "Much poontang down there then?"

A hesitation then, his voice distant, he said, "There was one ..." An image of Lisa flashed before his eyes, her face twisted with rage and her eyes burning with fire. He had to shake his head to dislodge the disturbing vision.

"Knew you'd get some; you always do, you jammy twat," Perry was saying.

Han forced out a hollow laugh and arched his back, stretching out a nagging ache. "You got a way with words, buddy."

"Fucking lyrical gangsta, me!"

"Knob."

"Charming!" Perry shouted as he squeezed teabags and added some milk. Bringing two mugs through, one *The Empire*

Strikes Back and the other with the masked face of *Hannibal Lecter*, Perry continued, "I take it you weren't that much out in the sticks not to hear about that crazy shit up in Northumberland?"

Han nodded and without looking at his friend, took the Hannibal mug. Staring into the steaming tea, he muttered, "They do have TVs and radios down there, you plonker." As an afterthought, he added quietly, "Terrible business."

"That sorta crazier-than-fiction shit would make a helluva film, eh?"

Han ignored him, still staring at his tea.

Casting the subject aside with a shrug, Perry said, "So, what's next then?"

Han glanced at him as the question sunk in. It was something he hadn't even considered since his fraught escape from Haydon into Scotland. What could possibly come next after Haydon? Until now, he hadn't even thought it possible that there could be a next.

He found that his gaze had drifted back to Gene Wilder. Blinking, he looked back to his friend and said, "I'll just walk the Earth."

Sitting down, Perry smiled knowingly. "What ya mean, *walk the Earth*?"

Han sighed, but managed a more sincere smile this time. "You know, walk the Earth, meet people ... get into adventures. Like Caine from *Kung Fu*."

"Or Jules, eh?"

They both laughed – Han's more of a snort – then both took sips of their tea. Han glanced up over the rim of his mug to study his friend. Perry was Perry, the Tarantino wannabe. Nothing had changed, well, not here anyway. He had changed. Haydon had changed him.

The image of a hulking, monstrous form, emerging out of the storm flashed across his vision.

biography

Rod lives in the beautiful North East of England with wife,
Vanessa. He also dabbles in a spot of acting.